## DEADLY AMBUSH

"Listen," Hooker Jim said, rising from the knee-high sage and turning his head to catch the distant sounds. "A wagon is coming along the road, going into town."

"He won't pass," Curly Headed Doctor vowed. When the settler came into sight, the shaman motioned to Hooker Jim to go to the other side of the road and make a diversion.

Crossing the road was enough to get him noticed. The settler, on his way to town for supplies, slowed his mules, then reached for a shotgun.

"Who's there?" he called, trying to find Hooker Jim in the tangle of undergrowth along the road. Distracted from the point of real attack, he never saw Curly Headed Doctor draw his knife and jump up. Something gave the attacker away at the last moment.

The settler turned and fired, but his shot missed. The shaman's thrust did not. The tip of the knife slid between the man's ribs, then drove upward with savage power to rupture his heart. Blood exploded from the settler's chest and drenched Curly Headed Doctor's knife hand and arm. He jumped into the wagon box and continued slashing at the now dead settler, gouging the heart from his chest and then mutilating him.

Drenched in his enemy's blood, Curly Headed Doctor stood up in the wagon, threw back his head and let out a cry of victory that was more animal than human.

"We have more to kill," he told Hooker Jim.

# BOOK YOUR PLACE ON OUR WEBSITE AND MAKE THE READING CONNECTION!

We've created a customized website just for our very special readers, where you can get the inside scoop on everything that's going on with Zebra, Pinnacle and Kensington books.

When you come online, you'll have the exciting opportunity to:

- View covers of upcoming books
- Read sample chapters
- Learn about our future publishing schedule (listed by publication month *and author*)
- Find out when your favorite authors will be visiting a city near you
- Search for and order backlist books from our online catalog
- Check out author bios and background information
- Send e-mail to your favorite authors
- Meet the Kensington staff online
- Join us in weekly chats with authors, readers and other guests
- Get writing guidelines
- AND MUCH MORE!

**Visit our website at**
**http://www.pinnaclebooks.com**

# THE BATTLE OF LOST RIVER

## *Karl Lassiter*

**PINNACLE BOOKS**
Kensington Publishing Corp.
www.pinnaclebooks.com

While based on actual events, this book is a work of fiction.

*For Mike & Liz.*
*Thanks for all the glimpses of past*
*(albeit medieval) times.*

The names of the Indians are not mentioned in the records, so that their skulls cannot be identified. But the circumstantial evidence points to their being the skulls of Captain Jack, Schonchin John, Black Jim, and Boston Charley. . . .

In all probability the bodies were buried, possibly at the fort [Fort Klamath] after the execution, and only the skulls sent to the museum.

F. N. Seltzer, head curator,
Department of Anthropology, Smithsonian Institution
January 26, 1949

# Prologue

"You're gonna kill 'em all, Ben?" The grizzled man scratched his chin, then grinned broadly, showing a broken front tooth. "Now ain't you the card!"

Ben Wright puffed up his chest and looked around the southern shore of Tule Lake. Waves lapped gently along the shoreline, and a hesitant fawn darted from the woods to drink, fearfully looking around but thirstier than frightened. Sated, the alert deer caught the men's scent and vanished into the thick undergrowth of tule and sagebrush, leaving behind only hoofprints in the muddy shore. The soft wind blew through the pine forest at the base of the eastern Cascade Mountains, giving a false sense of serenity and warmth to the new day's reconciliation of old grievances. Good. Wright wanted everything to be peaceable-seeming when the murdering savages showed up.

"Zeb," Wright said to his lieutenant, "bring up the wagons and get them unloaded. Them Modoc will be here in an hour or two. I want the cookin' to be 'bout finished then. No need for 'em to steal our recipes." Wright laughed at his own joke, one shared by his lieutenant.

"You're gonna show 'em good, Ben. Yes, sir. I cain't wait."

"Don't be too eager. They are bloodthirsty murderers, and

I don't want to scare 'em off." Ben Wright looked into the shadows of the forest, trying to spot the fawn that had been drinking at the lakeside. The animal had vanished as if it had never existed, just like the Modoc when they were killing and scalping. Wright's anger mounted. The savages!

They had attacked his and Emma's wagon train making their way along the Oregon Trail without warning. He had tried to save her. But the memory of the Indian towering over her, bloody knife clutched in his hand, was forever burned in Wright's memory and soul as a monument to his failure. The Oregon Indian Authority up in Salem had told him the attacking Indians might have been Klamath, but Wright did not care. Klamath. Modoc. Warm Springs. They were all murderers, and his best efforts to stop their predations had come to naught.

Until today.

"I ain't gonna spook 'em, Ben. Trust me," Zeb said. "I got my own score to settle. You know how they killed Little Zeb."

"Your wife survived. You can have more sons," Wright said, reliving the heart-stopping second when his darling Emma had died with the wicked knife in her breast. He shook himself out of the horrid reverie, his resolve hardening. Some in his band said what he planned to do was wrong. How stopping the damned red niggers could ever be wrong eluded him. No more would these Modoc loot villages, kill settlers, and attack wagon trains.

He was saving innocent women and children, women like his Emma and children like Little Zeb.

"Here's the first of 'em comin' in already, Ben," Zeb called.

"Treat 'em good," Wright said coldly. Then he put on a false smile and walked from his camp, hand out to shake. The Modoc approached hesitantly, a white flag on a wood stick showing their intention to parley.

"You are Wright?" asked the older man beside the young boy carrying the truce flag.

"I am. You must be Schonchin John. And who is this young lad?" Wright looked at the boy, who insolently returned his stare without blinking his dark eyes once. Wright felt a little uneasy at how the youth seemed to bore into his soul and see his real intentions.

"Kintpuash," Schonchin John scolded. "Do not be so bold."

The boy averted his eyes, but his attitude remained. Wright wanted to strangle the impudent little jackass with his own hands. But he smiled and thrust his hand out a bit farther for Schonchin John. The Modoc looked from the symbol of friendship to Wright, then shook hands hesitantly.

"This is a good day," Schonchin John said, releasing Wright's grip. "There is too much killing. We can be friends. We are already friends with white settlers."

"Around Yreka," Wright said, the words bitter on his tongue. Why those greedy fools tolerated the Indians was beyond him. He suspected they traded with the Modoc and certainly treated them as equals. Murderers. The redskins were nothing but killers of innocent women.

"Why do you want peace?" asked the boy Schonchin John had called Kintpuash. "You are the one who kills my people, cutting off noses and ears."

"And fingers," Wright said before he thought. He caught himself before he said anything more. He could not let this boy needle him. "These kinds of attacks should be over, in the past, things we need to resolve."

"It would be good taking your scalp," Kintpuash said, pointing to Ben Wright's long hair. "But you dress funny."

This took Wright aback. He looked down at his ornate clothing.

"Why, folks tell me I'm a real spiffy dresser. What's wrong with the way I dress?"

"You look funny," Kintpuash repeated. He dodged the blow as Schonchin John tried to cuff him for his impertinence.

"He is young. He will learn." Schonchin John glared at the boy.

"Then let's learn together over a fine meal me and my boys

have fixed to celebrate this truce. We got ourselves a fine chance to bury the hatchet."

Schonchin John nodded brusquely, then turned and motioned. From the woods came forty-four more Modoc. Ben Wright blinked at the sight. He had not expected them to be this close and waiting unseen. No wonder the murdering bastards had been so hard for him to find. They were more like ghosts than real people.

"Come on and let's chow down," Wright greeted them, putting his arm around Schonchin John's shoulders. The Modoc chief edged away slightly. Kintpuash followed close behind, the truce flag dragging in the dirt as he went.

"These times have been real terrible for us all," Wright said, sitting in a chair set up at the head of a crude table already brimming with food. Wright glanced in Zeb's direction. The man smiled, showing his broken tooth, and nodded.

Wright rested his hand on the pistol tucked into his belt when he saw Kintpuash's attention focused on the huge stew-pots and the way the cooks stirred the savory contents. Motioning to Zeb, Wright turned and whispered to the man, "You put the strychnine in?"

"Enough to kill all them rats," Zeb said.

"Good." Wright turned back to the table and beckoned to the Modoc standing around, looking hungrily at the food already on the table. "Come on, my good men. Sit, eat, enjoy our bounty. It's my grand pleasure to welcome you all to break bread."

Kintpuash sat beside Schonchin John on a long bench to Wright's left. The boy sniffed, his nose wrinkling. Wright felt an irrational urge to whip out his thick-bladed knife and cut off the twitching nose to add to his collection. He restrained himself. Better to get them all than to give in to a moment's temptation.

The boy sniffed again when a plate of stew was dropped in front of him. Then he said something in Modoc to Schonchin John. The older man shook his head. Kintpuash was not to be denied. He spoke loudly, so all the Indians heard. Several pushed back from their plates of food.

"Eat hearty," Wright said. "Eat up or I'll be offended you're not acceptin' my hospitality."

Several of the Modoc began eating, slowly at first, and then with greater hunger, stuffing potatoes into their mouths and mopping up the stew with bread.

Kintpuash spoke again.

"Boy, if you want to talk, do it in lingo I can understand," Wright snapped. "It's not polite to yammer on so's your host can't understand."

Kintpuash thrust out his chin and asked, "Why aren't your men eating, too?"

"Not polite for the host to eat 'fore his guests. I'd've thought even a sprout like you'd know that."

"There's something in the food," Kintpuash said to Schonchin John.

This time all forty-six of the Modoc stopped eating. A few who had eaten the fastest belched and clutched at their bellies.

"Kill 'em, shoot 'em down like animals!" cried Wright, pushing back from the table and whipping out his pistol. Schonchin John lurched forward, caught Wright's wrist, and shoved the pistol away so it discharged harmlessly. Then Wright dropped the empty gun and grabbed for his knife.

Ben Wright swung the knife, opening a long bloody cut on Schonchin John's chest. Kintpuash tripped him, giving the older man a chance to escape. All through the camp echoed the sharp reports of pistols and muskets firing and Indians crying out as they died. It was music to Ben Wright's ears. But he wanted a trophy or two of his own.

He'd lost the chief, but the young boy's ears would make fine trophies. Wright grabbed Kintpuash's wrist and jerked the boy around, only to lose his grip. Blood turned the boy's arm slippery. Wright regained his balance, roared, and tried to impale Kintpuash. He barely missed as the boy agilely slipped away. Then Wright found himself grappling with a Modoc warrior closer to his size.

He felt a surge of delight as his knife cut into the Indian's belly and angled up into his heart. But by the time Wright shoved the body away, Kintpuash and Schonchin John had disappeared into the sheltering forest, joining the fawn.

"Kill 'em, kill 'em all!" Wright cried.

Ben Wright and his men killed forty-one of the forty-six Modoc. His only regret was how badly he had failed in his attempt at poisoning. He would have enjoyed watching the Indians puke out their guts before they died.

# Mistrust

*Northern California*
*December 22, 1869*

"You will never get Captain Jack to agree," warned the interpreter. Frank Riddle paced back and forth at the edge of the Modoc village on the shore of Tule Lake, wringing his hands. "I know how important your mission is, Mr. Meacham, but you're going about it all wrong."

Alfred Benjamin "AB" Meacham heaved a sigh. His breath came out in a feathery tangle that quickly disappeared when the wind blowing from south out of Oregon caught it. AB pulled his coat tighter around his portly frame and tugged at his hat to cover his bald pate. He towered over Riddle and his Modoc wife, Tobey, who seemed impervious to the cold wind. Maybe tall white men felt the winter nip more than short ones—or Modoc women. Tobey had a wool shawl pulled around her broad shoulders. Otherwise, she gave no hint that the winter was growing colder by the minute.

"He is the big *tyee,* isn't he?" asked Meacham. "Deal with him, get the treaty signed, and all the trouble with the Modoc will be only a dim memory." On one point, Meacham shared some of Riddle's uneasiness. They had left behind the wagon with all its supplies and the squad of soldiers so their entrance into the Modoc village would not be seen as threatening. Now Meacham wished he had some of those men with him, especially Oliver Applegate or even their half-breed scout Don McKay. McKay was a vicious fighter, perhaps even a murderer, and Meacham had brought him along only because the commander at Fort Klamath had demanded it. But nothing said Meacham had to have McKay accompany him into the camp; McKay was better suited to guarding their supplies.

"You know they distrust these parleys," Frank Riddle said.

"Bloody Point and Ben Wright," Meacham said, struggling against a long memory among the Indians. "That was seventeen years ago and Wright met his fate, whether deserved or not." Meacham shuddered, and this time it was not from the cold. Ben Wright had been feared and hated by red man and white alike, but his massacre at Bloody Point had gained him control of the Oregon Indian Agency. A year after he slaughtered the Modoc under the truce flag, he had gotten drunk and stripped an Indian woman, beating her along the streets with a whip.

She had killed him and eaten his heart.

Meacham forced away the thought of a bloody heart held high before becoming dinner and looked toward the *wikiups* of Captain Jack's band. He longed to be out of the wind, but the *tyee* chose to let his visitors stand in the cold wind.

"You do not know?" asked Tobey Riddle, looking at Meacham curiously. She moved closer so her words would not be swallowed by the wind. "Captain Jack was there. He escaped with Schonchin John."

"I've spoken with Old Schonches, and he will sign the new treaty if Captain Jack does," Meacham said. "Schonchin John is his son and will go along with him, won't he?" Meacham shivered again. "I had never heard that Captain Jack was there at Wright's massacre."

"Kintpuash," she said. "Kintpuash is Captain Jack's real name, not his white man name."

"He couldn't have been too old. Why, the man's hardly thirty now."

"A boy," Frank Riddle agreed. "It turned him as cold as a

witch's tit toward the white man's treaties. And little wonder."
He looked at his wife, his gaze softening a little. "Tobey is
his cousin and was only eight when Wright killed most of her
family, hers and Captain Jack's."

"I'm sorry. I did not realize," Meacham said. He thought-
fully stroked his dark, full beard, patterned after President
Grant's. Meacham had been Indian Agent for some time but
felt he served the cause of the Modoc and other tribes better
in Washington, D.C., where the reins of power ended. Coming
south from Salem had only brought more trouble, or so he
felt. There were too many alliances and promises and hatreds
for him to straighten out, even with the able help of the Riddles.

"Tobey agreed to translate only because there has been too
much killing," Frank Riddle said. "It's time to put an end to
it and get her people settled peacefully."

"Thank you," Meacham said sincerely. He wished he had
more support from the Klamath Indian Agency—or Washington. But he did not. Wheels within wheels, boxes inside boxes.

He looked up as Captain Jack came out of the *wikiup* and
motioned to him. Captain Jack was a handsome man, short,
solidly built, with sharp, penetrating black eyes that never
missed a detail. Meacham tried to read something into the
Modoc leader's impassive expression but could not.

"He fights for control of the Modoc," Tobey whispered to
him as they entered the *wikiup* by climbing clumsily down the
swaying rawhide ladder into the stifling interior. Meacham
found it hard to breathe in the hot, humid interior. Two fires
blazed, filling the large structure with heat enough for an entire
cabin. After the wait in the winter outside, any warmth might
seem this oppressive, but Meacham did not think so. Captain
Jack wanted him to feel uneasy.

Meacham saw how those with Captain Jack were armed and
ready for trouble. That did not bode well. He had come to
negotiate a treaty and thought Captain Jack would agree to the
terms, but avoiding the currents of anger and outright hatred

would not be easy. Meacham held his tongue, waiting for Captain Jack to speak.

"What do you want from us?" Captain Jack finally asked. He crossed his arms over his broad chest and looked down his nose at Meacham.

"Peace," Meacham said promptly. He saw two older men behind Captain Jack moving around. He wished he could ask Frank Riddle who they were because they seemed to have a superior attitude that goaded Captain Jack into being so arrogant and rude. These might be the others Captain Jack struggled with for control of the tribe.

Captain Jack snorted, and the man immediately behind him spat into a fire. The spittle sizzled and hissed, sending a small whirling spiral of steam up to a smoke hole.

"Curly Headed Doctor agrees with me. White men lie and kill."

"That has happened," Meacham admitted freely. "Ben Wright was an evil man, but he is dead. I am here to bargain in good faith. I bear no arms. I come only to establish peace."

"By hiding us on the Klamath reservation," Curly Headed Doctor said angrily. "We are not friends with the Klamath. They are our enemies!"

"They are your brothers," Meacham said, shocked at the intense anger he heard. He knew of raiding back and forth between the Modoc and the Klamath, but calling them enemies flew in the face of all he knew. The Klamath chief David Allan always spoke of peace and had led Meacham to believe he could soothe the Modoc—and had already. Meacham had ventured out from Fort Klamath with orders to bring the internecine squabbling to a halt and stop raids against the white settlers. If he failed, the cavalry would begin a campaign of subjugation. That was something no one wanted, red or white.

"We are brothers only to the sun, sky, and earth," said the other man.

"That's Bogus Charley," Frank Riddle said quietly, ignoring the glares of Captain Jack for speaking out of turn and only to Meacham. "He can talk the fish out of a lake, but he's right. The Klamath are enemies."

Meacham considered what to say. The military commander at Fort Klamath seemed completely unaware of this and had told him how the Klamath and Modoc could get along just fine, given the right incentive. But then, the man's idea of incentives tended toward bayonets and bullets.

He eyed the Modoc and realized the extreme danger he had walked into so foolishly with his eyes wide open and armed with only vague promises and outright lies from the U.S. Army. Curly Headed Doctor and Bogus Charley both wore traditional war paint, white streaks and red ocher circles on their cheeks.

"There is plenty of land on the Klamath Reservation," Meacham said carefully, "separate from the Klamath. You can both live in peace alongside Old Schonches' band of Modoc." He directed his words toward Captain Jack, who kept a poker face.

"We live in peace now *off* the reservation," Captain Jack said. Meacham tried to imagine the thoughts that ran through the Modoc chief's mind. He had been betrayed by the white man over and over and had led more than one raid against nearby settlers and wagon trains coming along the Applegate Trail north of Tule Lake. But Meacham saw no hatred in Captain Jack, not like the hatred he saw in Curly Headed Doctor.

"You have agreed to treaties before," Meacham said.

"Never!"

"Twice before, you have taken goods from our government, the big *tyee* in Washington. Do I need to bring out those who saw you make your mark on these treaties?"

"Lost River," Captain Jack said obliquely, "is a lovely place."

"It is not on the Klamath Reservation," Meacham said, turning Captain Jack back to the issue.

"I am friendly with Link River Jack," the Modoc leader said, again skirting the issue. Meacham recognized the name as a Klamath, in spite of Captain Jack just naming the Klamath

Indians as his enemy. This might be the Modoc's way of offering a peace they both could live with.

Silence fell. Meacham's eyes adjusted to the curiously dancing shadows cast by the fires, and he saw more warriors in the *wikiup* than he had originally thought. The hunchback was Captain Jack's brother, Humpy Joe, and his other brother, Black Jim, spoke in hushed tones with Schonchin John. From their scowls, they were not in favor of any treaty with the white man.

*"Mekigamblaketu!"* cried Curly Headed Doctor.

Meacham leaned over so Tobey could translate.

"The shaman says they won't go. Curly Headed Doctor tries to force Captain Jack to agree with him and go on the warpath."

Meacham saw the tide rising against him. He jumped to his feet and shouted at Captain Jack, "You already agreed! I have seen the treaty you signed. Wagons are on the way here to take you all to the reservation."

Meacham swallowed hard when he realized what he had said and how it sounded. But Captain Jack smiled slightly and shook his head.

"I would be ashamed to fight so few of you with so many of my warriors."

Meacham blanched. He had come too far to back down.

"If you don't go, many more soldiers will come to force you onto the reservation."

Captain Jack shook his head. "I will never fire the first shot, but I am not afraid to die."

Meacham had nothing to say to that. Captain Jack stood and pointed to the smaller fire at the side of the *wikiup*.

"Will you share Modoc food?" Captain Jack asked.

"Thank you for your offer, but we will retire to our camp. Perhaps you will join us there for breakfast?"

"Perhaps I will."

Meacham left, Frank and Tobey Riddle following closely.

Once outside in the cold wind, Meacham heard Frank Riddle release a long-pent-up breath.

"That was close," Riddle said. "Schonchin John and Curly Headed Doctor wanted to kill us. Captain Jack outmaneuvered them by offering us food."

"I think he will agree to go to the reservation," Meacham said. "Did you notice the quality of their food? Very sparse, no meat, only some fish from Tule Lake. He will come to take breakfast with us, and we will convince him then of the folly of resisting. We can show him how well his people will eat if they settle on the reservation."

"Mr. Applegate and McKay will have set up camp for us," Tobey said, "but we should not sleep tonight. Stay alert."

Meacham did not like the sound of the woman's advice, but he took it. Throughout the night, every coyote's howl, every whisper of the wind, even the sound of fish jumping about in the lake magnified into a gunshot or twang of a released bowstring. Meacham was never happier to see dawn and the arrival of their supply wagon.

AB Meacham inhaled deeply, and smiled. The scent of breakfast cooking up was sure to sway the Modoc into going to the reservation. He had gone without food since the day before and knew he would have agreed to almost anything to get a plate of eggs and bacon along with the griddle cakes Oliver Applegate whipped up. The settler had decent relations with the Indians, especially Captain Jack, but had stayed in the background because he thought it would only muddy the water if he tried to settle the treaty.

Meacham had to agree. He was an outsider. Curly Headed Doctor and Schonchin John would accuse Applegate of wanting to steal the Modoc land so he could bring in more white settlers. Meacham had no vested interest in anything but peace.

"Kill the bastards, thass what you need to do," grumbled Don McKay. "They'll double-cross you. Mark my words." The weasel-faced man's pale eyes darted around, as if the Modoc were sneaking up on him to cut his throat. His nervous gestures made Meacham uneasy, as if McKay might come unwound and begin killing to take the edge off his barely suppressed hatreds.

"Enough, Mr. McKay," snapped Meacham. "You will not say such things when Captain Jack and the others come to our camp."

"They'll come to lift our scalps," said McKay. He tipped his head to one side and squinted at Meacham. "Those of us what have scalps to lift."

"Mr. Meacham, they are coming," called Tobey. The Modoc woman hurried into the camp and hunkered down by the fire.

"Go and alert the soldiers, Mr. McKay, and do not return unless I summon you."

"Keepin' them cavalry boys bottled up ain't right," McKay said.

"Those 'cavalry boys,' as you call them, can't keep any bottle corked," grumbled Meacham. There had been considerable drunkenness in their ranks on the trip here from Fort Klamath.

"I'll look out for yer best interest, even if you won't," McKay promised.

"Yes, yes, Mr. McKay," Meacham said, distracted. Approaching their camp came Captain Jack, strutting boldly with his chest thrust out like a rooster. With him were his two brothers, as well as Curly Headed Doctor. The shaman muttered under his breath constantly. Curses? Hexes? Meacham neither knew nor cared.

"Welcome," Meacham greeted them, turning his back on McKay and any problems with the scout. "I do not have a pipe to smoke, but I freely share my food." Meacham saw the way Captain Jack's nostrils flared at the smell of the savory food.

"You are generous to share such bounty," Bogus Charley said.

"Then come join us. All of you." Meacham saw to it that

the Modoc received generous portions, but he noticed Captain Jack and the others did not eat. He glanced at Frank Riddle, who made eating motions. Meacham understood then. Ben Wright. Poisoned food under a truce flag.

Meacham began eating with a hearty appetite. Only when the other whites ate did Captain Jack and his entourage tentatively sample the food. Meacham had a second helping before the Modoc fell to eating with a gusto born of enduring near-starvation for too long.

As Meacham ate, he spoke with Captain Jack of signing the treaty.

"Old Schonches has agreed to the treaty. The Hot Creek Modoc will settle, if you do, too."

Curly Headed Doctor grunted, then spoke rapidly in Modoc to Captain Jack, who shrugged as if nothing mattered.

"Curly Headed Doctor is the leader of the Hot Creek and says they will never go to the reservation. The white man is a liar and scoundrel."

And so went the discussion for the rest of the day, accusations followed by conciliatory words. Finally, Captain Jack said, "We return to my village. We will decide the matter there in council."

"Give me good news to carry to the big *tyee* in Washington," Meacham said.

Captain Jack grunted, then started back for his village, the others following and arguing among themselves. Meacham saw Captain Jack climb to the top of his *wikiup* and begin a long speech. Tobey Riddle sat beside Meacham and watched for a moment before speaking.

"This might take all night," she said. "Curly Headed Doctor will speak. So will Bogus Charley. Bogus Charley likes you and your food. But Schonchin John wants only war, but he does not like Curly Headed Doctor."

"Whoa, wait," Meacham said. "I don't want to get too mixed up in tribal politics. Captain Jack is well liked by the settlers around Yreka, and they hope he stays the Modoc leader, but as long as the Modoc go peacefully to the reservation, I don't care who is the *tyee*."

"You should," Tobey said. "Captain Jack is an honorable man."

Meacham started to ask if she thought the others were not, but a sudden thunder of hooves brought him to his feet.

"What's going on?" he cried. Meacham barely got out of the way of the attacking soldiers. Sabers flashed. Riding at the flank of the cavalry, Don McKay shrieked like a banshee and lashed out with a short whip, cruelly cutting men and women near him as he galloped through the Modoc village.

The Modoc scattered. Meacham did not have to be told what they were saying.

The white man was a liar and again showed nothing but treachery.

"Stop it, stop it!" cried Meacham. But the soldiers were drunk and not inclined to listen to anyone spoiling their fun, especially with McKay egging them on.

Ten minutes later, the soldiers had rounded up over a hundred Modoc and disarmed them. Not a shot had been fired, but Meacham realized he had witnessed the beginning of a long, bloody conflict.

Captain Jack and Curly Headed Doctor were among those who had escaped, and they would not trust him again.

# Ambitions

San Francisco
December 24, 1869

Joshua Harlan swung along the street just south of Portsmouth Square, whistling a jaunty tune. He slowed when he saw a commotion in the Square. A reporter, even the most junior one for the *Alta California,* had to stay alert for the story.

The Story.

He needed the big story that would scoop others on the staff to get the editor's attention. Otherwise, he was destined to stay at the bottom of the ladder, doing hardly more than sharpening the pens for the real reporters.

Josh pushed through the crowd, using his shoulder to wedge between others, then a quick, lithe twist to move past them. He was a short man, hardly five-foot-eight, and slight of build. The jam, turn, and ooze through was a technique he had learned from another reporter of greater stature, but Josh found it worked as well for him as it did Crandall Benson. He got to the front of the crowd and his heart fell. The chance for a big story a day before Christmas was dashed.

"Oofty Goofty! Oofty Goofty!" the crowd chanted.

"What's he doing this time?" Josh asked a well-dressed man beside him.

"Anyone with a dollar can hit him over the head with that

board." The man laughed at the antics of the hairy man gyrating wildly and pretending to be crazy. Or maybe he was crazy. Josh didn't care to speculate on it.

Oofty Goofty had made quite a stir in San Francisco months earlier at a Market Street sideshow. He had been locked in a cage and fed hunks of raw meat. Billed as the "Wild Man from Borneo," he had allowed himself to be covered in tar, then coated in fur. Rattling bars and yelling "oofty goofty" at passersby had given the man his cognomen.

The sideshow had closed when Oofty Goofty had fallen sick. Josh had done a small story on it. The tar had prevented the performer from sweating, and doctors had struggled to remove the tar without removing his skin, also. Since then, he had forsaken the sideshow and gone to work at Bottle Koenig's, a Barbary Coast dive that appealed strangely to the reporter in Josh. He felt there were thousands of stories lurking in the darker elements in the beer hall, even if his editor did not agree.

"Gimme a dollar, hit me with the plank!" Oofty Goofty jumped about in a reprise of his wild-man act. At first, the crowd shied away from him. Finally a sailor stepped up and handed the man a dollar.

Josh cringed when he saw how hard the sailor swung. The board broke over Oofty Goofty's head, staggering him and causing a cut to bleed as if an artery had been severed. But Oofty Goofty bounced back, laughing and urging another to hit him for a dollar. The next taker used his fist.

The crowd roared in approval, of what Josh was at a loss to say. He saw nothing to report, edged away, and quickly hurried to a four-story building a block from the Embarcadero. Glancing up, he sucked in a deep breath, adjusted his tie, and smoothed the wrinkles from his threadbare coat, then went into Murdoch and Sons Shipping.

"Top of the morning," he said jauntily to the secretary. The man glanced at Josh, made a sour face, and jerked his thumb in the direction of the president's office.

"Miss Murdoch's inside with her father."

"Don't sound too happy, MacMillan. It's only the day before Christmas." Josh laughed. The secretary made no secret of his dislike. For all that, no one in the company showed Josh much respect, except Faith Murdoch. And she was going to marry him.

Josh started to knock on Sean Murdoch's door, then hesitated. He had no reason to dread seeing the man who was going to be his father-in-law. Other than that he was cold and cold-hearted and obviously thought Faith was marrying below her station. Josh summoned his courage and knocked.

"Who is it?"

"Joshua Harlan, sir. Is Faith with you?"

"Yes. Come in." The "damn your eyes" went unstated.

Josh stepped into the lavishly appointed redwood-paneled office and saw Sean Murdoch presiding behind his cherry-wood desk. A furniture company in Boston had built the desk specially for Murdoch, then shipped it around the Cape at a cost that could have kept Josh and Faith in food and lodging for a year. But the desk was impressive, almost as impressive as the bulky man behind it.

Sean Murdoch had been a dockworker much of his life. The muscles still bulged, but prosperity and working behind a desk had turned some of that muscle to fat. Murdoch was physically imposing, but his pale blue eyes were intimidating. They bored in on Josh—and found him wanting. In all respects.

"Dear," Faith greeted Josh. The red-haired beauty came to him and lightly kissed his cheek. "I wondered where you were. We were going out to dinner, weren't we?"

"A special one, just the two of us," Josh said. He turned to Murdoch and added, "But not as special, of course, as Christmas dinner tomorrow at your house."

"You're one hell of a liar, Harlan," the shipping magnate growled. He pulled out a cigar and lit it, puffing out a cloud of blue smoke that might have been vented from a railroad locomotive's stack. Josh would have found that oily black engine smoke more tolerable. The cigar smoke choked him as Murdoch blew great clouds in his direction.

"Perhaps I should get you a watch for Christmas, Joshua," Faith said. "You are ever so late."

"Only a few minutes," he said, not wanting to get into a tiff with her in front of her father. "Let's go. I have to stop at the office before we go to the restaurant, but that'll take only a minute."

"Office," snorted Sean Murdoch. "You call that broom closet you have at the *Alta California* an office? Why don't you chuck it and come to work here? Put in a good day's work, earn a decent day's wages." Murdoch looked at his daughter. "Faith says you're good with numbers. Maybe we could use you in the accounting department, or out there on the dock making sure those damned pirates don't try to steal us blind when they unload cargo."

"That's a generous offer, sir. Thank you for making it. Again." Josh had dodged the issue successfully so far. Being locked in a small room doing nothing but adding endless columns of figures—or even being on the docks piled high with smelly fish and even smellier cargo from the Orient—was not in the least exciting.

"You'll never amount to a hill of beans with any newspaper. Reporter!" Sean Murdoch snorted again, disturbing the haze of cigar smoke surrounding him like a storm cloud now. "That's no fit occupation for a man who's going to marry my little girl."

"Yes, sir. Come along, Faith. See you tomorrow, sir."

"You know where it is," Murdoch said gruffly.

"Yes, sir, of course. The big house on Russian Hill. I've been there before." Josh tried to hide his sarcasm but couldn't. Not entirely. Only Faith's presence kept Josh from a more aggressive argument with Murdoch over the way he treated him.

Sean Murdoch growled like a bulldog and began pawing through the stacks of papers on his desk. Josh took the moment of distraction to usher Faith from the office. He almost gasped in the fresh air outside.

"You were so curt with Papa," Faith said tartly. "He only has your best interests at heart."

"He has *your* best interests at heart. I'm surprised he approved of our marriage."

"He would never deny me anything I want," Faith said, taking his arm as they walked away from the dock area. "And I want you."

"I love you, too," he said. "I wish I could say your brothers shared your feelings toward me." He saw Faith's two brothers, Michael and Morgan, glaring at him from a second-story window in their office building. He waved, smiled, and hurried on, knowing they returned his cheery greeting with obscene gestures. As they always did.

If he didn't love Faith so much, he would never have tolerated the Murdoch family's behavior. Even so, Josh wondered how he could handle them after the marriage.

"Let's elope," he said suddenly. "A Christmas wedding. It would be so romantic!"

"Oh, Joshua, you foolish man," Faith said, gripping his arm a little tighter. "You know that cannot be. There is so much to plan, so much to do. Why, my wedding dress alone will take *months* to sew."

"Have your father hire an extra seamstress. Or two more. That'd make five working on it. They should finish in no time at all."

"But not by tomorrow. Anyway, we are expected at dinner. There would not be enough time."

Josh wondered if Faith was joking. He could not tell. And it hardly mattered to him. She was the loveliest woman in all San Francisco, and she wanted to marry him. He loved her, she loved him. That was enough. Except for wanting to be a full-fledged reporter.

"Just a second while I check for messages. You never know if the city editor wants me out on a big story." They went into the *Alta California* office, Faith looking put out at having the evening interrupted in this fashion.

"You never get any assignments, Joshua. They ignore you. Come work for Papa. In no time at all, you'd be promoted to vice president and be earning a real salary."

"I get five dollars a week at the *Alta*," he said. His eyes lit up when he saw a flimsy yellow telegram stuffed into his tiny mailbox. He grabbed it and tore open the envelope.

"What is it?" Faith asked. "Not some bad news? I always dread telegrams. They always bring me bad news. Someone has died, there is a crisis in the family back in Boston, horrid things."

"I'm not sure what to make of this," Josh said, reading the telegram again. "An old friend of my family is a negotiator with the Modoc Indians." A catch came to his voice. It was a stretch saying he even had a family now, his parents long dead, his brother and two sisters victims of a fire. AB Meacham had been his father's friend but had done so much to help Josh that he felt Meacham was *his* friend, too.

"Oh, those savages? I read of the way they *killed* people in the most brutal fashion possible. You don't want anything to do with them, do you, Joshua?"

"There might be a clash brewing up north, on the Oregon border." His heart pounded. "I might get to cover a war!"

"Oh, silly. They'd never let you go. Why, you're not even a full reporter. Only—what did they call it?"

"A cub reporter," he said, irritated with Faith for pointing this out. "But I have an in. AB—that's Alfred Meacham—is a personal friend, and that would give me a source others wouldn't have. Wait here, Faith. I won't be long."

"Joshua!" she cried, but he had started up the broad stairs leading to the editorial offices, taking them two at a time.

"Mr. Billingsly, can I have a word with you?"

"What's it this time, Josh? Something better than giant sea creatures pulling down ships, I trust."

"That was a bad lead, sir. I know now that the man was

only trying to drum up business for his melodeon show. But this is important. There's a full-scale Indian war brewing up at Tule Lake. See?" He pushed the yellow telegram into his editor's hands.

"So? There've been shots exchanged up there before."

"This has all the earmarks of a major war. The *Alta California* can have a man on the spot, sending daily reports. With my connection to the Indian Agent, the paper can scoop all the others."

"That's only if shooting starts. The Klamath are peacefully on their reservation. The Modoc, the ones your friend refers to in the telegram, don't number more than a few hundred. What earthly threat could they pose?"

"Mr. Meacham says two of the leaders have escaped capture by the cavalry and are intent on starting a war. Sir, the *Alta* can scoop the other papers. That could boost circulation!"

"A good war always does," Billingsly mused. "Very well. Go up, nose about, then send me some good copy from—what town's nearest?—Yreka? Linkville? Your best reporting or nothing. If I like it, you can stay on the scene and report. If there's nothing of merit, come back right away. You understand?"

"Yes, *sir!*" Josh felt ten feet high. "And Merry Christmas!"

"And to you," the editor said, his mind already on something else.

Josh hurried back down the broad marble stairs, his feet hardly seeming to touch the ground.

"Faith, you won't believe it!" he cried, grabbing her and spinning the redhead around and around. She grabbed at her hat to keep it from flying off. Faith backed off from him as if he were a crazy man, one like that horrid Oofty Goofty person he'd mentioned to her on the way to the *Alta California* offices.

"Whatever has happened, Joshua?" she asked. "I'm not sure I will like it."

"Mr. Billingsly sent me to Yreka to report on the Modoc War!"

"Well, how nice for you," Faith said in a low voice. "I hope this does not interfere with dinner tomorrow."

"Of course not. I won't leave until after. What will I need? I have to pack. I can't forget a notebook and pencils. And—"

Josh never noticed how Faith Murdoch kept her eyes straight ahead and clutched at her tiny purse as they walked along the twilight street, going to the restaurant, nor that she barely spoke throughout the meal. He was too excited with the prospect of being a reporter. A real one.

# Parley and Thrust

*Yreka, California*
*December 28, 1869*

Joshua Harlan was exhausted from the rapid trip from San Francisco to Yreka, first by train to Sacramento and then north by stage, but he felt strangely exhilarated. The cold, crisp mountain air was part of it, so different from the fish-laden scent that pervaded all of San Francisco. No piles of garbage stood uncollected along the narrow streets, but the streets were mud and dirt, frozen in patches. The paved streets of San Francisco, with gaslights hissing, did not permit a moment's inattention to turn to disaster. Josh had barely emerged from the coach before he stepped into a deep pothole and sank to midcalf in cold mud.

"AB!" he called, waving to Alfred Meacham, standing safe and dry on a rickety boardwalk near the stagecoach office. Josh knocked gobs of sticky mud off his boots, then forgot entirely about such cleanliness. That was something Faith always hounded him about. Now there was no rug to track dirt onto. He was on the real frontier now, doing a reporter's job.

"Good to see you, Josh. Been a while."

Josh felt awkward at that. The last time he had seen AB Meacham was at his parents' funeral. They had died of cholera down in Sacramento. Not long after, he had moved to San

Francisco to find fame and fortune. Or at least fame. As a reporter for the state's biggest newspaper.

Josh bucked up and grinned. "Tell me all about it, AB. Every little detail."

"You don't waste any time, do you, Josh? Is that what they teach you to do as a reporter?"

"My editor's waiting by the telegraph key for me to send him a story that'll knock his socks off," Josh said.

"Come along, then. We can eat after we've talked with Captain Jack's sister."

"Queen Mary?"

"You've done your homework well. She was caught when the cavalry rounded up everyone in Captain Jack's village."

"What about Captain Jack and the others who got away?"

"So far, they haven't caused any mischief, but I worry. Ivan Applegate is quite knowledgeable about the Modoc and their ways, as many of the other settlers are. Around Yreka, Captain Jack is a respected man, but Applegate fears him, and rightly so, in my opinion."

"Why did the cavalry attack?"

Meacham walked along for a spell before answering. When he did, his lips pulled back into a thin, angry line.

"McKay wants blood. He told the lieutenant in charge of the troopers I had ordered the attack. The soldiers, mostly Oregon volunteers, were so liquored up and ready to fight, they would have believed a snake hissing at them was my order to fight. I fear Captain Jack distrusts me now to the point there is little hope of a peaceful solution."

"So you're trying to get Queen Mary to be your emissary?"

"Something like that," Meacham said. "Perhaps I should recruit you to help, Josh. You're quicker on the uptake than most of them around here. All they think about is fighting."

"You cannot blame them too much, AB. Look at how many wagon trains have been attacked, how many people have been slaughtered."

"By white and red alike. There are hotheads on both sides.

For every Don McKay we have, they have a Curly Headed Doctor with his chants and ceremonies. Rumor has it he has taken up the Ghost Dance credo."

"The Ghost Dance? What's that?" Josh began scribbling with his blunt pencil, trying to write and walk at the same time.

"There's time for you to fill in the details. I've put Queen Mary up in this boardinghouse. The widow woman running it is less inclined to think of all the Modoc as savages."

"I thought the people of Yreka were approving of the Modoc."

Meacham laughed harshly. "They like them just fine, but not as guests sleeping in their beds."

They entered the neatly kept house and went into the drawing room, where a Modoc woman sat staring straight ahead, as if she was a statue. Josh looked at Meacham, who motioned him to a chair.

"Queen Mary, this is my friend from San Francisco," Meacham said. "He is here to listen to your words and then write them so others can understand."

She looked at him with dull eyes. "Other white men?"

"Yes," Josh said eagerly.

"Do you lie to one another as you lie to the Modoc?"

"Truth is my business," Josh said earnestly.

"Queen Mary," Meacham said softly, "help us end this without bloodshed. Your brother will certainly be injured and probably killed if he does not lead your people to the reservation."

"We don't like the Klamath. They kill us. Captain Jack should not listen to David Allan's words. He lies to kill us, too." Queen Mary turned so she stared straight ahead again, a statue of living flesh.

"How many warriors can Captain Jack field? Enough to fight the cavalry?" Josh asked.

Meacham frowned and tried to silence the young man. Josh pushed on. He felt the story rippling all around him. He had to grab it, mold it, turn it into something sensational that would make Mr. Billingsly sit up and take notice.

"Will Captain Jack fight? Even if more soldiers are brought in?" Josh asked.

"Of course." Queen Mary fell into uncommunicative silence, forcing Meacham to bid her farewell.

Outside, Meacham turned to Josh and said, "Don't incite her with such questions. I need her to take a message to Captain Jack that fighting *isn't* necessary. To intimate that soldiers will be flooding in only riles Captain Jack more and guarantees that he will fight."

"I'm sorry, AB. I wanted a story, and I think I have the start of a good one."

"I need stories about the Modoc—and the settlers—that will smooth ruffled feathers, not raise them. This is why I asked you up here, Josh. The power of the press is what I need to put pressure on the military, to calm their fears, to show them they don't need more troops."

"I can't report anything I don't see, AB. That wouldn't be honest reporting."

"Then report it and don't make it up," Meacham said tartly.

"I need to find a place to stay. Can you recommend one?" Josh looked over his shoulder at the boardinghouse, wondering if he might worm more information from Captain Jack's sister if he stayed there.

"The hotel is full up, but it only has a half-dozen rooms. Try the restaurant. I think Mrs. Atkins has a spare room. You can't go wrong staying anywhere that the owner makes such good peach cobbler, either."

"Thank you, AB. I'll try not to disappoint you."

"You'd never do that, son. Just be temperate in your stories. We want peace, not fighting."

"I understand," Josh said, wondering how he could do this when all he saw around him spoke of imminent warfare. The people in Yreka seemed to be carrying rifles and shotguns.

Many of the men even wore side arms, something he seldom saw in San Francisco.

He wandered the muddy streets of town, talking to people, getting a feel for the town's temper. Josh became more and more excited because of the undercurrent of distrust and outright fear he found. Already he was writing headlines about the Great Modoc War. Eventually his random walk brought him to the small restaurant.

"Mrs. Atkins?" he asked, stopping in front of the cafe. The woman obviously ate well, passing pleasingly plump many years ago. Her mousy brown hair was pulled back and held by a snood as she swept the mud from the boards in front of the restaurant doorway.

"You must be the reporter fellow from San Francisco," the woman said, eyeing Josh from head to toe. "Word gets round quick-like out here. If you want a room, I got one out back. Fifty cents a day."

Josh swallowed hard hearing this. Such a princely sum was to be expected on the frontier, but it would strain his finances to the limit. He was not certain Mr. Billingsly would reimburse him for much more than that for an entire day.

"One meal included," she added.

"Then I can't go wrong," Josh said. "I'll take the room."

"Around back. See if it suits you, but I suspect it will." Mrs. Atkins went back to her sweeping. Josh slogged through ankle-deep mud and found the room at the head of stairs leading to the second story. The cramped room would have bothered him in San Francisco, but here it was perfect for a working reporter. He sat on the narrow bed and took out a new notebook to begin his first story. Josh had barely filled one page with his small, precise handwritten account when he looked up to see an Indian woman standing in the doorway.

"May I help you?" he asked, putting down his pencil. Josh was taken by the woman's exotic beauty. He could not help comparing her to Faith. Faith was delicate, of alabaster skin with a fragile flower's beauty. This woman, hardly more than a girl, seemed diametrically opposed in every way.

She stood unafraid, sure of herself, dark and lovely and possessing a power that captivated Josh.

"Clean your shoes?" She pointed to his muddy boots.

"Why, no, that is, how much?"

"Nickel."

"That seems a fair price," he said. "Come in."

The Modoc woman moved with the grace of a doe. She dropped to her knees in front of him and began working his boots off. When she looked up at him, her eyes were wide and clear and appraising.

"You don't have to take them off," Josh protested. "I can take them off."

"You can have me for two bits."

"What?" He recoiled, stunned at what he thought she'd said.

"Too much? I like you. A dime?"

"Are you offering yourself to me, uh, in a carnal fashion?" he asked, astounded and revolted. "That would mean you are a . . . a soiled dove."

"I do not understand."

"A Cyprian? A fallen angel." Josh steadied himself and realized the woman's English did not allow for such discreet distinctions. "A whore."

"I do not understand. All Modoc women work for money."

Josh let out a deep sigh. "I apologize for misunderstanding you. Of course. We all work for money. Your English isn't very good and my Modoc, well, that is nonexistent."

She rocked back on her heels and just looked at him. He noticed how lovely her eyes were. A deep, chocolate brown.

"What is your name?" It was all he could think of to break the uncomfortable silence that had fallen. He was not certain he had misinterpreted her overtures.

"Isabella," she said. "I can cook for you. Clean. Clean clothes, everything."

"I have so little money," Josh said, agonizing over the situation. "If you don't charge too much, perhaps I can hire you on. And perhaps you can tell me about the situation with Captain Jack and the other Modoc. Yes, that would be good. An interpreter."

"Like Tobey?" Isabella asked.

Josh searched his memory, then remembered something AB had told him. He nodded.

"I work for you. Interpret. Tell you things. Make your bed. Sleep in your bed."

Josh laughed uneasily at the pretty woman. The language barrier was going up again. But he thought she would be a much-needed source of information for his stories. If Isabella told him enough, he was sure he could get his editor to reimburse for her services.

He rocked back on the bed and let the Modoc woman take off his boots and begin cleaning them. It took him longer than he expected to finish the story he was to telegraph back to the *Alta California* because Isabella proved so distracting. But it was more than a story, Josh thought. It was a *good* story, filled with threat, promise of bloodshed and warfare, and even had a lurid description of Captain Jack's daring escape from the cavalry.

# Capitulation

*Klamath Reservation*
*December 31, 1869*

Queen Mary sat stolidly, looking glum. She huddled under her shabby wool blanket and cast sidelong glances at her brother. Captain Jack sat on a three-legged stool in the middle of the Applegate cabin. Ivan Applegate looked uneasy having the Modoc *tyee* inside but said nothing to upset Meacham's careful diplomacy.

Joshua Harlan took notes, sharing Applegate's uneasiness but for another reason. This was the first time he had seen Captain Jack, and it might well be his last. The Modoc chief was talking about going peacefully to the Klamath Reservation in exchange for promises of food and supplies.

"Will all your people go, Chief, uh, Captain Jack?" Josh asked, pencil poised and ready to take down the man's every word.

All he got was a brisk nod. Josh wrote a more florid, lavishly expressed sentiment of a betrayed people seeking nothing but peace from the great *tyee* in Washington. The embellishments flowed until Josh checked himself. Sending so much via telegraph would cost a fortune.

He had to come to grips with Captain Jack's total surrender.

There would be no war to report. That meant Joshua Harlan had to find another story to give him the big break needed to crowd out so many other young reporters on the *Alta California*. He sucked in his breath, then settled down to write a good story. It might not make page one, it might never be a banner headline, but he would do a yeoman's job or know the reason.

"You might not get along with the Klamath, but you *can* live there peaceably, can't you?" Meacham asked anxiously.

"Old Schonches has settled his people on the reservation," Captain Jack said. "I can live with him. He is an honorable man."

"I am glad you respect your elders," Meacham said, "but he is getting up there in years. What if Schonchin John takes over?"

Captain Jack shrugged.

"Very well," Meacham said. "We will cross that bridge when we come to it. If you live in peace, we will protect you from your enemies, even those in your own tribe."

"Schonchin John is not my enemy," Captain Jack said, but Josh heard the slight tremor. That might be true, but it was not the entire story. Schonchin John had fought Captain Jack for control of his band, and the political infighting continued. Captain Jack had moved past distrust of the white man after the Wright massacre. Older, more bitter, Schonchin John had not.

"This day is a special one for my people," Meacham said. "With Mr. Applegate's approval, we will have a big feast tonight to celebrate the new year. You and any of your tribe who wish to attend are welcome."

Josh thought Captain Jack was going to laugh in Meacham's face, but the *tyee* sat for a moment, then nodded.

"We will come to show our friendship and to seal the peace between our peoples."

Captain Jack glanced at Josh, his eyes unreadable. The Indian stood and walked off proudly. AB Meacham heaved a deep sigh when Queen Mary followed her brother from the cabin.

"That is a relief," Meacham said. "Well, Josh, you have your story."

"I do," he said, trying not to sound too dejected.

"Buck up. War has been averted. People who might have died will live—and in peace. There might be some trouble between the tribes on the Klamath Reservation, but nothing that cannot be handled. Am I right, Ivan?"

"I hope so, AB. Captain Jack broke two earlier treaties."

"That's a bit harsh, considering the circumstances around them," Meacham said, "but I am not going to argue details. I have his promise. Honor means a great deal to the Modoc, so I am sure he will move his people to the reservation as quickly as possible."

"I've got a feast to fix, AB," said the settler. "Better get the missus and the others to work."

"Leave the muskets hanging on the wall, Ivan. Please."

"All right, AB. You know what you're doing. I hope."

Meacham turned to Josh, a broad smile on his face. It faded a mite when he saw the reporter's expression.

"What? You don't think this is the end of it, Josh?"

"No, AB, not at all. I think it is the end, and the end of my story."

"It's been a good vacation, I suppose. Stay for the celebration. Then you can go back to that lovely fiancée of yours in San Francisco tomorrow. Give Faith my love. I hope to meet her someday soon."

"Yes," Josh said, but for some reason he thought more of leaving Isabella behind. The Modoc woman would have to fend for herself since she seemed to be without any family. The notion she might turn to whoring bothered Josh greatly, even if that was the way so many of the women survived. Perhaps he could see to it that she was moved to the reservation along with Captain Jack's band. Isabella would be guaranteed food and shelter then.

* * *

Joshua Harlan was happy to get off the ferry from Oakland. San Francisco Bay was choppy today, and he had been afflicted with more than a touch of seasickness. The trip back from Yreka had been quick, quicker than his trip up, but it had seemed to drag endlessly since he kept thinking of the lost opportunity in the north. Peace was not the stuff of headlines.

Josh smiled when he saw the feathery, flouncy vision of beauty that was Faith Murdoch. She stood on the dock, genteelly waving her lace hanky. The wind caught her red hair and carried it in delightful disarray. Even as he relished the small imperfection, Faith reached up and captured the vagrant strands, patting them back into place.

"Faith!" he called, tumbling over the side of the ferry and onto the dock. He might have taken a stage or the train around the southern end of the bay, but that would have added an extra day to the trip. Now he was home where his loving fiancée waited for him.

"Oh, Joshua, it is so good you got back from the frontier."

"I'd hardly call it the frontier," he said, chuckling. Faith had spent her entire life amid society and wealth. "But I'm glad to see you, too."

He started to kiss her, but she turned.

"If we hurry, you can get cleaned up and we will be able to make the soiree. I was afraid you would not return in time, and I would have to miss it. I simply could not be seen going in the company of one of my brothers, or even my father."

Josh shook his head as if to clear it of cobwebs.

"What soiree?"

"Why, the one at the Ralstons'. They are up-and-coming society figures destined to be prominent around town, mark my words. Mr. Ralston is owner of the Bank of California and—"

"I just got back from a long trip, Faith," Josh said. He was not prepared for a fancy dress ball crowded with social climbers making small talk and angling to be seen by the right people. "I had hoped for a quiet dinner with you."

"Quiet, Joshua, quiet!" she exclaimed, throwing up her hands. "It has been far too quiet with you gone. What did you want me to do over the Christmas gala season, go without you? The talk! A woman without a proper escort would be humiliated. Think of the gossip!"

"I'm mighty tired," Josh said, the excitement at returning fading quickly.

"Just don't yawn without covering your mouth. I am sure you will have *fabulous* stories to tell tonight. We will be the center of attention, I am positive of it. Now come along, Joshua. I have a carriage."

They climbed in, Faith rattling on and on about the parties she had missed and the upcoming ones through Twelfth Night.

"How's your father doing?" Josh asked, wanting to derail her constant talk of parties.

"Oh, better. He was hardly injured."

"What? Injured?" Josh sat up. "What happened?"

"Why, he was attacked by highbinders. Right here on the docks. Imagine that."

"Was he badly hurt?"

"Not too badly," Faith said, "but he used it as an excuse to avoid going to dinner with the Crockers. It would have been ever so good making social contact with people of their stature."

Josh frowned. Highbinders seldom left Chinatown. Something important along the docks must have drawn them. A clipper ship from the Flowery Kingdom bringing Celestials from opposing tongs? Josh perked up, wondering if a story might be found.

"What did he do?"

"Oh, he hired a few more Police Specials to patrol the docks. I bought him a brand new cravat that hid the cuts those yellow devils gave him on his chest and throat."

"We should look in on him," Josh said.

"Very well. It is on the way, and he said something about seeing you when you returned." Faith itemized all the people who were invited to the Ralston party, but Josh hardly listened. The carriage took them to the luxurious Murdoch house on Russian Hill. He helped Faith out, still engrossed in her planning for the evening. No military commander tended more to detail or plotted attack so diligently.

"Papa is in the sitting room," Faith said once they were in the house. "Go on in. I must see if my dress is ready. The maid had actually spilled something on it, imagine that." Faith flounced off, leaving Josh in the foyer.

Knocking on the door leading into the sitting room, Josh waited for Sean Murdoch's gruff command to enter.

"Sir, how are you? Faith told me of the attack."

"Yes, yes, that," Murdoch said, waving it off. But Josh saw the man's difficulty in moving his right hand. From the way his smoking jacket was pulled up around his neck, the cuts there might have been extensive. Chinese highbinders used vicious hatchets and long, slender-bladed knives.

"Can I get you anything?" Josh did not much like Sean Murdoch, but the man was pale and had lost more than a few pounds, showing how serious the injuries were.

"I wanted a word with you. This attack was a warning."

"The tongs are trying to take over shipping?" Josh eagerly perched on the edge of a sofa across from the leather chair pulled in front of the fireplace for Murdoch's comfort. He scented a story if the Celestials had grown so bold.

"What's that? How should I know? Those thieves wanted money, nothing more."

"What warning, then?" asked Josh, still curious.

"My own mortality, boy, my own mortality! I came close to dying. Didn't let Faith know, of course. She's too fragile to be exposed to that, but it made me realize how short life can be." Sean Murdoch fixed his steely gaze on Josh. "I've given you enough time to apply for a job with the company. Since you haven't come forward on your own, I have no choice but to tell you."

"Tell me what?" Josh didn't like the sound of this. "You aren't dying?"

"Not any time soon, I trust, but I need a son-in-law with a good job able to support my daughter. You will go to work in the accounting department Monday morning. No argument, now! The pay will be about what you eke out as reporter with the *Alta California,* but the advancement will be quick. I need you to learn every aspect of the business so you can take it over when I meet my maker."

"That'll be years, sir!"

"I know," Sean Murdoch said brusquely, "but there is much to learn, and you have to start right away."

"What of your sons?"

"What of those worthless louts? Those ne'er-do-wells? They are leeches sucking my lifeblood. The company might be named Murdoch and Sons Shipping, but *I* am the driving force, not those two tipplers. And I could never trust them to see that Faith is taken care of after I pass on. Why she chose a man as poor as a churchmouse to marry is beyond me. You must have some talents which are hidden, but I swear, I will bring them all out and you will do well by my daughter and my shipping company, or I'll know the reason!"

Josh opened his mouth, then closed it, not knowing what to say.

"Then it's settled. Monday morning, bright and early. See Edward Traylor in the accounting department. Now go. I need to rest. Everything tires me so these days."

"Yes, sir," Josh said, not sure what he was agreeing to. He left, to find Morgan Murdoch in the foyer, fists clenched and a look of pure hatred on his face. Without a word, Faith's younger brother spun and stormed up the staircase to the second floor.

Josh knew Morgan had overheard his father's tirade. Life was going to be even harder now. Not only was he being forced to give up his dream of being a reporter, he had to go to work in a company where the owner's sons would give him nothing but woe.

# Dissension
# and Violence

*Klamath Reservation*
*March 13, 1870*

"Pay for it," the Klamath brave said, sneering at Captain Jack. "The deer is not yours. It is *ours* and you must pay us for it."

Captain Jack eyed the arrogant hunter and considered how easy it would be to kill the man. The Klamath had fired his musket but had missed the deer that Captain Jack had brought down expertly. Still, to kill the Klamath meant trouble. Meacham had spent more than a week going from Modoc to Klamath and back with offers and counteroffers. Captain Jack was sorry he had agreed to settle near Old Schonches now because of all the trouble brewing. The Klamath insulted the Modoc at every turn. Old Schonches turned a deaf ear to the ridicule, but he was ancient. The sound of his joints grating and cracking as he moved drowned out all but the most strident Klamath.

Even then, the old *tyee* tolerated too much.

For once, Captain Jack agreed with Schonchin John. The firebrand had left the reservation and gone raiding against the white man's settlements. Captain Jack was not willing to go that far. He liked the people of Yreka, and they liked him. But those were not his lifelong enemies, in spite of what Ben Wright and others as bad had done.

The Klamath were the enemy of the Modoc.

Captain Jack never decided he ought not harm the overbearing Klamath. He simply acted to protect the game he had brought down with his own rifle. He stepped forward and swung the musket, the barrel catching the Klamath brave just above the left ear. The sick crunching sound of breaking skull told Captain Jack the Klamath was not likely to covet Modoc game again.

He stepped over the fallen brave and went to the deer to begin dressing it out. As he worked, his brother Black Jim and two others came up.

Black Jim said nothing about the dead Klamath brave. He dropped to his knees and began working alongside his brother. Bogus Charley and Scarfaced Charley huddled together, discussing the matter until Bogus summoned enough courage to ask.

"He said the deer was his. It wasn't," Captain Jack explained.

"Meacham will not like this. The Klamath won't, either," pointed out Scarfaced Charley. He nervously touched the bone handle of his knife, as if he might draw it and plunge the tip into the Klamath brave. "What are we going to do? Hide the body?"

"Why bother?" asked Bogus Charley. "They will know who killed this insect."

Captain Jack hefted the haunch he had cut off the deer. His brother staggered under the rest of the meat.

"We can no longer share the land with them." Captain Jack spat in the direction of the dead Klamath. "They insult us, they try to steal our women, now they think all the game on the reservation is theirs. I will not tolerate such outrages. They walk the earth as if it is theirs and theirs alone. They do not respect the Modoc."

"We can kill them," suggested Black Jim.

"Let them have their land," Captain Jack said. "We will settle along Lost River, where we belong. That is our proper land, not this, not surrounded by Klamath." He started back to the Modoc section of the reservation. Captain Jack left part of the venison for Old Schonches, knowing the old *tyee* would never leave with the younger members of the tribe. Then Captain Jack called out to assemble everyone near his *wikiup.*

"My people!" he said loudly. "Many counseled us against coming to the reservation with our mortal enemy, the Klamath, so near. I thought they were wrong. Now I admit they were right."

A murmur went through the crowd. Captain Jack did not often side with Curly Headed Doctor and Schonchin John. The shaman had a small band of followers settled a mile away, and Schonchin John had vanished, angered by the way the Klamath treated him. Now their *tyee* agreed. This was a day many had waited for.

"We leave?" asked a woman barely out of her teens.

"We will settle in the Yainax region, farther from the Klamath. Then we will see if Meacham supports us or takes their side."

"What if Yainax is not far enough away?" asked Bogus Charley. "We need to skip lightly and fast to avoid trouble from the Klamath. They would kill our women and children in their beds, then laugh about how brave they are."

"Yainax will be far enough. We will hunt without interference, and we will live as the Great Spirit intended." Captain Jack chased off the villagers to their *wikiups,* and then went to his own. He had little enough to pack for the journey of fifty miles.

Fifty miles was not much, but he hoped it would be enough. If it wasn't, they would all float canoes on the rivers of blood that would spring forth.

\* \* \*

"You can't imagine how difficult this is for me," Alfred Meacham said, exasperated. "It took me a week to find you, and now you hand me this sorry story about the Klamath trying to kill you."

"They refused us permission to hunt. They said those were 'their' forests. They said we hunted 'their' game. They said we drank 'their' water. You told me the Modoc would share with the Klamath. You did not convince the Klamath of that." Captain Jack stood with arms folded, glaring at Meacham, wondering if the white Indian Agent understood. The man had not lied. Not exactly. He had just not told the entire truth.

"It's all a misunderstanding. I'll work it out with them, but you can't stay here in Yainax. It's not the part of the reservation you were assigned."

"We stay," Captain Jack said firmly. "The land along the Lost River is Modoc land. *Our* land."

"The cavalry will come to force you back. I have no control over them, Captain Jack. You know that." What worried Meacham was the distance from Fort Klamath. The troopers would have to cross most of the Klamath Reservation to even reach Lost River. Such movement might create uneasiness among David Allan's band of Klamath, unrest that could bring the tenuous peace to a bloody end. Meacham fought on too many fronts—and was almost out of ammunition.

"I know that many of the soldiers are gone."

"True, General Sherman has transferred many of them to Arizona to fight the Apache, but many remain at Fort Klamath."

"Not enough to go to war with the Modoc," Captain Jack declared. "We will stay where our women are not raped and where we can hunt without hindrance."

"There will be trouble," warned Meacham. "This is close to white man's land now. Settlers are all around. You're not ten miles from the Applegate Cutoff, and you know how many wagons a month go along that trail."

"We can live in peace with them. I have many friends in Yreka. Maybe the Modoc should live there."

"No!" Meacham almost panicked at the thought. It was bad enough having them in an area along the Lost River not intended for the Modoc.

"We stay. If the Klamath come, we will kill them. Otherwise, we will live in peace. We will hunt and raise our crops— the weather becomes more favorable—and we will have many children. This is all I want for my people."

"Captain Jack, I know, I know," Meacham said, growing more agitated. "It just can't be. Not here."

"It will be," Captain Jack said confidently. "Or else many will die."

# Discontent

San Francisco
June 9, 1870

"Your columns are not properly aligned, Mr. Harlan," the head accountant said in his snippy, clipped tone. He peered through impeccably polished pince-nez glasses at Josh's work. His nose wrinkled slightly in distaste at what he saw all too clearly.

"Mr. Traylor, I am keeping them quite in a line. Are my additions wrong?"

"No, but you work too slowly. Take Gaines over there, for example. He does half again the work you do and ever as accurately."

"Mr. Gaines spends half again the time here that I do. The man does nothing but work!"

"Then, sir, you ought to consider doing the same, if that is what it takes to do an adequate job." Edward Traylor sniffed and looked down his nose at Josh. "You are poorly trained for this job, you know."

"Tell that to Mr. Murdoch," Josh said angrily. Everyone in the company knew why he had this job, and everyone, including him, agreed that he was doing poorly. To have Traylor point it out on a daily basis wore his temper down to the point where it would explode.

"Perhaps I shall. He put you under my tutelage as a trainee for a reason. I can see that you are not working out."

Josh glanced over his shoulder when he heard someone snickering. Michael Murdoch stood there, looking the dandy in his fine clothing, celluloid collar and fancy headlight diamond in the center of a silk cravat like a tinhorn gambler might wear. Faith's brother slipped away before Josh could say a word to him.

Ever since coming to work at Murdoch and Sons Shipping, Josh had lived a life of hellish hours and unutterable mistreatment from those working alongside him. They knew they were doomed to remain in this room earning their paltry wages until the day they died, which might be soon enough in such unheated quarters. Worse, they knew he was going to marry the boss's daughter and was on his way up the ladder, in spite of having no aptitude for the shipping business.

A few times Josh had looked over contracts but could not make head nor tail of them. The one time he had been put out on the dock, he had ordered the wrong ship unloaded. The owner of the cargo had thrown a fit. Only Sean Murdoch taking the owner to the Union Club as his special guest and getting him drunk as a lord had smoothed his ruffled feathers.

And accounting? Josh could never quite get the knack of the double-entry system invented by some Italian monk. Josh was sure the monk had gone crazy from isolation and had somehow left the accounting principles behind as a monstrous joke on the world.

"Joshua," came a voice that scrapped across his consciousness like fingernails on a blackboard.

"What is it, Faith?" he asked, not bothering to look up from his ledger book.

"You were supposed to be ready to go to the party already. I distinctly remember telling you how important this is to me."

"Mr. Traylor thinks I ought to work harder."

"Oh, pish." Faith stamped her foot. "Mr. Traylor, you can let Joshua go for the afternoon, can't you?"

"I certainly can't use him," the head accountant said nastily.

"Oh, good," Faith said, either ignoring or not hearing the sarcasm. "I knew you would see it my way. Come along, Joshua. We *must* go to the party. One of those railroad millionaires is having a quite festive picnic out by Sutro Rocks." Faith bit at her knuckle and frowned. "I do so hope those noisy seals don't make too much racket. They can be so disgusting, too, with what they do to the rocks."

Josh closed his ledger and stoppered his ink bottle, glad to be out in the summer sun, such as it was today. But even the wan sunlight filtering through the clouds was better than the tightly sealed room where Edward Traylor browbeat his minions.

"Mr. Harlan! Mr. Harlan, wait a moment," came the cry from Sean Murdoch's secretary. MacMillan hurried up, holding a letter. "This is for you."

"Thanks," Josh said, examining the envelope with anticipation. He had not heard from AB Meacham in weeks. Perhaps something brewed along the California-Oregon border, some new Indian trouble, a dispute, the hints of a war that might make the *Alta California* notice him again if he delivered a decent story.

"Mr. Murdoch wants to see you, too. Right away."

"Oh, bother. How can Papa keep me from the picnic like this?" Faith put her cool-fingered hand on his arm and said sternly, "Don't let Papa keep you long. I really must get to that picnic in time to see how all the women are dressed."

"Yes, dear," he said, almost happy to escape Faith and the prospect of yet another boring afternoon tea where the men played with empires and the women talked of European fashions and how hard it was to train new servants.

He went into Sean Murdoch's office, to find the man putting laudanum drops into a glass of water. He made a face as he swallowed, then looked up to see Josh.

"The pain," he said. "Can't get rid of it."

Josh knew the attack by the highbinders had taken its toll

on Murdoch but had not realized it continued to hold him in such torturing thrall.

"You wanted to see me, sir?" Josh almost hoped Murdoch intended to fire him. He would need a job, but at least he wouldn't be under Traylor's ink-smeared thumb in a boring job he barely understood.

"It's about time for you to move to other parts of the business, to round out your training," Murdoch said. He belched, downed the rest of the water, then lit one of his poisonous cigars. "Starting tomorrow, report to the orders office. Quinn will show you the ropes, how we take in orders, how we fill them, where, the bidding process, everything."

"Sir, I—" Josh didn't know how to tell the man he wanted to leave. It seemed that quitting the job also meant giving up Faith. What worried Josh the most was how indecisive he was about it. He was not sure losing Faith meant that much to him, especially if he had to be a part of Murdoch and Sons Shipping. A single day in the accounting department had exceeded his tolerance for boredom. Playing with orders might be a little better—it might take him two days before ennui set in.

"Can't talk right now. Faith said she had another of her socials to get to. Go on, keep her happy. Get out!"

Josh saw a wave of pain wash across Sean Murdoch's face. The man turned red and reached for the tincture of opium and more water.

Josh left, feeling robbed. He had wanted to be dismissed or at least given the chance to voice his problems. Outside the office, he stopped and heaved a deep sigh of resignation. He knew how a fly trapped in a spider's web felt.

As he clenched his hand, he heard paper crinkling. Looking down, he saw the letter from Meacham. Josh opened the envelope and read the small script with growing excitement. Captain Jack had left the reservation and trouble brewed, but hardly enough to justify going to the *Alta California* again to cover. He had quit there six months ago, as much because he had failed to deliver a decent front-page story as because of Sean Murdoch's offer to work for his company.

Josh reread Meacham's letter, trying to find meaning in what the Indian Agent hinted at rather than what he said. A single line at the bottom of the letter tore at his heart.

"Isabella sends her regards," Meacham had written. For Josh it reverberated in his head like a struck bell.

Then his head felt as if it came apart at the seams. Sudden pain lanced forward, starting at the back of his skull and going up and over the pate, driving him to his knees.

"Sorry," came Michael Murdoch's insincere apology.

Josh reached up. His hand came away bloody from the cut in his scalp.

"What did you do?" he grated out.

Michael smiled wickedly and cracked his whip. Morgan laughed and said, "You should be more careful, Michael. You're no mule skinner, no matter how much like a jackass he looks."

Josh sat on the floor, trying to stanch the flow of blood. The wound wasn't serious, but head cuts always bled profusely. He watched the brothers leave, whispering and then laughing. He knew he would have to watch his step. The brothers saw him as a threat to their inheritance and might consider killing him.

A new thought, born of the pain, hit him. Sean Murdoch's attackers had been Chinese, highbinders far from their usual haunts. What if his two sons had hired the Celestials to kill their father? They would inherit a business worth a million dollars or more.

Josh closed his eyes and wanted to be north in Yreka, tracking down a story that would carry his byline.

He got to unsteady feet, then left the office. Faith had gone on without him. He knew better than to let her attend the picnic alone, but he had to get a doctor to sew up his cut first.

The picnic was more excruciating than the stitches used by the doctor to suture his head wound.

# Death and Death Again

"She is sicker now than yesterday," Captain Jack said, looking down at his niece. The heat inside the *wikiup* made him sweat, yet the girl shivered under a thick blanket. "You have no idea where Curly Headed Doctor is?"

"None, brother," said Humpy Joe. "I looked everywhere for him. The Klamath claimed not to know, but they lie faster than a swallow flies. Old Schonches has not seen the shaman, or so he says."

"Old Schonches would not lie, especially when one of us lies near death." Captain Jack stared at the frail girl, remembering how she had laughed and played in the forest, gathering flowers and hunting for mushrooms only days before. She had been good at tickling fish, almost as good as Queen Mary. He was *tyee*. He was also her uncle and could not let her die.

"If Curly Headed Doctor is not here with his chants and medicines, then another shaman must be found."

"Another?" asked Humpy Joe. "A Klamath?"

"Comptowas is good," Captain Jack said. "Not as good as Curly Headed Doctor, but perhaps he is more trustworthy."

"Curly Headed Doctor is out stealing horses," Humpy Joe said with some disdain. "He lets the rituals go unsung so he can have new mounts."

"He lets Modoc die," Captain Jack said with some venom. He scooped up his niece and carried her lightness up the ladder and out of the *wikiup*. The sun had set, a bad omen. It warned Captain Jack of the fleeting life in the little girl. This lent speed to his trip down the Applegate Cut-Off, across Lost River, and north into the heart of the Klamath Reservation to find Comptowas.

"She needs immediate attention," Comptowas said, shaking a medicine gourd listlessly. Captain Jack nodded slowly, his eyes on his niece. The young girl no longer thrashed about in her fever. She simply . . . was.

"Curly Headed Doctor is nowhere to be found," Captain Jack said. "Can you help her?"

"Chants," Comptowas said. "Medicines, special medicines. It will take time." He stared at Captain Jack and sneered. "What will the Modoc *tyee* pay?"

"Anything," Captain Jack said. "Cure her."

Comptowas laughed, then began to chant, shaking his rattle with more authority and putting special white and brown powders into the small fire near the girl's pallet. Captain Jack stood to one side, watching anxiously. The Modoc had not gotten along well with the Klamath, but Comptowas was a shaman.

Why had Curly Headed Doctor gone off now to steal horses?

The hypnotic chanting lulled Captain Jack. His head dropped slightly. He jerked awake. The pungent odors from the powders put on the fire made his nose water. He blinked when he saw how Comptowas poked at the girl using a stick decorated with eagle feathers. He poked and prodded and acted as if he tested to see if an enemy was dead rather than to cure a sick little girl.

The shaman looked over his shoulder. He stopped chanting and put his rattle down.

"What? Is she cured already?" Captain Jack's heart raced. Not even Curly Headed Doctor, with all his talk of the Ghost

Dance and its protective powers, could have brought the girl back from the edge of death so quickly.

"Her spirit is gone," Comptowas said.

Captain Jack stood and stared at the shaman, then looked to his niece, so still and peaceful and dead. Captain Jack sucked in his breath, then did what his heart dictated.

Sheriff Abner Wingate found himself backed into a corner in his own office. He hated sitting behind the desk in the uncomfortable chair, but he wished he were there now. He could keep the desk between him and the irate settler.

"Now, calm yourself, Mr. Applegate," Wingate said. "It might not be as bad as you think."

"Think!" cried Ivan Applegate. "I know Comptowas is dead and Captain Jack killed him. The savage took his knife and gutted him in his own *wikiup!*"

"This is the first I've heard of a killing," Wingate said. He was sheriff of Siskiyou County but what went on up at the Klamath Reservation was out of his purview. Thankfully. Let that military man from Fort Klamath deal with the Modoc.

"So I'm telling you now. Captain Jack comes and goes here in Yreka. He might be in town right now. Arrest him! Hang the red bastard before he kills us all in our beds!"

"Now, now, Mr. Applegate, don't get so riled," Wingate said. "According to the government, Captain Jack's a reservation Indian and I don't have jurisdiction over him."

"But he comes to Yreka!"

"Don't matter," Wingate said, liking this conversation less and less. Ivan Applegate was not the kind of man to let matters lie. None of the Applegate clan was since they thought they owned danged near everything. "What goes on amongst the Indians is their business, or that of the U.S. Army."

"Hold him for the soldiers!"

"Can't do that. American law doesn't apply. I'd be breaking the government law if I tried."

"He can't murder and get away with it. My Klamath friends are sure Captain Jack slaughtered Comptowas in cold blood. No reason, just upped and knifed him, then gutted him."

"I know how they treat each other," Wingate said, "but it is *not* my concern." The sheriff held up his hand to cut off further protest. "What I can do is send a deputy or two out to do some inquiries."

"What good will that do? Those saucy Modoc are turning dangerous—again. You have a short memory, Sheriff, if you don't remember how they killed settlers coming in on wagons not so long ago."

"That was years back, Mr. Applegate, but I understand how you can get so excited."

"Excited!" shouted Applegate. He turned and left the sheriff's office, slamming the door behind him. Abner Wingate sagged a little, then went back to real business, the law-keeping the citizens of the county elected him to do. Running off to the Klamath Reservation could wait—forever.

# Mistrust

*Yreka, California*
*August 21, 1870*

"Are we fools?" cried Black Jim. "If Kintpuash—Captain Jack—goes to this meeting, they will arrest him!"

"Please," AB Meacham said, trying to calm Captain Jack's brother. "We will only talk. Nothing more. There will be no lawmen there."

"They chase my brother as if he were a rabbit for their stewpot," Black Jim insisted. "The sheriff from Yreka and his deputies have no business trying to arrest him."

Meacham heaved a deep sigh, feeling years older every day this dragged on. Somehow, Ivan Applegate had lit a fire under Abner Wingate and gotten him out chasing after Captain Jack every time he ventured into town. Most of the townspeople liked the Modoc and their loose ways. Time and again Meacham had warned Captain Jack that many whites thought of Modoc women as nothing more than prostitutes, selling themselves. He had come to realize the Modoc saw nothing immoral in this; it was their way of life among themselves. How women valued themselves so little was something Meacham had never understood, although the Modoc women he talked to were anything but the soiled doves of white settlements. This had produced great friction between settlers intent on their religious beliefs and the Modoc, who simply did not understand.

But Wingate dogging Captain Jack's every step had taken on the air of a bad melodrama. Captain Jack claimed he had not murdered Comptowas, but Meacham had the feeling the Modoc *tyee* meant something different from what Applegate meant. A gut instinct told Meacham Captain Jack had knifed Comptowas, but had considered it his due for the death of his niece. Or was this what a *tyee* did when anyone from his village died at the hand of a shaman? More miscommunication? Or outright murder? Meacham felt a headache starting that would never go away until the Modoc were properly settled on a reservation—and stayed there.

The Modoc thought one thing was perfectly natural; the white settlers saw it as the end of the world.

What worried Meacham most was Wingate listening to Applegate and trying to arrest Captain Jack. This was the province of the military. The soldiers ought to be dealing with such serious crime on the Klamath Reservation, not the California county sheriff.

"We will talk. We must settle this matter soon or there will be great trouble," Meacham said. He spoke the truth but worried about the source of the trouble. With Sherman's transfer of so many soldiers to Arizona to chase Geronimo, the Northwest went almost unprotected. Any trouble boiling over now meant a rampage through the countryside, and the settlers were likely to be the first victims.

Meacham wished he could convince Ivan Applegate of the trouble he caused, forcing Wingate to go after Captain Jack.

"Talk," scoffed Black Jim. He crossed his arms and glared.

"I offer my sincerest word that nothing more will happen. Jesse Applegate has offered the use of his home for the meeting." Meacham did not like the idea of having Ivan's uncle involved, but it was the only way he could get the settlers to believe anything was being done to bring Captain Jack to heel. Meacham just hoped Jesse—or his hotheaded nephew—did not bring Sheriff Wingate and his trigger-happy deputies in. Blood would flow if the Modoc saw the gleaming silver badges.

"Captain Jack will talk. Nothing more." Black Jim challenged him. Meacham accepted.

"Yainax," Captain Jack insisted. "Yainax must be the Modoc Reservation. Everything on the other side of Lost River."

Meacham looked at the map spread out, showing the boundaries of the Klamath Reservation, trying to decide what he could promise and what would be nothing but hot air.

"And no more sheriff following me, scaring off the game I hunt," Captain Jack went on.

Meacham looked up, wondering if the arrogance came from a strong bargaining position or a weak one. Was Captain Jack bluffing?

"Did you kill Comptowas?" he asked bluntly.

"He killed my niece," Captain Jack said in his oblique fashion. "A shaman should not kill, he should heal. He was Klamath and the Klamath hate us."

"I can't argue with that," Meacham said, resigned to granting Captain Jack his wishes for a separate reservation. He was tired of the Klamath clashing with the Modoc. The Klamath Indians never violated the strict letter of the compact with them, but they did all they could to stir up trouble. More than once he had overheard a Klamath tell a Modoc that the fish in the lake were Klamath, but the Modoc could fish. For a while. But not to take too many. Trees were for the Klamath, not the Modoc. But the generosity of the Klamath tribe permitted the Modoc to cut timber. But only one or two trees, and then not the best. Everything the Klamath Indians did was condescending and contemptuous of the Modoc. Listening to this every day would try a saint's patience.

Meacham knew full well that Captain Jack was no saint.

"You must stop raiding the settlers," Meacham said. Behind

him he heard Jesse Applegate move closer, waiting for the Modoc *tyee's* answer. This was the crux of the matter for the white settlers. Ivan Applegate had goaded Wingate after Captain Jack more to stop the raiding than he did to avenge Comptowas's murder. If anything, Ivan would gladly see every Indian in California and Oregon dead and buried so their land would be opened to white settlement.

"The people of Yreka like me. I like them," Captain Jack said.

"But around Tule Lake, *we* don't like you!" cried Jesse Applegate. "You steal our horses and kill our livestock. You shot two men who tried to stop your raiding. You—"

"Mr. Applegate, please," Meacham cut in. He turned to Captain Jack. "No more raiding if you get your own reservation at Yainax."

"That is fair," Captain Jack said, after mulling over the offer.

"I will do what I can to get authorization for a Yainax reservation," Meacham said, "but you must go back to the Klamath Reservation until then. And no more raiding. No more killing of Klamath. Nothing but peace."

"Get a Modoc reservation," Captain Jack said.

"Then we have a deal," Meacham said, thrusting out his hand. Captain Jack shook, but Meacham wondered if they were agreeing to the same thing.

# A Touch of War

*Fort Klamath, Oregon*
*January 25, 1872*

"What do you mean that you'll not get involved?" Meacham stared at the officer in disbelief. "It's your job!"

"Go out amongst those savages?" The captain shook his head. "I've got no supplies for a scout against them. And to what end? What am I supposed to do? Force them to love each other?" The officer laughed harshly, shocking Meacham even more. There was no way this man was going to venture beyond Fort Klamath's stockade walls to force Captain Jack and his band back onto the reservation.

"The Modoc have refused to go back onto the reservation for over a year. We had an agreement. They are still raiding and creating dissent among the settlers."

"Can you blame them?" the captain said. "You promised them something you never delivered. Their own reservation? That's rich. The Indians already have too much land."

"It's Klamath land. The Modoc want their own," Meacham said, but he felt hollow inside because the officer had gone straight to the heart of the matter. Meacham had not been able to wrangle a separate reservation for the Modoc, although he had fought to do so both in Oregon and in Washington, D.C.

The Department of Indian Affairs turned a cold shoulder to his every demand, telling him to do what he could with the existing reservation system. With no power, Meacham could do nothing.

The impasse seemed complete. Captain Jack would not return to the Klamath Reservation because he wanted to go directly to one for the Modoc alone. Meacham could not even talk to the officials in Washington any more about establishing a Modoc reservation until Captain Jack was safely and peaceably sequestered on the Klamath Reservation.

Meacham knew his limitations here and back East. He left the captain's office and went to his quarters, uncharitably granted him near the stables. A sheet of clean paper and a pen taunted him. Meacham began writing to the military commander for the district. If the Civil War general could not help him, no one could.

"Brigadier General Edward R.S. Canby," Meacham addressed the impassioned letter, detailing how a war was brewing that would cause even the massive effort against the Apache to pale, if allowed to fester any longer. Captain Jack had to be forced back onto the reservation, no matter the cost, regardless of the number of soldiers needed for the unsavory chore.

"I regret very much the necessity of this action," Meacham concluded the letter, "but the peace and welfare of the white settlers and Indians demand that it be done immediately."

He signed his name with a flourish and dispatched the letter to General Canby. Meacham had done what he could. Now it was time for the military to act.

# Again the Reporter—
# Almost

*San Francisco, California*
*January 30, 1872*

Joshua Harlan felt guilty taking so long on a personal matter. He was supposed to be on the docks, supervising loading of laundry bound for the Orient to be cleaned. Sean Murdoch had been adamant about Josh personally supervising the loading after two earlier shipments had been lost due to poor packaging. The laundry in those shipments to the Celestial laundries in Hong Kong had not been packed in waterproof wrappings and had rotted away on the long, wet trip. Josh was not certain the Oriental laundries had not substituted rags for the clothing, but Murdoch was adamant about the loading.

Josh hurried along away from the Embarcadero, heading past Portsmouth Square with all its public orators and other zanies. He had heard Emperor Norton was supposed to make an announcement today of an alliance with Mexico for the express purpose of throwing the U.S. government out of California. At the outrageous thought, Josh had to smile. During the Civil War the self-styled emperor had written to President Lincoln offering allegiance with the Union and had been ignored. Then Emperor Norton had written to Jefferson Davis with the same offer.

He had received back a request for money to support the Southern cause.

Josh weaved through the crowd gathering for the afternoon's amusement. He checked his pocket watch and knew he would have to hurry if he wanted to check the cargo aboard the *Orient Pearl* before it sailed at evening tide. Replacing the watch, he checked his inside pocket for the crumpled letter he had received from AB Meacham a few days earlier. This had prompted him to surreptitiously contact Mr. Billingsly at the *Alta California* again.

He tasted the assignment of covering the war still threatening along the California-Oregon border. It had been two years since Meacham had invited him up, and it seemed more like centuries. Josh had worked through the accounting department, orders, receiving, and every other conceivable position at Murdoch and Sons Shipping. The only job he had not held was being dangled before him like a carrot—a vice president's job.

When he got that, Murdoch promised, the wedding would be scheduled. Josh knew the real delay in marrying Faith came from back East. Her Boston relatives wanted to come to San Francisco for a high society wedding, but her aunt had been sick for some time and was too frail to travel. Now that she was on the mend and the Transcontinental Railroad had been completed, she and the rest of the Murdoch clan would be on their way.

Months, Josh told himself. He could marry Faith in a few months. Her relatives would be even more impressed if he had an important job not given him by Sean Murdoch.

"June," he corrected aloud. "She wants a June wedding. Heaven knows she's been working on that damned dress long enough."

A man in the crowd turned and stared at him, as if he waited for more of this one-man argument. Josh muttered an apology, made it clear he was not the entertainment for the crowd, and hurried on to the *Alta California* offices. He stopped and stared at the building, a lump forming in his throat.

He should not be here, not like this, not sneaking about like a thief in the night. If he did not have the backbone to stand up to Murdoch, he did not deserve to be a reporter. He knew the man disapproved of such "silliness," as he called it often. Any ambition other than taking over the shipping company met with immediate criticism that Josh was unable to counter. Unable or unwilling. He had never decided. All he wanted in life was to be a reporter and to marry Faith.

Josh wiped his lips, then entered, going up the broad staircase to the city room on the second floor. At the top of the stairs he stopped and drank in the scene. The smells of ink and paper and the sounds of reporters at work, shouting at each other, offering advice and criticism, the editors barking orders, and the paper being brought together all happened here. Where he should be.

"Mr. Billingsly!" he called when he caught sight of the editor. "Can I have a word with you?"

The editor frowned a moment, then said, "I remember you. Josh Harlan, isn't it?"

"Yes, sir," Josh said, happy that the editor remembered him. "I was a reporter about eighteen months ago."

"Reporter? No, not that. Apprentice. Cub. A copyboy."

"Yes, sir, I did all that, but I got promoted above a copyboy." He was proud that he had transcended this lowest of the low positions, even if he had not been a full-time reporter on the *Alta California* staff.

"What is it? I have a paper to get to bed."

"Yes, sir, I know. You might want to read this." He held out Meacham's letter detailing the growing unrest on the Klamath Reservation.

"So? Any shots fired yet?" Billingsly demanded.

"Not yet, sir. But they are close to a massacre of heroic proportions. You see what the Indian Agent said? Mr. Meacham's request for military aid was turned down by General Canby. With Captain Jack off the reservation and refusing to go back, that means there must be looting and raiding and killing. The soldiers might have held down the trouble, but Canby's refusal guarantees a huge blowup."

"Does it now?"

"Mr. Billingsly, send me up there again. I can report this better than anyone else on the *Alta* staff." Josh knew this was a long shot, but he was impassioned.

Isabella's image flashed through his mind. He could use her contacts with the Modoc tribe even as he got vital information from Meacham.

"I have the contacts on both sides, both Indian and U.S. government. It will be one hell of a story when the region erupts in war."

"War sells papers," Billingsly said, a slight grin coming to his lips. This was the most congenial Josh could remember seeing the editor.

"That it does, Mr. Billingsly, and I can deliver the goods better than any of your reporters. Besides," Josh said, hoping it was true, "they all have local beats to cover. You wouldn't want to send one of them. They'd be like a fish out of water."

"I wish I could agree," the editor said, turning and walking away. As he went he dropped corrections on the desks of reporters, who hurriedly read them over and rushed to change their copy for the last edition.

"Sir, wait!" Josh cried. "You'll be passing up a great story if you don't send me."

"I doubt it," the man said. "You think I'm stupid, Mr. Harlan?"

"What?" Josh was taken aback by the question.

"Seems that you do. I have a great paper to run. I don't do it in the dark, listening only to what these lackluster reporters feed me. I have sources of my own."

"Sir?"

"Listen, Josh," Billingsly said. "I hear things from all over. Before, my sources matched what you told me. But not this time. Just this morning I got a telegram from the sheriff of Siskiyou County about the situation. It's all blown over now.

Captain Jack is returning to the reservation as soon as your Mr. Meacham drafts an agreement. There's not going to be any fighting."

"No fighting, no story," Josh said, dejected.

"No story worth printing. Who wants to read about peace? But I like your determination." Billingsly looked at him like he was a bug under a magnifying glass. "You want your old job back? I have an apprentice position opening soon. Not much like covering an Indian war. Only tidbits around town."

"You'd probably have me covering the high society doings," Josh said, seeing this as punishment worse than eternal damnation in hell. "Sorry, but no, thanks. I have a job."

Billingsly shrugged and immediately forgot about him. Josh read it in the editor's eyes. The man had a paper to get out. Josh only wished it had his byline on a front page story.

He walked down the broad steps, dejected, heading back to the docks. He had dirty clothes to check before they were sent to the Orient for laundering.

# New Mistakes

"I serve at the whim of the Department," Meacham said, dejected. "I still regret turning over the agency to anyone else."

"Especially someone whom you hold in such contempt?" T.B. Odeneal looked down his nose at Meacham. "If you had dealt more aggressively with the Modoc problem, you would still be Indian Agent."

"I don't hold you in contempt," Meacham said, eying the smallish man with contempt. "What do you know of the situation?"

"More than you, obviously," Odeneal said, "or you would have resolved this mess. Letting the Modoc run wild! What an idea!"

"I wrote to Canby, trying to get military intervention. He said it was my job, not his." Meacham did nothing to keep the resignation from his voice now. He was tired, so very tired, but he toiled alone. The captaincy at Fort Klamath changed every month, or so it seemed, and the general commanding this military district wanted nothing to do with forcibly settling Captain Jack and his band on the Klamath Reservation.

Now Odeneal came in with no plans, no new solutions, only criticism.

"You did not phrase your request forcefully enough,"

Odeneal said. "It is about time to have someone in this office capable of energizing our forces and quelling such insurrection on the part of the savages."

"They are people, not savages," snapped Meacham.

"Such thinking is the reason for your failure. I have no starry-eyed misconceptions about the Modoc. They are not our friends. They are wards of the state and must be treated as such."

"Like children?" The thought of Odeneal dealing with Captain Jack as if he were a small boy amused Meacham as much as it appalled him. What trouble existed now would explode into real bloodshed if Odeneal pursued such policies and held such attitudes.

"You have been among them too long. You think of them as equals."

"I lied," Meacham said. "I *do* hold you in contempt."

Odeneal sneered. "All the more reason for you to surrender control of the agency."

"When are you going to talk with Captain Jack?" asked Meacham.

"Talk? The time for talk is past. You have shown that with your repeated failures. I am personally petitioning General Canby for troops to put down this rebellion."

"You aren't even going to see the Modoc *tyee?*" This surprised Meacham, and he had thought he was past such emotion.

"Use these vaunted persuasive powers of yours to convince him not to raid the settlers. He's only a child, after all."

"Childlike," Odeneal corrected. "All the more reason not to palaver with him, as you have."

"Try to corral him with soldiers and Captain Jack will simply go into the forests. Right now he is securely settled at Yainax."

"The wrong spot. You allowed him and his ragtag band to settle apart from the good Indians. They have to be put with the Klamath, as originally ordered."

"Captain Jack will run, mark my words," Meacham predicted. "And whatever you do, don't anger Old Schonches. The two of them together would be more than all the soldiers in the Northwest could handle."

Odeneal laughed heartily. Meacham packed the last of his belongings and left Fort Klamath, the mocking derision of the new Indian Agent ringing in his ears.

It came as no bombshell for Meacham when he heard two days later that Captain Jack and his entire village had left Yainax and vanished.

# Decisions

San Francisco, California
April 18, 1872

"Careful! Don't bang that around. It's fragile!" shouted Joshua Harlan at the longshoreman swinging a cargo net holding glassware being shipped north along the coast to Seattle. He cringed when the man ignored him and swung the net out over the bay. If one of the fraying ropes broke—and Josh had seen at least one a week do so—a valuable shipment would be lost.

At least he wasn't inclined to dive down in the muddy, murky water of the bay to rescue anything dropped there. Since he had supervised loading on the dock, he had seen two men fall off the piers and be eaten by sharks. If the vicious fish could not find garbage dumped into the bay, they were content with a human arm or leg or, in one dock-walloper's case, his head.

The load crashed to the deck of the ship. Josh heaved a sigh, and wondered if he ought to check it again. Such damage now might be remedied by arranging for new glassware from any of a half-dozen suppliers in San Francisco. Let it go and have it arrive busted into a million shining shards and no one would be happy.

Josh found himself tossed on the horns of a dilemma. Sean

Murdoch had ordered this load out fast. Replacing any broken glasses now would take days, missing the deadline.

"You want to check it, Mistuh Harlan?" the dockhand drawled. He did not care if he broke the glassware or sank the ship. He was getting paid. And probably not just by Murdoch and Sons Shipping. Josh had heard rumors of both Michael and Morgan Murdoch slipping the longshoremen a few extra dollars to make sure things did not go well for him. Once, he had been running down a checklist when someone bumped into him and knocked him to the edge of the pier. If he had not become tangled in a dangling rope, he would have plunged into the bay. While not necessarily a death sentence this close to shore, with sailors nearby to haul him out if they heard his cries, Josh could not get the image of the headless shark-bitten man out of his mind.

"You're doing a fine job," Josh said, waving the dockhand away from the winch. He had done as much damage as he could. Let the crew on the ship continue it now that the cargo was aboard. Josh felt a little guilty but knew he could always blame a rough sea or a careless captain or mate for any of the fragile glassware that did not arrive intact.

For all he knew, the ship might sink when it was out of San Francisco Bay. The weather this spring had been particularly violent and unpredictable. That made for higher shipping rates and bigger profits for Murdoch and Sons. It also made for greater losses.

Josh walked down the line of cargo ready to be loaded onto another clipper ship, this one headed for Hawaii, then stopped and frowned, wondering what was wrong. Then it hit him. The only sounds he heard were waves lapping hungrily against the pier and the ships creaking. An instant before seamen had been swearing and dockhands trying to top them in inventive cusses at the tops of their lungs.

But now? Silence.

He looked up and saw all the crew staring at him. Josh looked down, wondering if someone had splashed him with tar or paint. Then he turned and looked down the wharf and saw her.

"Isabella!" he called before he could stop himself. This set off a round of whispers among the men. He turned and barked at them, "Get back to work, you slackers. Mr. Murdoch's not paying you to gawk. Go on!"

Isabella stood in the center of the dock, hands at her sides and looking completely out of place. She wore a pale brown cotton blouse and a long buckskin skirt. Pulled around her shoulders to protect against the nip of the bay breeze hung a wool shawl decorated in the Modoc fashion. The expression on her face was impassive, but Josh saw a tinge of fear in her eyes. And little wonder. He could not imagine what had brought Isabella to San Francisco from her native woods around Tule Lake.

"Isabella, what are you doing here?" he asked going to her.

"Did I do wrong?" she asked.

"No, not at all." Josh shouted at his assistant. "Mr. Shelton, continue with the loading. I'll be back in a few minutes."

"Yes, *sir*," the young upstart said, leering at him. "Take all the time you want, Mr. Harlan."

Josh bit back a nasty reply. Every dockhand and most of the sailors could hear what he said. He didn't want to give them any more ammunition against him. Not a one of them respected him, knowing he was only passing through on his way to the main building as a company officer, a position none of them thought he deserved.

Worse than this, Josh had to agree with such an appraisal. In spite of the time he had invested in the shipping company, he had hated every second of it, and barely understood what was going on even now.

"They do not like you," Isabella said.

"You always were observant," Josh said, smiling. "That didn't take much figuring, though. Why are you here?"

"To find you," she said simply.

"Is something wrong?" Josh felt a surge of anxiety. "With Captain Jack? Or AB? Is AB hurt?"

"Mr. Meacham is unhappy."

Josh held down his impatience. He tried to remember all the interview techniques he had been taught when working at the *Alta California*. It was better coaxing the information from Isabella than shouting at her and possibly never finding why she had made the trip to San Francisco.

"What is AB unhappy about? Something I have done?"

"Oh, no, not that. He is very happy with you. He told me to give you a message."

"Well, let me see it." Josh saw Morgan Murdoch coming down the street in front of the Ferry Building and knew this chance meeting with Isabella would quickly get back to Sean Murdoch. Maybe even to Faith. That was worse than being fired.

"I have no message. Not written. He told me to let you know he was no longer Indian Agent. He has been replaced by Odeneal."

"Odeneal? I don't know him. Why did they replace AB— Mr. Meacham? He was doing a good job. Was he too ill to continue with the job?"

"He is healthy," she said. Josh wanted to throttle the information from her. Morgan turned and retreated, heading back to the main office. Whatever had brought him to the docks was less important than telling everyone Josh was entertaining a savage down on the wharf.

"And?" he urged.

"Mr. Meacham fears Odeneal will bring about a big war. Captain Jack has hidden in the woods. Old Schonches secretly helps him, and the Klamath are threatening him and those with him in their village."

"What does Mr. Meacham want me to do?"

Isabella looked blank. Beautiful and completely at a loss to understand what he meant.

"I only bring you the message Mr. Meacham told me."

"What did he say exactly? Why did you come here rather than send a telegram? That would have been easier."

"Mr. Meacham said for me to deliver the message. I do not know about telegrams, so I came." A little smile danced at her lips, and she averted her eyes shyly. "I wanted to see you again. You were nice to me. You paid me well."

"Here," Josh said, fumbling in his pocket. He had eight dollars to last him until payday on Friday. "Take this. You shouldn't have come yourself."

"You don't want to see me? I'll clean your boots again. And anything else you want, Mr. Harlan. Anything."

Josh blinked. Again he wondered if he misunderstood her. The Modoc had curious ideas of morality. The women sold themselves as easily as a settler might barter for a bag of corn-meal. But he had misinterpreted her before because of her imperfect English and the way she distracted him.

She was quite pretty, in an exotic, wild fashion, and Josh almost wished she meant what he thought. Almost.

"Joshua," came a sharp voice. "There you are. Papa said you were out here." Faith bustled up, whirling her parasol about. Only the fast rotation showed how mad she was. "I thought you would be working."

"Sorry, Faith. Let me introduce a friend of . . . Mr. Meacham's. He sent her to give me an urgent message."

Faith never looked at Isabella. She sniffed and turned her back, shutting out the other woman.

"I do hope you're not going to rush back north for no reason. A wild-goose chase, especially since you have obligations here in San Francisco. You haven't forgotten I wanted to go to dinner this evening, did you?"

"I . . . no, I didn't forget. It's just that I don't have any money."

"You may have this, Mr. Harlan," Isabella said, holding out the eight dollars he had given her for traveling so far to give him Meacham's message.

"Take money from the likes of her! Really." Faith's parasol

spun faster. She stumbled off balance when a gust of wind off the bay caught the flimsy lightweight umbrella. Josh steadied her, but she pulled away angrily.

"Isabella was just going," he said, looking at the Modoc woman, silently begging her not to make more trouble for him. Isabella lowered her head, backed away like a chastened servant, and then hesitated.

"Do you have any message for Mr. Meacham?" she asked.

"I'll get in touch with him. By telegram. Can you get back home all right?"

"Yes," was all Isabella said. She turned and walked off, head down like some defeated foe. Josh felt guilty for letting Faith browbeat her so, but Isabella retained her pride. It was just that she knew her place when dealing with whites.

Even as that thought crossed his mind, Josh felt the bile rising.

"You were rude, Faith. I'm surprised at your lack of manners."

"Rude? To an Indian? She was an Indian, wasn't she? One of those you wrote about up north."

"What brings you to the docks?" he asked, changing the subject. "You must want something more than to remind me of dinner."

"I should have mentioned it earlier, since you have become so recently impecunious. That was your money she had?"

"I owed AB money. She's taking it back to him," Josh lied, not knowing why.

"You trust a barbaric creature like her not to steal it?"

"Eight dollars is hardly worth stealing," he said. "It's not such a great sum." Josh fought to keep his temper because, to him, it was a princely sum. Having Faith remind him he was the poor relation rankled more and more.

"Let's not argue. It makes me so upset," Faith said. She kissed him lightly on the cheek. "I came down to tell you my aunt and cousins are planning on leaving Boston in mid-May.

That means they will be here the first week of June. For our wedding!"

"So you've decided on a date?"

"Don't sound so enthusiastic," she said, pouting prettily. "But then, the groom always sounds that way, doesn't he?"

"I wouldn't know. This is the first time I've gotten married," Josh said.

"Good. Then it is settled. I will tell Papa to rent the church, get the minister, do all that planning while I compose the guest list. Is there anyone you want to invite, Joshua?"

"Whoever you like, my dear," he said. Josh felt like a trapped rat and did not like it. He had a job he did not like and was marrying a woman whom he loved dearly, but who increasingly seemed like a stranger.

"Of course, Joshua, of course. I shall tell Papa to get you out of this weather and away from all the ruffians." She spoke of the dockhands, but glanced over her shoulder in the direction Isabella had gone. "You'll be in a fine office as the newest vice president tomorrow morning!"

Faith turned and went off, muttering to herself about engravers and wording on the invitations. Josh stared after her, then shifted around and wondered where Isabella had gone and how she would fare.

# Wedding Bells

Josh stood stiffly in his formal coat. He struggled to loosen the tight celluloid collar but couldn't. He swallowed and immediately regretted it as his Adam's apple caught on the collar edge, choking him. He tried to stop coughing but could not until someone clapped him on the back and he regained his composure.

"Big day for you, isn't it?"

"AB!" cried Josh. "I didn't think you would make it."

"After receiving your telegram, how could I refuse being your best man. The missus would never have let me forget about it if such a good friend of the family had to pick any of these, uh, other gentlemen to stand up as witness with you." Meacham pointed to the gently undulating sea of guests in their fancy cutaway coats or dress gowns, all friends or business acquaintances of the Murdoch family.

"I don't have many friends," Josh said uneasily. The truth was worse. He had no friends outside Murdoch and Sons Shipping Company, and these were more business acquaintances and men seeking him out to further their own ambitions. When he worked on the *Alta California,* he'd had several friends among the reporters, but none of them could attend.

"There's one of the reporters. No, several," Meacham said,

pointing to a tight knot of men working furiously to write in their notebooks.

"Social-page reporters, not real reporters."

"Not like you, eh?" Meacham clapped him on the back again and said, "Cheer up, old son. You look like this is your funeral rather than your wedding. You're marrying one of the loveliest girls I've ever seen."

"She wouldn't let me talk to her this morning," Josh said.

"Tradition, that's all. You'll make a good husband, Josh. You're dedicated and know your trade."

Josh said nothing. He still felt as if he knew nothing of the shipping business and hardly more of reporting. But he wanted to work for a newspaper, not smell of fish and yell at longshoremen all day long.

"I hope I'm not too out of date. It's been a while since I squeezed into this monkey suit." Meacham tried to suck in his waist and didn't do a good job of it. The buttons threatened to pop.

"Here's the ring," Josh said, handing it to Meacham.

"That's quite a rock," Meacham said, admiring the large stone.

"Mr. Murdoch bought it. Faith didn't like the one I bought— the one I could afford."

"These people do things a tad different. You'll get used to it," Meacham said, but he didn't sound any surer than Josh felt about it.

"Those are Faith's relatives from Boston. Her Aunt Angela is the rich one. The rest are cousins along to look after her. This was their first trip across the country on the railroad."

"I envy them," Meacham said. "I'll be going back to Washington soon. I hope I can ride the Transcontinental rather than wasting time in the saddle and waiting for river transportation."

"Are you going back East for good, or are you returning back here?" asked Josh, trying to keep his mind off how scared he was. He remembered the first time he had seen Captain

Jack. The Modoc *tyee* had tried to look imposing—and he had. But Josh was nowhere near as frightened of a warrior who might scalp him as he was of the hundreds of guests assembled in the church. His hands shook and his knees threatened to buckle.

"Odeneal is a complete failure dealing with the Modoc," Meacham said. "He refuses to talk to them. The matter has come to a head, as I knew it would. Canby has sent a new officer to command Fort Klamath, a Major James Jackson. He's an aggressive officer and not one I would have chosen for dealing with Captain Jack. But you don't want to hear this. You're getting married."

Josh had to be pushed gently out in front of the altar. He turned and watched as the organ began playing and Faith and her father appeared in the narthex and walked slowly to the main entrance. Faith paused for a moment, all eyes on her. Josh wondered if he would die of a stroke then and there from the way his heart raced. Then the future Mrs. Joshua Harlan walked down the aisle, slowly, methodically, locking eyes with those on either side until she reached the altar.

Josh was not sure what happened after that. He felt AB poke him once or twice and he grunted, made mumbled statements, and turned, and eventually found himself with a ring on his finger and the huge diamond on Faith's, then kissed her. The cheering from the guests shook him back to reality.

He stared at his bride. Faith looked radiant. Her red hair contrasted beautifully with the white lace of her veil and gown. Her green eyes gleamed, and he had never seen her looking more radiant, her alabaster skin glowing.

"I love you," he said in a low voice.

"Yes, Joshua, I know," she said, then turned to begin greeting people crowding in.

"Back, all of you back. Form a reception line!" bellowed Sean Murdoch. "We're doing this right. I'm not paying a fortune for you to mob the bride—yet."

They walked back down the aisle until they reached the

front steps of the church. The bright California sun beat down on them, moderated by a gentle, cool breeze off the bay. Before the relatives and friends of the Murdoch family came through to kiss the bride and shake his hand, Josh felt a tug on his elbow.

"A word, son," beamed Sean Murdoch. "You've been working hard."

"Thank you, sir. I—"

"As a wedding gift, to you and my daughter, I'm not going to let you dangle as a vice president."

A thrill ran through Josh. Sean Murdoch was letting him go to be a reporter.

"No, son, my daughter deserves more than a mere vice president. I'm making you a junior partner." Sean Murdoch pumped his hand and pushed him back into the receiving line. On top of all the other shocks of the day, this one left Josh completely speechless.

As Morgan and Michael Murdoch came by, they tried to crush his hand with their grips. He hardly noticed the pain, but Josh was haunted by the utter hatred blazing in their eyes. They knew he now shared the ownership of their father's company, and they were not happy.

# Battle of Lost River

*Lost River, Oregon*
*November 27, 1872*

"Are you sure, Mr. Applegate?" asked Lieutenant Boutelle. The cavalry officer hitched up his gun belt and looked at the settler closely. There had been too many wild-goose chases in the past months to trust anyone, especially anyone named Applegate. Ivan Applegate was the flighty one in that family and had too much contact with Odeneal for Boutelle's liking. If Jesse Applegate had brought the information to him, Boutelle would have hurried it to his commander.

"Of course I am sure, you fool!" Ivan Applegate threw his hands up in the air as disgust possessed him. "Tell Major Green. Now!"

"Proof, sir," Boutelle said. "I need something more than your word that you have located Captain Jack."

"I've located his whole damned tribe! Well, his band, at least," Ivan Applegate said, calming a little. "Me and a couple other settlers were out hunting and I saw his brother. The hunchbacked one. We followed him back to a new village on the Lost River. We watched, and Captain Jack's there!" Applegate's anger rose again. "Tell the major or, by God, I will go over his head and write General Canby himself!"

Frazier Boutelle heaved a deep sigh and tried to keep his temper. He knew Odeneal had sent Applegate with this message. It was a transparent ploy on the part of the Indian Agent to get the military even more involved than they were in the hunt for Captain Jack. Boutelle was no stranger to politics in the ranks. He had been a captain during the war, and had reverted to the ranks afterward, rising slowly to lieutenant once more. He respected General Canby and was glad for the man's command over the past two years, ever since Crook had been moved to the Southwest to fight the Apache.

The military had reasons for doing what it did. Boutelle was more suspicious of civilians.

"The weather is not good for such an expedition," Boutelle said, staring past Applegate into the parade ground of Fort Klamath. The morning mist had turned into a cold, punishing rain. Before noon, it might turn to sleet. This was no fit weather to begin a major campaign against Captain Jack, and with no advance planning or supply. Boutelle had tried to track the Modoc *tyee* several times and had been disappointed each time.

"It might be your only chance to catch him and get him back to the reservation," Applegate said belligerently.

"You'll accompany us? Will Mr. Odeneal come, also?"

"Odeneal?" From the expression on Applegate's face, Boutelle knew he had been right about who had put the settler up to coming to Fort Klamath. "Why, no, he's already left for Yreka. He is too far out of touch to get in time."

"I see," Boutelle said. And he did. "I will give your information to the major. Make yourself comfortable, Mr. Applegate."

He disliked bringing such secondhand information to his commanding officer because "Uncle Johnnie" Green had come to the post so recently and seemed more inclined to buck for promotion than do the right thing. Boutelle preferred James Jackson and wished he had continued as fort commander. Major Jackson had a background similar to his own, being promoted during the war, then reduced to the ranks and working back into command after the need for so many officers had passed. More than this, Jackson had received a Medal of Honor for his bravery. Boutelle would follow him anywhere, even in this messy weather, even after Captain Jack.

But Green, with his heavy German accent and almost slavish obedience to men like Odeneal?

"Sir?" Boutelle called to Major Green. "I'd like a word with you." Frazier Boutelle spent the next twenty minutes outlining everything he had been told by Ivan Applegate, then added his own suspicions that Agent Odeneal had fed the settler the information so he would not be involved personally.

"Never liked Odeneal's notion that even talking to the Modoc was somehow giving in to them," Major Green said in his heavy accent. "But Ivan Applegate—and Odeneal—are right. It's time to move Captain Jack back to the reservation. He's been raiding too much."

"And if we don't find him, sir?" asked Boutelle.

"If we don't find him this time, that'll make it a sight easier to ignore Applegate—and Odeneal—the next time, won't it, Lieutenant?"

"Remember what General Canby said, sir. Any move against Captain Jack will be seen by the Modoc as an act of war. We need a man like Meacham back to negotiate directly rather than turn tail and run at the mere hint of dealing with the Indians."

"The time has come for action, Lieutenant. Tell Major Jackson to get his men in the field and chase Captain Jack back."

"Yes, *sir!*" Boutelle said, saluting smartly. "I'll get a company ready for maneuvers."


"I'm sorry I doubted you, Lieutenant," Major Jackson said to Boutelle. "I even got Uncle Johnnie's orders in writing." The major held up the sheet with florid writing on it. "We're to track down Captain Jack, using Applegate's information, and escort the renegade Modoc band back to the Klamath Reservation. With thirty-eight men. I'm glad you're going along with me, Lieutenant. I need all the experienced soldiers I can find."

Boutelle sucked at his teeth, wondering how far they could bend the written orders. Nothing but trouble would come of sending so few after Captain Jack. This had to be an all-or-nothing campaign. If the entire post did not go after the Modoc, success would never be theirs. Even if Green ordered more soldiers into the field, even then success might elude them.

"We'll ride to Linkville," Jackson said, "and meet with Odeneal. Scuttlebutt has it he went there rather than Yreka. There's no reason not to go to the horse's mouth for instructions on finding Captain Jack."

"The horse's mouth, sir?" asked Boutelle.

"Or some other part of a horse's anatomy," Jackson said, grinning crookedly. "Mount the troop, sir!"

They reached Linkville and Odeneal's house by sundown. The major went in. Boutelle was not surprised when Applegate appeared, as if by magic, and went in, also. He was only mildly curious about what was discussed inside. When Jackson came out, he had somehow acquired Applegate as guide and translator.

"We have our orders, Lieutenant," Jackson said, looking as if he could spit. "We will not shoot unless fired upon."

"Sir? I thought we were supposed to escort the Modoc back to the reservation."

"To Yainax, for the time being," Jackson said, looking even more forlorn. "But we are to fire only in self-defense. Pass the order along, Lieutenant."

"Yes, sir," Boutelle said, doing so. This was war. The Modoc would see any company of soldiers riding into their hidden village as an invasion. It was crazy waiting for the Modoc to shoot first, especially when the troopers had to *find* Captain Jack's village.

Through the night, they struggled through thick sagebrush.

The intermittent rain froze on their coats and made their advance a nightmare. Just before dawn, Jackson ordered a halt.

"Lieutenant Boutelle, Mr. Applegate tells me we are only a mile from Captain Jack's camp. Prepare the troop for advance. Have the men adjust their saddles and be sure their arms are in good order."

"Major," warned Applegate. "Mr. Odeneal's orders—"

"I know, fire in self-defense only. There is nothing in his orders about being ready to return fire, however. Lieutenant. See to the men."

"Yes, sir." Boutelle was glad Jackson led them. He could see Green blundering forward with the men still cloaked in their wet, half-frozen coats and on saddles slipping about after a night of difficult travel. He went among the dispirited men, cheering them the best he could, seeing to the equipment used by less experienced troopers, and getting them ready for what might be an extremely dangerous advance.

"Lieutenant Boutelle, we will trot forward and enter the village before the Modoc know we are even in the vicinity."

"Yes, sir," Boutelle said, skeptical of such a plan. He was worried Jackson's order might be more for Applegate's approval than one born of reason. Why Applegate now wanted to coddle the Modoc was beyond him. At Fort Klamath the settler had been clamoring for their blood.

Unless Applegate knew there was no way in hell Captain Jack could be returned to the reservation peacefully.

The lieutenant shrugged it off. He was a soldier and obeyed orders. Major Jackson was a good field officer, and this was hardly his first fight, if it came to that. Boutelle tied his coat to the saddle cantle, mounted, and gave the order to advance quickly.

They had gone less than a quarter mile, and reached Lost River, when Boutelle saw a Modoc sitting on the riverbank fishing. The Indian looked up, then stood.

"Mr. Boutelle, halt the advance," Jackson ordered. He glared at Applegate, then went to greet the Indian.

Boutelle joined his commander and Applegate as they spoke with the Modoc.

"Hello, Bogus Charley," Applegate called. "We're looking for Captain Jack. Is he around?"

Boutelle had dealt with Bogus Charley before and knew he was fluent in English and a sly customer.

"Why do you want to see him?" asked Bogus Charley. The sun came up, cloaking his face in shadow as he turned his back to the pallid warmth. At least the rain had stopped.

"I have an arrest warrant."

"I do not understand this," Bogus Charley said. Boutelle saw Jackson was getting mad. The lieutenant grew edgy. Bogus Charley understood all too well and was playing for time.

"It doesn't matter if you do," Jackson said angrily. "Where's Captain Jack?"

The sharp report of a rifle spooked Boutelle's horse. He fought to control it and see who had fired.

"There, on the river. In a canoe!" he cried. Boutelle recognized the Modoc who had rowed across the river as Scarfaced Charley. The Modoc fumbled with a rifle, and then fell from the canoe into the water, dropping the weapon into the lake.

"Lieutenant, circle the village with one platoon. I'll ride straight in with the other," Jackson said, knowing that Scarfaced Charley's shot must have alerted the Modoc in the encampment.

Boutelle got his men riding hard to get to the far side of the Modoc camp to cut off escape. Already men and women stirred, heads poking out of their *wikiups* to see what the commotion was all about. Boutelle got into position, then formed his men into a skirmish line.

"No shooting," Boutelle ordered. Then he cursed such orders under his breath. Most of the men coming from the *wikiups* were armed and looked belligerent. How many soldiers did he have to lose before he could justify returning fire? One shot, self-defense, easy orders for a man like Odeneal sitting warm and dry and safe in his house back in Linkville.

Boutelle saw Applegate dismount and leave the skirmish line Jackson had formed at the other edge of the village.

"Captain Jack, come on out!" Applegate shouted. He looked in *wikiup* after *wikiup* hunting for the Modoc *tyee.*

"Dismount!" ordered Boutelle, seeing Jackson doing the same with his troops. "Order arms. Forward march!" He started a slow advance, wondering if he ought to search the *wikiups* he passed. When Jackson did not, Boutelle kept his men moving. The major knew what he was doing.

Scarfaced Charley stumbled past Major Jackson, yelling at the top of his lungs in Modoc. Boutelle leveled his pistol but did not fire on the angry Indian.

"What's he saying, Applegate?" demanded Jackson, drawing his pistol.

"Wait, Major, I'll shut him up. He's telling all the Modoc warriors to kill us, that we're outnumbered and can't fire."

Major Jackson drew his pistol and aimed at Scarfaced Charley.

"Halt! You are under arrest!"

Scarfaced Charley ducked into a *wikiup.* Jackson wiped his lips, spun, mounted, and rode to Boutelle.

"Mr. Boutelle, what is your evaluation of our position?"

"There's no way to avoid a fight, sir. The quicker we get ready for it, the fewer men we'll lose."

"Prepare, sir!" Jackson rode back to his platoon.

A Modoc came out of the *wikiup,* waving a rifle around.

"Shoot over his head, men!" ordered Boutelle. He saw there would be bloodshed. If he shot one Modoc, maybe he could shock the Indians and save the mission with a minimum of killing.

The echo of the volley had barely died when Scarfaced Charley popped out of the *wikiup* and turned on Boutelle. They both sighted and fired simultaneously. Boutelle yelped, spinning around when a sharp pain in his elbow rattled him. He looked down and saw a thin trickle of blood. Scarfaced Char-

ley's bullet had only scratched him after tearing out the elbow
of his uniform jacket.

Boutelle looked up and saw Scarfaced Charley standing
stock-still, eyes wide. Boutelle's bullet had ripped through a
bandanna around the Modoc's head. He had not even drawn
blood.

Boutelle tried to capitalize on the Indian's hesitation. He
fired again, this time knocking Scarfaced Charley to the
ground. He shot again as Charley scuttled off into the sagebrush. Boutelle was not sure if Scarfaced Charley had been
winged, but as he started after him, motion out of the corner
of his eye forced him to turn.

Another Modoc drew back an arrow, the sharp-edged ar-
rowhead gleaming in the morning sun. Boutelle reacted instinctively. This time his aim was good. The bullet tore through
the Modoc's chest. The released arrow flew off target.

For the first time, Boutelle realized the extent of the fighting
all around him. The white pall of pungent gun smoke hung in
the air, choking him, reminding him of the war and its day-long
battles. Men shouted and sobbed and moaned as they died in
pain. The disorder was everything he had come to expect from
combat. He sought out Scarfaced Charley, but the Indian had
fled.

From the other side of the village Boutelle heard Major
Jackson shouting, "Fire! Fire! Fire!"

The roar ripping from the throats of the Modoc warriors
chilled Boutelle. The Indians had somehow come together and
charged Jackson's position in a coordinated attack that would
have done any West Point graduate proud.

Boutelle saw his platoon edging away, getting ready to break
and run. He took a deep breath, then yelled, "Forward! Attack!"

On foot, the lieutenant ran into the center of the village,
firing as he went. He wondered if his platoon had abandoned
him. Then rifles barked behind him and hot lead sang into the

rear of the Modoc force attacking Major Jackson. His men had responded to his attack!

Boutelle, heartened, broke through the rear echelon of Modoc fighters. Rather than fight, the Indians began to mill about, confused. Then they began to make way for Boutelle and his platoon, allowing him to split them into two sections. Jackson went after one part of the attacking Modoc force. Boutelle swung his men about and pursued the other.

"Cease fire!" Boutelle called. "Round 'em up, men. Get them together."

Breathing hard, Boutelle watched as the soldiers began the chore of forcing the women, children, and beaten Modoc warriors into a tight knot at the middle of the village. Applegate came over to him and thrust out his hand.

"Sir, you have saved us all."

Boutelle shook the settler's hand.

"I wish I could have saved more. I count eight dead."

"But we killed more of them than they got of us," Applegate said. "Scarfaced Charley's dead. Captain Jack's nowhere to be seen. He must be dead. And his brother, Black Jim. Dead. Curly Headed Doctor. Dead. We routed them, Lieutenant, we whupped them good!"

Boutelle felt good. Then he surveyed the camp for Major Jackson and felt less confident.

# Yearnings

San Francisco, California
November 27, 1872

Joshua Harlan spread the *Alta California* in front of him on the desk and eagerly read the snippets reported about the Modoc returned to the Klamath Reservation. He frowned, thought, and read on when he saw the reporter had missed so much that Josh knew to be true. The article, hardly more than three column inches on page six, was nothing more than a piece praising Odeneal for his fine work as Indian Agent.

In another part of the paper, Josh found an even shorter notice of renewed Indian attacks near Tule Lake. Nowhere did he find mention of Captain Jack or how the *tyee* had been off the reservation for more than six months, raiding at will. AB Meacham had told Josh of hundreds of horses stolen, cattle slaughtered, even settlers' houses burned.

Josh pushed back and stared at the paper in wonder. How could Mr. Billingsly accept such shoddy work? Josh knew the entire northern region was a skyrocket with its fuse burning. At any moment it would erupt into the sky, spewing sparks and death behind it as it flew, bringing an unholy, unhealthy light to the dark sky.

He scribbled a quick note to Meacham, asking for more information. How he wished he was up north in Linkville with

Meacham where he could report firsthand on the Modoc situation.

Josh looked up guiltily when Sean Murdoch came into the office. The portly man walked with a slight limp now, the product of yet another attack on the docks. A sailor, some said a drunk one, had fired at Murdoch. The sailor had missed, but the slug ricocheted and nicked Murdoch's kneecap. Josh had asked around but could come to no firm conclusion that Murdoch's sons had arranged the attempted assassination.

But in his gut he knew the truth.

They should not have paid the killer in advance. He had gotten liquored up and missed.

Josh shook himself. He was reading a great deal into this. Too much, perhaps. Everything that happened had to have a story attached to it, and the attacks on Murdoch were not random. However, Josh could not prove his suspicions that Morgan and Michael were behind them.

All he knew for a fact was how diligently he had to watch his own back. Accidents happened around him constantly, accidents of suspicious genesis, since he had been made a junior partner with a ten-percent equity interest in the company.

"You getting the itchy foot again, son?" asked Murdoch, seeing the paper and the way Josh had circled the articles concerning the Modoc situation.

"Well," he hemmed. For some reason, Josh had trouble being forthright with Murdoch. The man never encouraged it, and Josh had yet to summon up enough courage to tell him.

To tell him he wanted to quit this boring make-work job, that he wanted to be a reporter, that—what else?

Josh bit his lower lip in frustration. That he wanted to get away from Faith? The few months they had been married seemed like an eternity now, in spite of the fine house and the servants and his exalted position with one of the most successful shipping companies in San Francisco.

Josh had never realized there were so many socials and galas and parties and society picnics until after he married Faith. And she had to attend them all "to maintain her position."

"I thought so," Murdoch said, pushing aside Josh's feeble attempt to speak his mind. "Look. There's nothing going to happen up north. The Army has the Indians you're so taken with on the run. It's only a matter of time before they catch them and pen them all up on that reservation."

"Captain Jack is a wily opponent," Josh said weakly. "I know. I—"

"I was a young man once, though I am sure it is hard for you to believe." Sean Murdoch ignored Josh's protest and chuckled at what he thought must have been a joke. "I understand the urges. Take the forty-niners. They sought gold. Most of them failed. Many died. After all the hardship and so-called manly adventuring, most left without realizing their dreams.

"Now, son, you have a chance to do more, something for the good of the entire city, the entire state, and perhaps even the country! Forget this newspaper business. Concentrate on a *real* profession. Shipping. Hell, when you get to be my age, if you've done well with the company, you can *buy* a newspaper and let others run it for you. That's where the money is. Owning businesses."

Sean Murdoch looked at him shrewdly, then said, "You need more to occupy your time. I want you to go to Chinatown. Get me some solid leads on new contracts to the Orient. I don't care what it is. Anything, anything but fireworks. I won't lose another ship filled to the gunwales with those dangerous things."

"Mr. Murdoch," Josh began, his mind a jumble. He had so much to say and no idea how to phrase it. And he wanted to be a wordsmith for a newspaper!

"Glad you like the idea. It'll get you out of the office and into the fresh air. That'll bring you around faster than a shot of good whiskey. Now finish off your contracts, then get out there and scare up new business for Murdoch and Sons!"

Josh opened his mouth, then closed it. Sean Murdoch was

already hobbling from the office, muttering to himself about building a new cargo ship. Josh sagged, knowing he had to show more backbone than this. He never managed to tell Murdoch what he thought, and always let the man railroad him.

Just like his daughter.

Josh shoved the contracts hidden under the *Alta California* into his top desk drawer, then left. He might have to talk to every store owner up and down Dupont Gai, what some had taken to calling Grant Avenue, but he could find one or two new customers to please Murdoch.

# Pursuing the
# Will-o'-the-Wisp

*Along Lost River*
*November 27, 1872*

Ivan Applegate stared at the retreating Modoc, mouth agape. He turned to Major Jackson and cried, "You can't let them go like this. They're taking the horses they stole from us!"

"Let them go," Frazier Boutelle said coldly. "We don't need more trouble than we have right now." He was bone-tired from the fight and saw that his men—the ones who had survived— were not inclined to fight anymore. Better to let the Modoc go than rile them and have a real battle on his hands.

"You were supposed to escort them back to the reservation," protested Applegate. "We whupped 'em fair and square, you reported to your commanding officer, and now you're supposed to get those savages back to the reservation!"

"We weren't supposed to lose eight men," Boutelle said. "Go on, Applegate, go home. We have to report to Major Green." Boutelle saw that the silent Major Jackson was only slowly realizing the full extent of the fight, and how they had come out the losers. Eight troopers dead. Eight. And the fight had gone out of the remaining two-thirds of their company. The Modoc had been run off, but the real losers set about putting the torch to the small encampment.

* * *

Applegate started to say something more, then clamped his mouth shut and stalked off to find his horse. If the damned savages hadn't stolen it, as they had all the mounts they rode off on. Applegate mounted, and rode hard for two hours until he reached his brother Oliver's house. He hit the ground hard and stormed inside, as mad now as when the soldiers had let the Modoc get away.

"Ivan, you're a sight," Oliver's wife said.

"Where is he? I need to talk to him. And anybody else you can find."

"What's wrong?" she asked.

"This is something Oliver and I—and the rest of the settlers—need to discuss."

"He's out mending fence with a couple fellows from—" Mrs. Applegate spoke to thin air. Ivan hurried back to his horse, climbed into the saddle, and urged the tired animal to even more effort. He found his brother and three others working to rebuild a section of fence that had been knocked down by cows leaning against it.

"Ivan, you're a sight," Oliver started, his words identical to his wife's greeting. Ivan was in no mood for pleasantries. He was telling Oliver and the other three settlers what had happened before he dismounted. Fifteen minutes later, out of breath and red in the face, he finished.

"They let them waltz off, after losing *eight* soldiers? That don't make a lick of sense," Oliver said. "What about Captain Jack? I like him, but the others . . ."

"We have to get them Indians onto the reservation," Ivan said doggedly. "You and me and you boys, too, if you're willing. If we don't stop the Modoc now, they'll steal us blind and the Army's not going to lift a finger to help. Today's raid on Captain Jack's village showed that."

"They do seem a mite confused who's paying their salaries," Oliver allowed.

"I got me a shotgun," a settler said. The other two had rifles.

"We can pick up a couple more shotguns back at my place," Oliver said. "Think you can track those red varmints, Ivan?"

"By their smell I can track them," Ivan said, smirking. For the first time today he felt something positive was getting done.

"How many do you reckon are there?" asked Oliver Applegate.

"I count five or six. I recognized two of the men. One's Hooker Jim. The other's that son of a bitch Curly Headed Doctor. Bag them and we'll have done a good day's work."

"You boys ready?" Oliver looked to his three friends. They clutched their weapons tightly, but all, in spite of their grim expressions, were up for what had to be done.

"They're not twenty yards that way," Ivan said. "You can even smell their cooking fire."

"Why'd they camp like this?" asked one settler. "If they knowed how the soldiers burned their village, wouldn't they start running and keep running?"

"They weren't in the village," Ivan said. "They must have been on their way to join Captain Jack."

"Curly Headed Doctor's a dyed-in-the-wool horse thief, that I know," grumbled another of the settlers. "He done robbed me three times of horses. If 'n it had been a white man, he'd have been hung a long time ago."

"Now's our chance," Ivan said. He hefted a shotgun, checked to be sure he had more shells in his pockets, then started through the heavy sagebrush, trying to make as little noise as possible. Although no woodsman, he got to the edge of the clearing where the Modoc camped before anyone in camp noticed him.

"Get 'em, don't let 'em escape!" Ivan cried. His shotgun

roared, both barrels discharging at the same time and knocking him ass-over-teakettle to the ground.

Oliver, startled by Ivan's sudden fall to the ground, cried, "My brother's been hit. Kill 'em all!"

Curly Headed Doctor was first to respond. He fired an old Remington pistol three times before it jammed. Another Modoc sent an arrow winging through the dusk to sink into one settler's arm. The man yelped and fired his rifle reflexively.

Then Oliver and Ivan got their wits about them and began methodically firing, one reloading while the other took carefully aimed shots into the Modoc camp. It took them almost a minute before they realized no one was firing back at them.

"We got them," Oliver said, face red with excitement.

"Let's be sure." He and Ivan advanced cautiously, the other three covering them from the shelter of the nearby trees. Bodies lay on the ground. Dead bodies. Unmoving. Silent. And small.

"Damnation, we killed a woman and her baby," Oliver said in a choked voice.

"Two more women over here by the campfire," Ivan said, sounding exactly like his brother. In a more desperate tone, he asked, "Where are the men? I know that was Curly Headed Doctor I shot. And Hooker Jim. Where'd they get off to?"

Oliver dropped to the ground and examined it for footprints. He found a few scuffs but nothing to show the direction taken by the Modoc warriors. He looked up and shook his head.

"No sign of blood. If we'd winged 'em, they'd be bleeding like stuck pigs."

Oliver and Ivan stared at the three dead women, but also at the dead baby. They backed off, then gathered their friends and rushed back to Oliver's house. Somehow, the fight got bigger and the danger greater by the time they eventually went their separate ways at sunrise.

# Reports

*Fort Klamath, Oregon*
*November 28, 1872*

"You officers have performed admirably," Major Green said, seated behind his desk. "I have prepared the report to General Canby, based on your information and all Mr. Applegate had given."

"Sir," Boutelle spoke up. "I'm not sure Applegate got it right."

"Nonsense, Lieutenant."

Boutelle looked at Jackson, who shook his head, urging his subordinate to silence. Boutelle could not do that.

"We lost eight soldiers, sir, but the only confirmed Modoc casualty was the one I shot. The one who tried to kill me with the arrow."

"Scarfaced Charley," Green said. "You shot and killed him. And—"

"Sir, I don't know if I even wounded him. He lit out and disappeared in the sagebrush. Before I could hunt him down, all hell broke loose in the village."

"My report to the general stands, Lieutenant," Green said coldly. "No fewer than sixteen Modoc were killed. Major Jackson properly set fire to this renegade village. I concur with your decision to let the women and children go. We can round them up and return them to the Klamath Reservation as we see fit. Moreover, your men required medical attention available only at this post."

"An old woman was killed in a *wikiup*," Jackson said. "That was an accident."

"Yes, yes, of course it was. This is a complete victory. And it is being reported that way. Now, gentlemen, go see to your wounded."

Both Jackson and Boutelle saluted and left Major Green's office. Outside, they stopped and looked around Fort Klamath.

"Three more of my men will probably die," Boutelle said. "They got bad wounds."

"It's all his fault," grumbled Jackson.

"Applegate?"

"Odeneal," snapped Jackson. "He's already left Linkville, heading north as fast as he can run. We got the Modoc back to Yainax, and started a war."

Boutelle had nothing to say. He trusted Major Jackson—and he had to agree with Jackson's appraisal. They had just fought the first battle of a war neither of them might live to see finished.

And all because Indian Agent Odeneal had refused to talk to Captain Jack, preferring to let the army do his dirty work.

# Escape to Hell

*The Lava Beds*
*November 29, 1872*

Captain Jack stood stolidly, watching the women and children from his burned village come to where he camped on the northern bank of Tule Lake. He counted slowly, trying to guess who had been killed and who had not. None of this made sense to him. The soldiers attacked while he was away, then burned the *wikiups,* but did nothing to escort the women and children and handful of men who had been trapped in the village to the Klamath Reservation.

Bogus Charley came up, chattering like a yellow-billed magpie and waving his arms like flapping wings. When he saw Captain Jack, he rushed over, the urgency of his words causing his voice to go shrill.

"They killed Watchman!" Bogus Charley cried. "The lieutenant shot him, but Watchman died well. He tried to fire an arrow, but was gunned down."

Captain Jack nodded, then asked, "Who else? How many others did they kill?"

"No one but an old woman trapped in a burning *wikiup,*" Bogus Charley said. "Even Scarfaced Charley got away. Scared like a rabbit by the lieutenant's shots, but he was not hurt. He claims to have shot the lieutenant, but you know what a liar Charley is."

Captain Jack had to laugh at this. Of all the men in his band, Bogus Charley was the one most likely to tell a tall tale—or, as he put it, squeeze the truth until it barked.

"They destroyed our belongings but let everyone keep their horses?" Again, Captain Jack made no sense of it. He wondered if the bluecoats knew what they were doing.

"We killed eight of them, fully a quarter," Bogus Charley boasted.

"Where were you during the attack?"

"I was fishing by Lost River when they came. I stalled them to give the others time to prepare, but when Scarfaced Charley came ashore in his canoe from his trip back to the reservation to gamble with the Klamath, it was all over. He was drunk and dropped his rifle. Then the soldiers attacked."

Captain Jack tried to puzzle it out but could not. The white men argued among themselves and were, when he considered everything carefully, crazy.

"What are we going to do?" asked Bogus Charley. "We can fight. All the men are coming here. We can kill the settlers."

"Why?" asked Captain Jack. "If we kill the *boshtin,* whose cattle do we steal? Will wild horses ever roam these lands for us again? No. We must take them where we can. From the white men." Captain Jack thought about it, then added, "Only the settlers hate us. The white merchants in Yreka like us."

"They like our women," Bogus Charley said without a hint of malice.

"You killed eight soldiers," Captain Jack went on, thinking aloud. "They cannot permit us to settle again on Lost River— or at Yainax. They will hunt us down and kill us."

"Or force us to settle with Old Schonches with the Klamath," said Bogus.

"That is the same as killing us. Old Schonches gets along with the Klamath. We do not, although I might find some common ground with David Allan. Of the Klamath *tyee,* he is most amenable."

"What about going to Shacknasty Jim?"

"The Hot Creek people would aid us," Captain Jack said, although he did not much care for Shacknasty Jim. Then he looked across Tule Lake and knew the answer. He walked to the lakeshore until the water lapped gently against his boots. Captain Jack turned and called in a loud, clear voice.

"My people, I am your *tyee*. We have been attacked and have fought off the white soldiers. But they are like ants. They creep and crawl and will return to nibble at our every morsel." Captain Jack paused to let this register with those whose homes, albeit temporary ones, had been destroyed by the troopers.

"We dare not surrender to them. They will kill us all. Going back to Yainax is no answer. That was never home for us. Our land is along the Lost River, and this is being denied to us."

"They'll hunt us down like animals!" cried a warrior already decorated with the white lines and red circles of war paint.

"Let them hunt us," Captain Jack said. "Get canoes. We'll cross Tule Lake and go into the Lava Beds to the south. They will never find us there!"

Great discussion went on, but Captain Jack prevailed. His dark eyes fixed on the far shore, and he knew the *boshtin* would never come after the Modoc now. He had heard one of the settlers, one of the Applegate clan, call it "hell with the fire burned out."

Let them follow the Modoc to hell!

# Lynch Mobs

*Linkville, Oregon*
*November 30, 1872*

John Fairchild felt a cold chill run up his spine when he heard his friend Pressly Dorris ticking off all that had happened in the past twenty-four hours.

"You're sure of this? A massacre?" Gooseflesh rippled along his arms and down his back again. "This is terrible. How many were killed?"

"I don't know," Pressly told him breathlessly. "I came as soon as the news hit town. I got to tell you, folks are getting mighty stirred up. Eight soldiers slaughtered and the rest forced to retreat or the whole company would have been goners."

"Major Green never was much of a military man, no matter what his record said."

"From the way everyone's so riled, they might just go after the Hot Creek Modoc. I know you and Shacknasty Jim are friendly and thought you'd want to warn him."

"This is Captain Jack's doing. Those were his people that killed the soldiers, wasn't it?"

"The story everyone's telling about how wild he's become makes me think they'd lynch him if they caught him. One man said that Ivan Applegate told him Captain Jack was responsible for four of the men getting killed. Scalped the soldiers and then ran off into the woods, whooping and yelling and holding the dead men's hair up high as he went."

"Shacknasty Jim is friendly with Captain Jack," Fairchild mused. "But if this happened a day ago, I know he had nothing to do with the scalping. He and a few of his men were in town. I saw them."

"Your memory'll be better than anyone else's," Pressly said. "They're whipping themselves into a killing frenzy and won't remember who was where, only that they want blood."

"Will you ride with me to the Hot Creek village? It's only a couple miles off."

"I wouldn't have come this far, John, if I wasn't willing to go the whole way with you. I like Shacknasty Jim. Hell, I like Captain Jack and can't believe he did any of the killing they claim. Not that he's incapable of it. Just that none of the killing sounds like his doing."

"But Curly Headed Doctor," Fairchild said. "I'd believe anything of him."

Pressly Dorris shrugged, then nodded. Fairchild went into his house and grabbed his rifle. Press already had a Winchester. The two rode fast for the Hot Creek Modoc settlement a few miles outside Linkville.

"I hope we're not too late," Fairchild said, bending low as he urged his horse to greater speed. "Things like this get out of hand fast."

"There's the camp," Press said, pointing ahead. "Doesn't look as if anything unusual's happening."

As the two settlers rode into the Hot Creek village, curious women and children poked their heads out of the *wikiups* and watched. John Fairchild greeted a few by name. The welcome he'd expected was missing. It was as if he had become a complete stranger instead of someone who sometimes fed and always supported the Modoc.

"Shacknasty Jim!" Fairchild called. "You here, Jim?"

A woman shuffled forward. She looked up at him with big

eyes and said, "Him not here. Him and other fellows out hunting."

Fairchild turned to Dorris, anxious at this information.

"Is Shacknasty Jim in town?"

The woman remained impassive.

"Where's Captain Jack?" Press asked. The flash of emotion on the woman's face told the men she knew where their *tyee* was.

"Don't know." The sullen lie told them more than they wanted to know. All whites were excluded from the friendship of the Hot Creek Modoc now.

"Is Captain Jack in the Lava Beds?" John Fairchild saw the way she blinked before turning and almost running away. He heaved a deep sigh and said to Pressly, "Jim might be off to join Captain Jack. If they get into the Lava Beds, there's no way we can get them."

"I got lost there once, right after I moved here," Press said. "It took two of the Modoc a full day to find me. I swear, they have every turn and hollow and cave memorized. I had no idea where I'd got myself to."

"Maybe Shacknasty Jim went to town." Fairchild looked around and saw how the Modoc had all popped back into their *wikiups* like prairie dogs sensing danger. "If he did, he's going to need some help. You still with me?"

"All the way, John. You've helped me when I needed it." Pressly Dorris looked at the village and said, "For all that, so have the Modoc. Jim showed me how to hunt these woods. And Captain Jack showed me woodsmanship I'd need to live. They're good people. That's what makes me think the stories got exaggerated."

"Exaggerated or not, there will be trouble if our neighbors believe even one word of the gossip."

The two men headed for Linkville but got only a half mile before they encountered a boisterous, drunken crowd on their way to the Hot Creek village.

"Hey, John, Press, come on and join us," a man barely able

to stand in the bed of the lead wagon called. "We're gonna stretch some red necks fer what they done."

"What *have* they done, Gordon?" Fairchild reached down, eased his rifle out of its saddle sheath, and laid it across his lap. Press did the same. "From the look of it, all you've done is get roaring drunk."

"Gotta take a snort or two, John. Bad news. So bad it tore me up inside without some whiskey to numb the pain," Gordon said. "Ain't that right, boys?"

The rest of the crowd, almost fifty men, all armed and looking mean and drunk, agreed with a loud cheer.

"What've they done? Them Modoc done upped and kilt half of Major Jackson's company, thass what. And we jist heard tell that Curly Headed Doctor and Hooker Jim attacked the Applegates. Them boys fought like wildcats and killed four Modoc before gettin' away with their scalps."

"This is serious," Fairchild said in a low voice so only Pressly heard. "I don't much like the Applegates, but if Curly Headed Doctor attacked him, there's no holding back this crowd."

"Which Applegate?" Pressly asked loudly. "That hothead Ivan?"

"Sure enough. He was translatin' fer the Army when they was attacked. Ambushed by Captain Jack! Ivan and Oliver was mindin' their own business when Curly Headed Doctor shot at 'em. Quite a fight."

"Quite a fight, indeed," said Fairchild, "if the likes of Ivan and Oliver Applegate could kill four Modoc warriors all by themselves."

"Wall, don't know they *was* braves that got killed," Gordon said.

"It don't matter!" someone else shouted. "We got to punish them all. It's the law!"

"Lynch law," Fairchild said, a deadly calm settling on him. He lifted his rifle and pointed it at Gordon, considering him to be the leader. Back the drunk down and the rest would dry up and blow away like autumn leaves.

"Hi-yah!" shouted the wagon driver, whipping his team and spooking Fairchild's horse. The rearing animal threw him to the ground. Pressly Dorris moved to protect his friend as the others rushed past. Fairchild's horse bolted and ran off.

"Give me a hand up," Fairchild called. He swung up behind his friend. Pressly's horse stumbled under the added weight.

"We've got to stop them, the drunken fools," Press said. "Any good ideas?"

"Shooting the lot of them in the foot might help," Fairchild said dourly. "Short of that, I don't know." He looked around, then pointed. "Cut through there, along the way my horse ran. We can get to the village before them, if they keep to the road."

"Stay on it? They might get lost on it, as drunk as they are." Pressly urged his horse to a trot, going down a ravine and through a grassy area that came out to the north of the Modoc village.

"There's Shacknasty Jim!" Pressly exclaimed.

"He's got my horse! Stop, stop, damn you!" shouted Fairchild. The words had the opposite effect on the Hot Creek Modoc. Shacknasty Jim put his heels to the horse's flanks and shot off like a rocket. Riding double, the two settlers had no chance of overtaking him. They galloped into the village, but this time there was a stillness that mocked them.

Fairchild looked around, then poked his head in a few *wiki-ups* before coming to a sobering conclusion.

"The entire village is deserted."

"Gone to join Captain Jack?" asked Pressly.

John Fairchild could think of no other answer. Shacknasty Jim had rallied his people and fled to the Lava Beds. Captain Jack's power grew with every additional Modoc warrior, every woman and child to be protected from the whites.

The drunken Linkville mob reached the village and became even angrier that they were cheated out of hanging any Indians.

They set fire to the village, not realizing or caring they were lighting the fuse to a keg of blasting powder that might blow them all to kingdom come.

# Rampage

*Linkville, Oregon*
*November 30, 1872*

"My women are dead," Curly Headed Doctor said, gritting his teeth. "They killed them. Theirs must die, too!"

"Death to all the white settlers! And their women!" cried Hooker Jim.

The two Modoc crouched low, cradled by the sharp-edged sagebrush as they pooled their ammunition. Between them they had fewer than forty rounds. Worse, Hooker Jim's rifle had jammed and then broken, leaving them only two pistols. Any killing had to be done close-up.

That suited both men. They wanted blood on their hands to avenge the deaths of the women and baby.

"Listen," Hooker Jim said, rising from the knee-high sage and turning his head to catch the distant sounds. "A wagon is coming along the road, going into town."

"He won't pass," Curly Headed Doctor vowed. The shaman methodically loaded his six-gun, then went to a ditch beside the road and hunkered down, waiting patiently. Less than ten minutes passed before the settler, driving his wagon pulled by a pair of mules, came into sight. Curly Headed Doctor motioned to Hooker Jim to go to the other side of the road and make a diversion.

Crossing the road was enough to get him noticed. The settler on his way to town for supplies, slowed his mules, then reached for a shotgun.

"Who's there?" he called, trying to find Hooker Jim in the tangle of undergrowth along the road. Distracted from the point of real attack, he never saw Curly Headed Doctor draw his knife and jump up on the other side of the road. Something gave away the attacking Modoc at the last moment.

The settler turned and fired, but his shot missed. Curly Headed Doctor's thrust did not. The tip of the knife slid between the man's ribs, then drove upward with savage power to rupture his heart. Blood exploded from the settler's chest and drenched Curly Headed Doctor's knife hand and arm. But the Modoc shaman was not done. He jumped into the driver's box and kept slashing at the now-dead settler. The body flopped into the empty wagon bed.

Slash. A new mouth appeared across the man's throat. Stab. Twist. Cut. The settler's heart was gouged from his chest with inhuman delight. Then Curly Headed Doctor began his mutilation in earnest.

Drenched in his enemy's blood, he finally stood in the wagon, threw back his head, and let out a cry of victory that was more animal than human. Curly Headed Doctor threw aside the heart he had clenched so fiercely and jumped to the ground to stand beside Hooker Jim.

"We have more to kill," the shaman said.

Together, they sought out more settlers and slaughtered them before being driven across Tule Lake into the Lava Beds by the outraged bands of roving settlers.


"Fourteen," Hooker Jim bragged. "We killed fourteen of them!"

Captain Jack stared at the man in disbelief. Then he saw how bloody both were—and neither Curly Headed Doctor nor Hooker Jim showed even a small scratch. The blood came from others. Many others. Fourteen others.

"Why?" Captain Jack asked. "Why did you do this?"

"They killed my women. They killed a baby. Not a one of them that died by my knife and pistol deserved mercy." Curly Headed Doctor thrust out his chest and strutted about.

Captain Jack turned from the shaman and looked across the Lava Beds. A mile or more to the west lay Tule Lake. A small stream meandered through the Lava Beds, more useful for drinking water in the spring than now. The sere grass and savagely edged lava rock spread as far as he could see, in deep valleys and ravines, in prominent hills, across the land no white man could travel. The Modoc knew this land well. Captain Jack had been drilled in its history, and knew every rock and turn by a special name, could tell a story about spires and coulees, sorrowed for those who had died at every point, and glorified those who had not.

This was his tribe's land. Every deadly square inch of it. And somehow, it seemed to be defiled by Curly Headed Doctor's wild killing spree.

"They shot down your women and the child?" he asked.

"We were there. We barely escaped their shotguns," Hooker Jim told him. Captain Jack knew Hooker Jim would lie as easily as he would tell the truth, but this time a ring of sincerity gave a steely edge to his words. Hooker Jim was not lying. The Applegates had murdered innocent women and a baby.

The cavalry had burned his village to the ground. This angered Captain Jack more than Curly Headed Doctor and Hooker Jim butchering so many settlers, perhaps even those who were friendly to the Modoc. The few warriors in the village had acquitted themselves well. Captain Jack wished only that he had been there rather than out hunting. Still, he had heard what had happened from both Bogus Charley, with his soaring, looping, sailing words, and from Scarfaced Charley. It was a pity Watchman had been killed, but eight soldiers for his life was a fair trade.

Captain Jack wished they could have given Watchman a decent burial. He was worried that the soldiers would take the body, defile and decapitate it, denying Watchman his spirit in the afterlife. The attack had been cruel and unexpected, far out of proportion to stealing a few horses and slaughtering a settler's cow when the village went hungry in the cold autumn.

"You will be turned over to the soldiers," Captain Jack said suddenly. He stood and stared down Curly Headed Doctor. "You cannot kill like this. It is wrong."

"You'd take us to Fort Klamath and let the soldiers *hang* us?" Hooker Jim sounded outraged.

Captain Jack feared hanging as much as any of the others. *Watchman, did your spirit survive?* he wondered.

"They will not hang you. I will see that they shoot you for what you did!" Captain Jack's anger flared. Curly Headed Doctor and Hooker Jim endangered all Modoc with their murderous killing spree.

"They might let you go," Bogus Charley said. "Who can say you weren't hunting to take revenge on the Applegates and got the wrong *boshtin?* You should be allowed to avenge the deaths."

"I will see that the Applegates are also tried," Captain Jack said. "They are responsible."

"And who is responsible for getting our village burned and chasing us to the Lava Beds?" demanded Scarfaced Charley. "They will kill us like rabbits."

"We need to talk," Captain Jack said. "There is too much spilled blood for anyone to be peaceable. If we find Meacham and talk, he will tell us what to do, how to make peace again with the whites."

"I wish they were all like the people in Yreka," Bogus Charley said. "They like us." He smiled and laughed. "I like them!"

"We will never surrender to any soldier," Curly Headed Doctor said. "Never!"

Captain Jack looked away from the shaman, distracted by a signal mirror used by a sentry near the lake. He left the arguing group and worked his way along tortuous corridors in the lava, deftly avoiding cutting himself on sharp protrusions of lava rock.

"Shacknasty Jim!" he called.

"Jack." The *tyee* of the Hot Creek Modoc greeted Captain Jack, then moved aside as everyone from his village made their way up from the lake.

"How many boats did you use?" Captain Jack asked.

"Twelve. We stole them, the ones we did not already have," Shacknasty Jim said. "We stole them from the settlers because they tried to lynch us!"

Captain Jack and Shacknasty Jim walked back to where Curly Headed Doctor argued loudly with Bogus Charley.

"Quiet," Captain Jack called. "We have guests." He saw the expression on Shacknasty Jim's face and amended the statement. "We have allies."

"Allies?" Hooker Jim scoffed. "Against the white soldiers, against the settlers? Do they look to turn us over to die, also?"

Shacknasty Jim cried to be heard amid the hubbub that went up when everyone tried to talk at once. Captain Jack shouted them to silence, permitting one after another to speak and forcing the rest to listen, however impatient they might be.

Captain Jack found himself receiving the brunt of the criticism, and his leadership was slowly eroded as each Modoc warrior spoke in turn.

Bogus Charley moved closer and said quietly, "They do not want you to turn Curly Headed Doctor or Hooker Jim over to the settlers. Not after Shacknasty Jim confirmed what we already knew."

"They want to exterminate us," Captain Jack said. "Why? Did Odeneal want this? Did he order it done by the soldiers? He will not even speak to me. Why should he hate us so?"

"He fears us. He is the kind of man who kills what he fears," Bogus Charley said.

The arguments bounced around, growing more strident, until Captain Jack saw his leadership was in jeopardy if he did nothing. The evidence presented by the Hot Creek Modoc was piled onto that offered up by Curly Headed Doctor and Hooker Jim that the settlers had turned murderous.

Captain Jack knew he could no longer get anyone to accept his belief that the soldiers' raid on his village was only a misunderstanding and that they could negotiate with them, possibly returning to Yainax but maybe getting to settle along Lost River as they hoped.

"What shall I do?" he asked Bogus. "Give up being *tyee?*"

"There is another choice. The council wants action. You know what that is."

Captain Jack did. He waited for the firebrands to burn themselves out with vicious cries for scalping all the whites before he stood and forced them to silence. At least he still had that much control over them.

Captain Jack looked around the circle of angry faces. He felt like a wood chip caught in the current of a powerful river. If he did not go along with the raging flow, he would be washed ashore and left behind. Who would lead the Modoc then? Captain Jack could not bear the thought of Curly Headed Doctor or even Schonchin John becoming *tyee*.

If it was to be war, let it be a war with him leading the Modoc.

"I have heard everything that has been said," Captain Jack said in his booming voice that reached out across the desolate Lava Beds and seemed to touch the sky itself. "Always we have talked and found common ground with the *boshtin*. This is no longer possible."

"They want to hang you for killing Comptowas," Curly Headed Doctor said. "Imagine anyone getting mad over killing a Klamath!"

Captain Jack glared at the shaman, silencing him. He knew how Curly Headed Doctor had resented the Klamath shaman. Then he went on. "Our problems only multiply. We have left the Klamath Reservation, but have not been allowed to live in peace. The soldiers followed us to Lost River and killed Watchman. The settlers killed our women and children. We have been driven into the Lava Beds for sanctuary. The Hot Creek Modoc have joined us for the same reason.

"Do you want me to lead you?" Captain Jack waited as a hush fell over the assembled warriors. He knew what had to be added. "Do you want me to lead you in war?"

The uproar was deafening. Captain Jack had his answer. Now it was time for him to cement his shaky alliances among the various factions.

"I will need all your skill, Shacknasty Jim, all your cunning and fighting ability."

"It is yours!" the Hot Creek Modoc *tyee* declared, giving his allegiance to Captain Jack with those words.

"Can you give us magical protection, Curly Headed Doctor?"

The shaman paused, looked at Hooker Jim, then stood. "The Ghost Dance can protect us in fighting. We can make the Lava Beds invulnerable to attack from any not following the teachings of Wovoka."

Captain Jack knew the mere name of Wovoka inspired fear in the whites. The Ghost Dance promised to return the land to the Indian, bring back the vast herds of buffalo, and drive out all who were not believers in the Great Spirit.

"Lead us in the Ghost Dance," Captain Jack said. "Make us invincible!"

Curly Headed Doctor began the two-day-long Ghost Dance, chanting and dancing, drumming and weaving around, until he was the last of the warriors to fall to the ground exhausted— and ready for war.

# War in Hell

Joshua Harlan spread four different newspapers in front of him on his desk. He compared the stories of the massacres around Tule Lake by the Modoc and found them all wanting. Not a one, even the *Alta California* story, had direct evidence or interviews with Captain Jack or other Modoc leaders.

Josh slammed his hand down on the desk and leaned back. "I should be there!" he said in disgust. Instead, he languished behind a desk, doing hardly anything. The winter weather had restricted ocean shipping for the past three weeks and was not likely to let up any time soon. He had delivered the new accounts Sean Murdoch had sent him into Chinatown to find, for all the good it did with the clipper ships docked and unable to venture beyond the Golden Gate.

Worse, he now spent more time looking over his shoulder, jumping at sudden noises and worrying that Faith's brothers might finally have found a way of killing him without anyone finding out their culpability. He had tried to alert Sean Murdoch to his sons' treachery, but the man refused to believe either Morgan or Michael would harm a hair on his head.

Murdoch had even gone so far as to tell them of their brother-in-law's fears. As far as Josh could tell, that might well have sealed both his and Sean Murdoch's fate. It made the two brothers more determined to hide their murderous ways.

If he was going to be killed, he wanted to die as a reporter and not a glorified clerk behind a desk. Josh's imagination soared. Troops moving in precise columns. The Modoc sniping at them from behind trees, and then running away into what Meacham called the most inaccessible land in all of North America.

"The Lava Beds," he muttered. He had not seen much beyond Yreka. What did the battleground for the Modoc War look like? He could describe it better than the second-rate stringers the *Alta California* had reporting.

Or any of the other papers. He could get the real story, even if some editors might not like it. Josh knew the Modoc could not be entirely to blame just from the way he had seen them treated the short time he was there along the California-Oregon border. While no saint, Captain Jack was not the diabolical murderer the papers made him out to be. Josh read the stories and saw how they were slanted. Propaganda, not real reporting, showed up in headlines.

It all made him want to be there, to be a part of it, to see and smell and feel and *report.*

"You reading about the massacre up north?" asked MacMillan, seeing the newspapers strewn about Josh's desktop. The secretary clutched a sheaf of papers for him to sign and couldn't locate a clear space to fling them down before leaving. Sean Murdoch's secretary had not taken well to Josh's promotion to junior partner any better than Murdoch's sons had.

"Not any longer," Josh said, coming to a decision. He grabbed the papers from MacMillan's hands, scribbled his name across them, then said, "I'll be back when the war's over."

He left, the secretary's mouth gaping.

* * *

Aching and sore from first the train ride, and now the time spent in the saddle reaching the southern outskirts of Linkville, Josh was about ready to admit he was not cut out for the life of a frontier reporter. Then he heard the baleful roll of drums marking cadence and the crisp crunch-crunch-crunch of military boots all hitting the frozen ground at the same time.

Old Glory showed above the vegetation far down the road leading into Linkville from the east, and slowly became larger, flapping in the brisk wind bringing winter out of the Arctic. Josh caught his breath, took off his hat, and waited as the soldiers marched into full view.

He counted as the troops went by, their ranks a little ragged from the long march, but nonetheless inspiring in their military precision. At the head of the long columns rode a full colonel, his uniform spotless in spite of the mud and sleet mixed in with the light rain that had fallen most of the day.

Josh watched the colonel ride past, and counted and kept counting. Company after company went into Linkville. Two hundred soldiers, all with .52-caliber Spencers on their shoulders, and the officers with sabers and pistols at their waists. Behind rattled supply wagons groaning under the weight of supplies. Tarps hid the contents, but Josh guessed at the vast amount of ammunition that could be carried in the wagons. General Canby had prepared for a real war, a long one with considerable fighting if even half the wagons were laden with ammunition.

The final element of the column passed through the crossroads where Josh watched. He urged his tired horse after it, going into Linkville. He fell back when he heard crowds cheering. A reporter had to be invisible, collecting facts and finding out the truth, not be part of the story. If it looked to the citizens of Linkville that he was with the military column, it would change the way they spoke to him.

It might help him get a story or two, but Josh felt it would only hinder his quest for the facts. Mr. Billingsly had not been receptive to the idea of signing Josh on as a reporter of any standing but had said he would look at whatever Josh wrote with an eye toward printing it in the *Alta California*.

Billingsly would pay by the piece, but the newspaper would not reimburse Josh to go to Linkville or to live there while ferreting out the juiciest stories about the war and its combatants. Josh was on his own, paying for the trip out of his own pocket.

Josh smiled crookedly. He might be paying in more ways than with money. Faith had been furious with him for leaving before the Christmas social whirl began, and his father-in-law had thought he was joking. When he found out how serious Josh had been, the empty junior partner's office mute evidence of his departure, he might well be inclined to revoke the part ownership of the company as quickly as he had bestowed it.

Josh stood to lose a fortune, and perhaps even his wife, because he had come north. Somehow, he didn't care. He rode into Linkville ten minutes behind the arrival of the soldiers, and felt good about it, damned good.

For the first time in months, he was doing more than simply existing. He was coming alive, driven by the challenge of being a reporter.

Dismounting, he tied his horse at the rear of the general store, and hurried to the street to catch the last of the soldiers marching by. Josh ran to talk with the sergeant marching beside the platoon. The man, his chin clean shaven but his face sporting a bushy walrus mustache, looked at Josh as if he might be some kind of insect.

"What you wantin', mister?" the sergeant demanded.

"How soon do you think you'll see action?"

"Saw action already," the sergeant said. "On the way here. A wagon got stuck in the mud. Danged near froze my balls off waitin' fer 'nuff men to push the wagon out."

"But the action?" Josh pressed.

"That was it. And don't go talkin' to my men. They got real jobs to do." The sergeant laughed and looked forward, dismissing him. Josh slowed and knew dealing with the enlisted

men might be harder than he anticipated. The officers would
be in constant conference over the impending maneuvers. He
slowed and finally stopped, letting the last squad of soldiers
tramp onward. He scribbled a few notes, but it was more for
show. He knew others in Linkville watched him and counted
on him for information.

"Who's that colonel up there in front?" asked one man.

Josh had no idea who commanded the soldiers. But before
he could speak, a soft voice said, "Colonel Wheaton."

He spun and saw Isabella. He grinned from ear to ear seeing
her again.

"You heard already?" he asked her, ignoring the man who
had inquired. "What more have you found out?" Josh was as
eager as a puppy, but he wasn't sure what drove him now.
Whatever it was, he was glad to see Isabella again.

"There will be another troop of two hundred commanded
by Colonel Mason."

"Four hundred men against Captain Jack?" Josh whistled.
"How can he defend himself against so many soldiers?" He
read an answer different from the one he expected. "What else
do you know, Isabella? Please. I need to know!"

"I can introduce you to Captain Bernard. He is Colonel
Mason's second in command."

"I could kiss you!" Josh stopped, horrified at what he had
just said, but Isabella took no notice of it. "I . . . I need a
place to stay. This time the *Alta* isn't paying for me, but I've
got enough money to stay for the duration of the war."

"There is no place left in town," Isabella said. "So many
people." She looked forlorn, lost at the crush of people into
Linkville. "Even in Yreka, there is no place."

"I need to be near the fort," Josh said. "Maybe I can get a
tent and camp outside Linkville."

Isabella laughed at him, irritating him.

"You don't think I can survive on my own, just because I'm
from San Francisco?"

"I saw your city with its fine buildings. You would freeze

your toes off the first night if you camped out." Isabella sobered and said, "I have a place you can stay."

"I knew I could count on you," he said. Then Josh saw her expression and knew what the lodgings were. It wasn't right for him to live with her, not under the same roof, but where else could he stay?

Josh took Isabella's hand when she reached out to him, leading him to her small room behind the town bakery.

# A View of Hell

"You are sure Captain Bernard will be out there?" Josh asked Isabella. The Modoc woman sat on a rickety chair beside the door, staring at him with her wide-spaced dark eyes.

"I heard this," she said simply.

Everything she did made Josh uneasy. She had offered him her bed, and if he had been inclined, she would have climbed in beside him. Josh did not like the Modoc openness with something so personal, and he was a married man. He might have fights with Faith over her tastes in entertainment, especially the opera, and her constant need to be seen in new and ever more costly dresses at San Francisco social events, but he loved her. He had married her.

Why had she married him?

Josh shook his head. This mental churning got him nowhere. His relationship with Isabella was platonic, open and innocent. She had sources of information closed to him and, if he gained her trust, he thought she could even get him an interview with Captain Jack. He would be the only reporter to speak with the Modoc *tyee* on the eve of a major fight that would crush the Indians totally.

"Will he speak to me?"

"Why not?" she answered.

"Thank you, Isabella. I don't know what I'd do without you." This caused Isabella to brighten. She started to say something more, then lowered her eyes and nodded assent. He hurried to get pencils and notebooks stuffed into his coat pockets, then drew on gloves and pulled a fancy wool scarf Faith had given him around his neck and up to cover his mouth and nose. The weather had turned frigid overnight.

"I'll see you get more wood for the stove," he told Isabella on his way out.

"I can get it."

"I insist," he said. "If it hadn't been for me being so cold all night long, we wouldn't have used so much."

Again she demurred to him. Josh saddled his horse and rode out of town, heading to the road leading southeast to the Lava Beds. He had heard about them constantly since coming to Linkville, but he had yet to see them. The Army patrols along the roads blocked most movement, but he had gathered plenty of information for his first story in town. Now it was time to see what the soldiers faced.

"Halt!" cried a sentry from the side of the road. "What's your business?"

"I am supposed to see Captain Bernard," Josh said, phrasing it in such a way it sounded as if the captain had summoned him. "I'm a bit late because I can't seem to find him."

"Late?" The sentry reached into his jacket and scratched himself as he considered what Josh said. He kept his hand inside for the warmth there, leaving his rifle butt-down on the ground and held in his left hand. If Josh had wanted to attack the guard, he would find it simple to overwhelm him and ride on. He waited for the sentry to think it through.

"The captain's on down the road, 'bout three miles. Up on the hill, looking over the Lava Beds."

"Thank you, Sergeant," Josh said, knowing full well the sentry was only a private. Still, the brevet promotion pleased the man and gave Josh a chance to ride on.

He rode hard until he found a tight knot of soldiers sitting around a fire, warming their hands. They looked up but did not challenge him. From the way they talked, they were Oregon volunteers, with a few Klamath Indian scouts sitting silently off to one side.

"Where's Captain Bernard?" Josh followed the detailed directions given him by the sergeant—an actual sergeant—and made his way up a winding trail through sagebrush and thornier vegetation until he came out on a butte looking out over the Lava Beds.

For a moment, he simply stared west across the lava flows. He thought he had gone too far and reached the Pacific Ocean, but closer examination showed this was not an undulating body of water. It looked like rolling hills or surging waves—but it was solid rock. Solid and black and unlike any terrain Josh had ever seen.

"There're down there," a man said in a deep bass voice. "We look but we don't see 'em. Do you?"

"Sir?" Josh jerked around and saw an artillery captain standing beside him, field glasses dangling from a cord around his neck.

"I've been here all day and haven't spotted a single Modoc. Captain Jack's men know the terrain better than I ever will, and I have maps." The officer tapped a cylindrical black case slung at his hip.

"It looks so peaceful down there," Josh said, "but I can see how difficult it would be to cross. The deep gorges, the rocks themselves. What kind of plants grow down there?"

"Same as up here on the heights," the captain said. "Who might you be, if I can ask?"

Josh introduced himself, then said, "You must be Captain Bernard. I've heard such good things about you, sir, it's a pleasure to meet you."

"Nobody in my command says good things about me. If they do, I'll have my sergeants drill it out of them." In spite of the words, the officer was obviously pleased with Josh's compliment. "You a reporter, eh?"

"For the *Alta California,* sir."

"A decent newspaper. You must be out of San Francisco?"

"I am, sir. That's why this land seems so . . . alien to me. It's like another planet."

"The face of the moon," Bernard said, nodding solemnly. "I look at the moon at night, then compare it to the Lava Beds. I'm not sure the moon isn't better ground to fight on."

"Lots of caves and hidden areas?"

"Large ones, from the maps I have. Captain Jack and his entire tribe can camp out in some of the open areas and never rub shoulders. Huge parts of that volcanic landscape for hiding, for living, and we cannot even spot them from here."

"When are you going in, sir?" Josh asked.

"Colonel Wheaton has more than four hundred soldiers, half on this side and half on the western edge. He is confident of going into that rock foam sea."

"And your opinion, sir? What do you think?"

"See how there are swells running north to south? They look tiny from here but are more than twenty feet high. To go from one tiny ravine to the other requires travel of more than a hundred yards. A soldier has to circle round—no one goes *over* those swells without being torn to ribbons on sharp rock."

"The entire area is a maze, sir," Josh said.

"I agree. There is hardly a spot not twisted into knots by that damnable rock. And the ones that are clear and flat, the Modoc occupy them. I think."

"You don't sound confident about going in after Captain Jack," Josh said. "What's Colonel Wheaton's position?"

Captain Bernard started to make an obscene retort. Josh saw it on the officer's face. Then Bernard caught himself and said, "The colonel feels we will make short work of the Modoc. Our superior training and arms will carry the day."

"Fighting down there will be hard, especially against an enemy who intimately knows the country, sir."

"We are putting in howitzer batteries on these very heights to cover the approaches. Colonel Wheaton feels the howitzers will prevent the Modoc from escaping. I think we will need their covering fire to advance. My imagination fails, thinking of hauling our howitzers into that rocky morass."

Josh wrote it all down, questioned the captain further on more personal points for background, then excused himself to ride all night and return to Linkville to file his story with Mr. Billingsly.

His account was printed on the front page of the *Alta California*.

# Confidence

"You should not be here," Captain Bernard said to Josh. The officer looked around and didn't see his commander. Josh knew Colonel Wheaton stood at the top of the bluff, looking far into the Lava Beds, and out of view of his subordinate. He was not going to tell Bernard that, however, if it meant he would be chased off before the barrage began. "But there's no reason you can't stay, if you keep out of the way."

"Yes, sir," Josh said, anxious to be where the action was. All around him soldiers had dug their way into the rocky cliff to place their howitzers. Beside each cannon stood a man with a thick rag tied to a long wood rod. He would dip the rag in a bucket of water, then slosh the water all over the short barrel to keep it cool after firing. Another stood with the firing lanyard in hand, practicing how he would face away, take a step forward, and fling his hand forward, setting off the howitzer. The other two men were entrusted with charging and tamping the cannon after every round.

Bernard used his binoculars to scan the rugged terrain stretching for miles in front of them. To their right lay Tule Lake, a barely seen sliver of shimmery blue water. Reaching it from this vantage point was impossible, either by foot or by artillery shell. The two main tracks leading westward into the wild lava rock countryside had been assigned to Bernard to protect with his battery of four cannon.

"You might want to cram bits of rag or cotton into your ears. It gets noisy once the firing begins," Bernard warned.

"Why doesn't Colonel Wheaton have earplugs?" Josh asked. He had stayed clear of the commanding officer, not wanting to be chased off. But the colonel had never noticed him, confidently going about his job of getting the artillery into position.

"He doesn't think the fight will last long," Bernard said. "The colonel believes the cannon will only fire once or twice before Captain Jack surrenders."

Josh hesitated. From all Isabella had told him of the Modoc *tyee,* this did not seem likely.

"What is it, son?" demanded Bernard. "You look skeptical."

"Well, sir, my sources say Captain Jack's in a fight to keep control of his tribe. Several aggressive men close to him want to become chief and replace him. That doesn't sound like a situation where a man, any man, would surrender quickly. He'd be inclined to fight, to see if he couldn't get rid of the annoying power-seekers, if nothing else."

"Send the firebrands into the teeth of the howitzers and kill them off," mused Bernard. "You think Captain Jack's that smart?"

"Smarter," Josh said without hesitation.

"I'm afraid you are right and the colonel's underestimated the fight ahead of us. My two scouts into *that,*" Bernard said, pointing to the Lava Beds, "brought back sorry tales. We can't march in and get Captain Jack out. He's got to surrender, and firing a couple shells at him won't do it."

"You can't even see his camp, can you, sir?" asked Josh.

He read Captain Bernard's answer by the sour expression. The officer turned and began barking orders to the howitzer crews. Josh scribbled furiously, only to look up and blink as sunlight glinting off a mile or more of gold braid dazzled him.

"You," snapped Colonel Wheaton. "What are you doing here?"

"Looking for you, sir," Josh lied. He knew Bernard would get into a stewpot of trouble if the colonel found out he permitted reporters on the battle line. "I need a comment about the fight. How confident are you about driving out the Modoc from their stronghold?"

"I am positive this skirmish will last only the day. I am sanguine about our victory. You may quote me. Be sure to spell my name right."

"That's Colonel Wheaton, right?" asked Josh.

"It is." The colonel peered over Josh's shoulder to double-check the spelling of his name, then shooed him away.

"Can't I stay with you, sir?" begged Josh.

"Get off the bluffs immediately," Wheaton ordered, puffing up his chest and looking very military. "I will not permit civilian casualties. Go and stay with the Oregon volunteers. You will be safe among them, if you do not drink their vile coffee!" Colonel Wheaton laughed at his little joke.

"At the foot of the cliffs, sir?" Josh felt like he was the rabbit being thrown into the briar patch. When he got no answer from the colonel, who turned and spoke rapidly to Captain Bernard, Josh made his way down a winding path to where the company camped. He had passed them on his way up the hill earlier in the day, but Josh had wanted to keep to the high ground to follow the bombardment. From the soldiers' camp, he could hear the artillery but not see where the shells landed in the Lava Beds.

"Kill the whole danged red lot of them," he heard one sergeant saying as he walked up.

"Who's that, Sergeant?" he asked. "I'm reporting for the *Alta California*. Care to give a statement?"

"Wall, shore, glad to talk to anyone of the press about us Oregon volunteers. We're gonna go into that Modoc stronghold and kick some red ass all the way to the ocean. When we git 'em there, we'll kick 'em all the way back! Them redskins don't cleave together, no, sir. Why, half our number is made up of Klamath! We're gonna see Indians killing Indians 'fore the day's out."

"Kick 'em?" said another. "I intend to *eat* them. Scalp 'em and eat their flesh. That'll show 'em."

Josh wrote slowly, hardly listening to the volunteer brag about how good he and the rest of his fellows were at fighting Indians. He saw a shadow moving, strangely positioned for this time of day. The shadow flitted around the edge of the Oregon volunteers' position, and none of them noticed. Josh started to say something, then bit back the words. What did he know? He was only a civilian and a reporter.

He'd gotten his story and that was what he wanted most.

# Vote

*The Lava Beds*
*January 15, 1873*

The Modoc brave froze, then tried to sink back into deeper shadow when he saw the white man staring directly at him. Heart hammering, he reached for the knife at his belt. If he had to fight the soldiers, he wanted to take at least one with him. More if possible. His heart raced, then settled down when it became apparent that only the one not in uniform had seen him but was not going to point him out to the loutish soldiers.

He did not understand this. Did not all the whites think like the settlers and soldiers? Murdering Modoc was all they sought to do, shotgunning innocent women and babies.

Moving slowly, as if the wind blew him along through the dense undergrowth, he moved around the Oregon volunteers' encampment where he could listen to the ones with stripes on their uniforms speaking. Sergeants, Captain Jack had told him, were the brains of the white Army. They moved the men into position and did the real fighting while the officers lingered behind lines and pretended to win battles.

He settled down and listened as the Oregon volunteers boasted of their strengths and how easily they would pry the Modoc from their positions in the Lava Beds. He counted soldiers and determined what supplies they had and where the wagons bringing ammunition were parked. He could have stolen many horses and mules but did not.

Retracing his path, he again saw the one without a uniform talking with the sergeant. He was not sure if the man saw him again. Probably not. Not daring to linger anymore, seeing there was nothing more to learn from the blowhards, he dropped behind one of the lava rock swells, went down a narrow, twisty ravine and then got into the center of the flows where he could run without worry.

His ground-devouring stride took him in and out of the sharp-edged rock and down into arroyos that eventually lead to a wide-open space where Captain Jack's entire band camped. He looked around and saw the *tyee*. He went directly to him.

Captain Jack looked up from a crude map scratched into the thin dirt and said, "You have learned much?"

"I have," the Modoc scout said. He quickly told his *tyee* all he had seen but held his tongue when it came to telling Captain Jack about the Klamath volunteers among the Oregon soldiers. He did not like the Klamath and wanted to see them all killed. His caution about relating this was answered by Captain Jack a few minutes later.

"Will they attack soon?" asked Captain Jack.

"They are ready," the scout answered.

"We need to hold off for a week, perhaps more. By then the Snake and the Klamath will join us. The soldiers will never fight three tribes."

"The Klamath? They leave their reservation to fight alongside the Modoc?"

"Of course they will," Captain Jack said. "David Allan has promised me much help from his tribe. He will come, bringing warriors and enough supplies for us to last for a year."

"And you trust Allan?"

Captain Jack nodded. "He speaks with Old Schonches, who would join us if he were able. But David Allan will not fail us, although he is Klamath." He looked past the scout when

Schonchin John came strutting up, looking belligerent. He wore full war paint and carried a rifle.

"When do we kill them?" Schonchin John demanded. "You *are* going to attack, Kintpuash? You will not let them bottle us up here?"

"We are not trapped," Captain Jack said. "They are. Where can they run, their backs to the cliffs? Their big guns aim down on . . . emptiness. If they venture in, their soldiers will die. Why do you think we are trapped?"

"We have been forced off our land along Lost River. We are denied even Yainax. We run here like frightened rabbits when our village is burned and our women killed. You are not fit to lead, Kintpuash!"

Captain Jack rested his fingers on the bone-handled knife sheathed at his belt. Schonchin John was always a hothead but now had gone too far. Captain Jack knew how tenuous his hold over the others was. If challenged, he had to fight to remain *tyee*.

"You would see all our people die," Captain Jack accused. "I can defeat the whites. You would kill the Modoc in your wild attacks."

"You believe their words. You signed treaties. The whites broke those treaties," Schonchin John said angrily. "Remember Ben Wright! Under a truce flag he killed. You were there. I was, too. *We* saw how treacherous the white man is, and you want to avoid fighting? Pah!"

Captain Jack saw a small circle of others looking to be leader of the Modoc had gathered. Scarfaced Charley spoke up, surprising him.

"Captain Jack is right. We wait. When more tribes join us, the whites will never dare fight. They will run away! Listen to Captain Jack, listen to Kintpuash!"

"We must fight!" shouted Curly Headed Doctor. Like Schonchin John he was decked out in full war paint. He waved a rattle in the air, shaking it noisily. The shaman danced about and stopped in front of Captain Jack, his face just inches away.

"We cannot wait. To let the whites attack us now is to lose! We must attack them first!"

"Vote!" someone cried. "The council must vote! War now or later."

Captain Jack was worried at the choices. He wanted to avoid bloodshed. Curly Headed Doctor was crazy and Schonchin John wanted only to fight. Neither of them had seen the power of the white man's howitzers. Those mighty guns were on a bluff too far away to harm them, but the shelling could be disconcerting. Captain Jack had a hundred women and children to consider.

"We vote," Captain Jack said. "We smoke a pipe, we talk, then we vote." It was the best he could do to keep control. Better to vote on war than on who was to be *tyee*. Captain Jack was not sure Schonchin John might not win, should that be put to the vote.

All day they smoked and talked and argued. Then they voted.

One by one the warriors cast their vote. Captain Jack saw quickly how it was to be.

"Thirty-seven for war. Fourteen to wait," he said. Captain Jack got to his feet and said in a loud voice, having no choice if he wanted to continue leading the Modoc, "Prepare for war!"

# Burning Bridges

*Linkville, Oregon*
*January 15, 1873*

Josh wandered through the Oregon volunteers' disorganized camp, noting how many Klamath Indians were interspersed among the ragtag white soldiers. The two groups did not mingle any more than water and oil, but the Klamath seemed as intent on killing Modoc as the whites did. Josh wished he knew their language. Maybe Isabella knew enough Klamath to translate some of the phrases he heard being bandied about like slogans, always greeted with laughter and jeers. He wrote them down to jog his memory later, when he got back to Linkville.

Seeing that nothing much was going to happen, he mounted and rode slowly back along the road toward town. He made sure he stopped to talk with the sentries, dropping the names of Colonel Wheaton and Captain Bernard liberally to reinforce in their minds that he was friendly with their commanders and ought to be let in again. It cost him a bag of tobacco and some jerky, but he thought the time spent with the bored sentries along the road was worthwhile. Let the other reporters, who huddled in Linkville making up their stories, match what he found out firsthand.

Josh rode faster once he left the bluffs looking over the Lava Beds, glad to be away from the odd volcanic terrain. The blackness, spotted here and there with sere vegetation growing, or trying to, in the winter cold and obdurate rock, made the hair stand on the back of his neck. Going into that vast wilderness would not be as easy as Colonel Wheaton thought. Captain Bernard had a better idea what it meant to pry out Captain Jack and all his allies.

Artillery would not be enough. Troops had to enter that hell-hole.

Writing his story mentally, he hardly realized he had returned to Linkville until shouts all around him shook him from his reverie. The reporters whooped it up, spending their per diem money on whiskey and loose women. Josh ignored them and went to the telegraph office, where the operator sat by his "bug" listening to the rapid clicks and clacks.

"Be with you in a minute," the telegrapher said, not even looking up as he wrote hurriedly, translating the incoming message from code to words readable by mere mortals.

"There's no hurry," Josh said, sitting at a small desk and carefully writing out his latest dispatch for the *Alta*. Mr. Billingsly would run this one on the front page, too. He had to. It set the stage for what might turn out to be one bloody fight.

Josh finished and then drew out a new sheet. He stared at the blank white page, dipped his pen, and wrote slowly, carefully, choosing his words well. This telegram went to Faith, telling her he was staying in Linkville to cover the Modoc War and had resigned his position at her father's shipping company. He was not certain what her reaction would be, but he knew her brothers would be out celebrating into the wee hours when they heard. Their rival had given up and gone away, leaving them the sole heirs to the prosperous business.

"I got a clear line for a few minutes. You ready for me to send?" called the telegrapher.

"Yes, sir, I am," Josh said. He handed the telegrapher the story intended for the *Alta*, but held the letter to Faith, reading it again and then a third time. Twice he started to correct a

word—or was it to throw away the entire letter?—but then he
passed it over and said, "Send this one, too."

The telegrapher looked through reading glasses, counting
the words. He made a quick notation on a pad and said, "If
that's it, you owe me four dollars and nineteen cents."

Josh left four dollars and two bits on the counter and left.
He stepped out into the cold, crisp winter dusk with Linkville
alive all around him. The tension in the air invigorated him.
The idea he was actually reporting something significant
thrilled him.

Most of all, sending the telegram to Faith had broken invisible shackles. Humming the jaunty tune "Gary Owen," he
went off to find Isabella. He needed her to translate the Klamath phrases he had written down and to see if she had heard
any more about the Modoc plans.

# The Ghost Dance

*The Lava Beds*
*January 16, 1873*

"If the Ghost Dance does not kill our enemies, what good is it?" demanded Bogus Charley. "We need allies, not dancing."

"We will be invincible after the dance," Curly Headed Doctor declared, glaring at Bogus Charley. "The way to regain our land is to fight and kill, not to fight and die."

"So the soldiers' bullets will miss us?"

"They will not kill anyone who takes part in the Ghost Dance," Curly Headed Doctor said firmly. "I can protect the entire area." With a flourish, he reached into his pouch, pulled out a thin red rope woven from tule, and held it high above his head, as if displaying a killed snake for everyone to see.

"What will this do?" asked Captain Jack, in spite of himself. He had avoided Curly Headed Doctor since the council vote went against him, but he found himself intrigued by—perhaps even believing—what the shaman had said about the Ghost Dance.

"It will create a barrier against those who would harm us. No one will be able to cross the rope, no one will be able to shoot a gun past the barrier!"

Curly Headed Doctor began chanting. When he settled into

a rhythm, he started unrolling the coil of rope, circling the large clearing where Captain Jack's band camped.

"No Modoc can be harmed if we stay within the tule rope?" asked Bogus Charley, his nose wrinkling in contempt.

"Perhaps not, perhaps so," said Captain Jack. "What can it hurt to try? We need all the potent medicine we can get." The *tyee* began dancing along with Curly Headed Doctor's chanting, following closely as the shaman played out the red rope. Another took up drums and began the soul-satisfying beat.

In a few minutes the rest of the warriors had joined Curly Headed Doctor in the Ghost Dance, even the skeptical Bogus Charley. After all, what harm could it do?

# The First Battle
# for the Stronghold

*The Lava Beds*
*January 17, 1873*

"Fire!" cried Captain Bernard. He turned from the belching howitzer as it sent a shell arcing into the wastelands of the lava flows. The distant explosion rocked the ground. "Fire!" he ordered again. The cannon barrel sizzled as the swabber laved it with water. The two soldiers at the muzzle struggled to load powder and cannonball. The man yanking the lanyard forgot to turn away when Bernard again gave the order and was knocked flat by the howitzer's concussion. He sat, stunned, staring into the distance at nothing in particular.

"Cease fire," Bernard ordered. "Tend to him, Sergeant." He lifted his field glasses, peered into the Lava Beds, and cursed. The fog drifting over the rolling landscape obscured his vision. He had no idea about range, much less target.

"Captain!" shouted Colonel Wheaton. "Cease fire. The shelling will do no good if we cannot see what we're firing at."

"Yes, sir," the captain said, having already reached that decision. He had precious little ammunition to waste. Throwing it willy-nilly into the emptiness only wasted it.

"Leave your sergeant in charge of the battery and assemble with the rest of your men at the base of the bluffs."

Bernard's sergeant gave him a curious look, then said, "Sounds like you're off to fight a war hand-to-hand, Captain. You want us to get the cannon down the hill so we can take 'em with us?"

"It does, indeed, seem to be in our future to go into the Lava Beds, but the colonel said nothing about bringing the howitzers," Bernard said, not thrilled with the idea of fighting the Modoc on their own territory, without artillery support. He took a final look at the twisting maze of the Lava Beds and saw nothing but uniform, gently swirling gray now. The fog had come in low and thick, blocking all sight.

To fight in that meant many good soldiers would never return to camp.

Bernard made his way to the bottom of the bluff where he had established his artillery positions and found Wheaton already mounted and impatiently waiting at the head of a crowd of Oregon volunteers. Bernard frowned. These weren't soldiers as much as they were a mob. And the Klamath scouts were nowhere to be seen. They had estimated their chances in the Lava Beds and wisely vanished.

"Prepare yourself, Captain. We go in after the red bastards in ten minutes." Wheaton checked his watch.

"A coordinated attack, sir?"

"We come in from the east. Another unit will attack from the west. We will catch the Modoc between the elements and crush them."

"Yes, sir," Bernard said, doubtful this would happen. He mounted and urged his skittish horse forward, to the narrow path leading into the Lava Beds. It reminded him of a cattle chute in a slaughterhouse. Bernard forced the image from his mind, checked his pistol, then made certain his saber slid easily in its sheath. He hated the heavy weapon and would not have carried it had not Colonel Wheaton insisted. For combat it was almost useless. Better to carry a second pistol or a knife for close-in fighting.

Better yet to sit on the hill and lob shells five hundred yards at his enemies.

"Column, forward!" cried Wheaton, his saber dull silver in the fog.

Bernard let the senior officer lead the way into the turns and bends of the lava flows, staying farther back with another company of the Oregon volunteers. He saw a sergeant had rounded up the Klamath fighters, but they emulated his caution, preferring to let their white comrades enter first.

Who commanded the Klamath Bernard did not know. He found an eager company of volunteers and got them marching forward in a semblance of order that quickly vanished in the fog. Less than a hundred yards into the Lava Beds, he found himself shut off from the rest, riding blind, aware of men only a few yards ahead and behind.

"Stay together!" he called. "Follow the man in front of you. Don't wander off or you're sure to be lost."

He tried to follow his own advice, but mounted, he found it hard to keep the foot soldiers in view. As he rode, he came to think of the fog as his ally, a friend shielding him from the Modoc's prying eyes. Wheaton had not adequately scouted the paths into the Lava Beds, thinking the Army would have observers on the top of the bluff alongside the howitzers to guide them.

The cold fog worked its way under his collar, dripped down his back, and turned his wool uniform clammy, but the fog was his ally. Bernard kept telling himself this, even when the soldier directly to his right yelped, spun, and fired wildly into the fog.

"There, there's one of them bastards!" the volunteer shouted. He kept firing, but all Bernard saw from his vantage astride the horse was swirling fog.

"Hold your fire," snapped the captain. "You're only wasting your ammunition. Reload. I'll cover you." He rested his hand on his holstered pistol, wondering if the soldier had seen something. Straining to see, Bernard made out indistinct ghostly shapes in the mist. Imagination? Or Modoc waiting to scalp them all? He couldn't tell. The Modoc could be five feet away and he would never know until it was too late.

This time the shiver up and down his spine came from fear, not the sodden wool jacket that suddenly felt like a target with a bull's-eye drawn on it.

Bernard drew his pistol and pointed it into the fog but did not fire. A light puff of wind swept away the gray tendrils and showed only . . . lava rock.

"There's nothing there," Bernard said. "Keep going. We don't want to get separated from Colonel Wheaton's company."

"Yes, sir," the man said, looking over his shoulder fearfully. He started walking, and had gone only a few paces when a single shot rang out. The man took another step, but this time his legs had turned to jelly. He fell facedown on the ground, dead before he knew it.

"We're being attacked!" cried Bernard, bending low to use his horse's neck as a shield as he tried to find where the hidden sniper lay. No other shots rang out. There was only the curious stillness of the eddying fog.

After a few minutes of unearthly quiet, Bernard dismounted and went to the downed soldier. Dead. Struggling, the captain lifted the man and draped him over the saddle of his protesting horse. Then Bernard led the horse with its death-still load on foot, the pistol clutched tightly in his hand.

He jerked up his pistol when he saw movement ahead. Then he relaxed. He had overtaken the soldiers ahead of him.

"Form up. I need to—" His orders were drowned out by a fusillade that sent slugs ringing off the rocks, ricocheting into the distance, swallowed by the fog.

"Form a line. Return fire!" Bernard tried to make sure none of the soldiers killed their comrades, but in the confusion of battle and the heavy fog, it was difficult. He got them into two lines, one kneeling and the other standing before they fired.

Volley after volley ripped through the fog and killed . . . nothing.

Bernard personally went to check. Not even a drop of blood from a wounded Modoc stained the ground.

"I'm coming back. Don't shoot me," he repeated constantly as he returned to where the frightened Oregon volunteers clustered like sheep in a storm. "How many men did we lose?"

"Three more dead, eight wounded, two pretty bad, Captain," came the report from a grizzled man with a beard shot with gray. "We got to get the hell out of this fog or they're gonna kill us one by one."

The words had barely left the man's lips when a single shot robbed him of life. The bullet went into his left temple and never exited. The bearded soldier wobbled and then fell, as if every bone in his body had turned to mush.

From far ahead came the sharp cracks of Spencers firing. Bernard knew Colonel Wheaton was putting up a fight, but was he accomplishing anything more than sending lead winging through the enshrouding fog? Fingers turning blue from the cold and from clutching his pistol so tightly, Bernard ordered the soldiers to advance, to catch up with Wheaton's command so they could join forces.

"What about them fellas?" asked one youngster, hardly in his teens. "You jist gonna let 'em lie here and rot?"

"Carry as many of them as you like, Private," Bernard said. He hated to leave behind any dead, but keeping the wounded with them was trouble enough. If they tried to bury the dead, digging in the lava rock would take hours. And they had so little time. Every shot at them was unexpected, unseen, a phantom of death. Bernard grew to cringe at the slightest noise in the fog, whether it was a soldier turning his ankle on loose rocks or a deadly bullet whining through the air at someone in his command.

"How long we been in here, Captain? Seems like forever,"

one man asked. Bernard took a few seconds to pull out his watch. He could hardly believe his eyes.

"Four hours. It's past noon already." He looked up into the fog. The diffuse glow gave no hint as to the real time. Worse, he had no idea how to get out of the maze. The ambushes and brief, fierce skirmishes they had fought had turned him around. For all he knew, they were on their way out of the Lava Beds.

Or were going in deeper.

"Sir, there's the colonel! I see his braid! Ahead, not twenty yards!"

"Colonel Wheaton!" Bernard called. "Don't shoot. It's Bernard!"

"Advance, Captain Bernard. How many men do you have left?"

A new thrill of fear passed through Bernard's body. This was not the question he had expected.

"Five dead, sir, another five wounded, some seriously."

"Damn."

That wasn't what Bernard had hoped to hear, either.

"Come on, man, come on. We need to set up a defense perimeter until this fog lifts. Damn it!" Wheaton waved his arms about like a windmill, as if he could blow away the cloaking mist.

Bernard advanced cautiously, wary of Wheaton's men shooting him by mistake. Their nerves were all frayed and everyone had an itchy trigger finger.

"How many Modoc have you bagged, sir?" Bernard asked. He swallowed hard when he read the answers in the senior officer's eyes.

"As many as you, I reckon, Captain."

"That's none, sir. None I can positively count. They come out of the fog on cat's feet, shoot, and then disappear like ghosts."

Bernard cocked his head to one side and heard distant drumming, an eerie, hauntingly rhythmic sound. Along with it came the scuff-scuff-scuff of moccasins and boots on the rock.

"What's that? A dance?"

"Who cares?" snapped Wheaton. "We can go toward it, unless you fear it is a trap."

"You're in command, Colonel," Bernard pointed out. "Right now, I'd settle for retreating to a safe spot so we can figure out where we are. I got turned around. Without the sun, I can't determine our location."

"At least the artillery is retired for the day," Wheaton said. "In this fog, they could never tell our position from that of the Modoc."

"Colonel!" screamed Bernard, jerking around his pistol and firing wildly at a Modoc in war paint who'd simply *appeared* out of the fog. The warrior knifed a soldier in the back, ducked low, and faded away. Bernard fired until his pistol came up empty, but he had no feeling he had even winged the Modoc.

"Dead, sir," an orderly reported, kneeling beside the soldier who had been attacked.

"Gather around," Wheaton called. "Form a circle. We have to orient ourselves and not get killed doing it."

Bernard worked his men into a double circle, half of them kneeling and the rest standing nervously, fingering their rifles and sometimes firing into the mist. He thought they did it to keep the Modoc at bay rather than because they had decent targets. The captain said nothing about this. It might work to hold off the Modoc.

It also ran through their ammunition fast.

"Sir," Bernard said after spending the entire afternoon praying for the fog to vanish, "it's almost sundown."

"Sundown and the fog is blowing away," Wheaton said. "How are you at traveling by use of stars, Captain?"

"Good, sir. I often used the stars to align my cannon at night for early dawn barrages."

"I have a map." They peered at it in the gathering gloom. The fog slowly evaporated, leaving them with a heavy overcast. Bernard was glad to see the fog go away. It had sheltered the enemy and given his soldiers no chance to defend themselves.

Peering up at the cloudy night sky seemed a fool's errand for the first few hours, but a higher wind whipped down on them and produced scattered patches of crisp, clear sky with diamond-hard stars burning brightly.

"There, there's the Pole Star, sir." Bernard hastily aligned the map and tried to determine where—and how—they had blundered through the Lava Beds all day. "This is the way. It looks as if we're better off heading north for Tule Lake and the shoreline than retreating through the lava flows."

"It appears that way to me, also, Captain." Wheaton closed his eyes and muttered a small prayer. "Let's get the men moving right away. Marching in the dark through these razor-edged rocks will be difficult, but dying out here will be worse still."

"Yes, sir," Bernard said. "I—" The bullet staggered him. He reached out for support from the colonel, but his hands were curiously numb. He sank to his knees, the world spinning crazily about him. "I'm hit, sir," Bernard said before he passed out.

By two A.M. the surviving soldiers reached Tule Lake and safety.

# Scalps

*Lava Beds*
*January 17, 1873*

Captain Jack stood motionless, cloaked completely in damp fog. He turned slightly and saw the bend in the lava rock where his grandfather had seen the white deer many years ago. The Modoc *tyee* moved forward a few paces and waited near the spot where it was always wet. The puddle from fog condensing against the rock over his head and dripping down gave him his bearings. In the distance he heard the loud shouts and angry curses from the bluecoat soldiers. He drew his pistol and waited.

As a white soldier blundered past, Captain Jack lifted his gun and fired point-blank in the man's face. The soldier reeled away. Captain Jack stepped past the puddle that was always wet, fitted himself into a smooth niche in the rock, and waited for the furor to die down. A few minutes later the soldiers rushed on, leaving behind their dead comrade.

Captain Jack followed, killing another and wounding two more before he had to reload. This was too easy. He let the soldiers flee as the fog began to thin. There was no reason to expose himself needlessly. With long, sure steps, he walked through the fog and returned to the clearing where his band camped.

He stepped over the red rope circling the encampment and

felt a small tingle. Was this caused by the guardianship given by Curly Headed Doctor's Ghost Dance or simply his imagination? To Captain Jack, it did not matter. Today the white soldiers had come into the Lava Beds and been routed.

He drank some water and ate from the meager provisions they had brought with them as he waited for the rest of his warriors to return. By ones and twos they slipped back into camp, each gingerly stepping over the red rope before going to their families. Captain Jack counted until all fifty-three of his warriors were back. Then he spoke to them.

"The colonel runs to the lake. The fog has lifted, and he has used his map to find his way out of the twistings of the Lava Beds. We have fought all day and not lost a single warrior. Is anyone injured?"

Laughter erupted, followed by Schonchin John's angry curses.

"What happened?" asked Captain Jack.

"Schonchin John's son Peter dropped his pistol. It went off, and he shot himself in the hand," Scarfaced Charley said with a laugh. "That is as close to being hurt as anyone came today."

Captain Jack forced himself to remain passive. If he laughed as he wanted at Schonchin John's clumsy son, it would only cause more trouble.

"See that the wound is tended. Curly Headed Doctor?"

"I will see to it," the shaman said.

"Queen Mary," Captain Jack called to his sister. "Lead the women to strip the dead. We need all the equipment and supplies, especially ammunition, that we can get."

"Scalps!" called Schonchin John, anxious to focus everyone's attention on something other than his son. "We have to take their scalps!"

"Take the scalps!" Captain Jack echoed, knowing he could not hold back the warriors. And he did not want to. They had fought well today and had driven off four hundred soldiers, with no injury. From what his scouts had told him, the Modoc had killed twelve and wounded twice that in their enemy's ranks.

The warriors deserved the scalps.

As Captain Jack started to join them, he stopped to see how Curly Headed Doctor fared patching up Peter's hand. Schonchin John's son glared at him, as his father would have. He'd learned quickly the sullen ways of his father.

"Your medicine is potent," Captain Jack told the shaman. "It protected us."

"No white man will ever cross the red rope. The Ghost Dance will keep our enemies away!" crowed Curly Headed Doctor.

"Good," Captain Jack said, still not sure if he believed in this medicine advocated by Wovoka. But today it had worked, and that was good enough for him. "Come, both of you. Let's take scalps!"

They melted into the black night to find the bodies of fallen soldiers and to relieve them of their hair, after the women had stripped them of their equipment. It was a good victory, a very, very good victory.

# Recriminations

*Linkville, Oregon*
*January 18, 1873*

Joshua Harlan contrasted the somber mood in Linkville with
the ebullience a few days earlier. The regular soldiers had returned and camped outside town, many too injured to reach
Fort Klamath farther north. He had tried to talk with Captain
Bernard, but the officer had been too badly wounded to allow
visitors, and the rest of his command was tight-lipped about
all that had happened.

But Josh found the Oregon volunteers, in particular, willing
to talk of the debacle in the Modoc Lava Beds.

Or was "talk" the proper way of describing it? Josh leaned
against the bar, sipping at a nickel beer and listening as the
soldiers swapped lies and accusations.

"Never shoulda gone in like that. I never seen such fog!
Thicker 'n my wife's pea soup, it was, and nowhere near as
tasty. Terrible," growled one man who wore a sling for his left
arm, but who seemed to have no trouble bending that elbow
when it came to drinking beer.

"Wheaton ought to have his head checked to see if anything
got knocked loose—before he ordered us in," said another,
equally angry. "No artillery? Why'd we spend the better part
of a week diggin' them cannon in if he wasn't gonna use
them?"

"Use them? In that fog?" asked the first soldier. "The gunners couldna see what they was shootin' at. We'd have been fightin' Modoc *and* be gettin' shelled by our own side. Disastrous, and we're damn lucky to have got out."

"My brother Jake didn't," said another, his voice low and sad. "Neither did my cousin Pierre."

"I heard total losses were twelve," spoke up Josh.

"Twelve dead. Twenty-five wounded so damn bad most of 'em won't make it. Not like me," said the one who sometimes used the sling for his injured arm. He shoved it back in now and clumsily used his right hand on the beer mug, having to turn it so the handle was facing in the opposite direction. It didn't take much to figure out he was naturally left-handed.

"Why do you think it failed? The attack?" asked Josh.

"It was them regular Army officers," opined one.

"And the soldiers. They were just as bad. They cut and run when we was in there gettin' our scalps lifted. And that's what the Modoc did! I saw a couple of the bodies brought out of the Lava Beds. Stripped nekkid and scalped!"

"The regular Army didn't support you?" asked Josh, fishing for more information from the volunteers.

"Not a bit of it. We went in and we got all turned around. Not a one of them officers showed our boys a map. We coulda found our way out, fog or no, if we had a map. They kept that for themselves."

"Rumor has it the Modoc had only fifty-three fighters," Josh said, having heard this from Isabella.

"Wouldn't have taken us more than a hundred men and true to pry them loose," said the first man. "Get rid of them regulars and let the Oregon boys do the work!"

A cheer went up. Josh paid for another round to keep their tongues lubricated and flapping. He wrote down few notes, not wanting to make it seem he was pumping them for information.

"I heard tell Colonel Wheaton admitted his failure," Josh said.

"He ain't tole none of us he's sorry for gettin' us kilt."

"Not that I heard," said another. "He won't fess up, no, sir. He'll put it all off on how we done wrong, when it's the other way. And them Klamath. What did they do to help us? They was supposed to be scoutin'. Not a one of 'em helped us once we went into the Lava Beds."

Josh went to the man who had lost a brother and a cousin. He seemed lost in thought—or memory.

"Pretty bad in there, wasn't it?"

"I fought a bit in the war. Pea Ridge and Honey Creek. I know what it's like going up against fortified positions. In there, *everything* is fortified. By nature. The Modoc know their way around in those ravines, and we didn't. That was enough to doom us."

Josh saw how the man's arms and face were scratched.

"From the rock?"

"Worse than tangling with a cactus," the man said. "Turn and not know what's there and the damned rock slashes you like a razor. Can't lean against a rock or you'll gouge out a hunk of flesh. Look at my boots. I reckon the Army owes me a new pair." He stuck out a foot.

Josh's eyes went wide. The boots were cut to leathery strips, and the thick soles were punctured in more than one place.

"Sounds as if they owe you more than that," Josh said. "What would you settle for?"

"Can't get my brother back," the man said, heaving a sigh. He lifted his beer and drained it. "A good drunk so I can forget? That might be enough. Or like that loudmouth James said. Cut us loose. Let the Oregon volunteers go in, and we'll clean out the red bastards in jig time."

"Would you let the Klamath go with you?"

The man turned. His eyes blazed. "They're all red bastards, as far as I care. Let them burn in hell, too." He made a wry face and shook his head. "No, not that. The Modoc're hiding out in hell already. Let us send them to *our* hell!"

Josh drifted around the crowded, smoky saloon, getting impressions and finally putting down in his notebook what details he remembered from the volunteers' bitter denunciations of Colonel Wheaton and the entire campaign.

When he heard the soldiers repeating themselves for the third and fourth time, Josh knew he had to harvest more fertile fields. He stopped by the town doctor's office, where many of the most severely wounded had been taken. The doctor sat on the front steps, smoking a cigar. The man looked up when he saw Josh coming across the street.

"You're that reporter fellow, aren't you?" he asked jovially.

"I work for the *Alta California*," Josh said proudly.

"Read a couple of your pieces, then. You do right by us, young fellow. I appreciate that."

"Don't know how the next few stories will read," Josh admitted. "The Battle for the Stronghold, everyone's calling it, was not a success and I have to report it truthfully."

"Depends on which side you're rooting for, calling it a failure. The Modoc did right well for themselves."

"You favor them over the U.S. Army?"

"Didn't say that. I know Captain Jack. He's a good man, but he's got a powerful lot of anger burning him up inside. Has ever since Ben Wright. And now?" The doctor puffed a big cloud of bluish smoke that caught on the wind and twisted to nothingness. "Now, he wants to stay *tyee* so he's got to fight."

"That's what I've heard, too."

"That Isabella is something else, isn't she? Knows pretty near everyone up here." The doctor laughed at the way Josh recoiled. "Son, in Linkville everyone knows everything about everybody. Don't take it wrong. We know how the Modoc are, especially the women."

"It's not like that," Josh said defensively.

"Nope, never is. But you aren't bending my ear because I have anything interesting to say, are you?"

"How are the wounded doing?"

"One of them has been asking after you. Captain Bernard."

"He's going to live?" Josh found himself thankful for this. Bernard had given him several good stories and had been open and frank. It had been hard hearing the captain had been severely wounded during the fighting.

"More than that. He's starting to get feisty again. That's a good sign, but it makes it hard to deal with him. Go on in and talk to him. I think he's got something for you."

"What is it?"

The doctor ignored the question, turning his head up and blowing a smoke ring that turned egg-shaped and vanished as a frigid new breeze sneaked down Linkville's main street.

Josh went inside, hastily closing the door behind him to keep in the heat. The wounded needed to stay warm. Nothing but cold entered with Josh.

"Captain Bernard?" he called. A dozen men were huddled under blankets. Josh could not tell which, if any, was the captain. From a small office to the side of the main surgery he heard an answer. Josh saw the captain seated at the doctor's desk, pen in hand. From the amount of ink smeared over his fingers, Bernard had written a considerable piece.

"I hoped you would come by, Mr. Harlan," the officer said. "I wanted to talk to you." Bernard leaned back, winced, and then controlled the show of pain.

"I am glad to see you are up, but should you be working so soon?" Josh pointed to the stack of papers on the doctor's desk, all fresh from Bernard's pen.

"This is for you, for publication, should you care to submit it," the officer said, shoving five sheets toward him. Josh read down the pages quickly, then looked up at the captain.

"This is explosive, sir. You are accusing Colonel Wheaton of malfeasance and poor planning."

"More than that, we ought never to have started this war. We have no business sending the Modoc back to live with their mortal enemies. Modoc and Klamath have never gotten along, any more than the Pit River and Wintu have. None of the tribes even shares a language. To put them together is to apply a blasting cap to dynamite. Deadly, dangerous, and utterly predictable."

"You say your men aren't capable of further fighting?"

"We were disheartened by the fight. I am not sure one in ten of the regulars would obey an order to return to those deadly lava flows."

"I've heard how terrible it was, unable to see because of the fog, the Modoc sniping at you, the very rocks cutting you apart."

"With artillery support, we might have succeeded. I don't know. Wheaton made a bad command error ordering us in. That much I know and that much I have put into a report to General Canby."

"If such a report is not well received, it could mean your career," Josh said.

"Then so be it. I am an artillery officer, and I go where I am ordered. But I swear by God, if Wheaton orders me into the Lava Beds again, I will not go. I will not lead men into such an abattoir! Let them court-martial me and execute me by firing squad, but I will not be responsible for one more death of any man in my command who trusts to my military judgment!"

"May I quote you, sir?"

"In full. Put it into a deposition and I will sign it in front of a notary public." Bernard slammed his hand down on the stock of papers. "Hell, I have already submitted my report to anyone in a position to do anything about it."

"May I send a copy to a friend? AB Meacham used to be Indian Agent before Odeneal replaced him. He is a good man and would agree with you." Josh missed Meacham, but the man's political star was rising. If it became ascendant, perhaps the fighting could end.

Perhaps.

# A New Course

Alfred Meacham straightened his tie, settled his thoughts, and then went into the office of the Secretary of the Interior. The secretary's aides hurried about their clerical chores, not giving him a second glance. In a way, that made Meacham feel good. It meant he belonged. He walked to the highly polished wood door leading to the secretary's office and rapped smartly.

"Don't stand out there all day. Come on in," Secretary Columbus Delano called. Meacham hurriedly went in, almost feeling that if he did not obey quickly, someone would find him out and chase him away.

"Good afternoon, Mr. Secretary," he greeted.

"AB, good to see you. Here in town to cast your electoral vote for the President?"

"Yes, sir, that I am. And I do it proudly. The general is a good man, one the nation needs."

"But you're here to see me on another mission, aren't you?"

"Word gets around fast, doesn't it?" Meacham grinned. Nothing got past the secretary. He was a political animal and firmly committed to President Grant. That made it easier handing him the letter from the Oregon delegation.

"Let's hear what you have to say," Delano said, leaning back.

He laced his fingers behind his balding head and looked as if he had been born to this office.

Meacham knew he had to get right to the point. No flowery speeches would do. That was for politicians out to sway crowds. Delano was hard-nosed and hardheaded and such a presentation would only turn him against the proper course of action.

"The military blundered going into the Lava Beds," Meacham said. "They lost too many men, and worse, morale was destroyed. Another foray will result in an even worse defeat because of the natural fortifications."

"You don't think this Ghost Dance had anything to do with the Modoc victory?" Delano looked at him sharply. For years the politicians had feared Wovoka and his Ghost Dance and what it might do to provoke Indian unrest. It was dangerous stuff preaching that the white man would be driven from the country, the buffalo would return, and any Indian killed defending the land would be resurrected.

"Not really. Military blundering and not enough jawboning. Those are the real causes."

"Blundering? Major Green has been put up for a Congressional Medal of Honor for his bravery."

"He might well deserve it, sir, but that bravery came at the wrong time in the wrong place. If Mr. Odeneal had bothered to *talk* to Captain Jack and the other Modoc *tyee,* the invasion of the Lava Beds would never have been necessary."

"Make them heroes or court-martial them," mused Delano. "Those are the only two courses of action allowed." He scratched his chin and leaned forward. "General Sherman is not pleased, and that means the President is not, either. Military defeats tend to cascade, one following another."

"Good money after bad," Meacham said.

"That's it, AB, that's exactly right. The president feels it is time to turn back to talk and away from rifles. For a spell."

"Then someone will be sent to negotiate with Captain Jack?"

"Not someone, AB, *you*. You will head the Peace Commission. Canby has been told to draw up all the proper papers authorizing it. This will be resolved by negotiation, not fighting."

"I hope so, sir. Thank you for your confidence in me."

"The president appreciates all electors, AB, especially you. Do well and there might be bigger things in the administration for you."

"A cabinet post?" Meacham said, grinning.

"If you have your eye on *my* office, forget it. Now get out of here. I have work to do." As Meacham reached the door, Delano called out, "AB? One more thing. Thank you for your levelheadedness in this, but be warned that Canby is recruiting Warm Springs Indians as scouts under that McKay fellow."

Meacham sucked in his breath and held it. The Klamath disliked the Modoc. The Warm Springs tribe went far beyond that in their hatred.

"I understand, and I won't fail. The Peace Commission will succeed."

"Good," Delano said, already turning to another report on his desk. "Good."

Meacham hoped it would be.

# Living in Sin

*Linkville, Oregon*
*February 1, 1873*

Joshua Harlan bent over the lapboard he used as a writing desk, scribbling furiously to finish another story for Billingsly before the deadline. So many other papers had sent ace reporters to Linkville that Josh felt the pressure of competition. *The Overland Monthly* had been particularly strident banging the drum for a war, wanting bloodshed to increase its circulation, and the *San Francisco Evening Bulletin* had made folks in Linkville angry by describing it as "a town of fifty inhabitants, two stores, a hotel, and an adequate number of whiskey bars." Josh knew he could do better by giving the truth, the straight facts, and letting the *Alta* readers decide the matter for themselves.

Sometimes Billingsly rewrote what he sent into more sensational news, but mostly Josh's reporting went through to the front page. For that he was grateful and felt a measure of pride.

A knock at the door made him glance up.

"Go away. I'm not here," he said, worrying about his deadline. If the telegrapher did not get the story before six P.M., the *Alta California* could not get the type set in time for the next day's edition.

"Is that you, Joshua?"

Josh dropped his pen in surprise when the latch lifted, the door opened, and in stepped Faith.

"What are you doing here?" he blurted out.

"That's a fine way to talk to your wife. I spent a perfectly ghastly three days getting here from San Francisco. I never saw such fearsome roads or ruder people. Why, the men positively leered at me!"

"Faith, you didn't have to come. This is no place for you."

"I can see you have at least kept this . . . place . . . clean. As well as you could, I suppose," she said, wrinkling her nose as she circled the perimeter of the small room. "I cannot understand why you left our nice house to come live here." She turned, tugged off her gloves, and dropped them on the bed. "For all that, I cannot understand why you left me."

"I'm a reporter, Faith. This is where the story is happening. The Modoc have—"

"Oh, bother," she said. "Who cares about those filthy savages? I certainly do not, and no one I know does, either. Come home, Joshua, and forget about living like one of those brutes." She sat on the bed and bounced, making a sour face. "You sleep on this? It's like a board! Why, it would kill my back to spend even one night here."

"I could never stand those feather mattresses you like so," Josh said. He shook his head. Arguing over mattresses would not get him anywhere. "I like being a reporter. I am good at it. Have you seen my byline on the front page of the *Alta California*? That's my name—your last name, too—in print. Are you the least bit proud of me?"

"Well, yes, I suppose so, Joshua. It's just that you walked out on a perfectly good job with Papa. He is ever so vexed and has been taking it out on me."

"Then there's no reason for me to go back," Josh said, trying to head off what he suspected was coming.

"Oh, no. I cried a little and I sulked for an entire week. He will take you back, for my sake," Faith said. She pursed her ruby-red bee-stung lips, as if showing how she had pouted ever so prettily to win him back his position with Murdoch and Sons Shipping.

"I don't want to go back, Faith. I'm doing an important job here. The people of San Francisco need to know about the situation here. Captain Jack and a handful of Modoc fighters defeated four hundred soldiers with artillery, and there will be deadly repercussions unless the Peace Commission is successful."

"Peace Commission?" She frowned. "I don't know what you're going on about, Joshua. Really."

"AB is going to head it. The government is willing to talk to Captain Jack now to get the Modoc back on the reservation. They might even give the Indians the land along the Lost River they want. If so, it will be—" Josh stopped in mid-sentence when the door opened. Isabella stood silhouetted in the light for a moment, then came inside.

"Josh, I have food for our dinner."

He looked at Faith. The redhead's eyes were wide with shock.

"It's not what it looks like, Faith. Isabella is my . . . is my servant."

"Servant? Is that what you call it, Josh?" Isabella batted her long dark eyelashes in his direction. "Will she stay in our bed, too?"

" 'Our bed?' " cried Faith, shooting to her feet. "You left me to come up here and to live in sin! With a barbaric woman like this! I have never been so humiliated in all my life."

"Faith, calm down," Josh said, seeing this wasn't going to happen. "Isabella and I aren't sharing the bed. It's not like that."

"This is my home," Isabella said. "That is my bed. There is no need to share. I give it to Josh."

"I am sure you do," Faith said, stamping her foot. Chunks of dried mud fell off. She angrily kicked at the muddy debris, then grabbed her kid gloves and pulled them on. Josh pushed aside his lapboard and put his pen down, to grab her arms.

"You're getting this all wrong, Faith. You're my wife and I love you, but I won't work for your father. Your brothers hate me and probably tried to kill me."

"Really, such an imagination," Faith said nastily. "The next thing you'll tell me, Morgan and Michael are trying to kill me, too!"

"No, but I suspect they've tried to have your father killed so they can take over the business."

"That's it. That's the last straw. I will stand for no more, Joshua Harlan! You have made your decision. For the life of me, I will never understand why you chose her over me."

"Good taste?" suggested Isabella, who weaved out of the way as Faith pushed past the Modoc woman, slamming the door after her.

Josh glared at Isabella, then grabbed his coat and went after Faith to try to talk some sense into her pretty head. Even as he left Isabella's room, he knew he had as much chance of that as Captain Bernard had of getting promoted after his scathing denunciation of Wheaton's invasion of the Lava Beds.

But Josh had to try. Faith was his wife, after all.

# The Peace Commission

Josh felt nervous at the prospect of going into the Lava Beds for the first meeting of the Peace Commission, but Captain Jack had vowed to accept no other place, fearing treachery. Josh knew how upset Meacham had been over this, because Captain Jack had mentioned Ben Wright repeatedly, and Meacham took this as a personal affront. Josh had to admit it was a stretch of the imagination comparing Meacham with Captain Wright, under any circumstances.

But in a way, he could not deny that the Modoc *tyee* had a point. If Captain Jack did not feel secure, he would not negotiate in good faith, but would lie, thinking he needed to if he wanted to escape the meeting alive. This way, Captain Jack could be honest about his intentions and give Meacham something to work with.

"We're about ready to ride in," Meacham said. He rubbed his sweaty hands against his trousers, then swiped at his nose.

"No need to be nervous, AB," Josh said. "You'll convince Captain Jack to come out of his stronghold."

"I don't head up the Peace Commission, Josh. I'm only a member, going along because I know the Modoc so well."

"What?" Josh was startled. "Who is heading it?"

"The man's name is Elijah Steele. He's a judge in Yreka

and seems fair-minded. He's said often enough that we should butt out of meddling in Modoc affairs."

"How many times are they going to try to sabotage the Peace Commission?" Josh asked. "Canby is hardly playing fair. It is as if he is doing everything he can to make sure we fail."

"General Canby is a cautious man," Meacham said in his most neutral politician's way. "He organized the Warm Springs Indians as scouts, in case they are needed."

"And he put Don McKay in charge of them. The man's a bloody-handed butcher, not fit to be in the Army under any circumstances, much less one as touchy as this," protested Josh.

Meacham smiled and said, "You sound like an actual negotiator, not just an observer and reporter, Josh."

"Thanks, AB, for letting me come along." Josh did feel as if he was taking part in history rather than only reporting it. He had never experienced such a thrill working at Murdoch and Sons.

"After seeing what the *New York Herald* reporter said about you—"

"Josh, Josh, you have to develop a thick skin. I don't care what they call me or the Peace Commission, as long as we succeed."

"Canby isn't helping," Josh said. "Replacing Wheaton was a start, but with a man like 'Cal' Gillem?"

"He got where he was by befriending Andrew Johnson, yes," Meacham said, "but Colonel Gillem is a war hero and knows the importance of negotiated peace rather than force of arms when dealing with the Modoc. He might be a better choice for overall command than Wheaton."

"Canby is breathing down his neck. I've heard rumors that the general came down from Portland and has set up a temporary HQ at Fairchild's ranch. Is that true?"

"I don't know much of the military side, Josh, and if I did, it wouldn't be my place to answer. Why not ask Fairchild? There he is now, with Pressly Dorris."

Josh went to the two settlers, who stood close together, whispering like conspirators. Fairchild looked up, irritated, when Josh stopped a few feet away. The man had made it clear he did not like reporters in general and Josh in particular. Isabella seemed to be the cause of this personal dislike.

"Mr. Fairchild, I have a few questions, if you have time to answer them."

"Not now, son," Fairchild said. "My friend here's gettin' ready to take a message to . . ." Fairchild's voice trailed off when he saw Josh's interest.

"To General Canby at your ranch, sir?" Josh asked.

"That's not for me to say." Fairchild shook Press Dorris's hand and sent the man on his way. "I've got a message for Mr. Meacham that needs to be delivered right away." Fairchild walked off, Josh following. He had a right to report anything said or done in public.

"AB," Fairchild called. "General Canby sends his regards."

"And what new surprises?" asked Meacham, not bothering to hide his contempt.

"Your choice of the Riddles as translators. The general doesn't like them and wants two others to go along with us."

"Who might that be?" asked Meacham. Josh saw the man tense, as if he knew the answer already.

"Bogus Charley and Boston Charley."

"Boston Charley's hardly more than a boy!" cried Josh. He had met Boston Charley earlier in Linkville. While the youth had a silver tongue and could talk rings around even the older Bogus Charley, he was hardly five feet tall, and was slender and something of a wag.

"Josh, quiet," Meacham said, his ire growing. "We can't trust the two Charleys." He looked around, stepped closer, and said in a low voice to Fairchild, "Boston Charley is a murderous son of a bitch, no matter how quick he is with that tongue of his. Frank and Tobey Riddle do not have mixed alliances. Using the Charleys is like having spies in our camp."

"Oh? Tobey is Captain Jack's cousin."

"She's married to a *boshtin,* also," Meacham said. "A white man. That makes her perfect for this job. She has blood relations with the Modoc and ties with us."

"The general is not going to like having your choice of translators shoved down his throat," Fairchild said, glowering.

"He can come and negotiate with the two Charleys as his translators. I want people I trust when I meet Captain Jack."

"Very well," Fairchild said. "We all want this to end well." He turned and waved to Elijah Steele. "Judge Steele, over here. We're almost ready to go."

Josh studied Steele as he approached. The Yreka judge looked unsure of himself, as if he had been talked into doing something he did not believe in fully. He was of moderate height, and had brown hair shot with streaks of gray, but the thing Josh noticed most was the size of Steele's hands. They were huge, as if used to hard work rather than swinging a gavel in a courtroom.

"Let's ride," Meacham said, waving to the Riddles. Tobey Riddle pulled her wool shawl around her shoulders, then let her husband help her mount. Her horse protested the sudden addition of weight, then settled down to the steady pace Meacham set through the Lava Beds.

Now and then Tobey motioned to Meacham, guiding him through the maze of the lava flows. It occurred to him that having the Riddles along solved another problem: navigating the trackless waste of the Lava Beds. Meacham had been right not wanting Bogus Charley or Boston Charley as interpreters. They might lead the Peace Commission in and then strand them in the deadly lava flows.

The path wound around, then dipped down by Tule Lake and back to a clearing a quarter mile away, where Captain Jack and a few other Modoc waited.

"Welcome," Captain Jack greeted. He seemed especially

happy to see Judge Steele, and welcomed the man warmly. Steele was more reserved, but soon settled down. Josh hung back with Meacham while Fairchild and Steele dickered with Captain Jack, Tobey Riddle translating as her husband looked on.

"It seems everything is going well," Josh observed.

"I hope so," Meacham said. He lifted his chin slightly, pointing out a small knot of Modoc warriors behind Captain Jack. "See them? The short one is Boston Charley, the one Canby wanted us to use as translator. A real killer."

Josh did not argue, though Boston Charley looked more like a small boy than a man to fear. The men around him, however, were painted for war and held their rifles tightly, as if restrained from killing the Peace Commission only by Captain Jack's authority.

"That one's Curly Headed Doctor," Meacham went on. "And Schonchin John is Captain Jack's rival for power. His father is Old Schonches and is still on the Klamath Reservation, but I've heard he is thinking of joining Captain Jack."

"What of the Paiute Snake?" asked Josh. "I've heard rumors."

"We hope to head off such an alliance. And Tobey seems to think the Klamath chief, David Allan, has made promises to Captain Jack, but that is—" Meacham cut off his sentence and turned his attention back to the men. "Look, Steele is concluding the negotiations."

Josh and Meacham went closer and heard Tobey translating, "An armistice. The Modoc agree to no more fighting if the white men do not try to enter the Lava Beds."

"Agreed," Steele said. "We shall see about getting Yainax back for the Modoc."

"It's all over, then," Josh said. Fairchild looked at him sharply.

"Don't believe it," Fairchild said. "I know them. I like the Modoc, especially the Hot Creek band, but Captain Jack's not telling the truth. He might not be lying, but there's more to this." He shook his head. "There's a considerable way to go before a treaty is signed."

"You will take this message to General Canby and then return with his answer," Tobey translated after Captain Jack rattled off a sibilant string of Modoc.

"I . . . I, yes," Steele said, obviously not pleased with this.

"This isn't good," Fairchild said. "He wants Steele back here for some reason."

"I'll return with him, for the story," Josh said. He glanced at Meacham, hoping to see whether the man thought this was bravado on his part or a reasonable way to report the story.

"Do that," Fairchild said. "You do that, boy."


"There's something wrong," Elijah Steele said, wringing his hands. The Peace Commission had left the Lava Beds and returned to Linkville, where Steele had contacted Canby. They had waited until dawn the next day for the general's reply. Now the stage was set for real peace, a treaty Josh hoped to cover firsthand.

"You have the general's word that there won't be any more military ventures against the Modoc," Josh said. "What could be wrong?"

Judge Steele looked Josh squarely in the eye and said, "You don't know what's really going on."

"What is? Captain Jack wanted you back to confirm General Canby's orders not to enter the Modoc stronghold. In return, you'll take Captain Jack's promise he won't cause any more trouble."

"Yes, of course," Steele said. "I hope so."

Josh rode alongside Steele without saying a word. Captain Jack had not requested anyone but Steele to return, including the Riddles. Their presence seemed to irritate the Modoc *tyee*. Like Canby, he'd insisted that Bogus Charley or Boston Charley could translate, and the two Charleys had remained in the Lava Beds with the other Modoc. Josh paid more attention to the route they took today, although the prior day's trail was easy enough to follow.

Since Wheaton's abortive attack, the fog had remained at bay and the weather had been crisp and clear.

"There they are," Steele said as they neared the clearing again. "I wish there was a boat on Tule Lake we might have used to get here. There's no hope of riding out, if Captain Jack changes his mind."

"He sounded peaceable enough yesterday," Josh pointed out.

"You keep quiet," Steele said sharply. "Let me do all the talking."

Josh fell silent. Judge Steele became increasingly nervous as the Modoc came up, as they had the day before. Boston Charley stood in front, grinning broadly and looking like a child. This time Josh saw the two knives sheathed at Charley's belt. Both handles showed bloody fingerprints.

The negotiations went quickly this time, Judge Steele assuring Captain Jack that Canby had approved of the armistice completely and that Colonel Gillem's men would not be sent into the Lava Beds. Then Captain Jack said something that perked up Josh's ears because it was such a curious thing to say.

Captain Jack did not bother with Boston Charley as translator but spoke directly to Steele in English. "We will all celebrate, like McKay, when this new treaty is forged between us."

Steele said nothing, letting the Modoc *tyee* continue.

"I want the rest of the Peace Commission to return to declare the new peace," said the *tyee*.

"All of them?" asked Steele. "Why is that necessary?"

"We will celebrate, the Modoc and you," Captain Jack said. "You can stay with us tonight, then go to Linkville with the good news."

"The good news," Steele said dully. He took a big breath, then let it out slowly. Josh felt the tension in the air and didn't know why it had built so suddenly. "There's no reason for me to spend the night here. Mr. Harlan and I can get back to Linkville before sundown and—"

"You will stay. You will not turn down Modoc hospitality," Captain Jack said flatly. The *tyee* spun and walked away. The rest of his party held their rifles but made no threatening moves.

"We should stay," Steele said uneasily. "It would rile them something fierce if we tried to go now."

"What's going on? I don't understand."

"I don't either, and I don't like it. The things he hinted at don't jibe with the way he spoke yesterday. I should never have agreed to head the Peace Commission!"

"They aren't making any threatening moves," Josh said. He saw how Steele pulled back his coat to show a six-shooter shoved into his belt. The judge turned back and forth, making certain the Modoc saw he was armed.

"Do you have a pistol or knife, Mr. Harlan?"

"No, I thought this was a peaceful mission," Josh said, more irritated than frightened. He had not bothered purchasing a firearm, unlike many of the other reporters, because he saw no need for it. He had never so much as held a pistol and would probably have done more damage to himself than the Modoc if he had brought one and tried to use it.

"So did I," Steele said. He took his bedroll some distance from the Modoc campfires.

"Should we join them? Captain Jack made it sound as if they wanted to entertain us. At least, they can feed us."

"No! Don't eat anything!" Steele said, frightened.

"Ben Wright?" suggested Josh.

"I can't say, but this is making me uneasy."

The Modoc did not approach them or offer any food. Josh did the best he could to build a small fire. Steele put his saddle against a lava rock outcropping, then half-sat, half-lay against it, his hand on his six-shooter. Josh tried to sleep but awoke several times during the night. Each time he looked at Steele he saw the judge rubbing his eyes and trying to stay awake, as if this held back an irresistible tide of savages.

In the morning, Josh was stiff and sore and badly in need of decent sleep. Steele sported bloodshot eyes and his hands trembled, whether from lack of food or fear Josh could not tell. When Captain Jack and a few others walked over, Steele leaped to his feet.

"Good morning," Steele called, as if the words would keep Captain Jack at a distance. "I think it's time for us to be leaving."

"You go?" asked Captain Jack, frowning. "Why?"

"To get the rest of the Peace Commission. We'll bring them right back. We can sign the treaty. I am sure Mr. Meacham and Mr. Fairchild will have it drawn up by now."

Josh said nothing. Fairchild and Meacham had nothing to do with drafting the treaty. That had to be approved by Secretary of the Interior Delano, and then on up to President Grant. Along the way General Canby and possibly General Sherman had to examine the terms. The actual treaty might take months to draft.

"You will bring the others back?" Captain Jack asked sharply. Too sharply, Josh felt. He wished he had a pistol to back up the judge.

"Yes, of course."

"You will return with them?"

"We're all on the Peace Commission, aren't we?" Steele tried to smile. He failed.

"No arms. You will all come back unarmed," Captain Jack insisted.

"If that is your wish," Steele said. He gestured to Josh to saddle their horses. Josh might have objected to being treated as a menial in other circumstances, but not this time.

"Return fast," Captain Jack ordered as they mounted and started out. Josh saw how tense Steele was as they rode. The judge obviously wanted to gallop his horse but held the pace down to the fastest possible that would not unduly tire the animal.

Josh had nothing to say to the upset, nervous man until they left the Lava Beds and headed toward Linkville. Judge Steele let out a huge sigh. Josh wondered if he had been holding it since they had left Captain Jack's camp. It sounded like it from the way Steele gasped. The man wiped his face of sweat and finally settled his nerves enough to talk.

"You get on back to Linkville and tell Meacham and the rest of the Peace Commission what has happened," Steele said.

"Very well, sir," Josh said, puzzled. "Where will you be?"

"I'm going back to Yreka, damned glad to still have my scalp."

"But you said you'd return with the rest of the Peace Commission!"

"I want no more of this." With that Elijah Steele turned to the road leading westward to Yreka, and this time did gallop his horse.

# Promises

*Fairchild's Ranch, California*
*March 1, 1873*

"You were right, AB. Here they come," said Josh, looking up from his notebook when he heard horses' hooves pounding on the frozen road leading to Fairchild's ranch house.

"Thank Isabella for the information," Meacham said, straightening his coat and going out to meet the two Modoc. "She told me how angry Captain Jack was at Steele for high-tailing it back to Yreka. Then she warned me this might happen."

"Will Canby see them?" asked Josh.

"Of course," Meacham assured him. "There's no reason for him not to. I hope he doesn't agree to too much." Meacham stopped, put on his politician's face, smiled, and went out to greet Queen Mary and Boston Charley. The two Modoc had ridden straight here from the safety of the Lava Beds unmolested.

"Good man, old AB, pleased to see you," Boston Charley greeted. He thrust out his hand. Meacham shook it, then drew back, as if wanting to count the fingers to make sure Charley had not stolen any of them.

"Pleased to see you and Captain Jack's sister," Meacham said. "You come to meet with General Canby?"

"We do," Queen Mary said, her words almost a growl.

"I'll be there, too, since I've been made head of the Peace Commission. A shame about Judge Steele having to leave," Meacham said, walking the two Modoc toward Fairchild's front porch where the settler and General Canby stood now. The general had only just arrived from his headquarters in Portland, and was still covered in mud and dust from his long trip.

"Captain Jack is angry that Judge Steele broke his promise to return. That no one on the Peace Commission returned."

"I'm sorry," Meacham said insincerely. "This is the first I'd heard that the Peace Commission was supposed to go back to meet with your brother. I'm sure we will work everything out with the general."

They went up the steps and talked briefly with Edward Canby and Fairchild. Josh worked his way closer so he could hear what was being said. He and General Canby had not gotten off on a good footing, but then Fairchild had had something to do with that. If it had not been for Meacham being appointed head of the Peace Commission, Josh knew he would have been sent packing long since. Scrabbling for stories piecemeal would have been more difficult from Linkville, the way the other reporters had to do it. He had a front-row seat and intended to milk it for all it was worth.

"Captain Jack will surrender. He will return to the reservation, where you want him, but you must send wagons." Queen Mary sounded adamant on this point.

"What sort of wagons?" asked General Canby. Compared with Boston Charley's youthful good looks, General E.R.S. Canby appeared plain, even homely. Josh had listened to the plodding, unimaginative officer enough to know that "homely" described both his face and his personality. He was well enough liked by his men, but more in the way the soldiers cared for a mongrel dog that had had a tail blown off, or some homeless crippled wight trying to make his way in the world. They had less respect than they did pity for their commander.

Still, Josh had heard nothing but good about Canby from General Sherman, who depended on Canby's reliable nature and his ability to follow orders without question. Their friendship went back to the Gold Rush and had won him command of the Department of the Columbia and all 1,225 men, although that number was more for bookkeeping purposes than an actual one. Too many soldiers had been sent south with Crook to fight the Apaches for Canby to muster more than a thousand, should they be needed.

Unless Sherman reinforced Canby's troops, as rumor had it.

"Captain Jack wants empty wagons, of course," Boston Charley said cheerfully. "We need to load our people and get out. Your troops sank all our boats on Tule Lake, stranding us."

"We have no wagons to send," Canby said.

"No wagons, no surrender. How can Captain Jack get out of the Lava Beds if he has to walk? That would not be right for a powerful *tyee*," Queen Mary said.

"What is your objection to sending the wagons, General?" asked a man dressed in a plain black broadcloth coat and looking as if he was ready to preach hellfire and damnation. He had stepped from inside Fairchild's house, and looked as if he wanted to take on the world.

Josh looked to Meacham, who stepped forward. "Allow me to introduce the newest member of the Peace Commission," he said quickly. "This is the Reverend Doctor Eleasar Thomas."

Queen Mary wrinkled her nose and looked away from him. Boston Charley hurried over and shook the reverend's hand, behaving as if it was a pump handle and he was dying of thirst. Reverend Thomas freed his hand from the grip and started to step back before thinking better of showing such weakness in dealing with the diminutive, ever-cheerful Boston Charley.

"My son," Reverend Thomas said warmly. "Pleased to make your acquaintance."

"Does Captain Jack want mules or horses to pull the wagons?" asked Canby, ignoring the pleasantries. He squared off in front of Queen Mary, as if he intended to fight her according to the Marquis of Queensberry rules.

"My brother is not a beast of burden to pull the wagons himself," Queen Mary said.

"We are supposed to make every effort at a peaceful settlement. Judge Steele's unfortunate, uh, withdrawal makes this request more difficult to refuse, doesn't it, General?" The reverend looked pleased with himself. Meacham moved to the man's side and spoke quietly. Reverend Thomas started to argue, but Meacham cut him off, deferring to General Canby.

"We have no wagons to send," said the general.

"No wagons, no peace," insisted Queen Mary. Boston Charley looked as if he was going to burst out laughing at any minute.

"Washington—the big *tyee* in Washington, that is," Reverend Thomas said in deference to Boston Charley and Queen Mary, "has ordered us to try to negotiate peace."

"How can we when you run away from Captain Jack and won't even send wagons so we can return to Yainax?" asked Queen Mary.

"Leave," Canby snapped. "Leave immediately. Tell your brother there will be no wagons. If he wishes to return to the reservation, he is free to do so without interference."

"No wagons, no return," Boston Charley said, enjoying the byplay. He laughed out loud when Canby did a military about-face and marched into Fairchild's house.

The two Modoc chattered between themselves for a moment; then Boston Charley jauntily waved good-bye to Reverend Thomas and Meacham. Chuckling, he and Queen Mary mounted and left.

Josh heard Canby's angry voice from inside. "Sherman *has* to permit force now. They were trying to dupe us, steal horses, and annoy us! I will not stand for it!"

Reverend Thomas had not heard Canby's outburst, but Meacham had and looked solemn. Josh had thought the Modoc

War was nearing an end. Now he realized it was only beginning, with both sides jockeying for advantage.

He had a story to do, one he found himself reluctant to
write because of what it meant in terms of more bloodshed.

# Violation of Armistice

*Fairchild's Ranch, California*
*March 3, 1873*

Josh and Meacham were riding side by side along the road from Linkville, heading for John Fairchild's spread, when they heard loud shouts and whoops from behind. The pounding hooves told both men they should get off the road and let the soldiers pass.

As the patrol swept past driving dozens of horses ahead of them, Josh got a cold lump in his throat.

"Those men were from Canby's personal command, weren't they?" Josh asked.

"They were," Meacham said in a tone matching the way Josh felt. "And those were not military horses."

"Mustangs? Could they have found mustangs running wild on Fairchild's ranch?" Even as he asked the question, Josh realized how stupid it was. The entire area had been settled long enough for any herds of wild mustangs to be caught, broken, and branded. The Applegate family made a special job out of rounding up wild horses.

"Look at the hoofprints left in the snow," Meacham said. "Unshod horses."

"Modoc?"

"Let's see for ourselves." Meacham whipped his horse into a canter, and Josh did his best to keep up.

It had been only two days since Boston Charley and Queen Mary had come to visit Canby and deliver their absurd demands for empty wagons. The longer Josh thought on that, the more he realized what Meacham had instinctively known. This was a ploy to irritate and steal. If Canby had been foolish enough to send the wagons into the Lava Beds, both horses and wagons—along with drivers—would have vanished. Captain Jack would claim he knew nothing, and how would the Peace Commission respond then?

Political infighting in Washington demanded new attempts at peaceful settlement of the Modoc on the Klamath Reservation, but Canby's every move was more aggressive, depending on military force. The general's nerves had become frayed at the way the Modoc laughed at him while saying they dealt honestly with the *boshtin*. It now appeared as if the general had sent out patrols to the Lava Beds to steal Modoc horses.

The general was not one to take kindly to anyone, white or Indian, laughing at him.

Josh arrived at the Fairchild house minutes after Meacham. AB was already on the porch arguing with General Canby and Reverend Thomas. Josh dismounted and walked up, not wanting to intrude but itching to know what was being said.

"You violated the armistice with the Modoc!" Meacham was fit to be tied.

"Troops patrolling the perimeters might have strayed in," Canby said in his stuffy fashion. "I hardly call that a violation of your precious armistice."

"But you took their horses," Reverend Thomas said, as if trying to work out a curious puzzle and failing. "Why did you do that? That's theft!"

"They have thirty horses fewer now to escape on," Canby said.

"I've been to Linkville and heard the rumors. I've seen the troop movements, also. You are reinforcing your position. Heavily. Are you going to attack them when you assemble enough soldiers, General Canby?" Meacham truculently thrust out his chin and waggled his bushy beard at Canby.

"Preparations for war are not your concern, sir," Canby said.

"What of the next meeting?" asked Reverend Thomas. "The one between the Peace Commission and Captain Jack?"

Both Canby and Meacham turned and stared at the reverend as if he had sprouted wings.

"What meeting?" the two men asked simultaneously.

"The one I arranged. Boston Charley came by earlier today. I agreed to meet with them."

"In the Lava Beds?" asked Canby, his eyes narrowing.

"Why, of course. That was the site of the first Peace Commission meeting. Captain Jack felt the next meeting could be similarly arranged."

"I'm head of the Peace Commission," Meacham said. "You do not negotiate on your own."

"I saw no harm."

"A moment, Mr. Meacham," Canby said. "Reverend Thomas did what he thought best. Perhaps we can turn this to our advantage. I need to see the Lava Beds for myself. Under a truce flag is a good way, and if I am present it shows our willingness to talk."

"I don't like this, General," Meacham said. "It smacks of an ambush. Boston Charley knew I headed the commission. Why else would he go to the reverend unless this was a trap? He knows I would never agree to such a meeting."

"We will make sure it is not a trap," Canby said. "Prepare your staffs, gentlemen. We will keep the rendezvous tomorrow. In the Lava Beds."

"He does look impressive," Josh commented, pointing to General Canby, all dressed up in his resplendent uniform. "The gold braid shines, even if those clouds look like rain."

"It'll take more than a few yards of braid and medals on

his chest to turn Canby into anything but a liability," groused Meacham. "This is a mistake."

"Reverend Thomas is anxious to go," Josh said. He remembered too well his second trip into the Lava Beds with Judge Steele and how they had ridden out, sure the Modoc were ready to scalp them. Some of his nerviness might have come from Steele's fear, but Josh thought the threat had been real. Captain Jack had not behaved the way he had the day before with the entire Peace Commission.

Would that make a difference now? He hoped so.

"I don't think he understands what is at stake, or perhaps he wants to see only the good in his fellow man. Whichever it is, Reverend Thomas is more dangerous to us than to the Modoc," said Meacham.

Josh considered how much of this to quote and decided against including any of it in a story to the *Alta*. He did not want to anger his sources, and Alfred Meacham was both a good friend and a good source. Without him, Josh would have been left behind more than once.

They rode the now-familiar trail into the Lava Beds, winding around as they went deeper, but this time Josh got confused. The leaden clouds hid the sun and robbed him of any sense of direction. North and south were the same as east or west in the confusing terrain.

"I hope Tobey remembers the path," he said to Meacham. "I'm all turned around now."

"Josh, there! Did you see him?" Meacham pointed to the top of a twenty-foot-tall lava rock.

"I didn't see anything," Josh admitted. "What was it, AB?"

"General! I saw a sniper to our right!" Meacham urged his horse forward, but the path turned narrow, necking down to a spot where only one horse at a time could get through the razor-edged rock.

"Tobey!" Meacham called. The Modoc woman reined back and waited for him to navigate through the passage. "In the rocks. They're going to ambush us!"

Tobey Riddle took Meacham's warning seriously. She stood in the stirrups and carefully studied the rocks, looking in places Josh would never have thought to look. Although his eyes weren't as sharp as hers, he still saw two Modoc with rifles, trying desperately not to be seen until the Peace Commission passed by.

Josh had horrible visions of the Modoc stepping out and firing into the backs of their enemies.

A heavy raindrop hit him in the face, forcing him to turn away. Another cold drop hit, this one larger and more insistent as the wind kicked up. Tobey made her way to the front of the line and spoke rapidly with General Canby. At first, the officer tried to dismiss her, then halted the column as she pointed to the rocks ahead on the trail.

The rain fell in cold drops that stung like tiny bees when they hit Josh's face. He pulled down the brim of his hat and caused a miniature rush of water that drenched his pants. Looking through the increasingly heavy rain, he saw how bedraggled Canby looked in his once-fine uniform. Josh thought he heard laughter from the rocks, but the sounds of the rain might have misled him.

Tobey Riddle rode forward alone. Coming from shadows like shadows themselves, three Modoc appeared. Josh recognized Hooker Jim right away, but the other two were strangers. Tobey argued with them for a few minutes. Then the three Indians vanished into the depths of the Lava Beds. The woman rode back to speak with a furious Canby.

The general wheeled his horse about and retreated, riding past Josh without so much as a sidelong glance. When Tobey reached him, Josh asked what had happened.

Tobey said in a low voice, "The general is plenty mad. Rain has ruined his fine uniform—and that saved us."

"What? How?"

"Hooker Jim was going to ambush us and kill us, then proclaim himself *tyee*. He is satisfied now with making a fool of the general."

"I'll trade that any day for getting scalped," Josh said. "Are we still in danger?"

"Not now," Tobey said, wiping rain from her broad face. She laughed without humor. "I even set up another meeting, this time halfway between Captain Jack's and Canby's camps. In an open area. Maybe neither will try to kill the other."

"Maybe," Josh said, but he wasn't sure about that anymore.

# Conditions

"I don't trust him," Meacham said, glaring at the back of Boston Charley's head as they rode into the Lava Beds.

"You didn't have to come," John Fairchild said irritably. "He invited us to talk with Captain Jack, and I, for one, don't think we are in any danger."

"They tried to kill us before," Josh said, uneasy but trusting in Meacham to get them out of any trouble, should it arise. "Hooker Jim wanted us dead."

"He wanted Canby dead," Fairchild corrected. "He also saw a chance to become *tyee*. Boston Charley is speaking for Captain Jack now, not Hooker Jim."

"Captain Jack's an honorable man," Meacham said, "as far as you can say any of the Modoc are honorable anymore. But you're right, John. We're in no immediate danger. If Hooker Jim or Curly Headed Doctor tried to harm us, it would reflect poorly on Captain Jack. It would look as if the Modoc *tyee* could not enforce his commands."

"Great," Josh said. "He gets even with them if they kill us. We'll still be dead."

"Shut up," Fairchild snapped. "I don't know why Boston Charley let you come. This is between the Modoc and the settlers."

Josh waited for Meacham to complain, to say the Peace Commission ought to be involved, but the man said nothing. As Josh rode through an unfamiliar section of the Lava Beds, he thought about this. If Captain Jack had wanted to kill them, he would have invited not only Canby but the entire Peace Commission to prove his power. The request to meet might be nothing more than Meacham believed: Captain Jack wanted to reach an agreement before Canby and the others on the Peace Commission could muck it up.

"Here we are," Boston Charley said in his cheery tone. "Enjoy the parley!" Laughing, he rode off into the twisting, turning ravines of the Lava Beds, leaving them alone in the clearing.

Meacham looked around, shrugged, then dismounted to wait. Fairchild followed him to the ground, but Josh remained in the saddle, hoping to catch sight of Captain Jack or other Modoc before they sneaked up on them. He tried and failed. Captain Jack appeared, seemingly out of thin air. Josh blinked, felt chagrined he had missed how the Modoc had accomplished such a dramatic entrance, then dismounted to join the others.

"We must talk," Captain Jack said. He dropped to his haunches, waiting for the others to join him. Meacham sank down painfully, his legs stiff from the long ride. Fairchild sat on the rough ground gingerly. Josh wanted to stand but saw this was not a good idea. He sat beside Meacham, enduring the places where lava poked into his rump. Riding back would give real discomfort—if Captain Jack let them ride back at all.

"We are always ready to talk to the great *tyee* of the Modoc," Meacham said.

Captain Jack made a dismissing gesture with his hand, as if brushing away such formality.

"You must know what the Modoc think," Captain Jack said. He launched into a recitation of all that had happened, starting with Ben Wright's massacre and finishing with his demands for the Modoc to settle along the Lost River, in their traditional lands. He spoke of how the Klamath hated them and how only war was possible if the Modoc were forced back to the Klamath Reservation, even the Yainax section, although that was better.

"Most hurtful is Odeneal's refusal to talk to us," Captain Jack went on. "He treats us like children. Worse. Are we so ugly he cannot bear to look upon our faces?"

"Mr. Odeneal does not enter into the negotiations now," Meacham said. "The Peace Commission is responsible for coming to an equitable solution."

"Equitable to the *boshtin?*" Captain Jack made a face. "Fairchild is an honorable man, even if he does not like me."

"We can come to some answer," Fairchild said. "I've never made a secret of liking the Hot Creek Modoc more than your band."

"Even when Shacknasty Jim steals your horse?" A smile crept onto Captain Jack's lips, then disappeared. "You do not hate all Modoc, not like Odeneal," Captain Jack said. "That is why I asked you here. We can find a place to settle along the Lost River and never bother you or the other settlers."

"I'm afraid that's no longer possible," Meacham said hurriedly, before Fairchild could respond. "General Sherman wants the Modoc to leave Lost River and go south to Arizona. You will be given a reservation there and—"

"Arizona?" Captain Jack barked like a dog. Josh wondered if he was laughing or showing disdain. "We do not know Arizona. *This* is our home."

"The government, the big *tyee* in Washington—demands it, Captain Jack," Meacham said. "Too much has happened for there to be any other solution."

"We will not leave our home," Captain Jack said flatly. "You want us to go to this Arizona so the white settlers can have our land. No!" He shot to his feet. "We will never leave. We stay in the Lava Beds!"

Josh saw Meacham grin at this. It was impossible to live in the Lava Beds. The barren land afforded no agriculture. Hunting of anything larger than a rabbit was unlikely. And the river that ran past the lava fields was dry and would remain that way until spring runoffs. The only reliable water came from Tule Lake, and if Canby wanted, he could post a hundred soldiers there to prevent the Modoc from drinking.

"You do not have to like Mr. Fairchild," Meacham said carefully. "But he will work with you if you work with him. There will be fairness on both sides. I will do what I can, but you cannot return to Lost River, and staying here is . . . difficult."

Captain Jack glowered and crossed his arms.

"We can talk more," he said.

Meacham nodded. "We need to, but this is a start, realizing you cannot remain here forever. And there is a condition for continued talks."

"What?" Captain Jack looked even more dour.

"Those who massacred the settlers must be turned over to General Canby for punishment."

"I won't talk unless you do that," Fairchild chimed in. "Friends were killed. Women and children. Fifteen innocents."

"I will not surrender any of my people to your justice," Captain Jack said firmly.

"You must. This is not negotiable."

"Then you must turn over to us those who shotgunned three of our women and a baby. Our justice is swift!"

Meacham and Fairchild exchanged glances, and silent communication passed between the men, a message Josh read easily. Canby would never permit a settler to be given over to the Modoc.

"We must talk more on this," Meacham said, rising. He dusted himself off. Josh and Fairchild got to their feet, also, showing the talk was at an end. "Come to Canby's camp and we can continue."

"At Fairchild's ranch?" asked Captain Jack.

"That's as neutral a place as we are likely to find," Meacham said.

Captain Jack started to speak, then clamped his mouth shut. Josh turned and looked behind them. In the rocks, unseen until this moment, stood four warriors, all in war paint and with rifles pointed in their direction. One man—Josh thought it was Curly Headed Doctor—obviously opposed any such talk.

"No," Captain Jack said. "It is too dangerous."

"I promise a truce," Meacham said.

"Like Ben Wright? Like the armistice Canby broke when he stole our horses?" Captain Jack stalked off. Josh tensed, waiting for the men behind them to open fire. When he looked over his shoulder, all he saw were shadows being sucked down into the black, porous rocks.

# The Truth . . .

*Linkville, Oregon*
*April 6, 1873*

"AB," Josh called, seeing the man leaving the telegraph office. "Wait a second." He hurried to catch up with his friend, who looked as if he were deep in thought. Meacham wrung his hands, and occasionally tugged at his bushy, full beard in consternation. Somehow, Josh shared this trepidation, even if he did not have a beard of his own to tug.

"Oh, hello, Josh. I missed you this morning."

"I had a story to send in to the *Alta*," he explained. "It took me most of the night to write it."

Meacham came out of his reverie and sharply looked at Josh. "What aren't you telling me?"

"AB, this is difficult for me. Mr. Billingsly is pushing me hard to report something more . . ." Words escaped him. He made futile gestures with his hands, as if this might explain it all.

"Something more dramatic?" supplied Meacham. "I've read the other reporters' stories. Sensationalistic, the lot of them. They are agitating for a war and don't care a bucket of warm spit about who might die. You're different, which is one reason I like you."

"I report the facts, sir," Josh said, still floundering for the right words. "But I need something, well, you said it. I need a dramatic turn or Mr. Billingsly is not likely to take more from me. The other San Francisco papers are increasing their circulation and the *Alta California* is not."

"Because you choose the truth over flagrant lies?"

"That sums it up," Josh said lamely.

"You cannot report what happened yesterday in the Lava Beds with Captain Jack," Meacham said flatly. "To upset the applecart at this stage of such delicate negotiation would be nothing less than criminal."

"I need *something*," Josh begged. "Don't tell me what to write, but give me something sensational."

"You know all that I do," Meacham said, turning cool toward his friend. "Do what you must, but if Captain Jack turns away from the Peace Commission and fights, it will be on your head."

"The public demands more, AB," Josh said, hurrying to keep up with Meacham as the man stalked off. "Is there anything I can write?"

"Just to keep your job? Even if this dire situation does not turn deadly, as it has in the past? What was it you called the unfortunate fight? The Battle for the Stronghold? So dramatic. It might just be that you'll have to rename it the *First* Battle for the Stronghold. Men will surely die if Canby goes into the Lava Beds again, white and red alike."

"I'm being fair, AB. I'm the only reporter not making you out to be a buffoon."

"So?" Meacham stopped suddenly and spun on Josh. "Call me a buffoon, if you must. I am past caring. Do not sabotage the peace talks, however, or you will find how spiteful this old buffoon can become! Good day." With that Meacham cut across Linkville's muddy main street and headed for the livery stable, undoubtedly riding to Fairchild's to meet again with General Canby.

Josh stood in the street, getting spattered with mud from passing wagons, and wondered what the hell he was supposed to do. The truth no longer seemed enough.

# A Vote . . .
# and a Warning

*Lava Beds*
*April 7, 1873*

Captain Jack watched Tobey Riddle ride up, her broad face impassive. He matched her expression, although he fought to do so. His heart raced and he wanted to blurt out the question: *What news do you bring, Cousin?* Captain Jack looked left and right. Curly Headed Doctor stood at his right elbow, and to his left, a half pace forward, Schonchin John waited with his usual impatience.

His rivals. *Two* of his rivals, Captain Jack corrected himself. Hooker Jim was off in the Lava Beds plotting and planning some treachery. Bogus Charley increasingly sought to position himself as a leader. And who else among the Modoc gathered today would kill him if it meant they would become *tyee?* Captain Jack wondered at this mad quest for power. He got only heartache and worry trying to do what was best for the Modoc. What drove his rivals? Blood lust? Hatred of the whites? Some inner need to be looked upon favorably by all the Modoc? Captain Jack had no answer for their ambitions.

He was too busy trying to preserve his power so the Modoc would not be slaughtered like cattle.

"Cousin," Captain Jack said in as neutral a tone as possible. "Welcome."

"Thank you, Cousin," Tobey greeted him, dismounting and coming over. She stood a head shorter, but her commanding presence spoke of confidence. Tobey had done well among the *boshtin,* Captain Jack thought, better than if she had married someone of her own people.

The others crowded around. Tobey took no notice of them, her words for Captain Jack alone.

"The Peace Commission has finished their plan and will present it to you for approval," she said in a low voice. This put Captain Jack's nerves on edge. If Meacham's plan had been completely favorable, Tobey would have announced it loudly.

"Tell me what they propose," he said.

Tobey began the recitation of the terms, including immediate departure from the Lava Beds and temporary settlement at Yainax again. Further discussion would be needed to determine whether the Modoc went to an Arizona reservation or remained near their ancestral lands. Other details flowed by, but Captain Jack barely listened. Meacham had presented a small peace offering in allowing the Modoc to return to Yainax while the Washington *tyee* argued among themselves. This meant Canby would be powerless to move the tribe for some time. From all Captain Jack knew of the white soldiers, Canby might transfer elsewhere, and the matter might be forgotten, allowing the Modoc to stay in Oregon.

Time was the ally of the Modoc and the enemy of the impatient *boshtin.* Meacham was giving them plenty of time.

"We need to vote," Captain Jack said, "after discussing the terms."

Tobey Riddle retired while the fifty warriors in camp circled Captain Jack. Animated discussion took place, turning more violent as Curly Headed Doctor began to tear the plan apart and question Canby's motives.

"He wants us out of our stronghold so he can kill us easily. Do you hear even a hollow promise of return to our land along

Lost River? No. The white general would lure us out into an ambush."

"I do not like the idea we might be sent to Arizona later," Bogus Charley said. "This is my land. Our land. We should never agree to leave without a fight."

"There will be no fighting," Captain Jack cut in. "We can live in peace while they argue among themselves. We must be unified against their division."

The talk ebbed and flowed, Captain Jack steering it toward acceptance. The Peace Commission plan was not good, not entirely, but it promised no fighting, return to Yainax, and possibly regaining their land along Lost River. Captain Jack was realistic in thinking this was only a carrot offered a balky mule, but living at Yainax was better than eking out a meager existence in the Lava Beds.

"How long can we live here?" he asked the assembled braves. "We can fight off Canby's soldiers, but only for a while. My belly rumbles. What of yours?" He looked around. "What of your wives' bellies? Do they growl, too?"

"It's a long way to Tule Lake for water," said a warrior in the rear of the group. "The stream's dried up."

"There won't be water flowing for a month or more," Captain Jack said. "We can survive here, but we cannot live. We can prosper at Yainax."

"A vote, a vote!" The chant went up, fed by Curly Headed Doctor and his allies. This worried Captain Jack. He tried to force more discussion but lost.

He lost the vote to accept the new treaty. Only eleven voted with him. Captain Jack felt his power slipping away unless he changed tactics.

"What does our *tyee* say?" Curly Headed Doctor asked loudly. He turned to challenge Captain Jack, thinking he would argue against the majority vote. Captain Jack knew what he had to answer.

"The treaty is rejected!" Captain Jack shouted. To have said anything else would have meant losing his power to Curly Headed Doctor.

Across the clearing, Tobey hung her head, then slowly walked to her horse and started to mount.

From behind her came a hoarse whisper.

"Nanooktowa," someone said, using her name as a young girl. "Strange Child," it had meant, showing she was special to the tribe. "Nanooktowa, tell Meacham not to come to the council tent again. He will be killed!"

She turned to see who offered such a warning, but only shadows stretched into the Lava Beds.

# Treachery Proposed

*Outside the Lava Beds*
*April 8, 1873*

"We expected Captain Jack to come to this conference," Meacham said, displeased that only three Modoc had come. Captain Jack had wanted to work out details with a solitary meeting in the Lava Beds and then, when Tobey had presented the details, rejected the treaty. This conference was the meeting agreed to when the Peace Commission, along with General Canby, had ridden into the Lava Beds and gotten drenched back in March.

"He is such a busy man," Boston Charley said in his almost-ridiculing fashion. Somehow, the bright grin and the flashing eyes defused the obvious insult. This made Boston Charley even bolder, since he felt he had gotten away with the deception. "He is bedridden with a terrible cold, also. It is hard for him to do everything in such a condition."

"We had agreed to meet halfway," Meacham said, trying to ignore the man's disdain for the peace process and all that had been agreed to already. "We are here. Are you the Modoc *tyee?*"

Boston Charley laughed heartily and shook his head, then looked at Bogus Charley and Shacknasty Jim, as if he might find a *tyee* there. He waved to two other Modoc some distance away, then threw up his hands in mock defeat.

"Nope, none of us is *tyee*. To meet with Captain Jack, you have to come to the council tent."

"In the Lava Beds?" asked Meacham. "This was not what we discussed."

"Captain Jack is plenty busy," Boston Charley said, smirking. "You want to make peace, you come to the council tent."

Meacham saw an orderly hurry up and give General Canby a note. He scanned it, then passed it to Meacham.

A scout had spotted twenty armed Modoc not five minutes away, hiding and ready for battle. Meacham folded the note and returned it to Canby, trying to keep his face impassive. He had no idea what scheme Boston Charley was hatching, but he wanted no part of it.

"We cannot go today," he said curtly. "Such short notice makes it impossible for us to leave when we had planned on conducting the negotiations here."

"When?" Boston Charley asked bluntly.

"We'll discuss it. If you will excuse us for a few minutes." Meacham wanted a word with Canby about this obvious plot to kill them. He waited for the Modoc to withdraw, his friends with him.

"They are treacherous swine," Canby said without rancor. "How do we deal with them?"

"Carefully, sir," Meacham said. "We can negotiate in the Lava Beds, as Boston Charley wants, but I doubt any of us would live to see the light of a new day if we tried."

"Nonsense," Canby said brusquely. "I know Indians. This is their way of frightening their enemy, which is the way they see us. They think only to unnerve us, nothing more."

Tobey Riddle had stood quietly listening until Canby spoke. She came up and said, "General, they will kill you if you go back into Captain Jack's Stronghold. A friend warned me."

"Who?" asked Canby.

"I . . . I cannot tell you," Tobey said. "But there was no reason to tell me this if someone did not plan to kill the Peace Commission—and you, General."

"Yes, right, of course," Canby said disdainfully. "They have no position of strength to bargain from. The Modoc are virtua prisoners in the Lava Beds, without supplies or any way out That is why they are trying to scare us with this gossip, th rumors that they think will make a white man quake in fear.'

"Sir," Meacham said, choosing his words carefully to con vince the general of the problem they faced, "the Modoc have a different way of thinking. If they lure you into the Lava Bed and kill you, they think they will have won. They believe w will simply give up, and they can then return to their lan along Lost River."

"Absurd. General Sherman would send someone else to re place me. Colonel Gillem would assume command until the and press the attack. They would gain nothing by killing me.'

"A *tyee* dying means the fight is over to them," Meacham said. Tobey nodded agreement, but Edward Canby ignore them. "Sir, if they kill you they think they have won, no matte what *we* think."

"I have spent most of my career fighting Indians," Canby said pompously. "The Navajo in New Mexico Territory, som Apache and Comanche, now the Modoc. I know how the think and how they fight. All those tribes have been defeated Washington wants a quick end to this furor, and by God, will oblige."

Meacham edged away, then went to where Boston Charle smoked a cigarette with Shacknasty Jim and Bogus Charley the other two Modoc looking enviously at the cigarette Meacham beckoned to the short man. For a moment, Bosto Charley looked fearful. Then his usual braggadocio returne and he strutted off with Meacham for a private talk.

"Why do the Modoc want to kill us?" Meacham aske bluntly.

"What are you saying? This is all wrong, no, no! Captai Jack wants to smoke a pipe with you, to parley. We want ou land and you can get it for us." Meacham knew a lie when h heard it, and Boston Charley was telling a whopper.

Meacham heard footsteps behind them. He turned to chase off whoever had interrupted their private dispute. Reverend Thomas stormed up, his face a dark cloud of anger.

"I have just spoken with Tobey Riddle," he said loudly. "She was warned that you people want to ambush us!"

Boston Charley recoiled, then looked at Meacham. The thoughts running through the Modoc's head might as well have been written in letters a foot high on his face.

"Traitors say things like," Boston Charley declared flatly. He pushed past Reverend Thomas and barked at Shacknasty Jim, Bogus Charley, and the other two Modoc, who trailed him from the conference area.

Meacham knew that Thomas had just signed Tobey Riddle's death warrant with her own people. It remained to be seen if the Peace Commission's goal was similarly doomed. Deep in his gut, Meacham thought it was.

# Threats

*Lava Beds*
*April 8, 1873*

"Winema," the Modoc boy said, "Captain Jack wants you to see him."

Tobey Riddle closed her eyes for a moment, then tried to compose herself so her voice would not show any anxiety when she spoke. Captain Jack had sent a boy to her, and she did not know what that meant. Were all the men unwilling? Did Captain Jack wish to see her secretly, not wanting Curly Headed Doctor and the others who opposed him to know they spoke?

"Why?" she asked.

"I do not understand, Winema," the boy said, using her tribal name again to show his respect and to prod her gently into obeying Captain Jack's request. *If* it came from her cousin, Tobey could not know. Since Reverend Thomas had blurted out how she had warned Canby of possible ambush earlier, and since Boston Charley's reaction on finding this out, she had known real fear. Boston Charley, Schonchin John, Curly Headed Doctor, and others unknown to her in the tribe all wanted her dead because they thought she was a traitor. Marrying Frank Riddle had been the start, but translating for Meacham and the Peace Commission had added to their ire.

Now that she had "betrayed" their plans for killing Meacham and Canby, she could never be secure.

If any of those men really plotted to kill Canby under a flag of truce. She did not know who had whispered the warning to her. And the person—man? woman?—had not mentioned that Tobey's life was in jeopardy.

"When does my cousin want to meet?" she asked.

"In the stronghold, near the camp, at midnight," the boy said, beginning to look nervous. Canby's sentries paced back and forth along their appointed circuits not ten yards away.

"Does Captain Jack guarantee my safety?"

The boy's eyes went wide, as if he had never considered that Tobey might be in jeopardy. This was enough for Tobey to believe she might be safe.

Maybe.

"Go," she said, when a soldier began to take notice of her and the boy. With a sigh of relief, the boy slipped silently into the night, leaving Tobey to make up her mind what to do. She knew there had to be wiser heads helping her decide, so she set off for Meacham's tent.

The head of the Peace Commission pored over sheaves of papers, scribbling in the margins and making more voluminous notes in a diary. He looked up when he saw her, then beckoned her to come in. Tobey sat on the man's cot, her mind boiling.

"What can I do for you?" Meacham asked.

Everything came spilling out, mostly in English, but some of her concerns in Modoc. Meacham let her ramble on before gently bringing her to a focus on what troubled her most.

"From what you say, Captain Jack wants to talk only with you. Is that right?" Meacham asked. Tobey nodded. "We cannot know if the boy was sent by Captain Jack or his enemies— and yours." Meacham chewed on this a moment, then said, "We should tell General Canby and see what he thinks."

"The general does not like me," Tobey said.

"I cannot argue that," Meacham said, "but he has to know

everything that happens. He is in command and officially on the Peace Commission."

Together, Tobey and Meacham went to Fairchild's house then knocked on the door. A captain answered, hand on his holstered pistol. It took a few minutes to get past the general's adjutant, but when they did, Canby was as effusive as Tobey had ever seen him.

"Talk only," Canby said. "Find out what you can about the encampment. How many men are there, if they have adequate ammunition for their rifles, how many rifles! There is so much to learn."

"Sir," cut in Meacham, "Captain Jack wants to talk with his cousin about something else. This isn't likely to be a productive scouting mission, from a military standpoint."

"But she must go. Definitely. Find out what you can from Captain Jack and return with the information."

Tobey looked to Meacham, tears in her eyes. She was afraid to go. Boston Charley was dangerous, as dangerous as Curly Headed Doctor and the others vying for *tyee.*

"Captain Jack assures your safety," Meacham said. "It will be safe enough for you since I doubt they would harm you knowing it would give us reason to launch new military expeditions against them. From what I gleaned from Boston Charley, they are willing to negotiate because they are not strong enough for a real fight."

"You think I should go?" Tobey choked back her fear.

"You will be fine," Meacham said, patting her on the shoulder. "You should go quickly, also, if you are to reach Captain Jack's camp by midnight."

Tobey nodded, then left Canby and Meacham to further discuss her mission. She stepped into the cold spring evening and looked at the stars, some vanishing behind wispy clouds promising rain toward morning. Tobey wondered if she would live to see the gentle rain and the blossoming spring.

And to see her family again.

She hurried toward her tent. Frank slept quietly, but it was her ten-year-old son Jeff that drew her. She cradled him in her arms as if he were once more a baby. He awoke with a start, and this woke Frank.

"What's wrong?" Frank asked, sensing the tension in his wife.

"Meacham and Canby want me to go to my cousin, in the Lava Beds. Tonight."

"No," cried Jeff, clinging to his mother. "You can't do it. Th-they will kill you. Boston Charley doesn't like you and he scares me, Mama!"

"He scares the hell out of me, too. Under that boyish exterior is a killer's black heart," Frank said.

"I will be safe. I must go. I must," Tobey said, "if there is to be peace. Kintpuash might want me to carry word of his agreement to the treaty."

They argued and wept and held each other. Then Tobey left.

She neared the Modoc camp a few minutes before midnight and heard the soft scurrying sounds all around her. Not rats, not rabbits, but other creatures, deadly ones she had hoped to avoid. Tobey reined back and waited before passing through the final narrow passage widening out into the clearing where Captain Jack and the rest of the Modoc lived now.

A shadowy figure moved to block her way.

"Kintpuash has given me his word," Tobey said. "I am to pass freely."

"You are a traitor," raged Curly Headed Doctor. "You told the *boshtin tyee* not to come talk."

"Cho-ocks," Tobey said, calling Curly Headed Doctor by his Modoc name, "know this! I am Modoc!" She jumped from her horse, drew a six-gun, and scrambled up onto a rock to peer down at him. "Yes, I told Meacham and Canby about your cowardly plot."

"How did you learn of it?" asked Curly Headed Doctor,

approaching her in spite of the woman's steady grip on her pistol aimed straight at him.

"One of your own men told me, but I'll never betray him!" Tobey didn't know who had told her, but she wanted to sow discord. For all she knew, someone loyal to Captain Jack had overheard Curly Headed Doctor or Schonchin John plotting and then warned her. "Shoot me, if you dare! I am Modoc and not afraid to die. I am better off dead than shamed by your cowardly acts!"

Tobey tensed. Rifles cocked all around her. She aimed straight at Curly Headed Doctor.

"Shoot me if you will, but I will die fighting. And you, Cho-ocks, will find your spirit tangled with mine!"

"Stop! Stop this!" came Captain Jack's angry command. He pushed past Curly Headed Doctor and put himself between the shaman and Tobey. "I will die alongside a brave woman, if you try harming her. She will kill you, Curly Headed Doctor, and I will kill a dozen more of you!"

Tobey heard muttering among those who had thought to ambush her. Slowly, they backed off until only she, Captain Jack, and Curly Headed Doctor remained. Then the shaman vented a loud cry of frustration, turned, and stormed back to the camp.

"I apologize for them," Captain Jack said. "I thought you could get in and out without trouble."

"What is it you wanted to say, my cousin?" she asked. She lifted her pistol when pebbles tumbled down toward her. Above on the rock with a rifle in his hand stood Scarfaced Charley. He smiled and disappeared.

"It is a sad day when even the *tyee* must have allies with him. Many more than Curly Headed Doctor would have died if they had harmed you, cousin," Captain Jack said. He paused, then said almost sadly, "I want to meet with General Canby in three days, under a flag of truce, no guns."

Tobey heard her cousin and saw his face and tried to keep

her hands from shaking. Captain Jack was trapped in some secret plot of his bitterest enemies.

"Will you sign the treaty?" she asked.

"Yes," he said. "Now go, quickly. They will not harm you. Scarfaced Charley will watch out for you until you are far enough from camp."

"Kintpuash," she started. Then Tobey sagged. "Good-bye," she said. "Good-bye until we meet again in three days."

"No!" Captain Jack said too loudly, too quickly. "Others will translate. Stay with your husband and son." He started to add something more, then thought better of it and headed back to camp, leaving Tobey alone.

She found her horse and rode as fast as she could back to General Canby with what she had heard and seen and felt.

Tobey told the general never to negotiate with Captain Jack or any of the Modoc again, but he ignored her worries. Alfred Meacham knew better than to doubt her instincts. Tobey was glad he understood. Very glad.

# Foolish Agreement

*Fairchild's Ranch, Oregon*
*April 10, 1873*

"Then we are agreed?" Meacham asked General Canby. "No meeting until we can be certain there will not be trouble? We can wear them down and get the terms we want without unduly risking our own lives."

"Yes, yes," Canby said, hardly listening to Meacham. "I must contact General Sherman for new instructions. The tone of his last directive was curt, as if he expected more."

"These negotiations cannot be rushed," Meacham said. "To make a mistake now will mean blood spilled for months or years to come." His lips thinned as he saw how little attention the general paid him and his valid concerns. He saw Canby treat Tobey Riddle with the same inattention and even contempt. Canby ignored her even when she had firsthand information to give because he considered her caught between two worlds and loyal to neither.

Meacham had found her story of going into the Lava Beds—and barely returning—quite chilling.

"Is there anything more, Mr. Meacham?" asked Canby, still distracted.

"I am going into Linkville for the day. My friend Joshua Harlan is feeling poorly, and I want to see him."

"The reporter fellow? Yes, go on. The Reverend Thomas will provide ample leadership in your absence."

"I am sure he will," Meacham said, knowing there was nothing to be decided while he was gone. It would be only a few hours. He left General Canby and rode quickly toward Linkville, worrying as he rode, as much about leaving Canby's encampment as about Josh.

"You are one smart fellow," Boston Charley told Reverend Thomas. "Lots smarter than Meacham. We like you and brought you presents." Boston Charley waved, and four Modoc carried gifts for the reverend, putting them on the table in the Peace Commission's tent.

"My, this is very generous of you," Reverend Thomas said, seeing baskets of woven tule and food that looked suspiciously familiar, as if the Modoc had recently stolen it but now gave it back. "I regret I have nothing to offer you in kind."

"Gifts, take our gifts as a thank-you for being so helpful," Boston Charley said.

"I wish there was something I could do for you fine gentlemen," Thomas said, stroking his chin. He saw Boston Charley start to speak, then bite back the words. "What is it? Tell me."

"Oh, that Meacham doesn't want to talk anymore. He is like Odeneal, afraid of us. Captain Jack wants to talk. Captain Jack wants to sign a treaty."

"Really?" Reverend Thomas's eyes glowed at the prospect of peace being so near. "Mr. Meacham never said anything about this. He even seemed frightened of talking with you again."

"We are harmless," Boston Charley said, smiling broadly. "We want only peace. Come to the council tent in the Lava Beds, and Captain Jack will sign the treaty."

"When?" Reverend Thomas felt a surge of eagerness. Peace was so close and was being offered up so graciously.

"We are afraid," Boston Charley said. "Not of you but of Canby and Meacham. We don't want them coming armed."

"Well, certainly not. And you would have to agree to come to the council tent unarmed, as well."

"Of course, of course," Boston Charley said, grinning even more expansively. "Tomorrow. Come tomorrow. It is a special day."

"It certainly is," Reverend Thomas said. "It is Good Friday, the perfect day for declaring peace between our peoples. This is splendid!"

"You will come? You and the general and the others of the Peace Commission?"

"Yes!" cried Reverend Thomas. "You have my word on it."

Boston Charley laughed delightedly. "I knew you were smart man."

"I have a perfect way of repaying your generosity and willingness to talk peace. Come with me to the camp commissary and I will see that you receive new clothing. Those rags you are wearing—excuse me if I am speaking out of turn—have seen better days."

"You will give us all new clothing?" This took Boston Charley by surprise. Then his head bobbed in agreement to such a generous offer. He spoke rapidly to the four Modoc with him. They all laughed and clapped Reverend Thomas on the back. "You have made good friends, good friends for the talks tomorrow."

"At the council tent," Reverend Thomas said, savoring the way the words rolled off his tongue. "On Good Friday," he said in a softer voice.

"It will be a good Friday," Boston Charley assured him. "Now where are our new clothes?"

Reverend Thomas led the five Modoc from the Peace Commission tent to the Army commissary and talked the supply sergeant into letting the Indians root through the boxes of clothing until they found shirts and pants that fit them.

* * *

Dusk fell by the time Meacham rode back to Canby's encampment at the Fairchild house. He frowned when he saw Boston Charley strutting around like the cock of the walk in brand-new clothes. He dismounted and went to him.

"Where'd you get those clothes?" he demanded.

Boston Charley sneered at him, then said, "Reverend Thomas gave them to us. For the heap big peace conference tomorrow. On Good Friday, the day of peace, he says."

"What?" Meacham pushed past Boston Charley and the other Modoc and ran to the Peace Commission tent, where Reverend Thomas sat with General Canby. Frank and Tobey Riddle stood off to one side, arguing in voices too low for him to hear.

"What's going on? Boston Charley just told me there's to be a peace conference tomorrow in the Lava Beds!"

"I arranged it. The timing is wonderful, don't you think?" said Thomas. "Our Lord Jesus Christ has sent a message. From all the killing will be resurrected living peace."

"Where?" asked Meacham, a sinking feeling in his belly.

"The council tent," Reverend Thomas said. "That is the only place Captain Jack feels at ease."

"I tried to avoid this. We can't go in there, not the entire Peace Commission. Let's change the date, move it, not send everyone," Meacham rattled on, his mind refusing to focus. He saw how distraught Tobey Riddle looked and knew why now. He had fought to keep them out of what had to be a dangerous situation.

"Don't be absurd, Mr. Meacham," said General Canby. "This is the very meeting you should have organized yourself. I take my hat off to Reverend Thomas for such fine work."

"This is a huge mistake," Meacham said. "We cannot go there without armed guards."

"No, no weapons," Reverend Thomas said. "That was one

point on which I was very strict, and one to which the Modoc reluctantly agreed. No one at the council tent will carry arms.'

Meacham knew what a trapped rat felt like now.

"I have permission to make the treaty," Canby said. "You are jumping at shadows. They are nothing but savages, but they are honorable enough."

"General, my cousin is honorable, but he is being forced to do things that are not," said Tobey. "And the others, the ones like Curly Headed Doctor! They are evil men!"

Meacham saw Canby's resolve harden. Tobey should not have spoken. The general disliked her so intensely, he felt anything she said had to be suspect. Now Meacham could never turn the officer away from attending the meeting, with the rest of the Peace Commission along to agree to the treaty terms.

"Perhaps it will be all right," Meacham said, hardly believing it.

"I will go," Tobey said. "You need someone to translate. You should not depend on either Bogus Charley or Boston Charley. I will not mislead you."

"Very well," Canby said, looking as if he had bitten into a green persimmon. "You may come. And you, Mr. Meacham, you *will* accompany us. After all, you do head the Peace Commission." With that Canby swept from the tent.

Meacham started to explain to Reverend Thomas what he had done, how he had put their lives into jeopardy, but the man looked too smug with his decisions for that. Slumping, Meacham left the tent, knowing he had to prepare for the meeting.

He went to his tent and sat on the cot, working to pull his new boots off. Meacham looked up when he saw movement at the tent flap. Boston Charley stood there, watching him like a hawk eyes a rabbit.

"Why are you changing boots?" Boston Charley asked. "Those are new."

"I want to put on my old ones."

"For the conference tomorrow? You would wear old boots?"

No, no, Mr. Meacham. Wear your new ones. This is a fine occasion, a special one." Boston Charley seemed almost distraught at the notion Meacham wanted to wear the battered, scuffed old brown boots.

Meacham knew why. It was better to steal new boots from a corpse than old ones.

# War!

"Boston Charley says we can do it. All is ready," Schonchin John said, looking around the guttering fire at the faces of the Modoc warriors. Many were already decked out in war paint. Good. He need not convince them. The others, the ones like Scarfaced Charley, who supported Captain Jack, needed more convincing. Or could he get a big enough vote so he could ignore them? Schonchin John thought he might, thanks to Boston Charley's honey-dipped tongue.

"This is not honorable," Scarfaced Charley spoke up. "We should wait for Captain Jack to return. He is *tyee.*"

"Where is he?" asked Boston Charley, throwing up his hands and looking around in his most theatrical manner. "For such an important meeting, why isn't our *tyee* here to give us his guidance on how best to kill the whites?"

"There should be no talk of killing until Captain Jack returns," Scarfaced Charley said steadfastly.

"We all know we cannot live forever in the Lava Beds. Look at our fire. We run out of wood. Our food is almost gone. The spring runoff is sparse and we need to go west to Tule Lake for water. If the *boshtin* soldiers line up along the lake, we will die of thirst," Schonchin John said.

"We grow hungry, too," Black Jim chimed in, supporting

Schonchin John rather than his brother's more moderate approach. "Captain Jack is too bewitched with the sound of his own voice when he talks to the *boshtin.*"

"We must fight," Boston Charley said. "Captain Jack's brother agrees. All we need is to figure out how to do it. I got them to agree to come to the council tent tomorrow. For them it is a special day." Boston Charley's eyes gleamed like a wolf's in the flickering firelight. "For us it will be an even more special day."

"It will be the day we kill their *tyee* and drive them from our land!" cried Schonchin John.

Scarfaced Charley moved to sit next to Black Jim. The two spoke in low tones, Black Jim obviously not agreeing with his brother's friend. Finally, Scarfaced Charley spoke again.

"They will weaken if we do nothing to annoy them. They are impatient and dart about. If we wait long enough, Canby will go away and the Peace Commission will agree to give us our land." Scarfaced Charley looked around to see if this argument would win. Only sneers met his suggestion.

*"Give us our land,"* taunted Boston Charley. "We are Modoc. Why should we depend on the charity of white settlers and soldiers? They drove us from our rightful land. We should take it back. Tomorrow. At the peace council!"

"Kill them at the council tent!" shouted Schonchin John.

"Kill them!" chimed in Hooker Jim. Slowly, others around the campfire began the chant. When Curly Headed Doctor stood and started his dance, the mood swung toward murdering Canby and the rest of the Peace Commission in cold blood.

"What's going on?" demanded Captain Jack, returning from a hunt. He dropped the two scrawny rabbits he had bagged and stepped into the circle of firelight and looked around.

"We will kill them tomorrow," Boston Charley said. "It is all agreed. Even your brother knows this is a good idea."

"We cannot kill them under a flag of truce," Captain Jack protested. "That's dishonorable."

"Like Ben Wright, like Canby stealing our horses, like so many other times they lied and cheated us?" Boston Charley had done all the agitating needed. He sat and crossed his arms, watching in satisfaction as Schonchin John and Curly Headed Doctor moved to convince Captain Jack.

"I can get them to agree to us living with the Hot Creek Modoc rather than sending us to Arizona," Captain Jack said. "They will listen to Old Schonches and—" He found himself outshouted.

"We all agree. Kill their *tyee* and they will go away." Schonchin John challenged Captain Jack for more than disagreement. If Captain Jack argued now, he lost control of the tribe. The Modoc had not formally voted for a new *tyee*, but he saw what had happened. Refuse to go along with the treachery and he lost out to Schonchin John. Agree and perhaps he could salvage something.

"What is agreed?" Captain Jack asked, hating himself for having to maneuver in this fashion. But he saw no other choice.

Schonchin John grinned.

"I will kill Meacham, me and Hooker Jim," Schonchin John said savagely. "Boston Charley and Bogus Charley want to kill their shaman, the one they call Reverend Thomas. If Colonel Gillem comes, Shacknasty Jim will kill him. Then there will be the Riddles."

"It is unworthy for Modoc to kill Modoc," Scarfaced Charley said, interrupting. "If you try to kill Tobey Riddle, you must kill me, too!"

Schonchin John and Curly Headed Doctor exchanged a quick look, then John nodded.

"No one will kill Tobey, if she is there. Her husband? Fair game."

"Who kills General Canby?" Captain Jack asked, although he knew the answer. He had arrived late at this vote, but the details were as clear to him as every hill and ravine in the Lava Beds.

"Our *tyee* should kill theirs," Curly Headed Doctor said, staring at his adversary. "Captain Jack, you will kill Canby!"

# Onslaught

*Lava Beds*
*April 11, 1873 (Good Friday)*

Captain Jack sat near the council tent, waiting for the Peace Commission to come. He glanced at the other Modoc, all checking their weapons and being sure they could hide them, then whip them out to slaughter the men coming under a truce flag.

"It is all over," Captain Jack said to Scarfaced Charley. Queen Mary moved closer and looked at him, obviously worried about him.

"You do not have to agree to this," Captain Jack's sister told him, but he only shook his head. Queen Mary saw how he had become trapped in dishonorable politics.

"I am ashamed of what will be done this day and my part in it. I never thought I would agree to such a thing only to remain *tyee*."

"You do what is best," Scarfaced Charley said, but the man's words fell flat. He obviously sympathized with Captain Jack and knew the *tyee* was right. This ambush was wrong, no matter what the white man had done before.

"I do it for my tribe," Captain Jack said. "I tell myself that, but is it true? Or do I only want to keep power?"

"What would happen with Curly Headed Doctor or Schonchin John leading us? The bloodshed would be immense," said

Queen Mary. "This way might not be honorable, but the whites will go away. We will win when Canby is dead."

Captain Jack was not so sure. The Modoc had lived among the whites for years, gotten along well with the settlers in Yreka. The Modoc wore white clothing and ate white food, strange as it was, and had been happy along Lost River. Women such as his cousin Winema married white men. Frank Riddle treated her better than a Modoc husband might. She was brave and good and lived in two worlds.

Two worlds.

That bothered Captain Jack the most. For all the years spent among the *boshtin,* the Modoc did not understand them. And from the way Canby—and Odeneal and so many others— acted, they did not understand the Modoc, either. The white settlers wanted Modoc land. That much was clear. Captain Jack was willing to fight them for it, as the Modoc did so many other tribes, but the rules were so different. If this meeting had been with the Klamath and Curly Headed Doctor and the others killed the Klamath *tyee,* the fight would be over. The Klamath would leave and the Modoc would be victors.

Captain Jack was worried this would not be so when they killed General Canby and the others. The whites fought with different weapons. How they viewed the world had always been a mystery to him.

"It is time for you and the other squaws to leave," Captain Jack told Queen Mary. Obediently, she gathered what she had brought and left. Captain Jack felt an even greater loss with his sister safely away now. It reinforced how treacherous this attack was.

"We will kill them and return to our ancestral land," Scarfaced Charley said, seemingly reading his thoughts. "You will lead us, Captain Jack, you will lead us out of this wilderness to a more plentiful life."

"Good," Captain Jack said sardonically. "My belly is empty more than it is filled. It's about time to eat."

Mentally, he added, *It is about time to betray a confidence and kill.*

Alfred Meacham rode with his eyes straight ahead. All he saw in the barren lava flow was death. Behind every dark upthrust of lava rock. In every rugged ravine. Across the few clearings dotted with knee-high fragrant sagebrush. Everywhere.

"You should go back before it is too late," Tobey Riddle said. She rode to Meacham's right and was as upset about this meeting at Captain Jack's council tent as he was. She had been warned and had told Meacham of the danger. But like him, she was caught in a web from which she could not escape.

"He looks as if he is the conqueror, the soldier who has won it all," Meacham said tiredly.

"Canby is a fool," Tobey said hotly.

"For not listening to your warning, just as I am for ignoring it," Meacham agreed. "But Canby is only doing what he thinks is best. It has worked for the Army before. He does not realize the Modoc don't fear him or the soldiers."

"Captain Jack fears him, but Curly Headed Doctor does not," Tobey said. "He thinks the Ghost Dance will protect all Indians. He is wrong. A bullet penetrates the strongest of medicines."

Meacham told her how Boston Charley had acted when it was obvious Meacham was not going to wear his new boots. From her expression, Meacham knew he had guessed right what it meant. Boston Charley had wanted those boots—after killing him in the council tent.

Meacham touched his breast pocket, his fingers tracing the outline of a derringer Fairchild had given him. This was a violation of the "no arms" agreement, but Meacham would never use it except in self-defense. It might be the only thing between saving himself and dying.

If he died, he had made John Fairchild promise that his body would be buried immediately, because he knew what the Modoc would do to a dead enemy's body. Meacham wanted to spare his family the horror of seeing his mutilated, scalped corpse.

"A good day, a Good Friday, indeed," Canby crowed as he slowed enough to let Meacham catch up with him. "We have won a marvelous victory."

"We should never have come," Meacham said. He glared at Reverend Thomas, who still did not understand the depth of his stupidity in agreeing to all of the Modoc's terms. Meeting in the Lava Beds was a major concession, but he had also allowed Captain Jack to set the rules for the meeting. Meacham had worked hard to avoid such a one-sided meeting, and now he rode into what Tobey Riddle was sure had been set up as an ambush.

He was sure. Tobey was sure. But neither Canby nor Thomas saw the danger.

Meacham hoped he was being an alarmist.

Canby pulled a watch from inside his dress uniform jacket and looked at it. "We are ahead of schedule. Almost ten A.M. and the treaty signing is not set until eleven. We shall be back in camp by late afternoon, with a telegram off to General Sherman. A fine day," Canby said, sucking in a lungful of springtime air and releasing it in a gust.

If they had not been riding into the middle of Captain Jack's stronghold, Meacham might have agreed. The day was gorgeous. The rain clouds from the prior day had vanished, leaving the ground damp and the flowers struggling to bloom. The air was fresh and the land, ugly as it was, appeared almost benign.

Meacham saw the entire spectrum of emotion among the others on the Peace Commission. Canby was confident. Reverend Thomas made notes as he swayed to and fro on his horse. Secretary Delano had appointed him without Meacham's agreement, and he held strange ideas Meacham could never share. Reverend Thomas was a Methodist minister and publisher of *The California Christian Advocate,* defending Quaker beliefs that if the Indians were always treated with generosity, they would respond in kind. Reverend Thomas's deep-set, pale eyes seemed almost lost under his bushy brows as he looked down at his diary. Unlike Meacham today, he had worn his Sunday-go-to-meeting clothes in an attempt to bring dignity to the meeting.

"At least he won't be scalped," Tobey said, seeing Meacham staring at the reverend.

It took Meacham a second to understand what she meant. Then he laughed. Reverend Thomas had almost no hair at all on his head.

Reverend Thomas felt their eyes on him and looked up, a beatific smile on his lips. "The will of the Lord will be done today," he said. Meacham was not sure what the man was talking about and did not bother responding.

"You cannot still miss the significance of this meeting, Mr. Meacham," said Canby. "We have won!"

"The will of the Lord will be done," Meacham answered, repeating what Reverend Thomas had just said.

"No, not that. You suspect treachery. They do not dare. I have my western force at Van Bremer's ranch, not three miles from Captain Jack's camp in the Lava Beds. And in this direction, why, we are only two miles away. Both elements are close enough to move in, should a field signal be given."

"You're planning on catching the Modoc between the two forces?"

"Not at all, but we are not alone, sir. I have scouts watching us."

"The Warm Springs Indians under McKay?"

"They are a part of the observation party," Canby said, uneasy at talking tactics with a civilian. "I did not rise to the rank of general by ignoring military concerns."

Meacham held his tongue. He had wondered how Canby had survived, much less risen through the ranks fighting Indians, since he seemed oblivious to the most blatant of facts.

"There," Canby said. "There is Captain Jack's council tent.

Do you see the Modoc?" He waved to the lead rider, a private, who trotted forward carrying the truce flag.

Meacham looked around but did not see the scouts Canby promised to have watching over them. As eager as McKay was to spill Modoc blood, Meacham doubted either the half-breed or his Warm Springs allies would venture out to rescue them if anything went wrong.

"Dismount!" Canby ordered, seeing the private's signal, the truce flag wagging back and forth twice. "Advance on foot!"

Colonel Gillem rode up from his position at the rear of the column and took his place beside his commander. The two officers exchanged words; then Gillem wheeled about and retreated. Reverend Thomas looked eager, and another man on the Peace Commission, a man named Dyar who was representing the settlers, seemed to be buoyed by the minister's faith. Both Tobey and Frank Riddle stayed close together. From the way Frank's hand twitched, Meacham knew the man was also armed, possibly with a six-shooter but definitely with a knife.

Canby had left even his saber back in camp, riding unarmed to the council tent.

Canby checked his watch, then snapped it shut. "They are late," he said.

"Not so late," Meacham said. The rocky basin where the council tent stood suddenly seemed to grow tall walls, sides like a huge grave. The Modoc appeared out of nowhere, paused, then came to some decision among themselves. Approaching, Captain Jack had with him all his principal rivals for power as the Modoc chief. Six braves stood behind them. Meacham swung around, then realized they had ridden down into the bottom of the rocky bowl, out of sight of the trailing scouts, even if they used field glasses.

"We should welcome them," Canby said, straightening his dress uniform.

"Count them," Meacham said. "There are three times as many of them as Boston Charley promised."

"So?" General Canby marched off, Reverend Thomas and Dyar hurrying to keep up, leaving Meacham and the Riddles to trail behind. Meacham took off his overcoat and laid it across his saddle, the heavy coat too warm for him now.

Meacham advanced cautiously, feeling more like a wolf's dinner than ever before, but to call off the council now guaranteed fighting. He had to trust Captain Jack and his ability to control the hotheads with him.

They went into the council tent, smoked a peace pipe, and each of the Peace Commission spoke briefly. Meacham was not even sure what he said. He felt like a rotted tooth wore on his senses, pulsing and paining him and blotting out everything around him. Somewhere in the middle of his talk, he looked out of the tent toward the northwest and Tule Lake.

Storm clouds.

Meacham did not believe in omens, but he found this almost too difficult to ignore. He hastily cut off his words, wanting the Modoc *tyee* to say his piece so they could sign the treaty and leave.

Hooker Jim suddenly jumped to his feet, speaking to Frank Riddle in Modoc. Meacham knew enough of the tongue to understand that Hooker Jim said, "Get out of the way!"

Both Captain Jack and Tobey spoke at the same time to Hooker Jim. "No!" they shouted. Then they looked at one another in horror. Tobey stepped across the tent and stood with the Peace Commission. Meacham read the movement to mean, "Kill them, kill me, too."

His hand rested on the derringer in his pocket, something not missed by Hooker Jim or any of the other Modoc.

For a moment, time stood still. No one moved, nothing was said. Then Canby spoke. "It is beginning to rain. We cannot talk while it is raining."

The pattering of drops on the canvas tent made hearing what was said harder but not impossible. However, Canby's words broke the spell that had gripped everyone.

"Who cares about the rain?" snapped Captain Jack. "You

stole our horses. You broke the armistice and are lower than a snake slithering through the Lava Beds! What do the Modoc fear from a little rain? You are better clothed than I am. Do you fear you will melt like snow?"

"You are being insulting," Canby said, his anger rising.

Meacham looked out the tent flap and saw Bogus Charley prowling about, as if he hunted for sagebrush to feed the council fire. For a moment, Meacham could not figure out why this bothered him. Then he realized the Modoc had brought no women with them to this meeting, as they had in the past. Hunting for firewood was woman's work, not that of a warrior.

Meacham looked at Frank Riddle, and then glanced outside so the translator would follow his gaze. Riddle's eyes went wide. Bogus Charley carried a rifle now. Hooker Jim jumped to his feet and went outside to join Bogus Charley. Both men pointed.

"Oh, no, what's going on?" Meacham groaned. The two Modoc had spotted a settler wandering about in the rocks. "Mr. Dyar," Meacham said. "Will you go out and see what is going on?"

"It's Clark. The danged fool is out here hunting for lost horses again," Dyar said. "I'll chase him off."

Meacham watched with bated breath until Dyar returned. The rain squall had passed as quickly as it had started, and again the day looked bright as a new penny.

The formalities began again, describing how the Modoc would act and what the government would do. Meacham conducted the talks but noted that Hooker Jim had returned but had not seated himself in the council circle. He paced like a trapped animal. He held a rifle now, also. When he ducked out of the tent again, he went to where the Americans' horses were tethered. Meacham saw Hooker Jim reach up and take the overcoat from Meacham's saddle.

"What are you doing?" Meacham called to Hooker Jim. "That's my coat."

"I'm old Meacham now," Hooker Jim said, looking admiringly at the coat. "Bogus Charley, you think I look like Meacham now?"

Bogus Charley came up, holding his rifle. Meacham found himself torn between the eyes fixed on him around the council circle and the two armed Modoc outside. He had to respond, but to make a mistake now would be deadly.

"Jim, if you want to look like me, you'd better take my hat, too."

"No," Hooker Jim said. He said something in Modoc to Bogus Charley. They both laughed.

Meacham looked to Frank Riddle, who had turned pale.

"Jim said to Charley, 'I will. There's no hurry to be an old man.'"

Of the Peace Commission, only Canby and Thomas missed what was really meant. They continued discussing the details with Captain Jack. Frank Riddle went to his wife and spoke at length with her. Tobey moved to the side of the tent, stretched and yawned, and then lay down as if she meant to sleep. From there she continued her translations. Meacham knew she was getting out of the way of bullets. Dyar had turned to stone. The man was marble-pale and rigid.

"Excuse me," Frank Riddle said. "There's something wrong with my horse."

Meacham watched the translator go out and position himself between his and Tobey's horses. Frank Riddle was getting ready to hightail it at the first sign of trouble, taking his wife with him.

Meacham turned to Canby and said loudly, hoping the general would understand what he wanted, "General Canby, tell Captain Jack how all your soldiers will be removed right away." Meacham wanted Canby to lie, to give them time, possibly to bring Captain Jack back to thinking a treaty was possible.

The general stood and struck a pose. "That will not be possible, removing all soldiers, because they have been sent by the President of the United States. But you need not fear them.

The soldiers will protect all Americans, red and white, and cannot be transferred without our president's order."

Meacham closed his eyes and shuddered. Canby had said exactly the wrong things to ease the tension. He rattled on about prior commands and Indian fights he had won. Meacham cringed when Canby told how he was the Indians' friend and another tribe had given him the name "Tall Man" because he was so much greater in height. Canby even went on to say that the Modoc would someday treat him as their friend, also.

Reverend Thomas began his speech, but Meacham was fixed on Captain Jack. He realized how the Modoc *tyee* was as much a prisoner as they were. Curly Headed Doctor and Schonchin John sat on either side of him, as if they guarded him and kept him from siding with the Americans. Meacham hoped that, when the fighting started, Captain Jack would come to their rescue.

Captain Jack suddenly stood and said, "I must go outside."

Meacham tensed, wondering if this was the signal for an attack. Or did the Modoc chief only have to relieve himself? As Captain Jack left, Schonchin John took Captain Jack's place.

The man's belligerence was at odds with how forcedly polite the meeting had been up to this point.

"Give us back Hot Creek," Schonchin John said. "And no soldiers. Take them all away."

Meacham saw Captain Jack stop in his tracks outside, then turn.

Meacham rushed to reduce the tensions again.

"Did Fairchild and Dorris tell you that you could have Hot Creek?" he asked Schonchin John. "They own Hot Creek. It is theirs, not the government's, to give away."

Schonchin John shouted, "Take away the soldiers! Give us Hot Creek! Give us Hot Creek or quit talking!"

Captain Jack walked slowly back to the tent. On the far side of the rocky bowl Meacham saw two young Modoc running out, each carrying a half-dozen rifles.

"Captain Jack, what's the meaning of this?" Meacham demanded.

Captain Jack ignored him. He pushed aside his coat and drew a pistol he had carried shoved into his belt.

"Now!" shouted Captain Jack. He lifted the pistol, cocked it, and pointed it at Canby's head. Meacham cried out when Captain Jack pulled the trigger.

The gun misfired.

The Americans stood around, paralyzed by the sudden attack. Captain Jack turned the cylinder and again pointed it at Canby's head. The general did not move, frozen by the treachery of the attack. The report as the gun fired filled Meacham's ears. Canby jerked back. The bullet entered his face just under his left eye, a killing shot this time.

Canby fell to the ground but miraculously thrashed about and somehow regained his feet. His face had turned to a gory mask, and he blundered about, blinded by pain and blood. The general stumbled from the council tent, Captain Jack and another Modoc, Ellen's Man George, hot on his heels. Canby got only a few yards before catching his foot on a hunk of rock and tumbling facedown. Meacham heard the general's jaw break from the fall.

Captain Jack quickly pinned Canby's arms, then plunged a knife into his throat. Canby gurgled and feebly kicked, not dead but definitely dying.

Captain Jack and Ellen's Man George started stripping his body, getting the general's uniform off him before it became too bloody.

"He's been killed!" Meacham shouted, struggling with Schonchin John. Outside he saw the Modoc boy, Sloluck, with the rifles toss one to Captain Jack and another to the warrior taking Canby's brightly polished boots.

Meacham struggled, kicked out, and forced Schonchin John to the ground, more by luck than skill. The Modoc was stronger and more agile, but desperation drove Meacham. He staggered in the same direction Canby had already taken, getting out of the tent. Meacham saw Captain Jack's brother Black Jim tearing out after Frank Riddle. Black Jim fired wildly, then skidded to a halt and looked behind him. Scarfaced Charley stood there, a rifle in his hand. The other boy, Barncho, had armed the remainder of the Modoc peace party.

Meacham could not tell if Scarfaced Charley would have shot Black Jim in the back had he killed Riddle, but the expression on Jim's face said that was possible. From behind, still in the council tent, Meacham heard Bogus Charley fire and Reverend Thomas gasp in pain and cry out, "Don't shoot me again, Charley. I'm dying anyway."

Meacham crashed into another Modoc warrior and bounced off in time to see Reverend Thomas stumble from the tent. Hope flared. Thomas was escaping! Then Meacham realized the Modoc were playing with the reverend the way a cat toys with a mouse.

"Turn the bullets away from your foul hearts," Boston Charley taunted. "Isn't your medicine as strong as ours?"

Reverend Thomas tumbled to the ground, tried to stand, and was pushed down.

"Maybe you will believe what a squaw tells you," Boston Charley said, for once towering over the reverend. A Modoc with a rifle came up, shoved the muzzle against Thomas's head, and fired. Then the Modoc and Boston Charley set to stripping his body.

Meacham swung with all his might and connected with Schonchin John's chin. A shock ran up his arm, and pain exploded in his hand and shoulder from the force of the impact. Meacham fumbled for the derringer and shoved it in front of him as Schonchin John recovered. Derringer against John's chest, Meacham pulled the trigger.

It misfired.

Meacham frantically tried again. Misfire. He shoved away from Schonchin John, stared at the temperamental two-barrel gun, and saw he had failed to cock it fully. Before he could fire, Schonchin John whipped out his pistol and fired.

Meacham ducked, hot lead ripping past his cheek and causing him to lose his balance. He reached up and felt where the bullet had torn his collar. A charred smell warned him that the nearness of the shot and the powder spewing from Schonchin John's gun had singed his full beard.

"Back, stay back," Meacham said, trying to retreat. He shoved the derringer out at arm's length and waved it about. Schonchin John emptied his pistol at Meacham, the shots going wild as the Modoc's anger mounted.

When John's pistol came up empty, Meacham felt a surge of hope.

"Stop," he said, threatening the would-be killer with the fully cocked derringer. Meacham saw John had a second pistol and was unlimbering it.

"Don't kill him, don't kill him!" shrieked Tobey Riddle. She tackled Schonchin John and knocked him to the ground, wrestling with him. The Modoc who had stripped Reverend Thomas's body hurried over and slugged Tobey with the butt of his rifle. Meacham tried to run, to dodge, to move. He stood frozen with fear.

Shacknasty Jim grabbed the rifle from the Modoc's hand and said, "I'll get him." He turned and aimed carefully at Meacham.

"Shoot me, you son of a bitch!" screamed Meacham. He tapped his chest. "Go on. Shoot me, you thieving coward!"

Shacknasty Jim squeezed back on the rifle trigger, but he had not counted on Tobey rejoining the fray. She knocked the rifle barrel up just as Shacknasty Jim fired. Meacham felt a lance of hot pain, but not in the chest. The bullet grazed the side of his head, hurting like the blazes and doubling his vision. He twisted about and fell heavily to the ground.

"I got him, I got him!" Shacknasty Jim boasted. Meacham realized he had one chance only in the middle of the massacre and had to take it. Blood gushed all over his face, but he was still conscious. Blind in the left eye, Meacham squinted through his right as Schonchin John came over, thinking the leader of the Peace Commission was dead.

Meacham rolled onto his side and fired point-blank into Schonchin John's chest. The Modoc gasped, clutched his breast, and fell. Then new pain ripped through Meacham's body as Shacknasty Jim shot at him again, this round tearing through his right arm. The derringer slipped from nerveless fingers. The world spun in wild and crazy circles as another round smashed into his skull. Meacham was more unconscious than alert. He felt his body twitching uncontrollably, but it was as if he watched someone else.

Eager hands ripped at his clothing, pulling it off his body. His scuffed boots were yanked from his feet, then someone sat him up to remove his vest. Buttons went flying. A distant voice, almost an echo in the back of his mind, said, "You don't need to shoot. He's dead. I want the shirt without any holes."

Shacknasty Jim? Meacham was not sure who took his vest and shirt. From the distance came Captain Jack's strong, distinctive voice giving orders in Modoc. But closer, Meacham heard Boston Charley say, "You white-hearted squaw. They all died. You are no Modoc. Go. Take care of this carrion."

Meacham drifted in and out of consciousness, unable to see because of the blood in his eyes. He heard rather than saw Captain Jack ordering retreat from the massacre. Then gentle hands dabbed away some of the blood on his face.

"You are alive!"

"Tobey?"

"Hush, don't move. They think you are dead." Tobey wiped away more of the blood, giving Meacham a view of the council tent and the area around it. Stripped naked, Edward Canby was undeniably dead. Blackbirds came to peck at his eyes and the softer parts of his body. Beyond him lay the half-stripped body of Reverend Thomas. Meacham could not tell if the man was dead or alive. Probably dead.

And he lay in his red-flannel union suit, head cradled in Tobey Riddle's lap.

Meacham had to use all his self-control not to shudder when he heard Boston Charley approaching. The treacherous Modoc said, "I want Old Meacham's scalp. That will make a fine addition to my collection."

Hooker Jim laughed and said, "What scalp? He's bald!"

Boston Charley pushed Tobey away. Meacham forced himself to lie still as death, because if Charley saw that he was alive, that condition would change fast. Strong, blood-covered fingers grasped the shock of hair on the top of his head and pulled. The sharp edge of a knife cut into his scalp.

"This is the best scalp I've ever seen," Boston Charley bragged.

"Be careful. If you drop it, you'll never find it again," Hooker Jim joked.

A half-circle cut lifted the scalp away. As Boston Charley moved to finish the cut, Tobey cried, "Soldiers! Soldiers are coming!"

Boston Charley and Hooker Jim ran away, leaving Meacham alone with Tobey.

"Soldiers," he said weakly. "We're saved."

"No soldiers," she said. "I lied, but they believed me. Guilty consciences." She held him, head in her lap, rocking him like a small baby, trying to soothe him.

The slaughter was over by 12:15 P.M. The Warm Springs scouts alerted Gillem sometime later, and the rescue party rode into the Lava Beds to find the body of the only general to be killed in the Indian wars, along with what remained of the rest of the Peace Commission.

# Victory Celebration

Captain Jack felt no triumph after killing Canby and the others in the Peace Commission. His warriors laughed and danced around their campfires while he brooded.

In the middle of the celebration, playing the role of conqueror, Schonchin John might have been *tyee*. Captain Jack considered challenging John to a fight to decide the matter, then knew it would not work. The tribe voted for *tyee*. If he killed Schonchin John, that left Curly Headed Doctor and so many others who thought they were better suited at being chief. Captain Jack felt the heavy responsibility on his shoulders of guiding the Modoc through increasingly dangerous times. Unlike Schonchin John and Curly Headed Doctor, he doubted the *boshtin* would go away because Canby had been killed.

"I have the prize!" cried Schonchin John, holding Canby's gold watch high over his head. The watch turned slowly on its gold chain, catching light from the fires like some alien beacon. "I will award it to the one who deserves it most."

Captain Jack got to his feet and dusted off his pants. It was time to lead. He stepped forward as Schonchin John began the presentation.

"For the courageous fighter who killed the white man's *tyee,* I give this watch to . . . Ellen's Man George."

Captain Jack froze, stunned at this perfidy. He had killed Canby. Ellen's Man George had only joined in stripping the body. It had been Captain Jack's knife that had slit the general's throat, his bullet that had blinded him.

The gathered tribe went wild, cheering and trying to touch Ellen's Man George as he came forward to take the watch. He looked at Schonchin John, then grinned, a broken tooth showing in front. Ellen's Man George let out a howl that rivaled any wolf's.

Captain Jack felt his authority slipping away. He pushed through the ring of warriors into the light. Nodding in Ellen's Man George's direction, he held up his hand for silence. Reluctantly, the Modoc quieted to hear what their *tyee* had to say.

"It was a good day," Captain Jack said, having no way to describe his shame at the slaughter. "Except Hooker Jim. He let Dyar escape." A murmur went up. Modoc slipped back, leaving Hooker Jim alone near the fire.

"It was not my fault he ran like a rabbit, too fast for even me to catch!"

"He escaped, and Dyar has the authority to bring the soldiers. Are we so safe here in the Lava Beds? The white men will be furious at us for killing their *tyee*. Meacham had friends among the settlers. Men like Fairchild who might have gone along with a treaty now see us as enemies."

"Do you think they will dare attack us?" asked Scarfaced Charley, helping his friend.

"Yes!"

The silence this time was complete. Wind blowing through the lava rocks whined mournfully. Drops of rain fell, causing hissing, swirling columns of steam to rise from the celebratory fires. Somewhere far off in the Lava Beds a coyote cried.

"What should we do?" asked Schonchin John, chin thrust out belligerently. Captain Jack's heart beat faster now. His enemies came to him for advice and leadership. It was time for him to toss them a scrap to keep them in line.

"Curly Headed Doctor," Captain Jack called loudly. "Protect us with your Ghost Dance!"

Whispers turned into outright agreement. The red tule rope still circled the clearing where they camped, protecting them all. But a new Ghost Dance would increase the security, and the shaman began to chant. Drums picked up the beat and a few danced fitfully. More joined. And more and even more when Curly Headed Doctor started the chanting in earnest.

Captain Jack joined the Ghost Dance, not sure if it would help. But it could not hurt.

# Out of Touch

*Linkville, Oregon*
*April 11, 1873*

"What can I do, AB?" Joshua Harlan asked his injured friend.

"You can get the hell out of the surgery and let him rest," the doctor snapped, glaring at Josh. Josh ignored the man because Meacham was trying to talk. A weak hand reached up and fell on top of Josh's.

"A moment, sir," Josh pleaded. "He's trying to talk."

"It was an ambush," Meacham said. "Jack killed Canby."

"We know all that, AB. Don't tire yourself telling me what Tobey already has."

"She's a real heroine," Meacham said, voice gravelly but growing stronger. "Saved me. Saw Reverend Thomas murdered. And Canby."

"Yes, yes," Josh said, heartsick at the condition of his friend. "Dyar got away and brought Colonel Gillem to rescue you." This was not strictly true, Josh knew, but it soothed Meacham hearing someone on the Peace Commission had tried to save the others. McKay's Warm Springs scouts had fetched Gillem with a warning of what had happened. Josh had to give the colonel his due. Once Gillem learned of the Modoc attack, he wasted no time moving a company of soldiers to the council tent.

"Don't let Gillem attack the Modoc. I don't think Captain Jack wanted to kill Canby, but he had to."

"He had to? I don't understand. Did the general attack him first? Was it self-defense?"

"No, no, the Modoc ambushed us. Captain Jack was only trying to keep his position as *tyee*. Hooker Jim and Schonchin John want to be chief."

"They'll all be dead soon enough," Josh said firmly. "I don't know what plans the Army has, but Canby's murder cannot go unanswered."

Josh waited for Meacham to get his strength back. He saw how badly wounded his friend was. Two head wounds, one bullet ripping off his eyebrow. But what fascinated and repelled him at the same time was how close Meacham had come to being scalped. The doctor had stitched the scalp back, but the cut was like an angry red beacon for Josh, symbolizing all that had gone wrong between the whites and the Modoc.

"Let me tell you what I know. Don't talk. Just shake your head if I have something wrong." Josh pulled out his notebook with the words recorded from the accounts of Tobey Riddle, her husband Frank, Dyar, and a few of the troopers who had ridden into the slaughterhouse with Colonel Gillem. The colonel himself had refused to comment, leaving Josh to find out what he could from other sources.

He methodically detailed the horrors, in spite of how pale Meacham became. He hated putting his friend through this but had to file his story quickly, getting the details right before the other reporters put out their sensationalistic stories.

Josh swallowed hard. The truth was sensational enough.

He finished, asking, "Is this all right, AB?"

"Yes."

"Get out or I'll have the marshal toss you in the clink," the doctor said, fingers like claws on Josh's shoulder. "I let you pester him enough. He needs to rest. Sleep. Lots of it."

"Yes, sir, I know," Josh said, closing his notebook. He

squeezed Meacham's hand. "I'll be back to see how you're doing."

Meacham already slept fitfully and did not hear the promise.

Josh left quickly, going to the telegraph office. It surprised him there was not a long line of reporters waiting to send their inflammatory stories across the country to New York and other places around the world. He went in. The telegrapher sat with his feet hiked up to his desk, reading a penny dreadful. The man pushed his green eyeshades back and looked at Josh.

"Won't do you any good," the man called.

"What's wrong? I need to send a telegram."

"The *Alta California?* Yep, figured it was. Sorry. The line out is down."

"When will it be fixed? This is important!"

"Figured it was," the telegrapher said, "but I can't send over lines that are down. Reckon the Indians might have cut the wires. If that's happened, it'll take days to find the break."

"Why? A rider can see if the line is cut," Josh said.

"Not that easy. They're crafty devils, them Indians. They tie rawhide strips on the wire and then cut it. The connection's broken but the wire's still up. Takes a man with good vision to see that's happened."

"Why do you think the Indians are responsible?"

"Might not be, but what do you think?"

"I've got to get this to my editor," Josh said, mind racing. This was the story of the century, and he had interviews with the survivors, something no other reporter had. He was torn between waiting for the telegraph to be repaired and getting the news to his editor.

"Yreka?" he asked. "What about a telegraph from there?"

"Might be all right. Can't say since—"

"Your line's down," Josh said in disgust. "Thanks."

He went straight back to the small room he shared with Isabella. Isabella looked up and smiled.

"You are back early," she said, although it was almost midnight.

"I've got to go to San Francisco. If I ride straight through, I can get the story to Mr. Billingsly in a couple days."

"The telegraph?"

"Down," Josh said, hastily packing. "I wonder if the Modoc are responsible or something else has happened. I wouldn't put it past other reporters to submit their story, then destroy the wires to keep anyone else from reporting. It's about time I talked face-to-face with my editor, anyway. I deserve more than the piecemeal assignment pay I've been getting." Josh frowned, realizing how distant Mr. Billingsly had become in answering his queries. It was almost as if the editor wanted to cut him loose but couldn't, because of the quality of his reporting. Josh couldn't make head nor tail of that.

"You go?" Isabella sounded devastated.

"I have to," Josh said. "I'll be back as fast as I can. I don't think the Army will get organized fast enough to attack within a week, especially now that General Canby is dead."

"I will miss you," Isabella said. She stood close to him, very close. Josh hesitated. He wanted to kiss her. Isabella closed her eyes and her lips parted slightly.

"And I'll miss you," he said, giving her a quick, unsatisfying hug. "Be back like a flash."

He left, feeling as if he had made a terrible mistake and not knowing what it was.

# Retaliation

"Mr. McKay," Colonel Gillem said, glaring at the leader of his Indian scouts. "Why have you not located the Modoc camp more precisely?"

"They've been movin' round a lot," Don McKay lied. "I got them Warm Springs Indians out to find them. The Modoc won't have anywhere to hide in another couple hours."

Gillem seethed. He turned and looked at the bluffs where Captain Bernard had worked so diligently putting in the howitzers and mortars. All day Gillem had had the artillerymen working to strike the positions and move all powder and shell down. The artillery would accompany any incursion into the Lava Beds. Leaving it on the bluffs wasted valuable ordnance. He wished Bernard had not been transferred to Fort Klamath, at the officer's request. Gillem appreciated an outspoken officer, even if Colonel Wheaton had not.

Gillem grated his teeth as he thought of Wheaton. The man was a thorn in his side, especially now that Canby was dead. Gillem's position was secure enough, having been assured by General Canby, but Wheaton commanded factions among the officers who supported *him*. Whatever happened now had to be done swiftly, with decisive force, and carried to ultimate success.

"Find them in those cursed lava flows," Gillem said. "I want my artillery to blow them to smithereens!"

"You'll get yer targets," McKay promised. "And, uh, Colonel, there's the matter of pay. The general kept saying he was going to give my scouts some money but never got round to it."

"What's that? The Warm Springs Indians are on the payroll, as are you. If you have not been paid, take it up with the paymaster."

"Well, Colonel, he said you had to approve the money."

"We shall deal with this after the Modoc are reduced to mewling babes!"

"Sorry, sir," McKay said, "but them's my people you're talking about." McKay spat. "Don't care for them, but that's got nothin' to do with me workin' for free."

Gillem had no idea if Canby had already ordered pay for McKay and the Indian scouts. He had been too busy working with the infantry to know such details.

"I shall speak directly to the paymaster," Gillem said, knowing he could put any payment on hold for weeks, if he chose. And he did. He disliked McKay almost as much as the man disliked him.

"What's the plan?" asked McKay.

"Cannonade beginning before dawn. I want my howitzers to commence firing by four A.M. Supplies are being brought in from Fairchild's ranch to give every foot soldier a three-day supply of rations. Wagons that will supply ammunition and more foodstuffs are being assembled now."

"You thinkin' on invading Captain Jack's Stronghold tomorrow?"

"After the artillery has softened the resistance," Gillem said. "Canby's death is a travesty, an affront that will not go unanswered."

"Got them orders from General Sherman, did you?" asked McKay, looking sideways at the colonel.

"Find the Modoc's main camp, sir," Colonel Gillem said.

"If your scouts are not out of the Lava Beds by four A.M., they might find it difficult ever getting out."

"Best get to it, then, Colonel," McKay said, giving a mocking salute as he left. Gillem stared at the half-breed Modoc scout's back and experienced even more anger. Every last Modoc was impudent and needed a strict upbraiding, and that included McKay with his attempted extortion of Army funds.

Gillem barked for his adjutant and assembled his senior officers.

"Send my regards to Colonel Wheaton," he told a courier, "and tell him I am following his invasion plan, with minor changes." The courier hurried off to tell Wheaton. When he was out of earshot, Gillem sneered and said, "The only difference is that, this time, we will crush them!"

He started assigning duties to his staff, preparing for the artillery barrage to be followed by an on-foot invasion just after dawn.

# No Longer Home

*San Francisco, California*
*April 13, 1873*

Joshua Harlan stood on the cobblestone street in front of his house. His and Faith's house. He looked at the large house with the eyes of an outsider. It was huge, in a classy neighborhood at the foot of Nob Hill, and cost more than he would earn as a reporter in a hundred years, but Faith had insisted, and her father had given it to her as a wedding present.

Josh touched the gold band on his left ring finger and knew he had been faithful to his wife, no matter what she thought. Still, Josh found Isabella blurring together with Faith in his mind. But the feelings he held for Isabella were so different from those for Faith. Faith was his wife, and he loved her.

It was very hard to walk to the front door. It was even harder to go in. Josh almost knocked, as if he were just a visitor and did not live here.

He went in and called, "Faith! I'm back. Faith!"

He heard rummaging from the direction of the study and went along the hall. He looked in and saw the lovely redhead industriously working at a letter. She was so engrossed, she had not heard him.

"Faith," he said more softly. This time she heard and jumped, startled.

"Joshua!"

"I came to town because the telegraph lines were down. I had a story to deliver to Mr. Billingsly, then I came by." The delight on her face faded as he spoke, and he realized why. He had thought more of his job at the *Alta* than he had of her. He had filed his story before coming to his wife.

"I see. It occurs to me I should have the lock on the front door changed."

"It wasn't locked," Josh said, taken aback by his wife's odd comment.

"It will be, from now on," she said, her nostrils flaring. "Please leave."

"This is my house."

"My father gave me this house. You hardly ever lived here."

"While I worked for him, I did. Faith, I—"

"Joshua, leave. Get out. I don't ever want to see you again. Go back to your . . . your Indian whore!"

"That's not fair," he said. "Isabella is no bawd, and I told you that we never—"

"Don't lie to me. I saw how you looked at her. You never looked at me like that. Go, Joshua, go or I'll call the police to have you removed."

"This is my house, too."

"Here," she said, rummaging through the papers on the desk. She found a thick booklet and shoved it at him, as if he might burn her if she so much as brushed his flesh.

"What is it?" Josh opened it and read quickly, then looked up. "You want a divorce?"

"It's all there. Sign it."

"I love you, Faith, though for the life of me, I cannot remember why." He glanced back at the divorce papers. "Why did you marry me?"

"I loved you, or the man you used to be."

"You married someone you thought would irritate your father," Josh said angrily. "You thought you could walk all over me and make Sean Murdoch realize you were no longer under his thumb. But it didn't work that way, did it? I refused to let him—or you—dictate to me."

"I thought you had potential," Faith said, a flush coming to her pale cheeks. "I was wrong. You want to do nothing but fritter away your time with your Indian mistress."

"I am a reporter, and the war up north is worth reporting. Everyone should know."

"Who *cares?*" Faith wailed. "Only you. When this so-called war is over, what then? You'll be off to another war? What about me? You left me alone." She made that sound like the ultimate insult.

Josh hesitated, then said coldly, "Not so very much alone. How often does your lover come by to service you?" It had been a shot in the dark, but when Faith wobbled slightly, turning faint, he knew he had hit a bull's-eye.

"How did you know?" She put her hand to her throat.

"I'm a reporter. I have sources," he said.

"It's all your fault! If you had stayed here, I would never have—"

"Faith," he said, suddenly drained of all emotion. "I never slept with Isabella. And I find myself totally uninterested in what you do." He put the papers on the desk, picked up the pen Faith had used to write her letter, and signed the divorce papers with a flourish.

"I'll be an outcast," she said in a choked voice.

"I'm heading back to Linkville right away. None of your precious society friends will ever hear of your indiscretions from me." He stared at her, trying to remember how he had once felt about her. It was all burned out. "Ask the social editor at the *Alta California* about your friends. He knows about their secret affairs. He probably even knows about yours."

"Joshua, wait," Faith said as he started to leave.

"It's all yours, Faith. All of it. The house, what belongings I've left, every bit of it. I have to get back north right away.

I can get there by tomorrow night, if I make the right train connections."

He closed the door behind him and stopped in the street. He wondered if Faith was looking out the front window at him. If he turned and saw her, would he go back into the house?

Josh never looked back as he hurried to the Embarcadero. He could catch the ferry to Oakland, get the train north to Sacramento, and pick up his horse again and see how AB Meacham was doing, what stage the war was entering, how the Modoc were reacting.

And there was Isabella. He knew now what his mistake had been when he had left her to come back to San Francisco.

# Attack!

*Lava Beds*
*April 13, 1873*

The cannon had fired constantly since four A.M. Colonel Gillem's head hurt from the sound, and he walked unsteadily because the very ground under his feet rocked with the impact of every shell out in the Lava Beds. Anyone—or anything—in the range of the guns had to be reduced to bloody parts by now.

Colonel Gillem had expected McKay to return with a report, but the scout and the Warm Springs Indians with him had never appeared. They might have been caught in the Lava Beds when the firing began, or they might never have gone on their scout. Gillem knew that such intelligence was important, but not vital. He would have no trouble finding the Modoc once he entered the Lava Beds.

He smiled wryly. Colonel Wheaton had experienced no trouble at all finding the renegades. His problem had been in killing them before they killed his soldiers.

Colonel Gillem was going to follow Wheaton's general invasion plan, but with one difference: He would succeed. He mounted his horse and looked out over the companies of nervous, restive soldiers waiting for the order to advance. Gillem had ordered his officers to do nothing to calm the troops. The sergeants had put them even more on edge. Gillem wanted the soldiers jumping at shadows, staying alert and alive. Wheaton's problem had been the damnable fog and the fear of the Modoc coming out of it, barely seen, firing and then vanishing as if they had become fog themselves.

The day was bright and clear. The only clouds to be seen were those caused by the wisps from his cannon. And the white smoke was carried off by a brisk wind blowing off Tule Lake to the northeast.

"Forward, march!" Gillem gave the order, and it was passed down the ranks in a ragged ripple of commands. He trotted off, the infantry coming after him. Gillem was as alert as any soldier in the ranks. He knew every detail of Wheaton's failure and vowed to avoid the mistakes made by his predecessor.

As the lava flows began to turn more rugged, Gillem passed the word back to the artillerists to cease fire, load their cannon and get the caissons moving up behind in support. They had done their work for the moment, blasting apart huge sections of the Lava Beds. No battle could be won with artillery assault alone. Land had to be occupied. The enemy had to be rooted out and either captured or killed. Nothing less would suffice in this war.

Gillem heard the muttering as he rode at the head of the column. The men feared what they would find in Captain Jack's Stronghold, as they had taken to calling it. He had to show them they had nothing to fear but their own officers' ire. From his vantage astride his dashing white stallion, Gillem kept an eagle eye on the land stretching ahead, the deep ravines, the ragged lava, the occasional clearing.

They reached the council tent where the massacre had occurred by ten A.M. without seeing any Modoc warriors or firing a single shot. Gillem took time to rest his men and let them see where the heinous murders had taken place.

He had four hundred soldiers in his detachment. A similar number waited on the western perimeter, posted to prevent the Modoc from escaping. If Captain Jack ran, it would be to the north, in an attempt to get across Tule Lake and return to the land claimed by the Modoc along Lost River.

"Sir, McKay sent a courier. One of them Warm Springs Injuns," reported a sergeant. "The scout lit out again, like somebody set fire to his, uh, his behind, sir."

"What did he say, Sergeant?" It surprised Gillem that McKay had even entered the Lava Beds, much less found anything to report.

"Modoc ahead on this trail, sir. Lots of 'em."

"Lots?" Gillem arched his eyebrow and smiled lopsidedly. "How precise. Tell your soldiers to stay alert. We move out in ten minutes."

Gillem mounted and rode around the clearing in the rocky bowl. The council tent was splattered with blood, the canvas ruined. The thirsty ground was stained red with the Peace Commissioners' blood. Gillem felt a coldness in his gut when he saw a rock near the tent covered not only with blood but also patches of hair. Was this where Canby had died so foully? Or Reverend Thomas?

Gillem saw how inept the butchery had really been. Too many of the Peace Commission had escaped. Some, like Alfred Meacham, had been seriously injured, but Dyar had escaped with only minor wounds. The Riddles were unharmed.

But Edward R.S. Canby was dead, and this caused Gillem's blood to boil.

"Move out!" he shouted, waving his arm in the direction that led deeper into the heart of Captain Jack's stronghold.

Less than a half hour later the first bullet sang through the air, winging a corporal in the leading company. Before Gillem could stop it, the soldiers had frantically returned fire—a hundred times over.

"Don't waste your ammunition," Gillem ordered angrily, "but take any good shot you have. Watch for those red devils and kill them! A bonus of ten dollars to the soldier who bags the first Modoc!"

The advance slowed when Gillem's men met with stiffening

fire. He ordered them into a skirmish line and met the Modoc fire with a withering fusillade that forced back the attacking Indians. Gillem sent out observers, who reported back when the Indians no longer shot at the soldiers.

"How many of them?" Gillem asked the corporal who had led the scouts.

"Eight, sir. That's all of them I seen. Eight!"

"Very good, son. Return to your platoon. Expect this kind of fighting until the Modoc are driven out."

"Sir, yes, sir!"

Gillem ordered his troops to advance, and they fought for every single foot. The Modoc had fired from fog and faded away when they fought Wheaton's troops. They tried to do the same now, but Gillem chased them. Without the fog, they had a more difficult time escaping, but escape they did, using their intimate knowledge of the Lava Beds.

Colonel Gillem was not discouraged. He knew the Modoc expected him to retreat as the daylight faded, but he did not leave. Finding a large clearing, he ordered his soldiers to pitch a camp. He posted twice the usual number of sentries, then went to the top of a tall lava rock with his signal flagman.

"Relay the message to the artillerists," he told the flagman. The long staff wagged from side to side, sending the message to another trooper just within the Lava Beds. From there an officer relayed the orders to the artillery officer commanding the slower-moving unit.

"Commence firing at sundown and fire all night long. Do not cease. Do not slacken the cannonade until dawn, at which time the troops in the Lava Beds will continue their assault on foot."

The flagman looked at him, eyes wide. Then he passed along the orders.

It was a long, frightening night. The howitzers thundered again and again, their shells rocking the ground under the tents pitched by the soldiers. The sentries jumped at shadows and occasionally shot at a rabbit—or one another.

Colonel Gillem listened to all the sounds, but the one missing pleased him. He heard nothing from the Modoc.

"If you aren't frightened yet, Captain Jack," Gillem said to himself, "you shall be. Very soon, you will become terrified!"

# The Second Battle for the Stronghold

*Lava Beds*
*April 15, 1873*

The ground shook, causing Captain Jack to clap his hands over his ears. Would the shelling ever stop? For two days Gillem's men had pushed deeper into the Lava Beds. Nothing Captain Jack had done had slowed their progress.

And the bombardment! The exploding shells were some distance from the Modoc camp, but the thunderous sound drove him to distraction. He could not concentrate with the whine of falling shells so quickly followed by the ground-shaking explosions. All night long the cannonade continued, and day brought more fighting with the soldiers. The first night, Bogus Charley and some of the others had gone out and taunted Gillem's sentries, hoping to lure them into a trap. It struck Captain Jack as dreadful irony now that the Modoc had mimicked artillerists loading and firing their howitzers. Little did they know that first night that Gillem would not retreat and would constantly pound at their senses with his blaring cannon.

"Gillem has stopped his advance," Scarfaced Charley reported. "We caught him at the place where the wind cries."

Captain Jack knew the spot well. Deep ravines and a twisting hairpin trail made the going difficult for a large group of soldiers. For a few fleet-of-foot braves it was simple to get through. From hiding spots in the pockmarked lava rocks, the Modoc could kill as they pleased. But retreat was difficult for them if Gillem went farther, stranding the Modoc snipers behind enemy lines.

"How many have we killed?" Captain Jack hoped to turn Gillem around and force the colonel out of the Lava Beds as they had done to Wheaton. But the weather worked against the Modoc now. No fog. Clear days let the artillery lob shells farther and farther into the wasteland, guided by Gillem's spotters. The first day, Captain Jack's braves had killed a few of those soldiers directing the artillery fire. Then Gillem had begun sending squads of soldiers out with them as protection.

Captain Jack jerked when the new barrage began. It tore at his nerves.

"Not enough," Scarfaced Charley admitted. "We fight and run. We have to. Our warriors cannot skirmish as they did against Wheaton's soldiers. Gillem's bluecoats stand and fight. He brought supplies with him, so he does not need to leave the Lava Beds to feed his troops."

"Be sure he gets no new supplies," Captain Jack said. He looked around with growing anxiety when he saw his brother, Humpy Joe, scuttling in from the north. The man's expression told Captain Jack he did not bring good news.

"Kintpuash," Joe said, out of breath. "Too many soldiers!"

"I know that," Captain Jack said, irritated. He knew he should not be angry with his brother, but the explosions all around his camp made him jittery. "Where's the water I sent you to fetch?"

"All gone. All the squaws you sent with me are gone. Captured by the soldiers."

"No water?" cried Scarfaced Charley. "We're almost out of water. What happened?"

"Two companies of soldiers, one coming from the east and the other from the west," Humpy Joe said, fearing his brother's wrath but spewing out the words to get them said. "They joined forces along the southern lakeshore. We cannot get water now from Tule Lake, not without fighting the soldiers for it."

"Cut off?" Captain Jack experienced a coldness in his belly that refused to go away. They had food. They could steal more from Army supply wagons, but water was a different matter. The spring runoffs had been sparse, forcing them to rely on water from Tule Lake. If the troopers blocked them in that direction, the Modoc would get thirsty mighty fast.

"They caught all the squaws and took them away," Humpy Joe said. "I hid. I came back to warn you."

"What do you say about this?" Captain Jack demanded of Curly Headed Doctor. The shaman and Schonchin John had come up to listen to the voice of impending defeat.

"He is lying," Curly Headed Doctor said flatly. "The Ghost Dance protects anyone going to the lake. He betrayed the squaws to the white soldiers."

Captain Jack looked up and saw a fiery streak above their camp. He had no time to cry out or to warn the others. The shell landed twenty feet away, in the middle of a campfire, and exploded forcefully enough to knock them off their feet. A crater a yard deep and six feet across remained where there had been a firepit.

"They are firing into our camp!" Scarfaced Charley hurried off to see if anyone had been hurt.

Humpy Joe struggled to get to his knees. His mouth hung open in dismay; then he said what had already occurred to Captain Jack. "The white man's medicine is stronger than the Ghost Dance. They are shooting at us *inside* the red rope!"

"He's right," Captain Jack said. "The great medicine of the Ghost Dance is gone."

"No!" shouted Curly Headed Doctor. "We can do another Ghost Dance. We—" He staggered when another shell landed fifty yards away, outside the red tule rope, but still near enough to shake the ground and upset the men like rocking tenpins.

Schonchin John grabbed Curly Headed Doctor's shoulder

and pulled him away from Captain Jack. The Modoc *tyee* felt a curious mixture of triumph and defeat. The soldiers were battering them with their artillery, and the Ghost Dance could not stop death from pouring on their heads. But Curly Headed Doctor and Schonchin John were discredited now. The greatest threat to his authority was wiped out. If any died, their attempt to take over the tribe was forever at an end. But would it matter if Gillem captured them all?

"What will we do about water?" asked Humpy Joe.

"Get men into the ice caves. Break off the ice and melt it."

"Will there be enough?"

"There has to be," Captain Jack told his brother. "See to it."

"Right away." Humpy Joe hurried off as Scarfaced Charley returned, looking grim.

"Has anyone been killed in the camp?"

"Not yet," Scarfaced Charley said, "but Gillem's spotters are only a mile from camp. They might not have found us yet, but it is only a matter of time. They send their shells crashing into the land all around us. If they learn one hit the camp . . ."

Captain Jack finished the thought in his mind. If Gillem got the range with his howitzers, he would blow them into a million pieces and deliver them to the Great Spirit.

"Send six braves to Tule Lake. Be sure my brother saw clearly the danger there."

"I'll go myself." Scarfaced Charley ran off, leaving Captain Jack to consider their position. He had counted on Gillem making the same mistakes Wheaton had. *That* had been a mistake. Angrily, he whipped out his knife and slashed at the red rope that was supposed to protect them. Captain Jack left only small pieces of the tule rope, then kicked at it.

It did not make him feel any better.

Dusk brought even more shelling, but the artillery aimed away from their camp. This was a small consolation to Captain

Jack, who knew time worked against them now. Humpy Joe had brought huge chunks of ice out of the caves, almost exhausting the supply. Melting the ice in the sun gave them enough water for another day, but the responsibility for the entire band's safety wore heavily on the *tyee.*

Captain Jack sat straighter when Scarfaced Charley returned. One look at his ally's face told him the sad truth. Humpy Joe had not been wrong.

Scarfaced Charley sank to the ground beside his *tyee,* then pulled his knife and drove the tip into the ground to show his displeasure.

"A hundred soldiers, perhaps more, block us from Tule Lake. We cannot escape there, or get water."

"Where are the men who went with you?" asked Captain Jack. "I want to talk to them, also."

"They were captured. We passed several Warm Springs scouts, who came after us. McKay leads them. I never liked him. The traitor!" Scarfaced Charley spat.

"How close to our camp were the Warm Springs scouts?" Captain Jack asked.

"Too close. They will find us in another day."

"Then Gillem will use his big guns on us." Captain Jack had spent the day working out plans. There was only one course of action to follow since he would never surrender. "I have told everyone to prepare to leave. We are going deeper into the Lava Beds. If we cannot kill enough of the soldiers, we have no other choice."

"We have killed six of them," Scarfaced Charley said, "and sorely wounded another seventeen."

"But the bluecoats captured six of our fighters and as many squaws trying to get to Tule Lake," Captain Jack said.

"No Modoc has died," Scarfaced Charley pointed out.

"Prepare everyone to scatter into the Lava Beds," Captain Jack said, coming to a decision. "We must slip past the Warm Springs Indians without them knowing we leave."

"Then I will stay with a few others and make it seem the

camp is fully occupied. If they attack, we can quickly escape, disappearing like lizards in the rocks."

"We will meet at the place where Old Winnea talked with the Great Spirit about her brother," Captain Jack said. Scarfaced Charley knew the place. They all did. Silently, they separated, each intent on his part of the mission.

While Scarfaced Charley kept the fires burning brightly, making the camp seem occupied, Captain Jack slipped the rest of his people past the inattentive Warm Springs scouts and into the most desolate section of the Lava Beds.

# Into the Stronghold

*Lava Beds*
*April 16, 1873*

"The scouts report we are close, sir," the captain reported to Gillem. "We can rush in and capture the lot of the Modoc in their main encampment."

"They must know we are near," Gillem said, rubbing his chin as he thought. "Is this a trap?"

"No, sir," the captain said. "McKay says we'll catch Captain Jack with his pants down. He hasn't bothered moving the camp, thinking we're too far off yet to do him any harm."

"That doesn't sound like the *tyee* who has taken out twenty-three of my soldiers without sustaining a single casualty of his own," Gillem said. "I don't trust McKay. He is a slippery fellow and not above lying to make himself look better." He stopped short of voicing his concern that McKay was playing both sides against one another. The Modoc scout might be swapping intelligence reports with Captain Jack in exchange for—what? There never seemed to be enough money in McKay's pocket. Or perhaps he still felt loyalty toward his tribe, as curious as that sounded.

Gillem saw no reason to ferret out the real answers right now. He just didn't—couldn't—trust McKay or the Warm Springs Indians any more than required.

"We captured a half-dozen of them at Tule Lake," the captain said pompously.

Gillem felt bile rising. He had ordered those units along the lakeshore to support him in the Lava Beds, not to go off on their own objective. Their commander had chosen to take matters into his own hands and had ignored Gillem. Cutting the Modoc off from their water had been a good maneuver, but it also jeopardized Gillem's main force. Had Captain Jack attacked in force at any of the narrow twisting, turning areas along the rocky trail, he could have delivered grievous damage and escaped without harm to his own fighters because Gillem's support would have been miles north at Tule Lake.

Things had gone Gillem's way, but because of luck rather than the obedience of commanders still loyal to Colonel Wheaton.

"The cannonade will cease fire at dawn," Gillem said. "How long will it take to move the entire force into the Modoc camp?"

"An hour, less," the captain said. "I can send ahead a platoon and the main body can reinforce them."

"No!" Gillem did not want to lose any more men. Better to move the entire detachment as a single body. "We go in together, supporting each other's flank. Is that clear?" From the look on the captain's face, Gillem knew he had found another of Wheaton's supporters.

"Yes, sir," the captain said, his tone implying it was not all right with him.

Gillem stewed until the howitzers fell silent, then led his troops forward, only to find the captain had disobeyed orders and plunged on ahead with two dozen men. As he rode into the clearing where Captain Jack's camp was, Colonel Gillem saw it was completely deserted. A few personal items were strewn around, as if dropped in a hasty retreat, but the tents remained upright and campfires blazed merrily, giving the impression of recent occupation.

"Captain!" he bellowed, getting the officer's attention. The captain ran over, a lopsided grin on his face. "I ordered you to wait for the entire force to back you up before initiating your attack on this camp."

"Sir, the Warm Springs scouts told us we had to strike fast if we wanted to stop the Modoc, so I ordered an immediate advance."

Gillem clamped his teeth shut to keep from bawling out the captain.

"Report!"

"Sir, we found three Modoc in the camp when we entered. All three were killed resisting our advance."

"Were you the one to kill any of the Modoc?"

"No, Colonel. Private MacNeal was the first soldier to make a kill." The captain barked an order that brought a short, stocky private with thin blond hair running over. The private saluted his colonel, showing an arrogance that made Gillem want to court-martial the lot of them.

"Private MacNeal, what happened?"

"I got me a scalp!" the man cried, holding up a bloody bit of hair. "It was Scarfaced Charley I got. He's one of Captain Jack's heap big fellows!"

"Show me the body." Gillem dismounted and let the private rush ahead. The captain trailed his superior, looking increasingly uneasy. Gillem should have accepted the report of victory and not gone to verify it firsthand.

"Here he is," MacNeal said, rolling over the mutilated corpse of an old Modoc.

"He must be seventy years old," Gillem said. "That's not Scarfaced Charley."

"It was somebody," Private MacNeal said defensively, "and I killed him."

"You took his scalp and then cut him up? Or did he put up that much of a fight against a strapping buck like you?" Gillem held his gorge down. The old man had been slashed to bloody ribbons.

"Got two others, too," MacNeal said, "but they was women,

o I didn't bother with them. Corporal Carson got one of them's scalps. And Ravelli got the other."

"You mean they scalped two women, women older than this poor fool whose only crime was to be too old to run?" Gillem shook his head. Sherman had said, "War is hell," but Gillem had not appreciated what more it could be until this instant.

MacNeal looked to the captain for support.

"Sir, we can get after them. Captain Jack is on the run."

"Form the troop and get them moving along whatever trail McKay can find," Gillem ordered. "I want Captain Jack caught or killed before sunset." He mounted and saw MacNeal putting the old man's severed head in the middle of the camp where every passing soldier could kick at it as he walked by. Gillem's stomach churned even more, but he wanted an end to the fighting more than he wanted to punish his own soldiers.

# Counterattack

"Are you sure the scouts have not spotted us?" Captain Jack asked anxiously. His ears still rang from the sound of the cannonade, but the howitzers were silent now and had been for a day—an entire day since Colonel Gillem had occupied the Modoc's old encampment.

Thoughts of the three old people the soldiers had killed caused Captain Jack's hand to tremble. He wanted this attack to succeed, for those who had died so terribly, for himself, to show Curly Headed Doctor and all the others that he was capable of leading.

Scarfaced Charley considered the question a moment, then nodded vigorously. "They are fools. They ignore the signs. McKay is not a good tracker. The Warm Springs Indians hate him as much as he hates us."

"That is hardly possible," Captain Jack said sardonically. "I can feel McKay's heat when he is close. If he hated any more, he would turn into the sun itself."

Captain Jack considered the lay of the land, where Gillem had camped for the night, all the ravines and ways to reach the clearing filled with almost four hundred bluecoats. There was only a handful of Modoc for the attack, but that was not a serious drawback. Captain Jack wanted Gillem's men shooting wildly, killing each other, then panicking as they retreated. Only a few snipers would be needed to kill the entire regiment then.

And in the attack? He needed no more than he had. Forty fighters dedicated to pushing the soldiers from the Lava Beds was all he required to win. He thought a quick, violent assault would take the camp in less than ten minutes. No need for protracted fighting or sniping.

"Where do we meet if the attack fails?" asked Scarfaced Charley.

Captain Jack wanted to tell his friend this rendezvous would not be needed, but he was a cautious man. The attack was bold, going against a force outnumbering his ten to one, but he needed a safe spot if the soldiers fought too well or luck turned against the Modoc. He had already seen how powerful the white man's medicine was.

"They cannot fire into their own camp without killing Gillem," Captain Jack said. "We should go somewhere close, so they cannot continue to drop their artillery shells on our heads."

Scarfaced Charley laughed. "We should sit in their laps and hope they *did* shell us!"

"I want to brag about this," Captain Jack said, smiling and feeling more confident than he had earlier. He sketched the terrain in the dirt with his knife point, and then showed Scarfaced Charley where he wanted Modoc warriors placed.

"When they hear me whooping, have them attack," Captain Jack said. "I will fire and scream and charge down this draw. The soldiers can't fire at me without shooting their own men in the back. If everyone attacks quickly, we can chase them out."

"Don't attack on these two paths," Scarfaced Charley said. "If they have no place to retreat, they will fight to the death."

"I would kill them all for what they have done," Captain Jack said, but he saw Scarfaced Charley's wisdom. He quickly reapportioned the attackers, strengthening two positions and leaving the soldiers a way to escape.

"They begin their evening meal now. What better time to catch them without their rifles?" Scarfaced Charley said.

"We will celebrate tonight," Captain Jack promised, then slapped his friend on the shoulder. Scarfaced Charley went to get two groups ready. Captain Jack got another to follow him.

On footsteps muffled by the soft wind whistling through the Lava Beds, Captain Jack advanced on Gillem's camp. He pointed out two sentries. They died quickly. The rest of Gillem's force ate dinner. The smell of the rations made Captain Jack's nose wrinkle. It had been too long since he'd had a decent meal. When they chased the soldiers out of their camp, he and the other Modoc would feast!

Captain Jack tucked a pistol into his belt, then lifted his rifle, giving a silent signal to those behind him. Then he leaned back so an unearthly howl left his throat and raced to the sky. Captain Jack fired his rifle and charged, deftly avoiding the sharp-edged lava rock that tore at the soldiers as they marched.

He exploded into their camp, firing as he ran. Behind him came a dozen other Modoc. For a heart-stopping moment, Captain Jack thought Scarfaced Charley had failed and the others were not in position. Then the Modoc erupted like the lava that had formed the rugged, ragged land. They fired into the soldiers nearest them, bringing down several.

Captain Jack saw that Gillem had not positioned his men in the usual Army garrison fashion. A thin line of men ringed the camp, cooking and eating. Most of the soldiers were clumped in the center of camp, formed into a square—and the Modoc stared down the barrels of a hundred rifles that erupted simultaneously.

"Kill them, kill them all!" Captain Jack shrieked. He saw that the spirited defense would drive off his fighters. His warriors were forced back to a point where he could get them under control. Bullets sang off the tough black rock and whined into the gathering night.

"Again," Captain Jack said. "We will attack again!"

Once more he charged, but this time all the soldiers had their rifles and fired in a steady, devastating barrage that cut through his men like a scythe through winter wheat. Captain Jack knew the surprise he had counted on to defeat the superior numbers of well-armed soldiers had vanished.

Whooping and signaling, he caught Scarfaced Charley's attention and motioned him to retreat.

They faded into the night, halfheartedly chased by Gillem's men, and regrouped not three miles away in the heart of the Lava Beds. Captain Jack said nothing. No one spoke to him; he spoke to no one. His hope of crushing the *boshtin* was gone, but Gillem had not killed him, either.

As long as Captain Jack breathed, the bluecoats would fight an implacable enemy.

# Different Offers

*Linkville, Oregon*
*April 23, 1873*

Joshua Harlan returned to Linkville tired and disheartened. The trip back from San Francisco had seemed a thousand miles long. He could not keep from dwelling on Faith and the divorce papers she had presented him. He loved her, but there had been too much interference from her father and brothers. Or was that only an excuse?

That thought kept Josh upset and awake at nights, as well as staring into the distance during the day as he took the train and then rode into Oregon. He had allowed Sean Murdoch to take control, or was that fair? Faith had had a hand in the breakup of their marriage, too. Josh had his dreams, and she had hers. They had not been the same, but this was no reason for her to depend more on her father than her husband. Josh had wanted to provide for her. He simply could not do it at the level she desired so ardently.

Shoulders drooping, Josh rode into Linkville and saw the way the town had grown in the twelve days he had been gone. Where there had been a dozen reporters, he now recognized hundreds. Tents along the road leading into town showed how Linkville had become a boomtown. He dismounted and went to the doctor's surgery, wondering how Meacham was getting on. The man had been recovering slowly from his wounds.

Poking his head inside, Josh looked around. The doctor glared at him.

"Mr. Meacham's long gone," the doctor said. "Don't know where to find him since all the trouble in the Lava Beds."

"Gillem launched an attack? So soon?"

"That he did. Been chasing that devil Captain Jack for almost a week now. From the casualties coming out of the Lava Beds, the fight is pretty one-sided."

Josh hesitated to ask which side was winning. His trips into the Lava Beds had convinced him this was indeed a section of Dante's Hell moved to Earth. Murdering Canby had ignited hellfires that would burn for a long, long time. But was Gillem the man to put out the fire?

"How many casualties?" Josh asked, probing for information. He straightened and reached for his notebook, forgetting—for the moment—about Faith and his divorce.

"Almost thirty so far. Gillem needs reinforcements bad, and I'm not sure General Sherman will give them to him."

Josh had the information he needed. He ducked out and looked around Linkville. AB Meacham was around somewhere, and he ought to talk to him about all that had happened since he had gone to San Francisco, but Josh decided to put that off and file a quick report with Mr. Billingsly. He had been out of touch since leaving San Francisco and wanted the editor to know he was back on the job. Their two meetings had been brusque, but Josh had been distracted, first wanting to see Faith, and then wanting nothing more than to leave San Francisco.

Crossing the muddy street, Josh went into the telegraph office. The telegrapher worked at sticking electrodes into his lead acid batteries.

"You wantin' to send a 'gram? It'll be a spell before I get enough electricity built up."

"How long did it take to fix the wires?"

"Oh, I remember you now. Haven't seen you in a while. Too many strangers running around Linkville." The telegrapher wiped his acid-stained hands on a rag. The strong smell of sulfuric acid made Josh's nose wrinkle. "Well, it took danged near a week to find the cuts. Not sure it was the Modoc who did the damage, but it hardly matters." The telegrapher pursed his lips and asked, "You Josh Harlan, right? Got a 'gram for you. It came in right after I got the wire up and singing again. Well, a few days back."

The telegrapher fumbled behind the counter and pulled out a flimsy yellow sheet. Josh took it and saw the *Alta California* editor had sent it right after he left San Francisco. He scanned the terse message twice before crumpling it and tossing it aside.

"Not bad news?" asked the telegrapher. "That's part of my job I hate."

"I've been fired," Josh said, shocked. His stories were worthy of top billing, front-page, above-the-fold headline stories. From the timing he thought Faith might have told her father about his visit, and Sean Murdoch had gone to Billingsly to get him fired. Murdoch was immensely influential and Billingsly, for all his prattle about integrity, was as prone to pressure as any other man holding a salaried job.

"Don't worry," the telegrapher said. "I get a couple 'grams a day from other editors asking if anyone can be a stringer for them." He dug about in the file under his desk and came out with a pair. "Try these fellows. The *San Francisco Chronicle* is hurting for good stories. So is the *Oregonian*."

Josh sent what small details he had learned since returning to Linkville to both editors, knowing one of them had to want a reliable source so near the scene of the Modoc War. Coverage of the war stretched from one ocean to the other now, leaving the public clamoring for more details, daily tidbits and tales of heroism and bloodshed.

"Thanks," Josh said, after sending the telegrams. "I owe you for that."

"Buy me a dinner sometime. Don't hardly get out of the office these days, and I get mighty hungry come supper time."

"All right," Josh said, grinning. He felt betrayed and abandoned and curiously optimistic. One of the papers would hire him. Maybe both.

It was time to find AB Meacham and get some real information, but Josh could not find his friend in town. No one had seen Meacham for a few days. One man opined that Meacham had gone to Fairchild's ranch to be close to the center of the military action, Meacham being the only remaining member of the Peace Commission. Dyar had quit, to no one's surprise, and the others were dead.

Josh sucked in a deep breath, then headed for Isabella's room, wondering what his reception would be there. He had left her fast and without much explanation. *Without good explanation,* he mentally corrected. It had to seem to her that he was running away from her.

As much as he hated to admit it, that was close to the truth. Then.

He stopped outside the door, started to knock, and hesitated. He was no longer married. Faith had done all she could to cut off ties to him, even to having her father sabotage his job at the *Alta.* He owed Faith nothing anymore, but still, they had been married and had loved each other. . . .

"Josh!" The door opened. Isabella stood inside. "I heard sounds. I hoped it would be you."

"I came back," he said lamely. They stood close to one another. He had missed her and knew how much in this instant. Isabella was so lovely. He reached out and touched her cheek.

Then he kissed her. For a moment, Isabella recoiled. Then she kissed him.

Faith had been right, in her way. Josh felt that he had finally come home.

# Massacre

*Lava Beds*
*April 27, 1873*

"Any luck, Lieutenant?" asked Colonel Gillem. He looked around the miserable clearing in the middle of the Lava Beds where they had camped almost a week. Supplies reached them now and then, whenever Captain Jack failed to stop the wagons that did not break axles or have their mules exhausted pulling along the rugged lava-rock paths, but most vexing was his scouts' inability to even *find* the Modoc.

"No, sir," Lieutenant Boutelle said. "I talked with McKay and am not sure he's being too aggressive about hunting for Captain Jack."

"I figured that out early on," Gillem said. "We cannot remain here much longer without finding that slippery snake."

Boutelle wondered who his colonel spoke of. It could be either McKay or Captain Jack.

"Sir, why not retreat, then let the cannonade drive out the Modoc?"

Colonel Gillem moved a little closer to Boutelle and said in a low voice, "That would be a good idea, Lieutenant, if we had the shot and powder. The early barrages used all we had, and General Sherman has denied me any more."

"Why, sir?"

"He hates me," Gillem said. The colonel motioned wildly.

"They all hate me. All my officers do. They disobey me. Did I order them to cut off the Modoc along Tule Lake? No, I needed them to reinforce my position. If we had entered the Modoc camp, the one with the red rope all around it, and had a fight on our hands, we would have died. Every man would have died because the troops I ordered to reinforce my position were miles off at Tule Lake."

"It worked well, though, sir," Boutelle said, uneasy at the sweeping condemnation Gillem made of his staff. Boutelle was hardly a big supporter of the colonel's, but he obeyed orders.

"We need a breakthrough in this fight, and I don't see where it will come from. Do you, Lieutenant?"

"No, sir, unless we can sweep through and happen on Captain Jack's new settlement." Boutelle paused a moment, then asked, "Where does he get his water, sir? We get ours from Fairchild's ranch and from Tule Lake. Captain Jack is cut off from those sources. Without runoff worth mentioning, where does he get his water?"

"The red bastard lives off the fog in the air, like some Pacific Coast redwood tree. Hell, Lieutenant, I don't know. The Modoc know every inch of this accursed land. It is their ally. Every sharp-edged hunk of lava helps them. For me, it is the enemy."

"Yes, sir," Boutelle said, not sure what else to say when the colonel ranted like this. Gillem's eyes went wide and wild, and he hardly seemed in control. A commander in this condition made serious mistakes. Boutelle had seen enough death in his ranks to know how deadly the Modoc were as fighters. If Gillem fell into a trap because he was irrationally screaming about how even his officers hated him, all the soldiers in his command might be at risk.

"Attack," Gillem said suddenly. "Send out a patrol. A big one. A company! Send out a company to reconnoiter. That will flush Captain Jack if they get anywhere near him. He'll think we've found him and run."

"Any particular direction, sir?"

"That way," Gillem shouted, pointing toward the west. "Send them west. If they meet up with the other element of my force, have them all come back through the Lava Beds. We must flush the Modoc soon."

"Yes, sir," Boutelle said, edging away to give the orders. It made no sense to him blundering about in the treacherous lava flows, but Gillem was in charge, even if he was not in control.

"How long have they been gone, Lieutenant?" asked Colonel Gillem.

"Four hours, sir. Hardly enough time to find Captain Jack, unless the Modoc are camped right next to us." As he said those words, a chill ran up Boutelle's spine. It might be true. The nature of the land made it possible for a camp only a hundred yards away to be completely hidden. He doubted Captain Jack would have camped this close and not taken the opportunity to snipe at the sentries, but the mere possibility plagued him.

Boutelle heard a sentry shouting. He made sure his pistol was free in his holster, then ran to the post to see what the fuss was.

"Sir, there," the private cried, pointing.

"Damnation," Boutelle said, throwing caution to the wind. He dashed away from the camp and dropped to his knees beside the sergeant clawing his way back. Boutelle recognized him as the company sergeant with the detachment Gillem had ordered out.

The company-sized detachment.

"What happened?" Boutelle demanded.

"Sir, we got ambushed. Terrible," the sergeant grated out. His front teeth had been broken off. He might have been hit in the face with a war club or kicked by a horse. Boutelle couldn't tell, and it did not matter. The noncom was in serious shape from a dozen other wounds, all caused by bullets.

"How far, Sergeant? Where are they?"

"Not a mile off. We found 'em, Lieutenant, we found 'em." He coughed up blood, then fixed his eyes on Boutelle. "Save our boys, Lieutenant. Please."

Boutelle held the man even after the sergeant died. Only when a few privates ventured out timidly from camp did Boutelle let the shaggy head down gently. He stood, saw that the sergeant was carried back to the camp, then went to muster a squad. He had to find the others and rescue them, if possible.

Boutelle ignored Gillem as he formed his platoon, then held the quartermaster at gunpoint to get all the ammunition those men could carry.

"I will not go out there unarmed or undersupplied," Boutelle told the quartermaster.

"I'll have to report this to the colonel," the quartermaster threatened.

"Do it. Then have him join me."

Boutelle saw that his men staggered under the load of ammo they carried, and got them mounted and trotting from the camp. Only then did Gillem see him and shout for him to halt. Boutelle ignored his commander. He feared that Gillem might go crazy and not order out a rescue party. Sixty-seven men's lives hung in the balance, and he would not let the sergeant's valiant effort to get help for them to be in vain.

Following the trail proved depressingly easy. All Boutelle needed to do was find new patches of slowly drying blood— the sergeant's blood marked the trail.

"Ahead, sir," called his platoon sergeant. "Hear it?"

"Prepare for battle," Boutelle ordered, pulling his pistol from its holster. His troopers got their carbines out and rounds chambered. Boutelle took a deep breath, then gave the signal to the bugler. The blaring sound erupting from the bugle caused his horse to bolt. Boutelle gave the animal its head, screaming as he clung to the galloping horse.

He burst into a small clearing and saw the dead and dying scattered all around. Boutelle fired as accurately as he could when he spotted war-painted Modoc stripping bodies. His men scattered and fought individual battles rather than putting up a solid front. Somehow, some of the madness that had infected Colonel Gillem now possessed Boutelle. He went berserk when he saw how the company had been cut down.

Only when his pistol came up empty did a semblance of sanity return. Boutelle shouted, and began reforming his men into a coherent fighting machine. They had to work together or they would be killed individually. He saw that quickly by the way the Modoc fired a few rounds, then faded from sight, vanishing into the tumble of lava flows.

Twenty minutes was all it took for Boutelle to get control and drive off the Modoc. Then he found himself in charge of a slaughterhouse.

"Build litters," Boutelle ordered. "We have to get the wounded men back to our camp. There's not much we can do for them here. They are in sore need of doctoring."

Boutelle walked around, counting the dead and comforting the wounded the best he could. Sixty-seven men had ridden out on Gillem's order. All the officers were dead. Their corpses had been scalped and mutilated and their uniforms ripped into tatters or stolen. Of the rest of the detachment, only seventeen men lived.

Seventeen. Seventeen out of sixty-seven, and none of these soldiers had escaped unscathed. Every one had taken at least one bullet wound. Most had several in their bodies.

"Lieutenant, we got to go now. Leave them behind. The wounded. Leave 'em."

"We will not, Sergeant. We came to rescue them." The image of the bloody, dying sergeant crawling back with the request for succor burned in his mind.

"Who's gonna rescue us?" The sergeant pointed at the narrow gap they had used to enter the clearing. On either side sat Modoc fighters. "We go back the way we came, we die. I seen at least a dozen."

"How many can't you see?" Boutelle wondered aloud.

"That's my point, Lieutenant. We go that way, with or without wounded, and we're all dead."

Boutelle looked around, wondering if there were other paths out of the clearing, out of the Lava Beds. North to Tule Lake? To the west? Gillem had wanted this patrol to link up with the element along the western rim of the accursed lava flows.

"We are not going to leave the wounded men," Boutelle said forcefully. "I wouldn't abandon you, Sergeant. We will not abandon them."

"No, sir," the noncom said reluctantly. He shuddered at the notion of being left here alive for the Modoc to finish off with their fiendish tortures. "I understand. I saw what them red bastards did to the officers. But where do we go?"

"We get out of here. Out of Gillem's Graveyard," Lieutenant Boutelle said bitterly.

Two days later, fighting every inch of the way, Boutelle and the survivors reached Tule Lake and safety.

# Change of Command— but Nothing Else

*Fairchild's Ranch, California*
*May 5, 1873*

Josh stood beside Alfred Meacham, wondering if he might have to help support his friend. Meacham looked years older, and for good reason. His wounds were beginning to heal, but they had been terrible ones. He wore a hat to cover his head where the scalping had left obvious scars. Where he had been firm and resolute before, Meacham now struck Josh as hesitant and even fearful.

He had been through hell and now had to watch others endure it, too.

"Here he comes," Josh said. He scribbled his notes, wondering which newspaper ought to get the scoop. The *Oregonian* had him on full-time pay, but he took a certain malicious delight in selling to the *San Francisco Chronicle*, to taunt Mr. Billingsly—and Sean Murdoch. He knew Faith never read newspapers, such plebeian pursuits beneath her station, but Murdoch would know how he was succeeding.

"Poor man," muttered Meacham.

"What do you mean? That his name's Jefferson Davis?"

"General Jefferson C. Davis," Meacham said. "He was one of Sherman's generals during the March to the Sea and made one command error after another. He burned a bridge, cutting off a passel of freed slaves looking to him for protection. The slaves were all killed and Davis barely missed court-martial."

"Is that why he got a command in Alaska?" Josh almost laughed at that. If a more distant post existed in the U.S. Army, he did not know what it was.

"Yes," Meacham said, "but he's back in Sherman's good graces. Anyone would look good compared to Colonel Gillem."

Josh saw the colonel standing on the front porch of John Fairchild's house, looking pale and haggard. Most of his command would have gladly drawn and quartered him for his inept leadership in the Lava Beds. If Colonel Wheaton's foray into Captain Jack's Stronghold had been a mistake, Gillem's had proven disastrous. No commander lost as many men as he had so publicly and survived in his command.

The reporters flocking about like bees to blossoming wildflowers sealed Gillem's fate. The Modoc War, as it was generally called in the press, was a nationwide sensation. Some papers took the Quaker viewpoint, as Reverend Thomas had, that a peaceable end might be had with the proper men on a new Peace Commission. The rest saw this as a war of extermination—and Gillem had failed to exterminate the enemy. Captain Jack had been reviled and portrayed as the devil incarnate. For some of the settlers in the area, this belief was repeated often. It did Josh no good to remind them that the people of Yreka had openly sought the Modoc's business, and many of the merchants there blamed the war entirely on military bungling and never spoke of Odeneal without swearing.

"If he doesn't get results fast, he'll be standing where the colonel is right now," Meacham observed as General Davis rode up. The officer dismounted and, amid a flourish on drums, marched up to the colonel and presented a snappy salute.

"Sir, I relieve you of your command."

"Sir, the command is yours." Colonel Gillem's hand quivered as he saluted. "Do you wish me to brief you on the status of our troops?"

"That will not be necessary," Davis said. "You have done as much as you can. It is time for another hand at the helm."

"He sounds more like a sailor than a cavalry officer," Josh whispered.

"He spent almost a month getting here from Alaska," Meacham said. "That might explain the way he talks, and why he smells of fish."

"Did Sherman intend to replace Canby? And Gillem just got in the way?"

"I don't think so. Davis was being transferred back East and had the misfortune to be the only senior officer in the area of high enough rank to assume command."

Josh tried to record the expressions of the officers lined up. Lieutenant Boutelle was the most unreadable of the lot. Poker-faced, the lieutenant went through the rituals of change of command like a machine. When Davis went into Fairchild's house to speak with the settler, Josh went to Lieutenant Boutelle.

"Sir, a word with you, if I might."

"Yes, Mr. Harlan?"

"Will General Davis's arrival change morale?"

"Morale cannot get worse," Boutelle said, not really answering the question. "It is my sorry duty to count the bodies as they return. I have been reduced to graves registration officer."

"You want to go back in, after Captain Jack?"

"I want the fighting to be at an end," Boutelle snapped.

"Sorry, sir," Josh said. "How can General Davis lift the troopers' spirits?"

"By convincing them they won't get their scalps lifted in the middle of the night. Too many of them fear Captain Jack so much they think he has become a ghost, a spirit drifting through walls and performing superhuman feats. Some of the soldiers sleep with their caps fastened on tight, to keep Captain Jack from scalping them while they are asleep. He is a man, nothing more."

"But the Lava Beds provide a sanctuary for him you cannot penetrate, isn't that right?"

Lieutenant Boutelle looked toward the horizon. He could not see the Lava Beds from here, but Josh knew the officer saw every body he had retrieved from those lava flows as perfectly as if they were laid in front of him now.

"He must be driven out of his stronghold," Boutelle said. The lieutenant straightened and pointed to a wagon rattling toward the ranch house. "Excuse me. I have work to do."

Josh followed and found a wagon loaded with bodies, a lot of bodies—and all wore blue coats. The fight in the Lava Beds continued unabated and was as one-sided as ever. Soldiers fought and died. Modoc warriors fought and lived. Fewer than fifty of Captain Jack's followers held an entire army at bay.

It almost made Josh believe in the powerful Ghost Dance medicine Isabella had told him about.

# Supplies

"I see it!" cried Scarfaced Charley, sliding down a rock and lightly jumping to the ground. He pulled a pistol from his belt and looked to Captain Jack for the order to attack.

"How many guards?" asked Captain Jack. He had bad feelings about this wagon train, but his people needed supplies. Worse, they needed water. He had mined every speck of ice from the caves and was now reduced to digging holes and waiting for ground seepage to turn the dirt to mud. He had hoped General Davis would pull back the soldiers along Tule Lake, but he had either ignored them or thought this was one thing Colonel Gillem had done right.

"A dozen," Scarfaced Charley said. "You want to attack?"

"I wish Gillem led them."

"He hardly gets out of their camp at Fairchild's," Scarfaced Charley said. "The *boshtin* are strange. Wheaton is still there. Gillem is, too. Do they collect them like scalps, except allowing their failures to live?"

"As if they needed bad examples," Captain Jack said, grinning. It still bothered him knowing Gillem remained, even if he was no longer in overall command. The man had done things badly, but he had blundered along in the right ways to make life terrible for the Modoc. Captain Jack rubbed his dried lips, longing for a long drink of water.

"This does not look like a trap? What do the wagons carry?"

"They are covered with tarps." Scarfaced Charley looked down at his tattered clothing. "New clothes would be worth the risk. Everyone's clothing is falling apart."

"Poor workmanship in white clothing," Captain Jack said. His own trousers were in bad shape, but he could still joke. A little. The feeling that he made a mistake attacking the supply train faded and resolve hardened. He nodded.

Scarfaced Charley let out a whoop that echoed through the Lava Beds. An answering cry signaled the other warriors' readiness to attack. Captain Jack drew his pistol and stepped out of hiding, placing himself squarely in the middle of the narrow road being taken by the wagons.

He lifted his pistol and fired at the driver the instant the wagon came around a sharp bend in the road. The driver threw up his hands and tumbled backward into the wagon bed. The other Modoc leaped from rocks and swooped down like eagles on the wagon and the few guards riding on it. The cavalry troopers struggled to get out their carbines, but Captain Jack's men had taken them completely by surprise.

"The other wagons," he called. "Get them!"

His warriors swarmed up and threw back the tarpaulins.

"Food!"

"Take what you can, burn the rest," Captain Jack said. If his people could not use it, then it had to be destroyed to prevent Davis's troops from enjoying full bellies. He worked to unhitch the mules on the leading wagon and swung up onto one balky animal's back. He felt like a *tyee* again, in spite of wearing rags a beggar would scorn and needing a long, cool drink of water.

"Got their canteens," Scarfaced Charley said, holding up a half-dozen sloshing containers.

"Burn the wagons and let's get out of here," Captain Jack

said. It had been a good day for the Modoc. They had more food, but they needed water and clothes. If Davis was as careless with other supply trains, Captain Jack was sure his people would get what they needed by raiding military shipments along the edges of the Lava Beds.

As they had today.

# Fame

Josh wrote quickly, embellishing the story of Captain Jack attacking the wagon train with a few personal anecdotes about the soldiers who had died or been injured.

"You know them?" asked Isabella, looking over his shoulder. She read slowly what he had written. He had worked with her, teaching her to read enough English to get by. Isabella had been helpful getting information about the Modoc, and now she was even more valuable, able to read documents and pass along information to him, because no one even noticed her. Josh did not like using Isabella as a spy around the Army encampment outside town, or even down at Davis's headquarters at Fairchild's ranch, but the officers left papers out where anyone could see them. They did not believe it mattered because they thought Isabella was illiterate.

Some of Josh's best stories had been sparked by things she had read in carelessly discarded reports.

"I've met them. I make a point of talking to the sentries, the guards, and the noncoms as much as I can. They might not know what their officers are planning, but they do know where they were and what the real story was. Captain Jack is attacking Davis's supplies wagons at will now."

"He kills many," Isabella said almost sadly.

"I know." Josh leaned back and looked at his story, one intended for the *Oregonian*. He had tried to make Captain Jack less the killer and more the romantic hero struggling for freedom. Alone of the reporters, he took the Modoc view, and now his editors were beginning to rail against his slant.

"That is why you are famous," Isabella said proudly.

"Famous?" Josh laughed at that. He was not famous. He was only a reporter doing his job. If he did it better than others, and he knew he did, that hardly constituted fame. "Why do you say that?"

"You get your name on so many stories." Isabella pointed to the clippings of his articles stacked on the writing desk he had put into the corner of the room. Two inches thick and growing daily. He had a body of work any reporter could envy. But famous?

"I'm not famous," he said. "If I were, I'd be rich."

For a moment, Isabella said nothing. Then she smiled and said, "I do not care if you are famous. I still love you."

He looked at her for a moment, his heart hammering in his chest. She was as lovely as any woman he had ever met. Intelligent, quick, she was what every man wanted in a woman. They were not married, but had done things only husband and wife should do, and this bothered Josh. That was not love, that was lust, illicit lust, and maybe his way of getting back at Faith for the way she had treated him.

Love meant more.

Josh realized then that he loved Isabella in every meaning of the word.

# Beginning of the End

*Sorass Lake, California*
*May 10, 1873*

"Gentlemen, we must become more like the Modoc if we are to win," General Davis said pompously. "They rob our supply trains, they snipe at us, they kill us and then fade into the Lava Beds where we cannot find them." He glared at Colonel Gillem. "I am sending a company into the Lava Beds to chevy them, retreating immediately if they are present in such force to deliver us grievous injury."

"We'll be running all the time," Lieutenant Boutelle muttered to himself. A captain recently transferred from Yreka glared at him, and Boutelle fell silent.

"General, we're ready. Let us go and you'll see them Modoc running like rabbits," Don McKay proclaimed. "Me and the Warm Springs scouts are ready for your orders!"

The captain sidled closer to Boutelle and asked in a low voice, "Is that the turncoat Modoc? The one who scouts for us?"

"Yes, sir," Boutelle said.

"My name's Hasbrouck. I need to find out everything here in a hurry or risk my men needlessly."

"Gentlemen!" barked Davis. "We have reinforcements from Yreka under Captain H.C. Hasbrouck. Lieutenant Boutelle, you will act as his second in command. You will scout with

the Warm Springs Indians working with Mr. McKay around
Sorass Lake, the mission being the interdiction of the Modoc
from any water source."

"Sorass Lake is nothing but an alkali pond," Boutelle com-
plained to Hasbrouck. "Captain Jack can't drink the water.
We're off on another wild-goose chase."

"You will be supported by an artillery unit I am sending
into the Lava Beds with you," said Davis. "Here are your written orders, Captain Hasbrouck. Good hunting!"

"Sir!" Hasbrouck took the envelope with the general's seal
on it, saluted, and left, Boutelle following. The captain read
the orders quickly, then handed them to Boutelle.

"It's about what I expected," Frazier Boutelle said. "This
might be our death warrant."

"Nonsense. Your attitude is not that of a field officer. We
*will* succeed."

"Yes, sir," Boutelle said. "But you might not say that after
you've seen the Lava Beds. It's terrible out there. Travel is
restricted, the grassy, sagebrush-covered areas are incredibly
fertile, but surrounded by almost impassable lava flows. The
ravines and caves hide Modoc at every turn. It's hell out there,
sir."

"We will see, Lieutenant. I want you to command the second platoon, with my best sergeant. Sergeant Kelly!" barked
Hasbrouck. The captain introduced the men. "Prepare to move
out in fifteen minutes," Hasbrouck ordered.

Boutelle looked Thomas Kelly over and saw a no-nonsense
sergeant. He needed men like that out in the field.

"Well, Sergeant? You heard the captain. Mount your men
and let's ride!"


Lieutenant Boutelle trotted forward and looked at Sorass
Lake. It was worse than he remembered it from an earlier
scouting mission. The scrubby bushes around the muddy flats
drew the horses. The animals nibbled a leaf or two and then

spat out the alkali-soaked leaves. Standing in his stirrups, Boutelle shielded his eyes and scanned the horizon.

Why Davis had sent them to this godforsaken place was beyond him. Hasbrouck was eager, not having seen battle with the Modoc yet. Boutelle reckoned the general had put the captain in command since his unit had no preconceptions about Captain Jack and how deadly his fighters were. Bit by bit, Boutelle studied the land and saw nothing.

"Sergeant Kelly," Hasbrouck ordered. "Have your men dig pits. Look for water."

"Sir," Boutelle said, "the only seepage you'll get will be undrinkable. And keep your horse from eating too much from the vegetation. It will kill a strong animal."

"The Warm Springs Indians are scouting to the south, aren't they?"

"I think so, sir. McKay tends to go where he wants, and that's usually far away from any fighting."

"Your opinion of the scouts is not appreciated, Lieutenant. Keep it to yourself. Now see to digging those water pits."

"Yes, sir," Boutelle said, dismounting. The muck sucked at his boots. This would be a terrible place to defend. Better to be with the artillery unit a mile back. Why Davis had sent howitzers into the Lava Beds was beyond him. He shuddered at the thought of Captain Jack capturing any of those cannon.

Venturing into the Lava Beds would go from deadly to impossible.

"Sergeant," Boutelle said. "Don't put all your men to digging. Put at least half of them on sentry duty. Keep a sharp eye out for any sign of the Modoc."

"But the captain wants—"

"Do it, Sergeant Kelly," Boutelle said sharply. A flash of gold caught his eye. He tried to find the source but couldn't. He glanced over his shoulder and saw Hasbrouck had ridden out of sight around the southern shore of the alkali lake. Walking slowly away from where Kelly's men labored to dig the useless pits, Boutelle scanned the horizon. Black rock boiled in the growing heat, sending up shimmery curtains that hid movement.

Then Boutelle saw the gold flash again. He hurried to his horse, fumbled in the saddlebags, and got his field glasses. Boutelle went cold inside when he saw the source of that gold reflection.

"Sergeant, form the men to fight off an attack."

"What's wrong, sir?"

"I saw something reflecting in the sun. It's the buttons on General Canby's dress coat."

"What? But Canby's dead and—"

"And Captain Jack stole his uniform. That's Captain Jack up there on the rock. That means he is directing his fighters right now, and we have only minutes."

The bullet that tore through the brim of Boutelle's hat put that estimate to the lie. He ducked involuntarily, dropped his field glasses, and grabbed for his pistol. Sergeant Kelly began yelling orders, but his men were in disarray.

Boutelle saw how indefensible their position was. The Modoc force came at them, probably in an arc to cut off escape either north or south along Sorass Lake. If they tried to retreat, it had to be into the muddy lake itself. That way lay only death, Boutelle knew.

"Sergeant, get a courier to Captain Hasbrouck. Get him back here. We can't run, so we have to fight!"

Kelly dispatched a private, who got only a few yards before being shot from the saddle. From the way the young man hit the ground, Boutelle knew he was dead.

"Here they come!" Boutelle fired at the line of Modoc warriors coming at them. He knew Captain Jack guided them from his vantage point. If Boutelle could have called in an artillery strike, he would send every last shell to the hummock where Captain Jack stood. Cut off the head, kill the beast.

Boutelle gasped as a bullet raced along his side, leaving behind a bloody crease that was more painful than dangerous. He dropped to one knee, struggling to get his breath. The world turned double, preventing him from aiming accurately. A Modoc fighter suddenly appeared in front of him, aiming a rifle at his face.

The dull click told Boutelle the Modoc had emptied the magazine, but that didn't keep the Indian from using the rifle as a club. He swung hard. The barrel caught Boutelle alongside the head, driving him to the ground. Everywhere he could see from his position on the ground, Boutelle saw Modoc fighters.

Laughing and howling like a dog, one Modoc stood out among the others. Boutelle lifted himself up on one elbow and blinked hard. He recognized that one. Meacham had told him about Ellen's Man George. Captain Jack had killed Canby, but Ellen's Man George had worked to mutilate the body. The way the Modoc acted, he commanded the attack directed by Captain Jack.

"Him," gasped out Boutelle. "Get that one." He fired his pistol until the hammer fell on an empty cylinder. Boutelle fell back to the ground, aware that he had drawn unwanted attention from Ellen's Man George. The Modoc stalked toward him.

Then a miracle saved Boutelle. Or outrageous courage. He heard Sergeant Kelly scream, "Who cares if we die! Get them, get them!" The sergeant mustered enough men to form a small wedge that cut through the attacking Modoc.

Kelly—or one of his men—fired point-blank at Ellen's Man George. The Modoc stiffened, a look of surprise on his face. Then he keeled over, dead.

"After 'em, after 'em! Attack!"

Boutelle tried to stand, but lacked the strength. He lay on his side staring at Ellen's Man George a few feet in front of him. The battle went away from him, returned, and faded once more. Boutelle struggled to roll onto his back, but experienced a lethargy that held him as firmly as iron shackles. He saw two Modoc hurry up, grab Ellen's Man George, and drag him away.

With a supreme effort, Boutelle rolled onto his back and

stared into the sky. He made out the different sounds of Spencers and the rifles used by the Modoc. The Indians ran out of ammunition, but Kelly continued to rally his platoon.

Boutelle had no idea how long he lay, but he heard a horse coming up and a distant voice, one he almost recognized, saying, "I'll look after him. Go on. Get Captain Hasbrouck."

Boutelle looked up and recognized the reporter.

"Mr. Harlan," he said weakly. "It's good to see you. It's good to see anyone, but why are you here?"

"You've won a great victory here today, Lieutenant," Josh Harlan said. He tipped a canteen up and dribbled water on Boutelle's lips. "I was with the artillery unit when one of McKay's scouts came in with word of the Modoc attack."

"You came alone?"

"I came with two companies of men," Josh said. "You're going to be all right."

"What happened? My men . . ."

"It looks like you sustained ten casualties. Five dead, five wounded, you among them. Sergeant Kelly saved the day for you. When he attacked, the Modoc broke and ran. They even left behind ammunition and supplies."

"How many did we kill of them? I saw Ellen's Man George die."

"Two, two, I think," Josh said.

"We lost five and the Modoc two. Such a victory," Boutelle said bitterly.

"It is a victory, the Army's first," Josh said. "These are the first two Modoc killed in battle. One of them was an important ally of Captain Jack's. It was a *great* victory. It'll make great reading when I send in my stories."

"Kelly deserves a medal. He saved us all," Boutelle said. Then he slipped off into a deep, exhausted sleep.

# Death in the Lava Beds

*Lava Beds*
*May 11, 1873*

"How near are the soldiers?" asked Captain Jack.

"Within a mile," Scarfaced Charley answered. "I just got back from scouting them. They are moving in more artillery. This time they have shells and powder for the big guns."

"They don't need to fire at us from the bluffs like Wheaton," Captain Jack said dully. "They can chase us with their cannon." He stared at the body laying on the funeral pyre. He had no great love for Ellen's Man George, but the death had sent a shock through the ranks of the Modoc warriors. Until now, the only casualties had been old men and women too feeble to fight. Ellen's Man George was the first warrior to die in battle.

The other Modoc who had died attacking the soldiers at Sorass Lake had been cremated hastily, not far from where he fell. Captain Jack realized more ceremony had to be given for Ellen's Man George, especially since Curly Headed Doctor demanded it. The shaman sat by the body, shaking his medicine rattle and chanting in a low voice. Ellen's Man George's family came with small bundles of wood and carefully laid them around his body.

This near the bluecoats, it would be impossible to give Ellen's Man George the funeral he deserved. Too big a fire would draw the soldiers.

"We didn't have enough ammunition," Captain Jack said. "I should have seen that."

"They didn't cut and run like they usually do," Scarfaced Charley said. "The sergeant rallied them after we killed their officers. Who would have thought Ellen's Man George would have been brought down so easily?"

"Where is the Ghost Dance medicine?" Captain Jack asked softly. As low as he pitched his voice, he still drew Curly Headed Doctor's angry attention. The shaman stood and began dancing around the funeral pyre. The pyre ought to have been larger, grander, more fitting for a warrior of Ellen's Man George's stature. But the soldiers camping so close made that impossible.

Captain Jack couldn't seem to think of anything other than how Ellen's Man George deserved more.

The chanting picked up in tempo, and the rest of the Modoc started a slow dance around the pyre. Curly Headed Doctor ritualistically ignited a small torch, then applied its guttering flame to the wood under Ellen's Man George. The wood, long since dried out, caught immediately and flared. Almost smoke-less, the fire grew until the flames licked at the body. Then greasy black smoke billowed up, showing that Ellen's Man George was being sent to the Great Spirit.

The chanting went on as the fire consumed the body, then died down until only Curly Headed Doctor continued the ritual. Finally, bones and ashes left, what remained of Ellen's Man George was gathered into a ceremonial bag and placed in a small cave in the lava rock where the white soldiers would never find it.

Captain Jack stood, numbed with the loss. He knew there had to be casualties, but Ellen's Man George had had a large following, an important faction that Captain Jack had depended on for support. Theirs had been an uneasy alliance, but a common enemy united them.

He looked up to see Curly Headed Doctor stalking up, a stormy expression on his face. Others came with him. Captain Jack braced himself for what might be another vote for leadership of the Modoc.

"You no longer can tell us what to do, Kintpuash," Curly Headed Doctor declared.

"You want a vote? Would you be *tyee?*"

"No! No vote!"

This startled Captain Jack. He had expected Curly Headed Doctor to force the vote. It would be close, but Captain Jack thought he could remain chief.

"What are you saying?"

"I am leaving," Curly Headed Doctor said. "I no longer follow you!"

"We're leaving, too," said Hooker Jim, pointing to Boston Charley, Shacknasty Jim, and Steamboat Frank. "We're going to Hot Creek."

"Do you think General Davis will let you stay there unmolested?" Captain Jack was astonished at their naive belief that the whites' commander would ignore them if they simply showed up at Hot Creek. "Even if you give him your parole?"

"We're going to Hot Creek," Curly Headed Doctor said. "You are no longer *tyee.*"

Captain Jack knew better than to argue. He had no power over them other than that placed in him by the entire council. Curly Headed Doctor and the others chose to leave the council, so he was no longer their *tyee.*

They hastily packed, gathered their squaws and belongings, and vanished into the maze of the Lava Beds, leaving behind a much weakened band and a disheartened Captain Jack.

He had lost only two fighters in battle, but those deaths might have cost him the war.

# Tightening the Grip

"That your squaw, boy?" asked a burly soldier. "I'll buy her from you for ten dollars."

Josh turned and looked up at the corporal, holding his anger in check. He felt Isabella's hand on his shoulder to restrain him, but he wanted satisfaction for such an uncouth offer. Josh knew the soldier spoke only to rile him, because the corporal's friends stood back a ways, snickering.

"What's your name?" Josh asked, taking out his notebook and a pencil. "I'm a reporter for the *Oregonian,* and I want to be sure I spell it right when I report how you turned tail and ran like a coward the first time you saw a Modoc."

"Why, you—" The corporal cocked back a meaty fist, ready to punch Josh, but one of the man's friends grabbed him and whispered furiously.

"Is it true? You a friend of Boutelle's?" the corporal asked, not wanting to brawl with anyone who knew the lieutenant.

"And of Sergeant Kelly," Josh said, seeing that he had more than a small opening offered now because of who he knew. "What does it matter? I demand an apology immediately." Josh held his ground.

"I'm sorry," the corporal said.

"Wait," Josh called when the soldier started to walk away. "You're not apologizing to me. You will apologize to her."

"To a damned Modoc squaw? Why—" The corporal's anger flared again.

This time the man hesitated when General Davis and his staff came by. Josh glared at the corporal, then called out, "General, can I have an interview?"

"Of course, Mr. Harlan. Anytime you want." Davis seemed oblivious to the situation around him, being lost in thought. Josh trailed behind the general, Isabella behind him.

"Is it true you are reinforcing the troops in the Lava Beds?" Josh asked.

"It is. After Captain Hasbrouck's stunning victory, we are sure the power of the Modoc is broken. We need only crush the last pieces of resistance to achieve a complete victory."

Josh did not bother writing down such blather in his notebook. Davis always spouted nonsense that he thought would sound good when put into a newspaper article. Josh knew better than to quote them intact since he did not want to make the general out to be a complete fool. He tempered the statements he quoted and let the facts speak for themselves. The Modoc were not broken, not yet, not after only two deaths. Captain Jack had inflicted more than a hundred casualties on the soldiers since taking refuge in the Lava Beds. The war would be won by attrition, not military action.

"Is it true the Modoc are suffering a lack of water and supplies?" Josh knew they were. Isabella had told him of Captain Jack's perilous situation, but he wanted the general to say it so he could get a decent story not based on hearsay from sources his editors would find unreliable. If a general said it, they believed it. If a Modoc reported it, there was not an editor alive who would believe a word of it.

"They suffer terribly, and we are going to capitalize on this as we step up our patrols. We have chased small bands of Modoc and captured several."

Josh knew the prisoners were women, children, and old men dying from lack of water.

"How many have died, sir?"

"Five. The patrols have rounded up five Modoc who subsequently died." General Davis pulled himself up and looked around the camp in the middle of the Lava Beds. The encampment had grown like Topsy in the past few days, now totaling more than three hundred soldiers. Josh and Isabella had asked around and determined over one thousand were in and around the Lava Beds, most guarding Tule Lake and the perimeter to keep Captain Jack from escaping, as if that were possible.

The Modoc still walked through the Lava Beds undetected and could leave any time they desired. But Josh knew no more secure stronghold, in spite of the lack of water.

"I have an announcement to make concerning command of troops in the field," said Davis. "Colonel Gillem has been transferred to the San Francisco garrison."

This caused Josh to scribble hurriedly. He had not heard so much as barracks gossip about this. Since Gillem had lost so many men in his ill-planned invasion of the Lava Beds, he had been on Davis's staff, contributing what he could to the current, more methodical campaign against Captain Jack.

"Replacing Colonel Gillem in the field will be Colonel Wheaton," Davis went on. "I feel this change of command will reinvigorate the soldiers and allow us to end the Modoc War quickly."

Josh glanced at Isabella to see how she reacted. She had came back from speaking with the starving Modoc who had been caught by Davis's patrol. The Modoc were her people, after all, but she stood impassively as the general outlined his plans for their destruction. She had kept aloof from the fighting and the bitterness among Captain Jack's followers. He was glad she had been spared so much heartache, even if the soldiers treated her shabbily.

She moved closer to Josh and said in a low voice, "You should talk with Mr. Fairchild."

"What? Why?"

Isabella smiled enigmatically. She said, "Big story will make you *real* famous."

Josh took her arm and slipped back from the still chattering general, getting their horses to ride to Fairchild's ranch.

# Surrender

*Fairchild's Ranch, California*
*May 21, 1873*

"Why won't you tell me what's going to happen?" Josh asked Isabella. She smiled and shook her head.

"It is a surprise. Big surprise. Get your notebook ready."

Josh dismounted and tethered his horse at the side of Fairchild's house. The bustle of soldiers around the house was unusual, even if Colonel Wheaton was expected soon. With Isabella beside him, he went to the door and knocked, expecting John Fairchild to answer. Instead, a junior officer opened the door.

"Oh, it's you," the lieutenant said.

"Glad to see you, too," Josh said, grinning. "What's going on?"

"We're preparing for Wheaton to come back," the lieutenant said, trying to hide his distaste for the officer.

"Were you with him when he went into the Lava Beds?"

"I was. My cousin was killed when those good-for-nothing Oregon volunteers turned and ran."

Josh glanced at Isabella, wondering if Wheaton showing up to give a boring speech rivaling Davis's was the reason she had urged him to come here. She stood on the porch, looking out in the direction of the distant Lava Beds, though not along the road they had taken.

"Where's Mr. Fairchild?" Josh asked.

"I haven't seen him. He lit out this morning like someone had started a fire under his butt."

"Oh?"

The lieutenant didn't know any more and was not inclined to waste time jawing with Josh.

"So?" Josh asked Isabella. "This is the big story?"

"That is," she said, pointing into the distance. Josh squinted as he saw a dust cloud working its way toward them. He wished he had a pair of field glasses. Shielding his eyes from the high sun was the best he could do until the slowly moving party got closer.

"My God!" he cried. "Come on!" He tugged at Isabella's arm to get her moving. Josh climbed onto his horse and galloped off, knowing how important it was to talk to Fairchild before anyone else got wind of this. He could have a story in half the papers in Oregon before any other reporter so much as found out.

"Mr. Harlan," Fairchild said. "I see news travels fast." Fairchild looked past Josh to Isabella. He tipped his hat to her politely.

"How many surrendered to you?" Josh asked, looking over the tight knot of Modoc. He was stunned by their condition. Men, women, children, all were haggard and dressed in ragged clothing. Many hobbled along, shoes or boots nonexistent. The sharp lava rock had cut their feet, and the wounds barely had healed before new cuts replaced them.

"Bogus Charley got in touch with me early this morning, saying he and a lot of others wanted to surrender. If I would be their spokesman, they would come in immediately and cease all warfare."

"Sixty?" Josh asked, counting fast.

"Sixty-three," Fairchild said.

Josh filled page after page with the details, noting that not only Bogus Charley but Hooker Jim, Shacknasty Jim, Steamboat Frank, and Curly Headed Doctor were among those surrendering.

"Will they surrender to Davis or Wheaton?"

"Whoever is at my ranch house," Fairchild said.

Isabella spoke up. "Colonel Wheaton arrives in a few minutes."

"Then the colonel receives their word not to fight again." Fairchild was pleased with himself, but Josh wondered if he knew how momentous this moment was. So many Modoc coming in from the Lava Beds robbed Captain Jack of his tribe. He might still be *tyee,* but no longer did he have enough warriors to fight effectively or squaws to feed the fighters and to find water.

"Here he comes," Isabella said. "Colonel Wheaton and his staff."

Josh fell back, riding to the side of the shuffling Modoc refugees. He wanted to talk to them but had to listen to the dialogue between Fairchild and Wheaton. The colonel's eyes were wide with shock at the surrender. He dismounted and walked forward, trying to figure out who spoke for the Modoc.

Bogus Charley stepped up, being the most fluent in English among the Modoc.

"I am delighted you have chosen the wise path, the path of peace," Wheaton said.

"We can fight no more," Bogus Charley said. "We are thirsty and tired. Too many of our squaws and children are sick."

"By returning to the reservation, you guarantee yourselves water, food, and medical attention." Wheaton stepped back when Curly Headed Doctor hissed and shook a medicine rattle at him. "I am sure your shaman will be able to make even greater medicine with our doctors working, uh, alongside yours."

This placated Curly Headed Doctor a little.

"In return for this aid, however, you must surrender your weapons," Wheaton went on. He eyed the rifles clutched in

Modoc hands with some suspicion. He tried not to look to his staff to be sure they could defend him if the Indians turned against him, but was unsuccessful. He glanced left and right to his officers. Their alertness eased his concern over personal safety.

"Each warrior will give you his rifle," Bogus Charley said. One by one the fighters came forward and laid their weapons at Wheaton's feet.

When they had disarmed themselves, Bogus Charley shuffled his feet as if trying to work up nerve. Curly Headed Doctor rattled off quick orders to him. Josh leaned close to Isabella for her to translate.

"They hate Captain Jack," she said. "They want to kill him."

Before Josh could ask any questions, Bogus Charley said loudly, "We want to help stop Captain Jack. Four of us." He pointed to Shacknasty Jim, Steamboat Frank, and Hooker Jim. "We no longer follow him as *tyee* and want him killed."

Josh saw the shock deepen on Wheaton's face. He was startled at the sudden surrender. The turn against their leader took him by storm.

"I do declare," Wheaton said, his mind racing. He stepped up and thrust out his hand for Bogus Charley to shake. "In return for your services, I will give you one hundred dollars a month. For it, all you need to do is bring in Captain Jack."

"Dead?" asked Bogus Charley.

"It doesn't matter," Colonel Wheaton said. "Just bring him in."

Josh realized the importance of this surrender and meeting. After a few more minutes getting information about the four "Modoc hounds," as Wheaton called them, Josh almost killed his horse riding into Linkville to send the story out on the telegraph to the *Oregonian* and the *San Francisco Chronicle*.

As the last clack of the telegraph key died away, Josh felt a curious sense of loss. His story was almost at an end, but that was not making him sad. Captain Jack had been a killer who ignored a truce flag to do his worst, but Josh still secretly admired him. The Modoc *tyee*'s days were numbered, and for that Josh mourned.

# Found and Lost

*Lava Beds*
*May 20, 1873*

Captain Jack sat on the lava extrusion, knees drawn up and arms circling them. He blended in with the black rock under him, having discarded the dress coat he had taken from Canby's body. The darkness of his clothing allowed him to blend into the countryside like a lizard, invisible to all but those he chose to greet.

Stalking along a path below him were the four hounds, or so he had heard the soldiers call the traitorous Modoc. Steamboat Frank slipped away like a puff of wind, silent and deadly. Behind him, Shacknasty Jim blundered about noisily, but Hooker Jim and Bogus Charley did nothing to quiet him. Captain Jack wondered if they cared. He lifted his rifle and laid it across his legs, now stretched out in front of him. If he had wanted, he could have killed all four men before they realized they were being attacked.

"What do you want?" Captain Jack asked. He tried not to smile as the four jumped as if someone had stuck them with pins. They looked around, hunting for him. Finally Hooker Jim spotted him on the rock.

"Captain Jack," Hooker Jim replied, trying not to look frightened. "We have a message for you."

"You don't talk to anyone I want to hear from," Captain

Jack said. His finger tapped restlessly on the rifle trigger. How easy it would be to shoot these four. How good it would make him feel. But they were Modoc, even if they had surrendered.

Even if they had sold out.

"General Davis and Colonel Wheaton want you to surrender," Shacknasty Jim said. He walked stiffly to the base of the rock where Captain Jack watched. Captain Jack noticed he wore new military-issue boots. All four were in old but clean clothing, but they all had new boots. His own toes poked through the toes of the shoes he had worn ever since escaping into the Lava Beds.

He should have insisted on taking Canby's boots, too, instead of letting Ellen's Man George have them. For all the good they had done the dead brave.

"He probably wants the sun to come up in the west, too," Captain Jack said. "That's more likely to happen."

"You can't hold out forever," Steamboat Frank said. "Davis is getting more soldiers every day."

"I will never surrender. The Modoc will never surrender."

"We are Modoc," Hooker Jim said defiantly. "And we surrendered."

"You are not fit to scalp. Dogs would choke on your flesh," Captain Jack said coldly. He tired of talking to them. In spite of what common sense dictated, he had hoped they were returning to rejoin the fight. *He* was *tyee* and led the Modoc.

"We have plenty to eat and drink," Hooker Jim said. "You don't. We know!"

"You know nothing. Get out or I'll risk poisoning the dogs with your carcass." Captain Jack lifted his rifle and sighted along the barrel, fixing on Steamboat Frank's chest. He had never liked him, anyway. Not that he cared much for Hooker Jim or the others, either.

The four "hounds" hesitated, exchanged frightened glances, then backed away.

"Davis will come for you. Wheaton will have your scalp!"

"Go back to your new tribe. See how they like you," Captain Jack said. "Probably no better than *we* liked you."

The four almost ran in their haste to get away. Captain Jack sat on the rock and thought hard, then jumped down and went through the rocky maze to the caves where the remaining Modoc hid. He had read the four "hounds" right and knew the soldiers would come fast on their heels. He had to ready his people for a fight.

"Colonel Wheaton, Colonel Wheaton!" shouted Hooker Jim, waving to the officer. "We found 'em. We talked to Captain Jack!"

Wheaton hesitated for a moment because General Davis had emerged from Fairchild's house and seen the four scouts. Wheaton had wanted to keep the "hounds" a secret, especially their mission of locating the Modoc camp. If he led a quick foray against Captain Jack and won, it would go far toward redeeming him in the eyes of, not only Davis, but even General Sherman. Somehow, Wheaton felt he had been tarred with the brush that had so disgraced Canby and his ill-conceived Peace Commission.

"What have these men found?" demanded Davis. Wheaton cursed under his breath. There was no way to hide the intelligence gleaned by the four turncoats.

"Sir, they carried a message to Captain Jack asking for his unconditional surrender. I was getting a report from them."

"He won't surrender, but you can beat 'em," Steamboat Frank said. "He doesn't have many men left."

"How many fighters still follow Captain Jack?" asked Davis.

"No more than twenty-four," Hooker Jim said, proud that he could count that high.

"What?" Davis was shocked. He looked at Wheaton and asked, "Can this be true? Captain Jack has only two dozen warriors?"

"Since Mr. Fairchild came out with most of the Modoc, it's not too far-fetched, sir." Wheaton wished Davis would let him mount the expedition, but he saw the calculations going on in the general's mind. Twenty-four Modoc meant an easy victory. There were already more than a thousand soldiers arrayed in and around the Lava Beds.

"Do you know where he is camped?" Davis asked the four scouts.

All bobbed their heads.

"Prepare to go after him, Colonel," Davis said briskly. "All available men. No reserves this time. We will throw our entire force into the Lava Beds. Two dozen fighters," he marveled, shaking his head. "I shall lead the expedition."

"Yes, sir," Wheaton said, disgusted. He saluted, glared at the four "hounds," and then went to muster the soldiers for an immediate campaign.

The last campaign in the Modoc War.

Boston Charley had never seen so many soldiers before. From the tight niche he had squeezed into, he watched rank after rank of the bluecoats tramping past. He tried to count and gave up when he hit fifty. There were many times that number in this single detachment, and he had heard others from Captain Jack's band say they had also seen many, many soldiers.

He lifted his pistol and followed one soldier after another, pretending to shoot them. Six shots, six dead soldiers. But Boston Charley did not fire. He knew what would happen if he did. He might kill six, but the hundreds of others would turn his body into a bullet-riddled mess.

He aimed at the last soldier in the column, then had his field of vision blocked by a man riding a horse. Boston Charley sucked in his breath, twisted sideways, and got out of the cranny. He stepped onto the path through the Lava Beds, and then pumped his short legs to catch up with the rider. Boston Charley reached up and tugged on the man's sleeve.

John Fairchild looked down, then jumped, spooking his horse.

"Charley!"

Boston Charley put his finger to his mouth, warning Fairchild to stay quiet and not alert the soldiers a few paces ahead. Fairchild dismounted and went to him. Fairchild was not a tall man, but he towered over Boston Charley.

"What do you want?" Fairchild asked pointedly.

"I heard how Hooker Jim and the rest were received. Even Curly Headed Doctor was given food and water and not put in a cell."

"That's true. They surrendered."

"I want to surrender, too," Boston Charley said. "To you. I don't want them to kill me." He aimed his pistol in the direction of the slowly vanishing soldiers. "I want to eat and drink good water." He tried to spit, but there wasn't enough moisture in his mouth.

"I'm sure I can talk to General Davis about this. He's at the head of the column. But you knew that, didn't you?" Fairchild saw that Boston Charley had seen the general go by.

"It doesn't do any good to kill the white *tyee*. More come," Boston Charley said. "We killed Canby but Davis came. We kill him and another will come."

"Pray that General Sherman does not personally take charge of the campaign," Fairchild said. "Or General Crook."

Boston Charley had heard of these men, and they were even bigger *tyee* than Davis. They were terrible fighters who never stopped. Truly, fighting the *boshtin* was like pushing sand along a lakeshore. The waves gently pushed the sand back and smoothed it, no matter how much work went into moving the beach.

"Can you speak for any of the others with Captain Jack?" asked Fairchild. "The more who surrender, the better the treatment you'll receive."

"Can I go to Lost River?" Boston Charley asked eagerly. "I want to be *tyee*. I'd be better than Captain Jack."

"Lost River is out of the question. Perhaps the government will allow you to settle back at Yainax, but I cannot say."

Boston Charley thought for a moment, then said, "Queen Mary and all the rest of the women will surrender, too."

Fairchild's eyes went wide with surprise. Having Captain Jack's sister surrender would be a major blow to the Modoc resistance. All the squaws giving up would mean only Captain Jack and a handful of warriors remained.

"I give you my solemn promise you will be treated fairly and well if you bring in Queen Mary and the other women," Fairchild said.

Boston Charley thrust out his grimy hand. Fairchild shook it solemnly.

Boston Charley vanished into the tortured rock to find the women and escort them back to where Fairchild waited.

# And Another . . .

*Lava Beds*
*May 29, 1873*

Josh looked around uneasily. He had never ventured into the Lava Beds alone before. Worse, he was not exactly alone. Isabella had insisted on coming with him to translate. Risking his own neck was one thing, but risking hers bothered him greatly. She showed no sign of nervousness as they rode slowly along the bloodstained path meandering through the lava flows. On either side of the trail Josh saw tortured rock with holes big enough to hide a man—or an army.

"Are you sure you understood him?" Josh asked for the hundredth time.

"Do not be afraid," Isabella said. "He promised no trouble. Only talk."

Josh jumped when a man stepped onto the trail directly in front of him. As alert as he had been, he had not seen Scar-faced Charley until the man chose to appear.

"Charley!" called Isabella. She spurred her horse forward, then slid from its back and went to the Modoc. The two talked rapidly for several minutes; then Isabella waved for Josh to join them. He dismounted and advanced slowly, still not certain this wasn't some elaborate trap. It made no sense for Captain Jack to ambush him. He was only a reporter. One of dozens in Linkville and Yreka. Maybe the Modoc *tyee* had it in for

Isabella, who had steadfastly remained among the whites—and in Josh's bed.

For the first time, in spite of all he had written for so long, in spite of living with Isabella for months, Josh realized he knew next to nothing of the Modoc, their customs, or what made them such fierce fighters.

"Scarfaced Charley says he wants to surrender. The others surrendered to Fairchild, but he wants you to speak for him with General Davis."

"Why me?"

"I've told him how you speak the truth, how the newspapers print your words and that you are famous. Scarfaced Charley wants a famous man to speak for him."

Josh laughed, but it came more from nerves than real amusement.

"Tell him I'll do what I can. I cannot make any promises, but I will speak to Davis and see if I can't get him terms of surrender at least as good as the others." Josh thought he could go to Meacham or even Fairchild and plead Scarfaced Charley's case, after he had interviewed the Modoc. Meacham or Fairchild would see to it that the soldiers didn't kill Charley outright, although it might be difficult to stop some who had lost friends and relatives to Modoc snipers. In spite of Captain Jack's reduced fighting force, Davis and his massive invasion had not brought the wily Modoc *tyee* to bay. Josh could not be certain but had heard Davis's troops had suffered more than a dozen losses, and this was after the four "hounds" had reported Captain Jack's army amounted to only two dozen fighters.

Two dozen minus one, if Scarfaced Charley surrendered.

"Scarfaced Charley has been one of Captain Jack's staunchest allies," Isabella said. "He regrets having to give up, but he will. He cannot go on any longer."

Josh saw that Scarfaced Charley was almost naked. Traveling through the Lava Beds was hard on clothing. The lightest touch against the razor-sharp edges slashed a sleeve or pants leg. Too much dodging or hiding in the caves quickly tore even the toughest canvas into strips. Scarfaced Charley showed patches of open sores and wounds that had never healed. And the shoes he wore were paper-thin. He did not so much walk as hobble.

Yet he had hidden completely until he chose to show himself.

"What of the conditions?" Josh asked. "Can he tell me how he has been living?"

Josh wrote as Isabella translated. His lips thinned to a line as he heard of the terrible conditions Scarfaced Charley and the others had endured daily. They were hardly more than walking skeletons, and yet they still kept the soldiers away. Even with McKay and his Warm Springs scouts and the four "hounds" Davis had recruited, Captain Jack remained a free spirit drifting at will through the expansive, deadly Lava Beds.

"No water since they were cut off from Tule Lake?" He hardly believed it was possible to live on ice chipped from cave ceilings, yet Scarfaced Charley said that was what they had done. Josh had no reason to doubt him.

Scarfaced Charley kept a steady stream of answers coming for Josh's questions until the reporter had asked everything he could. He had enough for a dozen stories—and he would see that everything was printed in some newspaper somewhere.

A curious thrill came every time he sold a story to a San Francisco paper, never the *Alta California* again, not after Mr. Billingsly had buckled under to Sean Murdoch the way he had. It was petty, Josh knew, and he reveled in it. He only wished Faith would see each and every word and know he was responsible.

He was the famous reporter.

"I can't think of anything more," Josh said, closing his notebook. "Does Scarfaced Charley want me to ride ahead to speak with Davis?"

Isabella talked for several minutes, then said to Josh, "They will accompany you—us. He trusts you to speak up for him when we find the general."

"They?" asked Josh. "Scarfaced Charley is bringing along someone else to surrender?"

Josh's mouth dropped open when Scarfaced Charley waved. From the rocks came eleven other Modoc warriors, including Captain Jack's archrival, Schonchin John. Half of Captain Jack's remaining fighters had turned themselves in to Joshua Harlan.

# Songs of Victory

Lieutenant Frazier Boutelle dozed in the saddle. Colonel Wheaton had put him on back-to-back patrols in the Lava Beds, and he was dead tired. He jerked awake when his sergeant hissed at him.

"Lieutenant, ahead. What do you make of it?"

Boutelle touched the pistol holstered at his belt, then relaxed when he recognized the Modoc in the path ahead.

"At ease, Sergeant," he said. "I know him. That's Humpy Joe, Captain Jack's brother."

"His brother! We should kill the son of a bitch!"

"As you were," Boutelle said sharply. "Joe's harmless enough."

"None of them Indians are harmless, or are you forgettin' how many of us they've cut down?"

"I know better than you, Sergeant," Boutelle said. He remembered every one of the men in his command who had been killed. He knew their names and had written letters of regret to their widows and mothers and brothers, all detailing how bravely their husbands and sons and brothers had died in combat. This chore was usually reserved for the company commander, but Boutelle had written his own to let the relatives know how much he appreciated the bravery the dead soldiers had displayed.

"Joe!" Boutelle called out. "You fighting today or are you surrendering?"

Humpy Joe came up, his hands empty. Boutelle tried to press the blurry vision of his near-sleep out of his eyes. Joe might be bait for a trap. Captain Jack had never done that before, using one of his own relatives to entice soldiers to their deaths, but these were perilous times. Boutelle's briefings all told of extreme hardship among the Modoc, but he had come to mistrust anything Davis said. The only ones Boutelle did trust were the reporter, Joshua Harlan, and the Modoc woman he lived with and used as interpreter. After they had escorted twelve of Captain Jack's best fighters in to surrender, he had spoken with them at length to find out what he could of the remaining Modoc forces.

Josh assured Boutelle that Captain Jack had fewer than a dozen men left. Humpy Joe was one of them. Boutelle knew the cruelty of war and how the Modoc had fought, Humpy Joe as fiercely as any of the others, but he could not find it in himself to be afraid of Humpy Joe. All he could do was pity the man.

"Want to surrender to Fairchild. Nobody else," Humpy Joe called in his gravelly voice.

"Surrender to me or no one," Boutelle said. "I don't want to bother Mr. Fairchild. He's a busy man, and I won't ride back to fetch him." This produced a chuckle from his sergeant and a few of the soldiers behind him.

"You won't get Fairchild?"

"Not today, Joe. What do you say to that?"

Humpy Joe turned and scuttled off, disappearing into the rocks before Boutelle realized he was not going to surrender to him.

"He surely did call your bluff, sir," the sergeant said.

"No bluff. Keep your eyes peeled, Sergeant," Boutelle said. "We've not seen the last of Joe today."

They rode for another twenty minutes. Boutelle halted the patrol when McKay and a few of his Warm Springs scouts came loping up on foot.

"What have you found?" Boutelle asked McKay. The half-breed shook his head and looked disgusted.

"Can't find hide nor hair of them. Might be Captain Jack's left the Lava Beds and gone to Yreka. Maybe I should go over there and look for him."

Boutelle laughed. "I don't think the gin mills of Yreka are hiding him, McKay. The caves and ravines around us do a good enough job." Boutelle's voice trailed off when he saw a solitary figure ahead in the road. It was nearing dusk and the shadows masked the man's identity. All Boutelle knew for a fact was that this could not be Humpy Joe. He stood too straight.

"Wait here," Boutelle ordered McKay and the scouts. He motioned to his sergeant to ride with him. Together, they slowly approached the lone figure.

Boutelle halted a few yards away.

"I come to surrender," Captain Jack said.

Lieutenant Boutelle accepted his surrender. The Warm Springs Indians led the way out of the Lava Beds, singing songs of victory all the way back to General Davis's headquarters.

The Modoc War had ended.

# Extermination!

*Linkville, Oregon*
*June 5, 1873*

General Jefferson Davis leaned back on the rickety camp
stool and read his orders again. He sighed deeply, then began
penning his reply to General Sherman. He looked up when
Colonel Wheaton entered the tent.

"Sit down, Colonel," Davis said. "We've got a bit of unpleasantness ahead of us, it seems."

"How's that, sir?" Wheaton still held a grudge against Davis
for taking the credit for the Modoc captures. He had been on
the front lines during the entire war and deserved some recognition, recognition he was not likely to get from the likes
of General Davis.

"I'm putting you in command of Fort Klamath," Davis said,
startling the colonel.

"Why, thank you for the confidence in my abilities, sir."

"You'll need every bit of diplomacy for this one. And not
a bit of ruthlessness, too."

"What do you mean, sir?" Wheaton frowned. Being put in
charge of Fort Klamath had sounded like a promotion. Now
it turned into a snake writhing around to bite him. He knew
Davis was intent on transferring back East and getting the hell
away from the West as fast as possible. If that meant foisting

off some dirty chores, he was not above it. Especially if Wheaton was the scapegoat.

"General Sherman's orders are quite precise. We are to court-martial and execute the Modoc leaders. All other Modoc will be tried by civilian authorities and hanged. Any remaining Indians, presumably small children, will be dispersed as widely as possible, perhaps to some desolate spot in Indian Territory, and all effort will be made to erase the name Modoc from the history books."

"This is most harsh, sir." Wheaton took some glee in hearing the punishment to be meted out to the Modoc. He had suffered at their hands. Now it was time for retribution.

"Yes, it is," Davis said. "I am a relative newcomer to this fight, but General Sherman's punitive measures are designed to reassure everyone that the war was never out of our control, that it will never happen again."

"The newspapers had a field day with it, sir. They made the Army out to be incompetents. They only reported how many soldiers were killed by the Modoc in combat, never letting the public know of our victories."

"That's because there were damn few victories," Davis said harshly. "Cutting the Modoc off from Tule Lake determined the course of the war, and that fool Gillem never realized it. He even filed reports detailing how the two commanders of those companies had disobeyed his orders. He wanted to court-martial them, not give them medals!" Davis turned angrier. "Until Ellen's Man George was killed at Sorass Lake, we had no victories. He and the other brave were the first battle casualties sustained by the Modoc."

"I am aware of that, sir," Wheaton said stiffly.

"You can redeem yourself by performing these duties without fail, Colonel," Davis said.

Wheaton had the feeling he was being used as a stalking-horse. Instead of stepping forward and publicly executing the Modoc himself, Davis wanted another layer of authority between him and the act. That meant Sherman might be gunning

for Davis—again. Sherman had sent Davis to Alaska for h[is]
mistakes during the March to the Sea. What new blunders ha[d]
turned Sherman against Davis?

"The name Modoc will cease to exist," Davis said firml[y.]
"You have your orders, Colonel. See that they are carried o[ut]
with dispatch."

"Yes, sir, right after I take command of Fort Klamath.["]
Wheaton played for time. A few days or a week would n[o]
matter. If the public wanted blood, they would get it. But onl[y]
when Wheaton examined his new role as closely and thor[-]
oughly as possible.

Davis could dig himself as deep a hole as he wanted. Whea[-]
ton wanted to be sure it didn't turn into a grave big enoug[h]
for the both of them.

# Countermanded

*Fort Klamath, Oregon*
*June 9, 1873*

Wheaton walked around his new office, appreciating the solid walls and the way the wind was held outside where it belonged. It rained almost constantly this time of year, and he no longer trooped around in ankle-deep mud. It was good being in command of Fort Klamath.

It was good until he learned of the full political battle going on over the Modoc and their disposition. General Sherman had not minced words in his original orders. When the Attorney General had countermanded the order, Wheaton had almost dropped the telegram because it was so vitriolic. He had never received a dispatch this long, this varied, or this critical of a commanding officer.

Sherman had obviously lost out to the politicians in Washington.

A knock on the door brought him around.

"Enter," he barked. Wheaton liked the way his every word echoed in the office. Out in the field, he had felt as if the Lava Beds swallowed his words and left them among the black, jagged rocks chewed like an animal with a bone.

Wheaton frowned. He did not want to talk with reporters right now, especially the one who came in. Joshua Harlan had been too lenient in his attitudes toward the Modoc, perhaps because he was living with a Modoc harlot.

"Yes?" Wheaton asked curtly.

"Sir, I heard the Modoc trials are to be canceled."

"Your friend Meacham had a hand in that, I am sure," Wheaton said.

"What is the new policy?"

Wheaton thought for a moment, considering how Sherman had acted and how Davis had played to the newspapers so well. They'd looked like heroes, and he'd ended up seeming to be the one persecuting poor, innocent Modoc women and children.

There was no reason he could not use the press as his superiors had.

"Sit down, Mr. Harlan, and I'll go over it with you. I must say, you are an alert young man. I only received the new orders from the Attorney General this morning."

"Word gets around, sir," Josh said. Wheaton found himself disliking this young whippersnapper more and more because of the power he wielded. A strike with the pen removed a name from the list of heroes. A few quick squiggles defamed even the best Army officer. And the spoon-fed, sensation-hungry public gobbled it all up, whether it was true or a complete fabrication.

"The Attorney General has requested a far more lenient position, one that I wholeheartedly agree with, by the way." Wheaton tented his fingers and rested his chin on the tips as he sat behind his wood desk. He should have had his orderly polish it better. Here and there dull spots made it appear as if this was not a completely military office.

"Why is that, sir?"

"War was never formally declared, a point I often mentioned in my dispatches to General Sherman. The Modoc were—are—a separate nation and Congress had to act. Military skirmishes, while deadly, were not governed by the rules of war. Not strictly."

"So you now view the Modoc War as . . . what? An insurrection?"

"An attempted civil war," Wheaton said with some gusto. "As a result, policies established during our previous unpleasantness will serve as guidelines. No civilian court had jurisdiction."

"But a military tribunal does?" asked Josh.

"Only over the acknowledged leaders of the, uh, insurrection. We are making all effort to give the Modoc leaders a fair trial here at Fort Klamath. In fact, we are rounding up all members of the Modoc tribe we can find and are bringing them here for the trial so they can see that our justice is quite fair and impartial."

"All of them? There aren't many, are there, sir?"

"We have found one hundred fifty-five so far," Wheaton said. "They will be quartered nearby and be allowed to attend every day of the trial, and, of course, witness the subsequent executions."

Josh said nothing. He stared at Wheaton until the colonel grew uneasy. What had he said wrong? Wheaton rushed on to explain how the trial would be conducted.

"The finest lawyers will be provided to defend the Modoc leaders."

"Before the leaders are executed." The way Josh said it, it sounded like a condemnation. Wheaton wasn't sure what he could say to sway the man. He wasn't even sure what he had said to incur such sarcasm.

"We will endeavor to bring out all aspects of the Modoc rebellion and each man's part in it. I solemnly assure you, justice will be done."

"How will they be executed?"

"Why, by hanging. That is the usual method."

"Are you aware how frightened the Modoc are of dying in this fashion?"

Wheaton sniffed. "I should imagine they are afraid of dying in *any* fashion."

"Not at all," Josh said. "My interpreter—"

*Your whore,* thought Wheaton, but he kept the insult to him self.

"My interpreter tells me the Modoc are sure their spirit will be trapped in their bodies if they are hanged. This mean their spirits—what we might call our souls—cannot go on t the Happy Hunting Grounds. They will be trapped forever o earth in a dead body."

"Buried alive, as it were?" Wheaton repressed a shudde The mere thought of such a fate frightened him.

"Yes," Josh said flatly.

"The method of execution will be determined upon convic tion and will be out of my hands. It is possible they will b acquitted."

"Or given lesser sentences?"

"Perhaps some might be sent to Alcatraz Island. Are yo familiar with that particular prison?"

"I'm from San Francisco," Josh said. Wheaton liked th way the reporter turned a little pale at mention of Alcatraz. had been transformed into a secure prison facility after th Civil War and would be an ideal place for the Indians, shoul the court choose not to follow orders and execute the Modo leaders.

But such a decision was out of the question. Wheaton idl wondered how many feet of rope would be needed for noose and how many board feet of lumber would be required to buil the gallows.

"If you will excuse me, Mr. Harlan," Colonel Wheaton sai "I have to put in a requisition for some . . . supplies."

# Trial

"Are they going to shoot us?" Captain Jack asked Josh. The Modoc *tyee* was shackled to Schonchin John. The two seemed to have mended whatever fences had been torn down earlier. Josh knew they were both in the same predicament, but now he had to smile wanly and shake his head. He looked at Isabella, who seemed confused at what was happening. She trusted him that nothing evil would befall Captain Jack.

"No, that's not a gun. Just stand still and wait." He stepped back with Isabella while the photographer vanished under the dark cloth dangling over the back of his camera. He fiddled for a moment. Then a loud click sounded. Captain Jack jumped, but Schonchin John remained impassive.

"Got it!" the photographer said. "Thanks."

"Come on," Josh said to Isabella. "This might be the only chance we get to really talk to Captain Jack."

Josh moved in before the guards hustled the two Modoc back to their cell. The entire trial had taken on the air of a Sunday social, white settlers from all over the area coming in to see the Modoc. Worse, Wheaton had insisted on bringing in every Modoc squaw and child he could find. The few men with them looked sullen, and with good reason. Their leaders were being tried for murder and insurrection. Josh had seen

Wheaton's orders to build a log stockade capable of holding "44 Bucks, 49 Squaws and 62 Children." They were virtual prisoners instead of observers.

"Are they treating you well?" Josh asked, walking alongside the two prisoners. Isabella translated for him when he could not phrase the words himself or the reply was too fast to understand.

"Good," Captain Jack said. A smile curled at his lips. "We will be in newspapers?"

"What? Oh, the photograph. Yes, yes, you will. I'll see if I can get you a copy."

This pleased Captain Jack. Josh wondered if he had any idea what was happening to him. It did not seem so.

"Have you spoken with lawyers? Men who speak for you in court?"

"I have spoken with American Indian Aid Association," Captain Jack said. Josh shuddered. Although their support for Indian causes was nationwide, they were more interested in their own agenda. The Modoc happened to come along at a good time for the AIAA to claim the trial was a farce, but Josh hated agreeing with General Sherman on one point. They were more interested in praying over the graves of American settlers than they were in saving the lives of Indians.

Too many congressmen had rushed to Fort Klamath for Josh's comfort. A circus, one reporter had called it. Josh was not sure if this wasn't worse. Some of the politicians attacked President Grant's Indian policies, while others wanted the matter put to a quick end. A quick end meaning the execution of all the Modoc.

The worst was the Congressman from California who wanted a complete and full investigation, with himself at the head of the inquiry. That would ensure his name being reported daily for months, at the expense of the Modoc.

As Josh walked along, he saw the Universal Peace Delegation arriving. Behind them came other missionaries, possibly another group of Quakers, intent on the stockade where Whea-on had put the Modoc not standing trial. Josh could not help wondering if the tribe might have been better off staying in the Lava Beds, fighting to the last brave, to the last squaw and child. This torture by the religious was becoming endless, each group with its own ax to grind. And not a one stopped to ask why the Modoc had fought or what they had hoped to win.

"Why did you fight?" Josh called to Captain Jack as he was being escorted into the jail block built specially for the Modoc.

"Old Schonchin came to me in the Lava Beds after the first big battle and said David Allan would join me. I wanted to surrender then, but Old Schonches told me David Allan would bring ammunition and we would fight forever. He told me the Peace Commissioners were liars."

Josh stepped back and spoke with Isabella, making sure he understood what was said.

"David Allan is a very important Klamath *tyee*. Captain Jack would listen to his words," Isabella told him. "In spite of him being Klamath, because Old Schonches vouched for him."

"But Allan didn't fight. He stayed on the Klamath Reservation with Old Schonches. Did he abandon Captain Jack or change his mind?" Coldness settled in Josh's belly when another solution came to him. "Or did he want to get rid of Captain Jack?"

"That is possible. There was always great trouble between the *tyee*."

Josh had seen that with Schonchin John, Hooker Jim, and Curly Headed Doctor. They had fought Captain Jack at every turn, but none of them could have done better than Jack. If anything, Curly Headed Doctor's Ghost Dance had done much to undermine Captain Jack's authority and make him risk too much, believing his warriors were invincible.

For a while, they had been. But it had come from their intimate knowledge of the Lava Beds, not the big medicine Curly Headed Doctor chanted.

"We should tell General Davis about this," Josh said. "I
David Allan was instigating the insurrection, then he is re
sponsible, at least in part, for all that happened. Especially i
Captain Jack wanted to surrender after the First Battle of th
Stronghold. Think of the lives that could have been saved.

He tried not to think of Boutelle's description of Gillem'
Graveyard and the moaning, dying soldiers.

Josh hurried off, Isabella falling farther behind as he ap
proached the general's office next to Colonel Wheaton's. Mos
of the action took place in the colonel's office, but Josh ha
to push his way through representatives from a half-dozen dif
ferent peace organizations all vying for the general's attentio
and approbation.

"Sir," Josh called. "Are you aware that David Allan encour
aged Captain Jack to fight?"

Davis looked as if he had bad indigestion. He started to sa
something dismissive, then saw how intent Josh was.

"Ladies and gentleman, please excuse me a few minutes.
have some important news to give this lad from the fourt
estate." He motioned for Josh to go into his office. Josh pushe
his way through the increasingly antagonistic crowd, an
heaved a sigh of relief when he and the general were alone
But outside, it sounded like the buzzing of angry bees.

"Sir, I just heard from Captain Jack that—"

"Sit down, there," Davis said, pointing to the single chai
in front of his desk. The general grabbed a handful of paper
and leafed through them. "It might surprise you, but thes
allegations have already been examined." Davis got a pair o
reading glasses and "hmmed" to himself as he read page afte
page, finally finding one that he passed to Josh.

Josh scanned the page, then looked up.

"David Allan denies everything," Josh said, surprised.

"He might be lying. But he was not in the Lava Beds wit
Captain Jack, killing my soldiers. From what he said, commu
nication between Captain Jack and those on the Klamath Res
ervation was common and frequent."

"David Allan said he was ill and could never have joined Captain Jack," Josh read from the page, then looked up. "But he promised that a considerable number of his people would reinforce Captain Jack."

"Mr. Meacham agrees that David Allan spoke against war with the settlers as long as four years ago. As to Allan being ill, who can say? I found his testimony suspicious and I questioned him sharply, but there was no way to implicate him. In any case, whether Captain Jack acted on his own or was duped by David Allan into staying in the Lava Beds to fight, U.S. Army soldiers died. Settlers died. Too many died because of Captain Jack's guerrilla war."

"What does Old Schonches say?" asked Josh. "If he agrees that David Allan's message was enough to keep Captain Jack fighting . . ." His voice trailed off when he saw Davis searching for another sheet in the thick file of testimony already taken.

"He denies he ever talked with Captain Jack about David Allan or Klamath support."

Josh knew the sound of nails being driven into a coffin when he heard it. Captain Jack was being shut off from the men whom he had respected and who advised him to stay and fight. Those *tyee* lied now to save their own hides.


The courtroom looked like any other court-martial trial. An array of officers sat along one wall. Captain Jack, Schonchin John, Black Jim, Boston Charley, and two boys sat shackled to a bench in the middle of the room, soldiers with bayonets at the ready immediately behind them. Frank and Tobey Riddle stood to one side to translate. Alongside Josh pressed other reporters and observers. He could not help noticing Hooker Jim, Steamboat Frank, Shacknasty Jim, and Bogus Charley were not only free and watching but seemingly enjoying the spectacle.

Josh had asked and learned that the four "hounds" had been

exempted from prosecution because of their role in finding Captain Jack and getting him to surrender.

Josh stood on tiptoe to see the prosecutor begin reading the charges. Every one was like a knife into Josh's side. Too many bitter memories were stirred as the prosecutor charged the defendants with "murder in violation of the laws of war" in killing Canby and Reverend Thomas. The second charge was the attempted murder of Meacham and Dyar.

"How do you plead, guilty or not guilty?"

It took a few minutes for the Riddles to translate for the defendants. Then Frank Riddle stated in a strong voice, "All defendants plead not guilty to both charges."

"Then, Your Honor," the prosecutor said to the judge, Colonel Elliot, "I call Mr. Frank Riddle as my first witness."

Josh frowned. It had to be unusual calling an officer of the court—Riddle interpreted for the defendants—as a witness against them.

"How well do you know the defendants?"

"Well, sir," Frank Riddle said, "I've known them all for years."

"How would you describe them, in terms of their influence in the Modoc tribe?"

Frank Riddle scratched his chin, then said, "Captain Jack's a *tyee*. That's a chief. His brother, Black Jim, is something less. Call him a sergeant. Schonchin John wants to be *tyee* and has some influence. Maybe 'sub-chief' is what you'd call him. Boston Charley isn't much of anything, and the two boys, Sloluck and Barncho, they ain't nuthin' at all."

"Describe what happened at the council tent where General Canby and Reverend Thomas were killed."

Josh could not bear to listen to Riddle retelling the slaughter. He pushed out of the courtroom to get some air. Hurrying across the parade ground in the direction of the courtroom was AB Meacham.

"AB!" Josh called. "You're back."

"Just got in from Salem. I must say, Josh, I am worn out from all the travel. How is the trial progressing?"

Josh looked at his friend and was worried about the man's health. Meacham was pale, had lost a considerable amount of weight, and looked as if he might keel over at any instant. A ring of sweat dribbled down around his hat brim, pulled down tightly to hide where he had almost been scalped.

"Are you feeling well, AB?"

"Yes, yes," Meacham said irritably. "What's gone on so far?"

Josh filled him in on the progress of the trial.

"What about lawyers?"

"There's a prosecutor," Josh said, "but Captain Jack and the others don't have lawyers. Colonel Elliot said he couldn't find anyone to defend them, and Captain Jack said it didn't matter."

"Did he understand?"

Josh did not reply. The answer to that was obvious. The white man's justice was a complete mystery to Captain Jack. The *tyee* enjoyed having his picture taken, and the good food and water came steadily, even as he rattled his leg irons and headed inexorably toward the gallows.

"I'll talk to Davis about this. The general can't let Jack be railroaded."

"He did everything they've accused him of," Josh pointed out. "You barely escaped. Canby and Thomas did not."

"Justice cannot be served if they are tried without a lawyer." Meacham pushed past Josh and went into the courtroom. Josh followed, wondering what Meacham was up to. He found out quickly when Meacham walked to the judge and spoke rapidly to him.

"Mr. Meacham, are you volunteering to be counsel for the defendants? This is highly unusual, especially since you are the aggrieved party named in the second charge against them."

"Do you have any objection since you have found no other lawyer willing to put up a defense?"

"No, sir," Colonel Elliot said. "I only pointed out how pe-

culiar this seems. You may have a few minutes to talk wit
your clients."

Josh moved closer, wondering what Meacham would say
He saw Captain Jack thrust out his hand and heard him cry
"Old Meacham! Good to see you!"

Meacham recoiled, looking at the outthrust hand, and said
"I cannot shake your hand, Captain Jack. It is red with Genera
Canby's blood."

"I shake," Schonchin John said, grinning.

"Nor can I shake yours. Your hand is red with *my* blood."

Josh wondered how vigorous Meacham was going to be i
the Modoc's defense if he could not even shake hands wit
the two worst villains among the defendants.

Josh saw how old Captain Jack looked in that instant. .
once proud warrior, he now shook like a leaf in a high wind
For all the good food and water, he seemed thinner somehov
Josh then decided it was not so much a thinness of the bod
but of the soul. Captain Jack's friends had abandoned him
leaving him to stand alone for his crimes.

"Captain Jack," Meacham said, "you must speak for your
self, for your tribe. I want you to take the stand and testify.

"Old Meacham, I do not know how. You do it for me."

Josh saw the expression on Meacham's face. How a ma
reluctant about shaking hands with his client could speak e
fectively for him was more than a curiosity. It was a travest

"No, I won't do that," Meacham said.

"Old Meacham, I cannot talk with chains on my legs."

Josh saw Meacham wobble a bit, paler than he had bee
earlier. Even if Meacham's spirit was willing, the flesh wa
not. He had not recovered enough from his wounds. Josh wer
to Meacham's side and put his arm around him.

"AB, you can't do this. Get one of your friends to defen
them. There has to be a lawyer among all the idealists here
the fort. You're not up to it physically." Josh hesitated to te
what he saw as the real truth. "You're not up to it emotionally.

Meacham shot a fiery look in Josh's direction, then sagge

"You are right."

Meacham turned and spoke with Colonel Elliot at length. Finally, the judge rapped the gavel and said, "Court is adjourned until tomorrow, at which time the defendants will have new counsel."

Josh helped Meacham to a seat as the Modoc were taken back to the guardhouse.

"You did the right thing, AB," he told his friend.

"I don't know, Josh, I just don't know what's right anymore," Meacham said.

Josh had to agree.

# Conviction

*Fort Klamath, Oregon*
*July 7, 1873*

"No one? You couldn't get anyone?" Josh was horrified at Meacham's failure. "What are you going to do, AB? You can't defend Captain Jack and the others. You're not up to it." He studied Meacham's face for some sign that he was joking. He saw only desolation at the failure to find another lawyer.

"I asked, but no one would do it. No one! Captain Jack said he will defend himself. I might give him some pointers, but I doubt that will do much good."

Josh knelt beside Meacham, who sat immediately behind Captain Jack and the other prisoners in the courtroom. Captain Jack seemed confused today, and well that he should be. Josh knew the trial would go fast because Captain Jack knew nothing of procedure. Somehow, that ignorance would not matter with the military men conducting the trial. The panel of officers entered and took their place in the jury box. Colonel Elliot came in soon after and gaveled the court to silence.

"It is my understanding the defendant will represent himself. Continue," the judge said.

Meacham whispered to Captain Jack, who stood. "Colonel, I cannot talk good with leg irons on."

"They stay. Do you have a witness to call?"

"I call Scarfaced Charley," Captain Jack said.

Josh paid little attention to the questions Captain Jack asked of his friend. They were rambling and had little bearing on the charges. When Captain Jack took the stand himself, his statement was an incoherent series of anecdotes. Josh was not sure any lawyer could have successfully defended the Modoc *tyee,* but Captain Jack's lack of defense or appeal to mercy from the court certainly damned him.

"I did all these things because of the Klamath," Captain Jack said. "They are bad. They forced us away with their taunts. Then David Allan lied, saying he would come to the Lava Beds with ammunition and warriors."

Josh straightened, staring at Captain Jack. He wondered what bearing this might have on the Modoc's defense. Even as the words condemning the Klamath came out of his lips, Captain Jack knew they were not doing him any good. The Klamath had served as scouts against him during the First Battle for the Stronghold. They had proven so ineffective that McKay and the Warm Springs Indians had been recruited.

On any front, deriding the Klamath Indians was a poor defense.

Captain Jack clamped his mouth shut for a moment, then said, "The four who hunted me down. The 'hounds' as they are called, are guilty. They should not have amnesty."

This produced a small murmur among the jurors. Again Captain Jack saw he had missed the target. Trying to shift blame was not going to save him.

"He's right," cried Schonchin John, jumping to his feet with a rattle of chains. "Bogus Charley and the others are guilty of as much as we are!"

"Sit down," barked Colonel Elliot. "You'll have your say later, if you choose."

Schonchin John did not say anything more, sitting with a sullen expression on his face. When Captain Jack left the stand, the defense, such as it was, ended.

"I charge you, the jury, with the need for careful deliberation in the matter before you," the judge said.

Josh spoke quietly with Isabella. "It won't take long. The facts are clear. The only thing that could have been worse for Captain Jack and the others would have been for Meacham to take the stand and remove his hat. The jury would have seen how he had almost been scalped by Schonchin John."

"They decide now?" asked Isabella, holding Josh's arm tightly.

He felt her warmth, but in spite of the stifling summer heat in the courtroom, he enjoyed it. Josh tried to keep his emotions away from the facts in the case but could not. He admired Captain Jack, but the man was a killer. Captain Jack had tried to do what was best for his tribe and now he had to die for it, and he barely understood why. Killing Canby and Thomas had been brutal, but in Modoc thinking, it ought to have ended the war, not prolonged it.

"All rise," called the bailiff. Colonel Elliot sat and waited for the jury to take their seats.

"Have you reached a verdict?" the judge asked the jury foreman.

"We have, Your Honor. All are declared guilty as charged."

"Thank you for your swift work," Colonel Elliot said. He looked stern when he addressed the defendants. "The court has pardoned those Modoc who served as scouts and thanks them for their fine work. Some might think it treason to their own race, but I personally believe there is no better way of teaching savages that treachery to those who wantonly kill is no treachery at all."

Colonel Elliot shuffled his papers and said, "I sentence all the defendants to death by hanging, such sentence to be carried out on October third, this Year of Our Lord. In view of their youth, Sloluck and Barncho's sentences are commuted to life imprisonment at Alcatraz Island."

He rapped the gavel sharply and left.

Josh saw that Captain Jack and the others did not understand what had happened until Tobey Riddle explained to them. Captain Jack cried out in rage at the sentence and had to be re-strained by three soldiers.

"He doesn't want to be hanged," Isabella said. "His spirit will be trapped forever in his dead body."

"I know," Josh said sadly. "I know how that feels." He left to file a story he wished he did not have to write, his spirit likewise trapped and unable to get free.

# Execution

Joshua Harlan stared at the gallows, trying to determine what he felt. To his surprise, he could not describe his emotions. He had been good at putting the words down that described, that conveyed to readers throughout the West, what it meant to fear the Modoc, what it meant to be Modoc, that his failure came as a shock. He had tried to show both sides of the conflict, even knowing how it would eventually end.

But what did *he* feel now? He had tried to be the dispassionate observer and report only the facts. What did he *feel*?

Captain Jack and Schonchin John and the other Modoc were killers, bloody butchers who mutilated and scalped and killed women and children. The killers of the settlers before Captain Jack lit out for Lost River had never been brought to trial. But for nothing else, killing General Canby was crime enough for most men to pay for. Canby had been the only regular Army general killed during the Indian Wars, and it had been done under a truce flag.

Josh knew why Captain Jack thought this was acceptable behavior. Captain Jack had been a boy when Ben Wright did the same to his own people. The Modoc notion that a *tyee's* death meant the end of fighting had convinced Captain Jack the whites would stop their war after Canby was gone. Different cultures, different ideas.

Captain Jack was guilty also of one other crime: trying to help the Modoc.

The last hammer had fallen silent weeks earlier when the soldiers built the gallows, but the echoes still rang in Josh's head.

"Soon," Isabella said, coming up behind him. "You will watch?"

"It's my job to report it," he said, mouth dry. "I wish I didn't have to, though."

"I do not want to watch. It is a terrible thing to do to a Modoc. Couldn't they just shoot him?"

"Military justice calls for hanging," Josh said. A firing squad would accomplish the same purpose and give the surviving Modoc some sense of relief that Captain Jack and the others were not forever bound to this world, that their spirits could migrate to the next.

Josh might have found some anger if the method of execution had been determined with malice. Colonel Elliot—and Davis and Sherman—did not care. They followed the law to the letter. Hanging. That was it.

"I—" Josh started to speak, but the words jumbled in his throat. He had so much work to do in such a short time. By now the chaplain, Father Huquemborg, had spoken with Captain Jack and the others in the guardhouse. When the crowd began to assemble, that would be the signal to interview, ask questions, find out what the onlookers expected.

This was not the question bubbling to the surface of his mind.

"Yes, Josh?"

"Isabella, we've been together for quite a spell," he said, struggling for the words.

"Yes."

He looked at her and saw fear and sadness. Tears welled at the corners of her eyes but did not run down her cheeks.

"We've been together but not as husband and wife."

"I don't understand."

"Marry me, Isabella. This is a terrible time to ask, but I love you and want you to marry me."

For a heartbeat, Isabella stood speechless. Then she swallowed hard and said, "I thought you were sending me away, th-that you were going back to . . . San Francisco," she finished lamely.

"You were going to say Faith. No, I can't go back to her. Ever. It's you I love. This is going to be hard on you, I know. I see how everyone looks at Tobey Riddle. She's caught between her people and Frank's. You'll be balanced on that same knife edge, too. I—"

"Yes." Now tears did flow down her cheeks.

"Yes?"

"I will marry you. I love you and have since I first saw you." She threw her arms around his neck and hugged him. He turned his face slightly and brought his lips to hers in a simmering kiss. Then Josh jumped back guiltily when a bugle sounded and drums rolled.

"I thought that was for us," he said.

"No," Isabella said. "It is for them." She hugged his arm tightly. They drifted through the gathering crowd of people as if an invisible bubble surrounded them, keeping everyone else away in some other world.

Josh stopped at the base of the gallows. Four nooses swung in the early morning breeze on a gallows designed for six.

"Sir, you'll have to go to one side," a soldier told him.

Josh saw that Isabella had already left. A dozen yards back stood the post adjutant, Lieutenant Kingsbury. Wheaton had lined the Modoc and some whites to the left of the gallows. Josh went in that direction to stand with the others. Josh made out Lieutenant Boutelle in the company to the north.

Immediately to the east, in the middle of the parade grounds, Colonel Wheaton and his staff assembled. Josh saw the fort's physician, Dr. McElderry, checking his watch. Josh looked at his own and wondered if the doctor saw the same time. Just a little before nine A.M. McElderry spoke quietly with Meacham and a few others off to the rear, then returned to his position and stared at the empty gallows.

Josh couldn't help but pick out the soldiers in the ranks. Captain Hasbrouck stood with the 4th Artillery Regiment, looking pleased. In a way this was his best vindication since Sorass Lake, where Ellen's Man George had been killed. Josh saw now that that was the true turning point in the war. Ellen's Man dying had robbed Captain Jack of his authority among the Modoc, and the battle had gone downhill from there for the Indians.

Josh jumped when the drum roll became more strident, more insistent. Then the tempo changed. The muffled drums joined the band playing the Dead March. From the guardhouse came the column, amid a great cloud of choking dust. Josh saw Boston Charley and Black Jim sitting in the front wagon. Captain Jack and Schonchin John were in the rear wagon, Captain Jack with a blanket pulled up around him almost to his ears, as if this would keep out the dread sounds.

The gallows had been built in an open field to the south of the stockade, as if the Army wanted to keep its boundaries pure and unsullied. Josh doubted that was possible this day.

Colonel Hoge, the post quartermaster, mounted the gallows and stood, arms crossed, waiting for the condemned to mount the platform.

From beyond the assembled soldiers came a loud whooping and cheering from the mounted Klamath Indians who had ridden in at dawn to see the execution. Several wagons came rattling up, filled with Oregonians eager to watch, also. Josh tried to do a quick head count and determined at least two thousand had assembled. Captain Jack and his cohorts would be executed in style.

The wagons with the prisoners came to a creaking halt at the side of the scaffold. Guards helped the Modoc down. Boston Charley, wearing a lieutenant's cap, took a plug of tobacco and bit off a chaw. Josh wondered if he understood what was happening. He looked nonchalant. As he started up the gallows steps, he took another bite from his tobacco. Black Jim followed him. The floppy brown felt hat he wore caught the wind and sailed off. He grabbed for it, but the chains on his wrists prevented him from saving it.

Schonchin John wore an army shirt and trousers. He paused a moment at the base of the steps, then lightly ascended, as if the chains on his ankles meant nothing.

Captain Jack had to be helped from the wagon. His legs seemed to have turned to water. He wore a striped cotton shirt open at the neck to reveal a red-flannel shirt underneath. The corporal with Captain Jack had to help him up the steps to the top, where the *tyee* sat beside the other three.

Four enlisted men worked to pinion the condemned as they sat, discarding shackles and using stout rope on their wrists and ankles. Colonel Hoge examined their handiwork and nodded curtly. He motioned to someone at the far side of the scaffold.

Josh saw Oliver Applegate and another settler, Dave Hill, mount and go to the Modoc. From the snippets he caught, the two men were explaining what was going to happen. Dogs under the scaffold began barking when Adjutant Kingsbury called the battalion to attention and read the verdict of military court which had tried the Modoc.

"By order of the President of the United States and the Secretary of War, it is hereby ordered that the execution will take place on this third day of October 1873, no earlier than ten A.M. or later than two P.M."

The adjutant went through the remainder of the orders, ordering Sloluck and Barncho to be brought forward and stood in front of the gallows. They were so close, Josh could have reached out and touched them, but they were not dead men. Not today. Immediately following the execution they would be sent to Alcatraz Island.

Josh looked up at the prisoners and tried to imagine what

vent through their minds. He tried and he failed. For the world
t looked as if they were enjoying the view of the assembled
roops, all except Captain Jack, who sat with his head bowed.

Father Huquemborg stepped forward. The Episcopal minis-
er began the service for the condemned. The gentle breeze
vhipped up, sending the nooses twisting about wildly now.
osh saw Colonel Hoge descend from the scaffold, take a drink
•f water from a bucket near the steps, then go back up. Josh
·igured the colonel's mouth was dry from nerves. Executions
lidn't happen every day.

"Bring the condemned forward," Hoge said in a voice that
:arried over the field. The four enlisted men, one behind each
·risoner, got the Modoc to their feet and pushed them forward
·o stand on the trapdoors. "Adjust the nooses."

Josh sucked in his breath.

"Hey, Jack," shouted a Klamath behind Josh. "What'll you
;ive me to trade places with you?"

Captain Jack jerked at the question. A tiny smile crept to
1is lips, a bit of his bravado returning. He shouted back, "Both
ny wives and all my ponies!"

"Not enough," the Klamath brave said, sparking a round of
aughter.

This was the last merriment to be heard.

"Hoods," the colonel said loudly, his voice quavering a bit
1ow. The hoods were improvised from black canvas haversacks
ind were secured over the heads of the four bound men. The
:olonel lifted a white handkerchief, looked to the corporal
standing at the side of the gallows, then dropped the handker-
:hief.

The corporal swung his hatchet, severing the rope holding
he trapdoors.

As one, the Modoc fell.

Josh let out his breath when he heard Captain Hasbrouck
it the rear of the parade ground bellow, "At parade, rest!"

Josh stared as the four bodies swung this way and that,
·risoners to rope and wind. Captain Jack and his brother Black

Jim had died fast. Schonchin John and Boston Charley continued to kick for several seconds, clinging furiously to life. Then they, too, were dead.

Slowly, the assemblage broke ranks and moved away. The Modoc were herded back to their stockade, and Colonel Wheaton and the others with him all left, all save the post physician who came forward to supervise cutting down the bodies.

Josh knew he ought to go write his story and get it on the telegraph. He had deadlines to meet and did not want other reporters beating him with this story, but he wondered why McElderry lingered. There could be no question that the Modoc were dead.

He waited a half hour until the enlisted men cut down the bodies and carefully laid them in coffins. Dr. McElderry fussed over the procedure like a mother hen shooing her chicks about, then got in the wagon and rode with the four coffins back into Fort Klamath.

Josh tried to talk with Sloluck and Barncho, but the soldiers with them refused to permit them to speak, to tell him what fears they had for their own future. Discouraged, tired in mind and body, Josh trudged back to the fort to find Isabella.

What a day he had chosen to ask her to marry him.

Just after nightfall, Josh became restless. Isabella puttered about, getting their belongings together for their trip back to Linkville in the morning. They had eaten and talked and shared the horror of the day, and somehow this had brought them closer together. Josh felt a curiosity about Dr. McElderry and how the man had behaved after the execution that he did not share with Isabella.

Leaving her to pack, he wandered through the fort. The post surgeon's office was still lit, and Josh figured Dr. McElderry would likely be there. He tried the door, but it was locked. He started to knock, then hesitated, not knowing why. He had learned not to be shy around people who tried to intimidate him—or locked doors that barred his way. Both held secrets a reporter could turn into usable stories.

Going to the side of the building, he wiped dirt off a windowpane and peered into the back room of the surgery. Josh felt a little faint when he realized all four bodies were stretched out on examination tables, partially hidden under black India-rubber sheets. For a moment, he thought his eyes were playing tricks on him. Then he knew his vision was fine.

The bodies of Captain Jack, Boston Charley, Schonchin John, and Black Jim had been decapitated.

Dr. McElderry came into the room, fussing with a sheet of paper, trying to write on it without putting it on a hard surface. The doctor finally gave up, placed the paper on a nearby desk, and made notes for almost a minute before leaving the room. Josh heard McElderry unlock the main door to the office and then walk across the compound.

Josh had to see what was going on. Trying the doorknob, he found McElderry had left it unlocked. He went in. The sharp smell of antiseptic carbolic acid made his nose wrinkle. He hurried through the office to the back room. His hand rested on the latch, shaking at what he knew was on the other side. Josh was not sure he wanted to see what had happened to Captain Jack and his comrades.

"Victory to the bold," he quoted, then went into the room. The formaldehyde odor gagged him. Pulling his coat lapel up to cover his mouth so he could breathe, Josh went to the examination tables and verified what he had seen through the window.

All four Modoc had had their heads cut off.

Surgically removed, he saw, examining Captain Jack's neck. A surgeon's scalpel had removed the head, severing the parts that had not been broken during the hanging. Gorge rising, Josh stepped back and stumbled into the desk.

He glanced down and saw the paper McElderry had toiled over. Josh read it twice, to be sure he had not mistakenly interpreted the words.

McElderry had removed the heads. Where they might be now, Josh could not tell from what had been written in this terse report filled with Latin phrases he did not understand. He looked around the room but did not see jars with the severed heads on any of the shelves.

The paper detailed how the four heads would be shipped back East to Dr. Henry C. Yarrow, Office of the Army Medical Museum, for detailed phrenological examination. The Army wanted to determine if the shape and character of Captain Jack's head had led to him being a killer.

Josh fought down a wave of revulsion. Then he backed away. Josh sucked in fresh cold October air when he got outside Dr. McElderry's office. He felt dirty, somehow, knowing that the Army had executed Captain Jack and then done this to him. They would bury Captain Jack and the other three in their plain pine coffins in graves near the fort, but no one would know of this atrocity.

Perhaps it was not so bad after all. Captain Jack had worried that being hanged would trap his spirit in his body. Decapitation might free that spirit and let it roam forever free.

Josh did not have the heart to ask Isabella if this might be so.

What a day he had chosen to ask her to marry him.

# Epilogue

The surviving Modoc were moved to Indian Territory (in Oklahoma), where Scarfaced Charley became *tyee*. After Quaker missionaries converted Scarfaced Charley in the 1880's, Bogus Charley finally achieved his dream of becoming chief.

Barncho died in Alcatraz of "scrofulous Adenitis" (lymphadenitis, an inflammation of the lymphatic gland), and Sloluck later was pardoned to join his people in Oklahoma.

In 1909, the Modoc were allowed to return to Yainax, although some still reside in Oklahoma.

Alfred Meacham's account of the Modoc War, *Wigwam and Warpath,* was published in 1875. In the manner of a Wild West show, he toured the country with Frank and Tobey Riddle, sometimes joined by Scarfaced Charley, giving lectures until his death in 1882.

During World War II, a section of land bordering Tule Lake was turned into an internment camp for Japanese-Americans. The Lava Beds became a National Monument in 1925, ironically accessible then only through a small town named Canby on Route 139.

# William W. Johnstone
## The *Mountain Man* Series

# The Wingman Series
# By Mack Maloney